PRAISE FOR *THE HEARTWOOD CROWN*

Rich and vivid worldbuilding, a diverse cast of characters, heartbreaking sacrifice, and a flying cat—*The Heartwood Crown* packs all that and more into a modern take on portal fantasy. It captures the fun and wonder of fantasy while unapologetically critiquing some of [the genre's] outdated tropes.

ALEX SHVARTSMAN, editor of *Future Science Fiction Digest* and award-winning author of "Explaining Cthulhu to Grandma"

I loved it! A great follow up to *The Crescent Stone*—not an easy feat considering how high a bar that book set! Magic, hard truths, and impossible decisions. Wit, snark, and love. You need to read these books.

M. E. GARBER, speculative-fiction writer

Is it cliché to say you're in for a massive treat? I don't care if it is. 'Cause you are. You were worried book two wouldn't keep up with the first in the Sunlit Land series? Fear not, friends. Matt Mikalatos has again nailed it. Compelling characters, a scintillating story world, and twists that will leave you guessing. Did I mention the Narnian flavoring? Buy it!

JAMES L. RUBART, five-time Christy Award–winning author

PRAISE FOR *THE CRESCENT STONE*

For Narnia fans who enjoy heavy snark, this is a must read.

KIRKUS

✦

Matt Mikalatos has built a compelling fantasy world with humor and heart.

GENE LUEN YANG, creator of *American Born Chinese* and *Boxers & Saints*

✦

Matt Mikalatos has penned a tale straight out of today's headlines that will tug at your heartstrings. *The Crescent Stone* is a compelling story that will get under your skin and worm its way into your heart.

TOSCA LEE, *New York Times* bestselling author of *Iscariot* and *The Legend of Sheba*

✦

The Crescent Stone hooked me from the first page! With the rich characterization of John Green and the magical escapism of Narnia, this book is a must read for all fantasy fans!

LORIE LANGDON, author of *Olivia Twist* and the Doon series

✦

This is what sets Mikalatos's epic world apart from so many other fantasy realms: the characters feel real, their lives are genuine and complicated, and their choices are far from binary. Mikalatos's creativity and originality are on full display in this epic tale for adults and young readers alike.

SHAWN SMUCKER, author of *The Day the Angels Fell*

✦

The Crescent Stone blends . . . glitter unicorns, powerful healing tattoos, and an engaging cast of characters into a funny and thoughtful story that examines the true costs of magic and privilege.

TINA CONNOLLY, author of *Seriously Wicked*

ALSO IN THE SUNLIT LANDS SERIES

The Crescent Stone

"Our Last Christmas Together:
A Sunlit Lands Christmas Tale"

THE SUNLIT LANDS

PASTISIA

KAKRI TERRITORIES

COURT OF FAR SEEING

TOLMIN PASS

WASTED LANDS

GINIAN SEA

N

THE SOUTHERN COURT

ALUVOREA

ALUVOREA
UDUHUM KOB
N
HANALI SAID
NO DRAGONS
BUT
ALLAE
ARAKAM
ANNAGINI VASAGI
ANUKOP
MAP NOT
TO SCALE
OR TREE
WOULD BE
HUGE!
AYARA ARDHA
INYULAP
ANYAR
A CURSED RIVER? OF COURSE!
BRING
YOUR OWN
MARSH
MALLOWS
KASKA SHRAM
CARNIVOROUS
FOREST—WHY??
RASKAN
WITH MY LUCK
THERE WILL BE A
SWAMP MONSTER
HERE !!
PATRA
KOJA

THE SUNLIT LANDS

BOOK TWO

THE
HEARTWOOD
CROWN

MATT MIKALATOS

wander
An imprint of
Tyndale House
Publishers, Inc.

Library of Congress Cataloging-in-Publication Data
Names: Mikalatos, Matt, author.
Title: The Heartwood Crown / Matt Mikalatos.
Description: Carol Stream, Illinois : Wander, [2019] | Series: The sunlit lands ; book [2] | Summary: Madeline's health continues to deteriorate after she returns home, bringing Shula and Yenil along, and she yearns to return to the Sunlit Lands, but the magic fueling that land is failing, threatening its inhabitants.
Identifiers: LCCN 2019000619| ISBN 9781496431752 (hc) | ISBN 9781496431769 (sc)
Subjects: | CYAC: Fantasy. | Sick—Fiction. | Friendship—Fiction. | Magic—Fiction.
Classification: LCC PZ7.1.M5535 He 2019 | DDC [Fic]—dc23 LC record available at https://lccn.loc.gov/2019000619

Printed in the United States of America

25	24	23	22	21	20	19
7	6	5	4	3	2	1

To Jermayne Chapman, who has been a generous friend and a wise guide along the way

JASON'S NOTES ON THE PEOPLES AND PLACES OF THE SUNLIT LANDS

PEOPLES

ALUVOREANS—Plant people. They have green or blue skin. Don't make jokes about weed killer. They do not like this.

ELENIL—I don't think they're jerks on purpose. It's just that they really like everything a certain way. And that way involves them being in charge and also dressing up in silly clothes. Loves: costume parties, prophecies, fancy food, haberdashery, making deals. Hates: high fives, irreverent jokes at their expense, the destabilization of their source of power, impertinent questions about the underlying philosophy of the magical economy, suspenders.

KAKRI—They love stories and live in the desert and are great warriors, and they are tall and tan skinned and have shining silver eyes, et cetera, but the most important thing is that Baileya is a Kakri, and she is the most beautiful, amazing, intelligent, kind, terrifying, and wonderful person I have ever met. Also, she can't read English, so I can say whatever I want about her here. (Insert heart emoji, insert smiley face with heart eyes, XOXOXOXO.) PS, reminder: do not teach Baileya to read.

MAEGROM—These little dudes have grey skin and have a whole underground kingdom. I don't know much about them, so I just make up stories about them. My favorite is called "Maegrom, PI." It's about a Maegrom named Thomas who solves mysteries in the Sunlit Lands. His best friend is a mole named Higgins. I want to get to know the Maegrom better, but honestly, at this point I think I'll be disappointed because they won't live up to my fantasy version.

PASTISIANS—Necromancers. I've said it before, and I'll say it again: HARD PASS. If you talk to the dead, don't talk to me.

SCIM—I think they're cute, and I don't care what anyone else says. In fact, as soon as I'm done here, I'm going to go give Break Bones a great big hug.

SOUTHERN COURT—You know that friend who tells you jokes and then he's the only one who laughs? Yeah, that's these guys. Also, they are lizard shape-shifters.

ZHANIN—I'm told Zhanin translates to "shark people," and c'mon, that's all we really need to know, right? Baileya was telling me, "These people are dangerous, for they kill all who threaten the balance of magic," and I was like, "Hey, as soon as you said 'shark people,' I knew to stay away from them."

PLACES

ALUVOREA—The great forest where the Aluvoreans live. Why am I writing this stuff down? I should be able to remember this.

COURT OF FAR SEEING—The fabulous city-state of the Elenil. Slightly less fabulous since me and Madeline and our friends busted it up by wrecking their magic and chopping off their leader's hand. Now they're trying to kill me, but I'm like, whoa, have you ever heard of forgiveness? You'll be happier if you try it, believe me.

GINIAN SEA—I hear it's nice this time of year. Maybe everyone should go hang out on the beach together for a week. Then there would be less fighting. Maybe the Elenil and the Scim could solve all their problems with a big volleyball tournament or something. The Zhanin live here, and they could be the referees or eat the losing team or whatever.

KAKRI TERRITORIES—It's pretty nice here if you like deserts and lots of wild animals that are smarter than Earth animals and trying to kill you. Oh yeah, and the Kakri people, who are also nice when they are not trying to kill you. Other than that, great place, highly recommended, five stars.

PASTISIA—They have death blimps. Baileya says not to call them that, but I know a death blimp when I see one.

THE SOUTHERN COURT—Imagine that one table of weird kids in the cafeteria who are nice and everything, but they are always laughing at jokes that make no sense whatsoever. Now imagine they are shape-shifting lizard people.

UNDERGROUND MAEGROM CITY—Not that I've been there, but I picture a big cavern with houses carved out of the rock. There are torches, probably, and the houses are warmed by magma flows. And maybe someone has painted a big yellow sun on the ceiling of the cavern. Just as a way to cheer up the other Maegrom, you know?

WASTED LANDS—Imagine the dumpsters at Disneyland and you know what the Wasted Lands are—the Happiest Place on Earth has to get rid of all its waste somehow. They try to keep it locked up and hidden away, but it's only going to work so long. The Scim live here. It's not great.

WESTWIND—This is the name of the Knight of the Mirror's castle, which is located on the EAST side of Far Seeing. When I was staying there, I would ask the knight once a day, "Hey, why is it called WESTwind when it's on the EAST side of the city?" And every day he would ignore me, but I could tell my daily question was getting to him and that one day I would ask and he would gently place his hand on my shoulder and explain it all to me. Only then would I be worthy to take my rightful place . . . as TOUR GUIDE TO THE SUNLIT LANDS.

ZOLTARNOG—The hidden wizards' island in the northern Ginian Sea. It is said that the wild magics of the Sunlit Lands will be tamed by the wizards of Zoltarnog— ha ha ha ha, I just made that one up and you totally fell for it, didn't you? ADMIT IT!

CAST OF CHARACTERS

AMIRA—Shula's younger sister

ARAKAM—a prophetic dragon who lives in Aluvorea

ARCHON THENODY—the chief magistrate; supreme ruler of the Elenil; crippled since being wounded by the Sword of Years

BAILEYA—a Kakri warrior; Jason's fiancée; daughter of Willow, granddaughter of Abronia

BEZAED—a Kakri warrior; one of Baileya's brothers

BLACK SKULLS—the elite fighting force of the Scim; there are three known members, one of whom is Darius

BOULOS—Shula's older brother

BREAK BONES—a Scim warrior once imprisoned by the Elenil, now Jason's ally

DARIUS WALKER—an American human allied with the Scim; Madeline's ex-boyfriend; a Black Skull

DAVID GLENN—an American human who was sent to Aluvorea by the Knight of the Mirror

DELIGHTFUL GLITTER LADY [DEE, DGL]—Jason's unicorn; can change size

DIWDRAP—a faerie

ECLIPSE—a Scim child

EVERNU—a gallant white stag who works alongside Rondelo

FATHER ANTHONY—a Catholic priest

GARDEN LADY—a mysterious old woman who has taken an interest in Madeline

GILENYIA—an influential Elenil lady; Hanali's cousin; has the power of healing

HANALI—an Elenil recruiter who invited Madeline to the Sunlit Lands

JASON WU (WU SONG)—an American human who followed Madeline into the Sunlit Lands; always tells the truth

JENNY WU—Jason's sister

KEKOA KAHANANUI—an American human who was sent to the Zhanin by the Knight of the Mirror

KNIGHT OF THE MIRROR—a human in his midforties; eschews magic; onetime guardian of the five Scim artifacts

KYLE OLIVER—Madeline's father

LAMISAP—an Aluvorean woman

LIN—an Aluvorean woman

MADELINE OLIVER—an American human formerly in the service of the Elenil

MAJESTIC ONE—the Elenil name for the magician who founded the Sunlit Lands

MALIK—Darius's cousin

MORIARTY—a brucok (gigantic bird from the Kakri territories)

MOTHER CROW—a Kakri matriarch

MRS. RAYMOND—an English human woman who runs the Transition House for humans in the Sunlit Lands; fifty years old

MRS. ROUHANA—a Syrian woman who used to clean for the Bisharas

MUD—the Scim leader of the anti-Elenil resistance

NIGHTFALL—a Scim child

NIGHT'S BREATH—a Scim warrior

OREG—a Maegrom tinker and rebel

PATRA KOJA—the antlered spirit of an Aluvorean marsh

PEASANT KING—the figure from Scim legend who founded the Sunlit Lands

REMI—the Guardian of the Wind

RONDELO—the Elenil captain of the guard in the Court of Far Seeing

RUTH MBEWE—a Zambian eight-year-old; the Knight of the Mirror's ward; accompanied Kekoa to the land of the Zhanin

SHADOW—a Scim child

SHULA BISHARA—a Syrian human; friend to Madeline; has the power to burst into flame

SOCHAR—an Elenil guard

SOFÍA—the housekeeper in Madeline's home on Earth

THASTLE—a faerie

VIVI—the father of Hanali, son of Gelintel

WALLACE—a sentient tunnel

WENDY OLIVER—Madeline's mother

WILFRED—yet another sentient tunnel

YENIL—a young orphaned Scim girl; adopted by Madeline and Shula

PART 1

If we're together, I won't be afraid.

**FROM *THE GRYPHON UNDER THE STAIRS*
BY MARY PATRICIA WALL**

THE VOLUNTEERS

Prepare yourself for the pain, and then breathe in. Hold it as long as you can, relax, and let the breath escape. Prepare yourself for the pain. Breathe in, let it out. Do it again. Again. Ask yourself how long you can keep doing this. Prepare yourself for the pain. Breathe in.

Madeline could scarcely sleep anymore. The once-automatic process of breathing now required her full attention, each inhalation an act of courage. When she'd left for the Sunlit Lands, she'd expected that she would come home stronger, healed, and would go back to school as a new person. Instead she'd come back broken, unable to get to school at all. Which, maybe, was for the best. The thought of going to chemistry class and seeing an empty chair where Jason should be, or not having Darius drive her to school or meet her after class, filled her with a sadness that tightened like a vise around her chest.

So she stayed home, tried to convince herself to get out of bed each day, to walk around the house, to play a game with Yenil, to sit with Shula and sip tea. She had outgrown school, anyway. Algebra wasn't much use when you were on a slow slide toward the grave. Madeline shuddered. Some days she felt at peace with the idea of dying, even wished for death to come faster so the pain could finally be over. Other days panic gripped her, and she wanted to burst out of the house, break through a window if she had to, and run. Some animal instinct was convinced that if she could move fast enough, go far enough, she would escape her disease. On those days she gripped the arms of the easy chair and willed herself to relax, told herself the story of what was happening, where she was headed, assured herself that it was terrible, yes, but it was also okay. Okay to be sad, okay to be scared, okay to be dying.

The garden looked grey and lonely most days, and Madeline turned more and more often to her memories, eyes closed, sifting through all the beautiful things she had seen and done and wishing there were more to come. But she knew better. There was more life behind than ahead. She hadn't expected to grieve her own loss, but many days that's what she felt. Grief. Sorrow for the future that was no longer ahead of her, sadness for the people she would leave behind. So she would try to focus on today, this moment, to be present in the present, not living in the past or worrying about the losses piled up in front of her. She had to be realistic. There were things to be done with the time that remained.

She made preparations. Not as quickly as she would like, but she could accomplish so little in any one day. She had registered Yenil for school. Madeline's mother had insisted on paying for private school, saying Yenil's experience would be better there. They had no birth certificate, Social Security number, or green card, and Madeline wasn't even sure of Yenil's age. But it had been less trouble than she had expected. The principal had made comments, but the woman at the desk had told Madeline it was no problem, that this happened from time to time.

Shula thought Yenil was about seven, and that seemed right to Madeline. So this week she would enter second grade. It would be difficult. She had just begun learning to read. She looked different than the other kids. She had long, black hair, brown skin that seemed to have an almost chalky grey undertone, and a mess of silver scars that covered her arms and hands—the scars that matched Madeline's own. But it had been almost six months, and the little girl so often burst with joy and happiness that Madeline could almost forget Yenil had lost her parents, murdered by the Elenil in the Wasted Lands.

Then, three days ago, something strange had happened in the garden. Madeline had been in her chair by the window, taking in the manicured but lonely expanse of it: the pond, the fountain, the winding white path, the maple where she had met the Garden Lady, the bench her mother had placed near there, the little faerie villages that Yenil built along the shore of the pond, the hedge that enclosed it all. Then she'd seen it. Beside the path stood a tall stalk of flowers, purple bells crowded onto a single strand of green.

It stood at least four feet tall and was blooming out of season. Not only that, but it was a plant her mother had never seen in the garden and hadn't planted. Foxglove, her mother said. A plant that only flowers in its second year. It should not have been there, should not bloom in the fall. Sofía went out into the garden and cut it, and put it in the vase on the kitchen counter. "A volunteer," she said, with a note of disbelief in her voice.

Madeline's mother frowned, first at the flower and then at Sofía. "One of the neighbors must have planted some. Or a bird dropped the seed in our yard. It feels wrong, having this flower in this season."

The next morning, Madeline made her way to the back window, stopping to breathe when needed, taking small and careful steps. Six more stalks of foxglove stood, heavy with purple bells, near the maple tree. Sofía, astonished, brought them in and put them in the same vase.

Then, last night, Madeline had a dream. She stood in the kitchen, near the vase of foxgloves, and heard a ringing, clear and clean, like a tiny silver bell struck with a tiny silver hammer. One of the flowers shook, and Madeline held her hand beneath the opening of the bell (how did she know to do this?), and a faerie fell out of the plant, landing in the palm of her hand. The faerie was tiny and weak, curled in upon itself. It had clothes made from bits of leaves and acorns. It wore a small twist of wood on its forehead, a tiny crown. It was breathing but did not turn to look at her. Its mouth moved, but no sound came out.

Then, more ringing. A second bell. A third. Then all the bells, all at once, a hundred flowers ringing, and she knew each was a faerie arriving, entering her house through the flowers. All of them trying to say something, all of them failing, each of them wearing a crown. A green glow suffused the kitchen, and a sharp pain came from Madeline's arm. The seed burned there, small and bright as a star. She put her hand over it, but the light shone through her fingers.

She woke gasping for air in the darkness of her bedroom and stumbled to the kitchen. She reached for the vase, but in her haste she knocked it to the floor, where the crystal shattered with a sound not unlike a thousand bells. She felt the cold wash of asphyxia moving through her, knew she would faint if she was not careful, and slid to the floor among the shattered glass and broken flower stems.

She could not avoid the pressing certainty that the flowers were a communication from the Sunlit Lands, that they were reaching out again. She wanted to be left in peace, left out of their wars and conflicts and injustices. She had nothing left to give. Her strength was gone, her breath, her hope, and she resented the Sunlit Lands intruding again, asking for her help. She was the one who needed help. A small part of her wanted to answer the summons, and that made her angry, because she was not able to do so. She turned her anger toward the Sunlit Lands. They knew this about her, knew she had left them with no intention of returning. She wanted them to leave her alone, leave Shula alone, leave Yenil alone.

She labored for breath, and when she was able, she gathered the foxgloves and pushed them deep into the trash can. She didn't have the strength to clean up all the glass. She dragged herself to the living room and slept beneath the garden window.

When she awoke, someone had cleaned up the glass and mopped up the water.

A hundred foxgloves grew in the garden.

She prepared herself for the ache in her chest and breathed.

1

HUNTERS

Where fear is planted, hate will grow.

AN ALUVOREAN SAYING

✛

Jason Wu had wedged himself into what he suspected might be a closet. It had never occurred to him that people who lived in a fantasy world would need a place to store their clothes, but of course they did. This particular closet was narrow and located in a dilapidated three-story house that had once been a mansion. There were holes in the roof, mold on the walls, missing stairs on the long, winding stairways. There were tapestries on some of the walls showing ancient battles between the Scim and the Elenil, among other things, and the hallways were lit with softly glowing stones in metal settings. Doors to certain rooms were missing, and others were locked. He had managed to find this closet, though, with its door still intact and unlocked, so he could slip inside and pull it quietly shut, certain his pursuers would not find him here, not given the size of this house.

Delightful Glitter Lady, Jason's kitten-sized rhinoceros, scrabbled impatiently on the floor beside him. Jason scooped her up and held her against his chest, trying to keep her quiet. He could hear the thundering footsteps of his pursuers outside. Dee let out a low whine, and the footsteps paused. "Dee," Jason whispered, doing his best to make it clear she needed to be silent.

"I heard him," a voice called. By now he recognized the distinctive sound of a Scim. He could tell by the guttural voice that the Scim had put on his war skin, a defensive magic all Scim had that allowed them to have thicker skin, heavier muscles, and a terrifying appearance.

Dee whined again. Jason pulled her tighter against him.

Outside the closet, all sound ceased.

Jason held his breath.

"In here?" another voice asked.

"I think so. I heard the unicorn." The people of the Sunlit Lands thought Dee was a unicorn. They were a little sketchy on zoological categories. Unfortunately for Jason, their tracking skills were fully developed.

A third voice asked, "Have you checked the closet?"

"Hold," said another voice, one Jason knew well. It was deeper, more resonant, than the others. Jason could practically feel it vibrating the house. It was the voice of Break Bones, the Scim warrior who had sworn to murder Jason and then kept incessantly reminding Jason about it. "I must be allowed to kill him. But each of you may say first what you wish to do with him when the door is opened."

"I will stab him in the liver," said the first voice, and cackles of laughter came from the others.

"I will break his arms," said another.

Jason shivered.

"I will crush him with my hammer," said the third.

Jason pushed as far back against the wall as he could, feeling with one hand for a crack, a hole, a way out. But there was nothing. He was trapped.

The door flew open, and three Scim shoved and pushed, all of them trying to get in the door at once. Dee let out a delighted squeak and struggled to get out of Jason's arms.

The Scim piled on top of him, laughing and cheering as they pinned him to the floor and tickled him mercilessly. Jason begged for them to stop, and after thirty seconds or so, Break Bones called the Scim children off. They bounced out of the closet, Delightful Glitter Lady gamboling at their feet.

"Six minutes," Break Bones said. "It is the best you have done so far."

"Is Baileya back yet?" Jason asked. Baileya was a Kakri woman, a powerful warrior from a desert tribe to the north. She also happened to be Jason's fiancée, ever since he had accidentally proposed to her nearly six weeks before. The last several weeks, since they had made this broken-down mansion their base of operations, Baileya had taken to going on long patrols of the area.

Break Bones held out a wide hand and helped Jason to his feet. "She is safe, Wu Song. No one is trying to kill her."

"She'd be safe even if people *were* trying to kill her." You shouldn't mess with Baileya.

"Everyone's trying to kill *you*, Wu Song," one of the children said.

"Not you, I hope," Jason said, wrapping an arm around the nearest kid's neck and wrestling him to the ground. Soon all three kids were grappling with him. These little monsters had been his almost constant companions since he, Baileya, and Break Bones had moved in here. Nightfall was the oldest, maybe ten or so, and he was delighted by Jason's refusal to ever tell a lie. He liked to ask Jason's opinion on awkward subjects in front of the adult Scim. Then came Eclipse, an eight-year-old girl who most often won these games of Hunter and Prey. Shadow, the youngest, was a boy of around six, with a nasty habit of biting.

"Enough," Break Bones said. Jason and the kids stopped wrestling. "What did Wu Song do wrong?" Break Bones asked the Scim children.

"He got found!" Shadow shouted.

"He hid somewhere obvious," Eclipse said.

"He made every person in the Sunlit Lands want to murder him." Nightfall grinned.

"Hey!" Jason said, but it was true. The Elenil wanted to kill him for his role in crippling their leader, the archon (not to mention the extensive damage that Jason and his friends had caused to the archon's palace, the literal pinnacle of Elenil architecture). The Scim wanted to kill him because one of their nobles had died so he could live. The Kakri were trying to kill him as part of his engagement process to Baileya. (It was a long story, but her whole family had a year to try to kill him before they got married.) There was even some group of people he had never met, called the Zhanin, who were upset because Jason had supposedly messed up the balance of magic or something. Still, it's not like *everyone* was trying to kill him. Those necromancers in the north didn't even know who he was . . . he hoped. And the creepy shape-shifters in the south had invited him to come to their land anytime. And the . . . well, he couldn't remember all the different people in the Sunlit Lands, but so far as he knew, only four groups were trying to kill him.

"Eclipse is correct," Break Bones said. "In a closet or under a bed—this is the first place most people will look. If you are being hunted, such places are to be shunned." He looked at Jason with pity. "For the Scim, at least. Humans are not known for their cunning in battle or survival."

"Hey!" Jason said again.

"Shadow," Break Bones said, "you are the prey now."

Shadow leapt to his feet and looked around shiftily.

"Run," Break Bones said, and the boy sped from the room. Break Bones gathered the two remaining Scim children and Jason in the center of the room. "This time you will hunt as individuals, not in a pack. Eclipse, you will take the ground floor. Nightfall, the second. Wu Song, the third floor and above."

"Why are we doing this again?" Jason asked.

"To help you survive," Break Bones said.

Oh. Fine. But it's not like Jason would be hunting anyone. If anything, he would be the one hiding, just like he was hiding now in this old house. It had belonged, once, to the family of Night's Breath, the Scim prince who had died so Jason could be healed of a mortal wound. Jason had come here hoping to make peace with that—and with Night's Breath's family. But as soon as Jason had arrived, Night's Breath's wife and children had left. The Scim prince's elderly mother still lived here, but she had made it clear she remained only to guard the house . . . from him. The children who remained were Night's Breath's nephews and niece. The kids had taken to Jason immediately, but the old woman showed no interest in him. Jason had to admit it hurt his feelings in a weird way. He was here, far from his own family, and when he tried to connect to this woman, she shut him out. She even turned her head away any time he entered a room. Not that it surprised him. He was terrible at family stuff. His own parents hated him and wanted nothing to do with him, so why should a family that wasn't even human be any different?

Meanwhile, Jason and Baileya had friends in danger, but Baileya wouldn't agree to travel to help them. Their friend Kekoa had sent multiple messenger birds asking for assistance, but Baileya said, "It is too dangerous at this time. One of my brothers is seeking our trail. Twice I have led him away. He is cunning and swift, and should he find us, I do not doubt he would succeed in killing you, Wu Song." Baileya's brother was named Bezaed, and Baileya spoke of him with reverence. He had killed one of their sister's suitors, and that was a Kakri man. He would make short work of Jason. At this point in the conversation, Jason had almost tried to explain to her about their accidental engagement. He had told her a personal story, not realizing the Kakri got engaged by sharing a story one had never told anyone else. Jason and Baileya were a month and a half into their yearlong engagement now, and he didn't want to break up with her. But he didn't want their engagement to be based on a misunderstanding, either. Plus, it was weird to be seventeen and engaged to a terrifying warrior maiden from a fantasy world. She wasn't even human—at least, her golden skin and shining silver eyes argued for something not quite human.

"Wu Song," Break Bones said.

"Hmm?"

"It is time to hunt," the Scim said, shaking his shoulder gently. "The other children have already begun."

Jason glared at him. "The *other* children?"

Break Bones grinned, his yellow, tusk-like teeth protruding from his mouth. "Prove me wrong. Be the first to find Shadow."

"I will," Jason said forcefully. He strode out of the room and immediately had no idea what to do. Finding a half-pint Scim in a dilapidated mess like this place would be a challenge.

Delightful Glitter Lady romped down the hallway. Jason followed her into what must have once been a ballroom. Or maybe something else, because Jason thought a ballroom would be on the ground floor, but this room was large, and there were many gigantic pieces of furniture covered with moldering cloths. The floor was tiled in blue and white, creating mosaics of the moon in various phases, but the tiles had been pried up in a bunch of places, revealing the wooden boards beneath.

Dee sniffed twice, then sneezed, almost knocking herself over. Jason had been keeping her at kitten size because he didn't trust the floors in this place. He worried she could fall through a rotten board in her larger sizes.

"I know you're in here, Shadow," Jason said. He could hear the uncertainty in his own voice. He shivered. Anything could be under these sheets. He yanked one off, letting it fall to the ground. It revealed a sort of low sofa with no arms. He pulled another sheet to discover a pair of chairs. He would have to uncover them all, he knew, because Shadow was exactly the kind of kid to hide under a moldy sheet if he thought it would give him even a minute's advantage in a game like this. There were at least thirty sheets. Jason sighed and got to work.

About ten sheets in, Dee made a high-pitched whine. "What is it, girl?"

She snorted and shuffled toward the back of the room. Jason smiled. She smelled Shadow. He bent down low and whispered, "Where's Shadow, girl? Do you smell him?"

Dee made a quiet, distressed honking, looking at another large sheet-covered item near the wall.

"In there?" Jason walked to the sheet. It had to be a cabinet or something like that. It was taller than Jason by several feet and nearly square in shape. He yanked on the sheet, and a cloud of moldy dust rained onto him. He sneezed, grumbling to himself, and tried to shake it off. He studied the wardrobe that had been revealed. It was made of some dark wood and looked ancient. A star had been carved into the front of it and painted silver. A slight shuffle came from inside. Shadow was exactly the kind of kid who would hide in a closet immediately after being told not to hide in closets.

Dee turned in a tiny circle, whining.

"What's the problem, girl?" Jason put his hand on the door. The kids liked to say all the terrible things they would do when they found him, delighting in making it sound as terrifyingly gory as possible. Since Jason didn't tell lies, his threats sounded lame in comparison. "When I find

Shadow, I am going to gloat about how I found him so fast and say that I'm better at Hunter and Prey!"

Jason flung the door open.

Shadow was inside.

A golden arm was thrown across the little Scim's neck. A young man with flashing silver eyes and loose, flowing clothes stood behind him. A knife point pressed against Shadow's cheek. Shadow struggled, and the man constricted his arms, pinning the Scim child.

"Be very quiet, Wu Song," the man said. "I have no desire to hurt this child. But if you call for help, I will." Jason opened his mouth, but the stranger's knife point pressed in, and a bead of blood appeared on Shadow's cheek. "I will take his eye if you scream."

"That is what a real threat should sound like, Wu Song," Shadow said. He had that defiant, almost nonchalant look he would get in his eyes right before he bit one of his siblings. Showing fear was not encouraged among the Scim.

"Well," Jason said, very quietly, "I did find you pretty fast. I am better at Hunter and Prey. Obviously."

The man's eyes flicked toward the room's entrance and then back to Jason. "There is room in here for one more," he said.

"Um," Jason said, "maybe if we were closer friends."

The man pushed on the knife again, and Shadow's eyes widened. Jason's hands clenched. He wasn't a warrior. He was terrible at Hunter and Prey. He needed to be protected, and he was useless with any weapon. But he wasn't about to let someone threaten a child and get away with it. He opened the second door of the wardrobe and stepped into it, Dee scrambling at his feet.

"Close the doors," the man said.

When the doors were closed, the stranger's silver eyes shone out with a powerful light. The man spoke, his voice steady and low. "My name is Bezaed. My mother is called Willow, and my grandmother, Abronia. I am here, brother, to kill you before you can marry my sister Baileya."

2
FIRST DAY

Anger is the seed of violence.

FROM "THE SEED," AN ALUVOREAN POEM

✦

Shula Bishara woke, panicked and disoriented, clutching her blankets.

The sound of a distant jet engine still echoed from her dream, and she was waiting for the whistling sound, the sound of a falling bomb. She pulled her sister close, but it was not her sister. It was Yenil. Where was Amira? Of course she knew the answer to that, but still a part of her asked because the answer was too terrible.

She put her hand on her chest, felt her heart hammering, tried to calm herself. *I am in the United States now*, she reminded herself. *I do not live in Aleppo anymore. My parents, my sister, my brother, do not live on the seventh floor of a cement building in a tiny apartment. I do not share a small bedroom and a bed with Amira. We do not heat the house with a diesel-powered heater or with the small wood-burning stove Baba found, not anymore.*

She took a deep breath and let it out with barely a stutter. She would not cry, not when she had just awoken. She refused to start the day in this way. She continued her litany of remembrances, forcing herself to face reality. *I live here now,* she reminded herself, *in an American house. A small mansion in a suburb, with central heat and a too-large yard and more bedrooms than people.*

It was too quiet here in this neighborhood. The neighbors too far. The sounds of life muffled by the thick walls and carpets. But still, the recitation of these remembrances calmed her. She forced her breathing to even out, her shoulders to relax. Morning had come, and it was time to get ready for the day.

Yenil had not stirred. Let her sleep a few minutes more.

Shula still wore her T-shirt and jeans from yesterday. It had been a hard night for falling asleep, with all Yenil's excitement about starting school today, and Shula had lain beside her until she slept. Shula's unruly mop of dark hair covered her face. She pulled it into a ponytail.

She stepped quietly down the hall, the plush carpet under her bare feet another reminder that she lived in a luxury home in the United States. Madeline's door, white and perfect, was closed. For once no coughing or wheezing came from the other side. Shula turned the handle gently, silently, and slipped inside.

Was Madeline breathing? She lay so still, unmoving. Then Madeline gasped, and Shula's muscles unknotted.

The windows had blackout shades on them, and Madeline's room remained midnight dark despite the weak sunrise. Except. Something in the bed glowed. Shula thought Madeline must have brought her phone into bed, but instead of blue, the light was a golden green.

Stepping nearer the bed, she could see that the light came from Madeline's wrist, that it burned from within the network of Elenil scars on her arm. But the light of Elenil magic had always burned silver, not green, and had flowed along her entire tattoo. This light seemed to be centered in her wrist but grew gradually dim, revealing only the tattooed lines closest to its center. Could this be because of the stone flower that had stung Madeline in the marketplace? Shula had never heard of such a response, but then again she didn't know all the ins and outs of the magics of the Sunlit Lands. The light came from a place near where Madeline had received the wound, and such a coincidence couldn't be ignored. But speculation seemed unimportant when Shula studied Madeline's face.

In the greenish-golden glow, Madeline's sunken eyes appeared more stark, the hollow of her cheeks more pronounced. She had been eating less and sleeping less with every month that passed. Shula put her palm on Madeline's forehead and swept the hair out of her face. Her skin was cold and clammy.

Shula decided to let her sleep. Yes, it was Yenil's first day of school, but Madeline rarely slept so deeply or so well these days. Let her rest.

The housekeeper, Sofía, had made an impressive American breakfast. Eggs and toast, pancakes and bacon. The smell of the bacon brought Yenil out, still half asleep, wrapped in a blanket. She settled happily at the table. Madeline's mother came out as well, already dressed in a perfectly tailored suit. She busied herself filling Yenil's plate and chirping along with small talk about the coming day that Shula could only half follow. But the happy warmth of it all—Sofía's loving meal, Mrs. Oliver's attempt to start Yenil's day well, Yenil's affectionate smiles between pouring too much syrup onto her plate—reminded Shula of her own loss. *This is not my mother*, she reminded herself. *No more long breakfasts with my parents and Amira and Boulos. No ful or za'atar, or olives and oil and cheese and makdous and pitas, no table filled to bursting with plates and small bowls and laughter.*

And yet . . . this was good. The winter sunlight slanted in and warmed them. The eggs were hot and fluffy, the jam reminded her of her mother's. Her mother had made the most amazing fresh apricot jam. When they had finished, Yenil scurried away to get dressed. Sofía cleared the table, and Mrs. Oliver set out to make Yenil a lunch. Shula loaded a plate of breakfast food and took it, quietly, in to Madeline.

Madeline's eyes flickered. "Morning," she said. Her voice had become so weak. Her breathing was often louder than her words.

Shula put the food on the nightstand, but Madeline didn't look at it. She gestured at the shades, and Shula opened them, letting in the light. She helped Madeline to the bathroom. Madeline insisted on getting dressed. She planned to drop Yenil at school. Shula helped her get ready. She had learned not to critique, not to suggest Madeline take it slow or rethink her decisions. She must be allowed to make her own choices—she was not a child. Not anymore.

Shula left her resting, sitting on the side of the bed. When Shula brought the wheelchair, Madeline still had not eaten anything. "You must eat," Shula said. Here she would draw a line. Madeline could make her own decisions, but she had no interest in food. Her body did not tell her to eat anymore.

Madeline looked at her glumly and forced down a few bites of her eggs. She drank a sip of orange juice. "I'll eat . . . when we get . . . back."

Shula scowled at her. "Promise."

"Yes, yes, okay," Madeline said, and she laughed. The coughing stopped her.

They took pictures in front of the house. Of Yenil in her school uniform—a blue plaid skirt with a crisp white blouse and a navy sweater. Shula thought Yenil could almost fit in. Sofía had styled her hair in a French braid down her back, and the long sleeves of her sweater hid most of the swirling black Scim marks on her skin. Yenil smiled for the pictures. She was nervous but happy. Sofía waved at them as they piled into the car. Shula sat in the back with Yenil, Madeline in front of her. Mrs. Oliver drove.

Yenil's English was much better than Shula's already. She latched onto the grammar and pronunciation with ease, while Shula struggled to remember the difference between *bed* and *bad*. There were so many vowels in English! Keeping them all straight was a chore. Yenil chattered away with Mrs. Oliver, while Shula let the words envelop her, and Madeline interjected a few labored words here or there.

The wide streets of the neighborhood and the perfect lawns reminded Shula of something from an American movie. Every house with its green grass (Madeline said that here the weather was so mild that the grass was actually greener in the winter than in the summer) and one tall tree in the front. The long driveways and the wooden fences. No apartment complexes crowding the roads, no motorcycles squeezing past, no tiny grocery stores wedged beneath and between the apartments. Madeline's house was at the end of a branching series of cul-de-sacs, and only one road drove through the middle, like the trunk of a tree.

"Oh dear," Mrs. Oliver said, slowing the car.

A heavy truck was parked diagonally, blocking the street. It was the sort of truck that American commercials showed being used for farm work—bales of hay being thrown in the bed (not the *bad*) of the truck. Here in this neighborhood there was no need for such a vehicle, but Shula saw people driving them from time to time.

A teenage boy, about her age or maybe a bit younger—seventeen or so—stood outside the passenger window, shouting. A teenage girl was in the cab of the truck, the window down. She also was shouting.

Beside Shula, Yenil tensed. Shula put a hand on her arm. When Yenil became upset, she put on her war skin. Her skin thickened, her hair thinned, muscles layered onto her, and thick, tusk-like teeth protruded from her mouth. It was a defense mechanism, and it made her look inhuman. Shula patted her hand. "It is okay," she said. "I have seen this boy yesterday. Sometimes he is near here."

"I should call the police," Mrs. Oliver said, her phone in hand.

"Mom," Madeline said, shaking her head.

They couldn't call the police. Madeline always said this. Shula and Yenil did not have green cards, or visas, or any identification. If the police asked for those things, they didn't know what would happen. Shula could be deported to Syria. And Yenil . . . well, they didn't know where they would send her. Not to the Sunlit Lands, certainly.

The boy reached in through the window and punched the girl in the face.

Shula flung her door open and strode toward them.

She did not allow this.

Mrs. Oliver honked her horn. Yenil's door opened. "Stay!" Shula said sternly, and the door shut again.

The boy saw her coming. "This isn't your business," he said. His bloodshot eyes darted toward the girl in the truck. She was screaming at him, holding her face. Her lip was split, and blood dripped down through her fingers.

The boy also had a bloody nose. So the girl had managed to hit him at some point too. Now that she was closer, Shula could see bruises on the girl's neck.

"Move the truck," Shula said.

"I would love to, but Tiffany there won't let me back in the cab," the boy said. He slapped his palms on the window, which the girl had wisely rolled up. He swayed, then turned his attention back to Shula. "What are you, Iraqi?"

She was not afraid of him. She had fought bigger men than him. She had fought Scim. The tattoo on her left wrist tingled. A single thought from her and the magic of the Elenil would course through her. She would feel the familiar bite of the flames as she lit on fire. She knew she could do it. She had tested it in the backyard more than once. She had made sure no one was watching, and she had felt the comforting prickle of heat as she brought the fire through her skin. The magic of the Sunlit Lands still coursed through her, despite being in America. This boy could not hurt her, could not even touch her unless she allowed it.

The honking again.

Shula looked back. Madeline's door stood open. She leaned against it, standing beside the car.

"Stay!" Shula shouted.

The boy sneered at her. "You think you're in charge of everyone, don't you? Telling people to move their trucks. Telling people to stay. I don't know what it's like in Iraq, but this is a free country."

Inside the truck the girl, Tiffany, was screaming, "Shut up, Josh! Just shut up!"

Shula looked in at Tiffany. "You drive away," she said. Her English was a problem. She hoped the girl understood.

Josh held his hand up and shook his keys. "She can't. She keeps locking the doors when I try to get in, but she can't go anywhere either."

"We are calling police," Shula said.

"Yeah, right," Josh said. He sneered. "They gonna believe me or you?" He dropped his keys. Swayed. Bent over carefully to pick them up. He was on drugs, clearly, but Shula had no idea what type. He would not be rational. She did not think she would be able to talk him out of this. They could not call the police. "You go get back in your car and go on home. Me and Tiff will be done here soon, and you can go do whatever it is you got to do." He slammed his palms against the window again. "Isn't that right, Tiffany?"

"Don't leave me with him!" she wailed. "Please, please."

"What is it you want, anyway?" he shouted. He pushed against the truck, rocking it.

Tiffany screamed, "I just want someone to love me!"

"Oh please," Josh said. He spit at the window. "You're high." He kicked the truck.

"You give her the keys," Shula said. "We go to school."

Josh's eyes refocused on her. She could see it, that moment the rage redirected. She had seen it before in men's eyes, recognized the way they decided that the person in front of them could be an outlet, that this person might be weak enough to make them feel strong. She planted her feet, ready to beat him.

"I'm calling the police," Mrs. Oliver yelled from behind her, and then, "Yenil, no!"

Josh swung, vicious and fast, but Shula stepped out of the way.

She heard the sound of small feet running on the pavement behind her, but she couldn't take her eyes off Josh.

He swung again, this time grazing her cheek.

Yenil burst past, leaping onto Josh's chest, knocking him to the ground. In her war skin she looked more beast than human, and her breath came in ragged, staccato wheezes.

Josh, terrified, tried to scramble away, but Yenil grabbed him by the shirt. She spun, gathering momentum, and threw him across the sidewalk, where he slammed into the wooden post of the neighbor's fence. Yenil screamed, a primal sound without words. Josh lay unmoving.

Yenil turned toward the truck. The girl inside shrieked, high pitched and terrified, over and over. Yenil struck the truck with her whole body, shoving it out of the middle of the road. The strength in that war skin body astonished Shula and frightened her. The Scim girl seemed more monster than person now, and Shula didn't know what would happen if she reached out for her, if she took Yenil by the arm and tried to steer her back toward the car or tried to pull her away from the boy's crumpled body.

Josh groaned. He was still alive, then. Shula exhaled, not realizing until then that she had been holding her breath.

Sirens sounded in the distance.

Yenil stared at her, chest heaving, tears in the corners of her eyes. "He hurt you," she said.

Her uniform was torn. Her braid had come free, and the tusks in her mouth made her words harder to understand.

Shula held out her hand to the Scim girl. War skin or not, this was still the Yenil she knew. At least, she hoped so. Still breathing hard, Yenil looked at Shula's hand. Shula held it steady until the girl reached for her, and Shula gave her hand a quick squeeze. "First day of school tomorrow," Shula said. "Not today."

Yenil nodded, wiping the tears from her face with the back of a thick hand. "Okay."

"Go to Madeline," Shula said, and Yenil ran to her.

The girl, Tiffany, was bent over her boyfriend now, sobbing. "You broke his ribs," she said. "He was just dropping me off at home, and you attacked us."

"I'm telling the cops," Josh said. "Pressing charges. You'll be back in Iraq soon."

"Your house?" Shula asked casually, tilting her head toward the house they had been parked in front of. "You live here?"

Tiffany's eyes widened.

"If you tell police," Shula said calmly, "I bring my little girl to visit."

"I'm not afraid," Josh sneered.

"Maybe," Shula said quietly, leaning in close, "I bring her father."

The sirens were close now. She walked to the car, not looking back at them. She could hear Tiffany and Josh again, screaming at one another. She settled into her seat. Yenil was curled in Madeline's lap.

Shula's hands were shaking as Mrs. Oliver turned the car around. Who would have thought that she would feel less safe here than in Syria? Or that she would feel like she fit in better in a fantasy world than in the United States?

The sirens grew closer behind them, but Shula did not look back.

3

THE WARDROBE

But the creatures did not harm the boy, perhaps
because they saw in his heart a sort of kin.
FROM "THE GOOD GARDENER," AN ALUVOREAN STORY

✛

Nice to meet you," Jason said. It was mostly instinct. He hadn't thought through the proper response to meeting your future brother-in-law who had come to murder you, had taken a child hostage, and then invited you into a confined space. "Well. Not nice, exactly. To be honest, I was sort of hoping to put the whole thing off until you weren't trying to kill me."

"You are not worthy of my sister," Bezaed said. His silver eyes flashed in the darkness. "She should not have accepted your proposal, knowing you to be so weak. It is no honor for me to kill a mewling child."

"Mewling? What does that even mean? Like a cat or something?"

Shadow shifted in Bezaed's grip. The warrior tightened his arm, and the Scim boy stopped struggling.

"You're gonna regret trying to hurt Wu Song," Shadow said, his voice fierce.

Bezaed laughed. "I've never regretted killing a suitor of my sister's." He scowled at Jason. "Let alone one who isn't even Kakri. It is not right to mingle the blood of the desert people with such weak stock."

Jason cleared his throat. "What if I promise we won't mingle our blood? To be honest, I am not great with blood. I get light headed."

"I spoke to our grandmother after your betrothal, when you and Baileya first fled into the desert. I told her I did not approve of a Kakri warrior marrying a human. I told her I would never accept you, but she said that you are my brother now. If I wish to prevent it, I may do as the Kakri have done for generations: kill my sister's suitor. I tell you this, *brother*, I will not fail in this endeavor."

It was a weird thing about the Kakri. Instead of "speak now or forever hold your peace," it was "you have a year to kill your sister's fiancé." Jason wasn't a fan of this particular cultural institution. "Remind me to thank your grandma at the wedding."

"You can thank her yourself," Bezaed said. "I have decided to bring you home to her before I kill you. It will please me to spill your human blood in the presence of the council. It will serve as a warning to the other Kakri not to seek marriage among the humans. I could kill you now, but instead you will join me beyond the Tolmin Pass, to die among my people."

"That makes sense," Jason said. "You did seem sort of slow at killing. I figured I had five, maybe ten, seconds once we got in the wardrobe."

Bezaed scowled, his knife biting into Shadow's cheek. "But how to keep this boy silent after we leave?"

Jason's eyes met Shadow's, and he knew what was about to happen. The boy had opened his mouth wide, the sharp yellow teeth and too-large tusks fully extended. He had seen Shadow take chunks out of his siblings' thick hides. The kid liked to bite.

Delightful Glitter Lady let out a plaintive whine.

"Oh, hey! Is that mewling?"

Shadow's vice-like jaw clamped shut over Bezaed's forearm. His sharp teeth sliced easily into Bezaed's flesh, and the Kakri warrior hissed and dropped his knife.

Jason threw his back against the wardrobe door, planted his feet firmly on the wooden wall opposite, and pushed as hard as he could. The doors burst open, and they exploded from the wardrobe in a tangle of arms and legs. Delightful Glitter Lady rolled out of Jason's pocket and slid across the floor. Shadow grabbed the knife before Bezaed could and skittered out of reach, grinning. Bezaed jumped to his feet, another knife already in his hand, grabbed from somewhere in his loose shirt.

Jason fell on his back. He didn't roll away or jump to his feet or grab a weapon or produce another one or do anything useful, really. Doing useful things was not his strength. On the other hand, all the stumbling, smashing, crashing, and rolling had made enough noise that the other kids were running from the other floors toward this room. Their shouts and stomping feet echoed through the hall.

"Think you can fight six of us?" Jason asked, glaring at Bezaed from his prone position, half in the wardrobe and half on the floor.

Bezaed gave him a cool glance, as if it was a stupid question. "Of course. Though I would prefer not to kill your companions."

"I'll roast your liver!" Shadow shouted.

Jason got to his feet. "What is it with you and livers, Shadow? There are so many other body parts—don't get hung up on using one as your go-to threat."

Nightfall and Eclipse came skidding into the room. They both stopped at the sight of their brother, knife in hand, and the Kakri warrior standing between him and Jason.

"What is going on here?" Nightfall asked.

"Jason made someone else want to kill him," Shadow said.

"Hey!" Jason said. "That's not true. This guy is from my original list."

Faster than Jason could blink, Bezaed leapt behind him and wrapped his left arm around Jason's neck, the knife in his right. The blade touched Jason's throat, pressed firmly enough that he could feel his own pulse. Bezaed dragged him backward. Jason grabbed hold of the wardrobe's edge with one hand, the other drifting to his pocket.

"Come no closer," Bezaed hissed, and the three children paused.

"He won't kill Jason here," Shadow said. "Wants to take him back to Kakri territory. Said so himself."

Bezaed's grip tightened. "I will kill him here if I have to. It is not my preference. I will be angry."

"*You'll* be angry?" Jason choked. "Hey, lighten up with the choking." Jason made a strangled cry as Bezaed's grip tightened again. Jason managed to choke out, "Dee!"

Delightful Glitter Lady had somehow ended up under a dust cloth. She burst out from under the sheet, her ears perked toward Jason. Her tiny black eyes found Bezaed. She saw him choking Jason and let loose the sort of sound that only an enraged kitten-sized rhinoceros can make: a tiny, high-pitched trumpeting. Her feet pattered across the half-rotten floor toward Jason and Bezaed.

"This," Jason choked out, "this is gonna hurt."

Bezaed laughed. "You are a lunatic, brother. That little thing—"

Jason's hand had reached, at last, the embiggenator he carried in his pocket. A small device, the embiggenator was a box with a red shell set in the center. Turned to the left, it could make Dee small as a kitten. Turned all the way to the right, it made her "magic war rhino" size—bigger than an elephant. He turned it as far to the right as he could.

As she ran, Dee grew larger. The size of a Labrador, then a horse, then a van. Bezaed, shocked, dropped Jason and got into a fighting stance. Jason rolled to the side.

Delightful Glitter Lady lowered her horn, then hit Bezaed like a locomotive hitting a watermelon. She didn't slow a little even after she made contact. The Kakri warrior was spread across her face like a bug on a windshield. She kept running, bursting through the wardrobe and turning it to kindling, then smashing through all the other furniture and eventually into the wall, which burst into splinters.

She managed to stop then, her head and shoulders outside the house. Her tail swung happily, and she backed up, snorted, and turned to face Jason, a goofy grin on her face. Bezaed was gone.

"Good girl!" Jason said, his voice warm with affection.

"You better shrink her," Eclipse said. "Quick!"

"Why?" Jason asked. The house answered with heavy groaning. The floor beneath Dee was buckling, her feet practically sinking into the wood. Jason's hand slipped on the embiggenator. Panicked, he yanked it from his pocket and turned the dial to the left, just as the floor gave way and Dee crashed through it in a shower of wood and tiles. A cloud of dust rose from the hole where Dee had been standing.

"Dee!" he shouted and ran to the edge.

He peered over the side, the jagged, unstable planks complaining under his weight. Delightful Glitter Lady was two stories down, on the ground floor, kitten sized again, and covered in dust. She shook herself twice, sneezed, and looked back up at Jason. She squeaked, and a small puff of dust rose up around her.

The three Scim kids rushed past Jason to the hole in the side of the house. They hung out, pushing each other to get the best view. Nightfall whistled. "Great job, Wu Song!"

"For a human," Eclipse admitted reluctantly.

Shadow snorted. "What did Wu Song do? I bit the Kakri, and Dee knocked him through the wall. Wu Song just turned a dial."

The other two children nodded solemnly. "That's true."

Jason wedged himself in the middle of them, straining to get his own view. Bezaed lay on his back, surrounded by plaster and shards of wood. His arm twitched, and he rolled to his side. Jason relaxed. "When He's still alive."

Shadow shook his head in disgust. "You are a terrible Scim, Wu Song."

"That's Baileya's brother. Wouldn't it be weird if I killed him?"

All three Scim shook their heads, but Jason didn't care. Sure, the Kakri had the whole "kill the fiancé" tradition, but he had to imagine it got weird at Thanksgiving if the fiancé managed to kill one of the siblings instead. Not that the Kakri celebrated Thanksgiving. Whatever.

"Children," Break Bones called. He stood at the entrance to the room, his massive stone ax in hand. "Report," he said, and Shadow told him in quick, succinct sentences all that had taken place. Break Bones crossed to them and glanced out the newly ventilated wall. Bezaed was on his hands and knees now, shaking his head. He stood, unsteady but determined.

"Take Wu Song to Baileya," Break Bones said. "When you find her, leave Wu Song in her care and return. If I come to you, all the better. If the Kakri comes instead, kill him."

The Scim children nodded. Eclipse grabbed Jason's hand and yanked him toward the door. "Wait a second," Jason said.

Break Bones didn't answer, just gave Jason a rough shove toward the door. He studied the ground outside for a moment, then jumped, his right hand still brandishing his stone ax.

Jason stuck his head out the hole. "Break Bones, don't kill my brother-in-law!"

"You're not married to Baileya," Eclipse said.

"Yeah, well, 'brother-in-law-to-be' is so long."

"You forgive too easily," Nightfall said, racing down the stairwell ahead of them.

"He tried to kill you," Eclipse reminded him.

"Well. Not very hard," Jason said. He didn't forgive too easily either. His stomach turned at the thought of forgiving his parents. If they hadn't pushed him and Jenny, his sister, in the particular way that they had, if they hadn't tied him up in knots so he was afraid to tell the truth about where she had gone the night she died, she might still be alive. And then to blame him! His father giving him the silent treatment, his mother walking through the house, trying to pretend nothing was wrong. Sure, Bezaed had tried to kill him, but at least he seemed to *like* Jason. A little. Which was more than he could say for his parents.

"I will find us some weapons," Nightfall said. "You two take Wu Song as far and as fast as you can."

"But Wu Song is so slow," Eclipse said mournfully.

"So don't hesitate. I'll catch up to you with the weapons." Nightfall split away from them with a quick wave, and the other two kids moved in front of Jason, each of them ahead and to one side of him. As they hit the ground floor, Dee came trotting over to them, and Jason scooped her into his arms.

"Better put Dee to war rhino size," Shadow said. "Maybe we'll be faster, right, Eclipse?"

"Oh no." Jason checked his pockets, shifting Dee from arm to arm. He had forgotten the embiggenator in his hurry to check on Dee and then look out at Bezaed.

Eclipse grimaced. "If only Wu Song wasn't so slow! No, we have to hope that Nightfall remembers it while he's gathering the weapons."

"Hey, that's the only magic I have besides my pudding bracelet! We can't just leave it."

"Where did you drop it?" Eclipse said.

"On the floor. I think."

"Did it fall through when Dee broke the floor?"

Jason stopped. It could have. The sounds of shouts and the clang of metal on stone came from the other side of the house—Bezaed and Break Bones fighting. "We have to look," he said.

Eclipse shook her head. "It's not safe here, and we have our orders. What if some of Baileya's other brothers are here somewhere? We have to find her so you'll be safe and we can find a new place to hide."

Shadow patted Jason's hand gently. "Me and Eclipse will come look for it later, if it's safe."

Jason looked back at the dilapidated mansion, with its rotting roof and peeled paint. The front door didn't hang straight, and the face of the house sagged inward a bit. It had been a fine house, once, the estate of a powerful Scim family—Night's Breath's family. Jason had come here hoping to make peace with his past, and the fact that Night's Breath had died so he could live. But Night's Breath's mother had rejected his apologies and his overtures of friendship. This house was a connection to a past in which the Scim were noble, wealthy, and powerful. But that time had passed, and what remained was only enough to serve as a painful reminder of the injustices heaped upon this family over the decades.

Eclipse tugged on his hand. "Wu Song, we must run."

Run. He knew how to do that. Baileya told him often: run if you can, hide if you must, fight if there is no other option. She had started him on a daily regimen of running to increase his speed and stamina.

"Let's go," Jason said, and the three of them set off, away from the forlorn house, away from Break Bones and Bezaed and their battle, and toward Baileya.

4

THE PRIEST

Age and experience had given her wisdom.

FROM "JELDA'S REVENGE," A SCIM LEGEND

✛

Shula was not given to fast friendships. Not anymore. She wasn't quick to bring people into her orbit. Madeline had been a notable exception. When Mrs. Raymond had brought the American girl into her room in the Sunlit Lands, Shula had been taken with her naiveté, her open heart, and the speed with which she trusted others. It had set off a desire to protect Madeline, a desire which Shula found simultaneously annoying and impossible to ignore. She so often had this impulse to protect people around her, even though she knew it was futile. Every new friendship, every loving relationship, every vulnerability was a guarantee of future pain. It could be predicted, measured, assured. Every new friend would leave you in time. A new relationship would end in distance or death. Vulnerability meant pain. This was merely the way the world worked, as predictable as winding a clock caused its hands to spring to life.

After leaving Syria, Shula had decided she was done with friendships. She had lost her family and had no desire to replace them. But Madeline had somehow found her way into Shula's heart. And now Shula felt, if she was honest, that she had been tricked. There had been no evidence Madeline was sick when they met, no way to know that she was not only sick but dying. Another dead loved one. Shula didn't know why this should surprise her, as every person she had ever loved had ended up dead. Her one bright spot of hope was Yenil. She was so young and strong. Yenil could be the one to outlast Shula if anyone could. Still, she found herself trying to hold back from the girl, struggling to keep Yenil out of the space reserved in her heart for a sister or daughter or even cousin. She tried to think of her as a neighbor kid, the one you babysit and see on the street when you go to buy bread.

She failed at this. Shula's instinct was to adopt Yenil, to treat her like part of the family. This morning, as Yenil got ready for school and sat at the breakfast counter eating the warm oatmeal spooned out by Sofía, Shula brushed Yenil's long, black hair. Yenil had been in school for three weeks now, and though she came home each day exhausted from speaking English and running with the children, it seemed she found the regularity of it soothing and that she may even have begun to make some friends. Shula could not help but think of her own family in Syria once upon a time, getting ready for school and work together. This hair brushing was a good example of how Yenil was slowly making her way past Shula's defenses. Yenil could brush her own hair, but Shula liked to stand near her, to pull the brush through her long tresses, to listen to her babble on in English or Spanish to Sofía. Yenil picked up languages with astonishing speed, and she laughed when Shula struggled to find an English word, or when she didn't know when Yenil was peppering her speech with Scim or Spanish. Yenil had even picked up a few French words when Madeline and Shula talked together.

Mrs. Oliver would take Yenil to school today. Mrs. Oliver had tried to get Shula to enroll in school, but Shula had told her she was eighteen and had graduated in Syria. It was a lie, but Shula could not stand the thought of leaving Madeline home alone during the days. Mrs. Oliver vacillated between smothering Madeline with too much attention, and then, with a suddenness that surprised Shula, announcing that she was going out somewhere. No doubt seeing her daughter in pain caused frayed nerves and stress. Madeline found her mother's nervous energy exhausting, and often the two of them would snap at one another. When this happened, Shula felt almost nauseous. If she could see her own mother again, she would never snap at her, never for a moment make her feel anything but loved and appreciated.

Here, again, Yenil came to the rescue. The Scim girl provided an outlet for Mrs. Oliver's nervous mothering energy, and Yenil accepted it with a warm gladness, cementing a relationship between her and Madeline's mother, who she seemed to see as some sort of benevolent auntie or grand-mother. Mrs. Oliver, in these last few weeks, had fallen into the rhythm of dropping Yenil at school in the morning, picking her up in the afternoon, and filling the middle of the day with other things: reading to Madeline near the window looking over the garden, going to the grocery store with Sofía, or making appointments with her friends, all depending on her mental state and how well she was coping.

Shula wondered again about Madeline's father. Unlike his wife, Mr. Oliver seemed to grow ever more absent. He woke before the sun and slipped out of the house and came home after Yenil had been tucked into bed. If Madeline was awake, he would kiss her on the cheek as he loosened his tie, and rummage in the kitchen for an apple or a bite of dinner. He seemed not to see Shula. His eyes slid over her as if she were a blanket thrown on the floor or a pair of shoes left on the fireplace. There was a momentary awareness that she should not be there, where she was, and then he looked away without a word of greeting or acknowledgment. As for Yenil, he behaved as if she were a ghost.

Today was a grocery day, so Mrs. Oliver and Sofía left together with Yenil. "Do you have everything you need, dear?" Mrs. Oliver asked as she walked out the door. This was her code, her way of saying, are you okay to be alone with Madeline? Or perhaps it was her way of saying, be sure to call me if something happens. Shula assured her she would be fine, and Yenil hugged Shula tight around the waist, and they were off.

Shula quietly padded across the carpeted floor to check on Madeline. The morning noise and activity in the house seemed to help Madeline sleep. In the darkest hours of the night she was restless, coughing, uncomfortable. But the morning sounds of Yenil singing, of Sofía cooking, of Mrs. Oliver moving about, seemed to relax her, to make her feel more at peace, and she often drifted off for an hour or two at this time. Shula went to make herself a cup of tea and found the kettle already boiling. Sofía had a way of predicting the needs of the people in the household. Shula's family had once had someone like Sofía who would come to their apartment when she was younger—Mrs. Rouhana. She went to their church, and when she was done with the cleaning and had made a meal for the evening, she would sit and read with Amira. Once Shula had even caught her playing a video game with Boulos. Mrs. Rouhana's family had left for Turkey when Shula was fourteen. She thought of Mrs. Rouhana from time to time, though, and Sofía brought fond memories of her.

Shula curled into an easy chair beside the garden window. She and Madeline had spent many hours in this spot, talking when Madeline felt up to it or watching out the window when she did not. Shula had taken to reading simple books to Madeline in the afternoons, which both filled the silence and helped Shula's English. Sometimes, when Yenil was home, they would read books from Madeline's childhood, and the Scim girl would stealthily enter the room, like a cat stalking prey, and curl up on the floor between them, listening to Shula's words, occasionally correcting her pronunciation when Madeline did not.

All told it was a peaceful life, and one Shula did not want to change. In time, she knew, Madeline would go the way of all the people Shula loved, and everything would be different. Madeline said Shula and Yenil could stay here in her parents' home, but Shula had seen enough grief and hardship to know that the promises of the dead do not mean much to the living and that the powerful tides of sorrow can cause even the kindest souls to be cruel. She did not know what she and Yenil would do, should the worst come. She knew this should terrify her, that she should be startled to action by it, but Shula knew that if such a thing came, she was strong enough not to break. She had been through much worse already, and the continual waves of misfortune in her life were just that—waves. One came, and another, and soon another, and you could not steel yourself against a wave. You could only wait for it to come and hope you could swim through it or rise above it and not be dashed against the rocks.

When her tea was done, Shula got her sketchbook and pencils and drew the flowers in the garden. Only in the last few weeks had her desire to draw returned, a full year and more since the death of her family. She rubbed the long scar on her face and considered the foxgloves. That's what Madeline called them, a whimsical name that made Shula and Yenil laugh. Madeline seemed concerned by the flowers. She would not let Sofía bring them in the house and had flown into a rage when Yenil had snapped a stalk off and brought it inside, tearing the flower away from the child and throwing it into the backyard before collapsing by the door, wheezing, and reaching to turn the lock.

Madeline wouldn't speak about it. Shula tried to get her to share her anger, to talk with Shula about it so she wouldn't explode in unpredictable moments or take it out on her mother. But when they got close, when they almost could speak about it, the conversation would touch so near to Shula's own grief and anger that they would cycle into frustrated silence, or Madeline would lose the strength to continue, leaving Shula unsettled and thinking of her family again.

As Shula sketched the trumpet-shaped flowers, she thought of Amira, trying to remember the good things and not dwell on the grief or pain. She thought about how Amira would sit beside Shula, too close, as she sketched, making it hard to get her lines straight, jostling her, asking a nonstop series of questions about what Shula was drawing. How she would beg for drawings of cats. Shula found it hard to get cats quite right, with their long bodies and the almost supernatural way their shape changed when they slept or stretched or sat. "No, no, a cat!" Amira would shout, laughing, every time Shula tried. It became a joke between them. When they walked the streets of Aleppo together, if a cat sauntered toward them out of the shade, Shula would say, "No, no, I wanted a cat!" and they would both laugh.

Shula's pencil stopped moving across the page, her eyes unfocused as she stared at the flowers. Her hand moved to Amira's silver cross around her neck, clutching it so hard that the edges nearly cut into her skin. Her other hand rose to her face, stroking the smooth line of the scar that descended from her left eye to the corner of her lip. Instead of flowers she saw flames, and her grip on the cross tightened, her lip curling up as her hand began to shake. A sharp pain built as she balled her fist tighter and tighter. She thought of Amira, of the last time she had seen her. Thought of her parents, and the fire, and the man who cut her face, and of her father, a pastor, praying to a God who did nothing, did not intervene or help or answer in any way. Her whole body shook, and she bit her lip to keep from screaming.

A ringing echoed in her ears. She hunched over, grabbing her right fist with her left hand.

The ringing again. A bell.

The doorbell.

Shula gasped, letting go of her cross, and the world rushed in again. She unfolded her hand, becoming conscious of a piercing pain in her palm. She had drawn blood this time.

She hurried to the door, hoping the doorbell hadn't woken Madeline. She shook her hand as she walked, pressing her thumb against the tiny wound on her opposite palm. The front door had windows on either side. She peered out at an older man in a black suit. He rang the bell again before she got to the door. She yanked it open.

"What is it?" she snapped, upset she hadn't heard it the first time, angry that he might have disturbed Madeline.

The man smiled, the wrinkles around his pale-blue eyes crinkling. His white hair was thin, and a pair of wire glasses perched on his nose. He wore a priest's white collar. "Ms. Oliver?" he asked, and when Shula didn't immediately answer, he asked, "Madeline?"

"No," Shula said, taken off guard. This priest had come at the exact wrong moment. Her palm ached. The feelings about her family had been stirred up again, and reentering the present took effort. She wasn't sure what to say, and her English wasn't good enough to produce a worthwhile sentence with all of the competing messages struggling to exit her mind.

The old priest's eyes fell to Shula's hands. She clutched them together, not wanting him to see the wound, but he was looking at her wrist.

"Ah," he said. "So you are Madeline."

Shula shook her head again and said, "No."

"It's okay." His voice held great gentleness. He pushed up the sleeve of his coat. He had a mess of old silver tracks around his wrist, the telltale sign of the departed magic of the Elenil. "I have walked in the Sunlit Lands too. I met your friend in the hospital. He told me you had made a deal with the Elenil, and I saw on the news how a young woman had disappeared from the hospital. Imagine my surprise when I overheard one of the nurses saying last week that you had miraculously returned. You have been back for some time, I am told."

"I am Shula," she finally managed to say. Her lip curled again. She was not like this, so weak. She prided herself on being strong. *I am a warrior,* she reminded herself. *I walk through fire and am not burned. I am strong. I have been through the darkness, I have crawled through collapsed buildings to get where I need to go. I have no reason to fear this man. I am more powerful than he.*

Shula stood straight and pushed her shoulders back. "Madeline is sleeping. She does not want to see a priest. She does not want your prayers or your words. She wants to be left alone."

"Shula," the man said, as if hearing her for the first time, realizing that she was not Madeline. He looked at her more closely this time, and something changed in his eyes. "Marhaban, Shula. Ismii Father Anthony."

Shula stared at him in astonishment. "You speak Arabic?"

He laughed. "Only a little. Where are you from, Shula?"

"Aleppo," she said, still in shock.

"I've never been to Syria," Father Anthony said. "I would like to go one day." He stepped forward.

Shula moved to block the doorway with her body, swinging the door halfway shut. A fierce protectiveness for Madeline settled on her. What was he doing here? He had found out about Madeline at the hospital, he said, but how did he get her address? What could he possibly want? "Madeline is sleeping," Shula said again, her arms loosely at her sides.

"Of course," he said. "I understand. Shula . . . I need to talk to her. To both of you. Whatever Hanali is planning, he's not worried about your well-being, I promise you that."

Mrs. Oliver's car pulled into the driveway. Sofía was driving. Mrs.

Oliver came walking up the sidewalk while Sofía fetched the groceries from the trunk.

The priest glanced back at them, then locked eyes with Shula. He held a business card out to her. "Call me, Shula. We need to talk."

"Why, hello," Mrs. Oliver said. "Shula, who's this?" Mrs. Oliver stopped, brushed a stray hair out of her eyes, and looked at the priest. She froze. "Tony? Is that you? But you look so . . . old."

"Wendy," he said. "What are you doing here?"

"This is my house, Tony. I live here." She put her hand to her head. "You're not a priest." Mrs. Oliver's legs started to give way, and she sank toward the ground.

Father Anthony grabbed hold of her forearm and helped her ease into a sitting position. Sofía raced to her other side.

"I don't want to see you, Tony," Mrs. Oliver said, her voice rising into a panicked wail. "I've told you a hundred times, Tony, I don't want to be reminded—"

Father Anthony leaned toward her ear and spoke some low, quick words. Mrs. Oliver went limp.

He looked at Shula. "Let her rest for a little while. When she wakes, give her water—as much as she will drink." He straightened, tugged his jacket into place, and walked down the sidewalk. Sofía watched him go, a scowl on her face.

The priest turned at the end of the driveway and walked down the street. Shula didn't see a car. She didn't watch him for long, though, because Sofía was helping Mrs. Oliver to her feet. With Shula's help they got her up the few steps and inside to the nearest couch.

Madeline stood in the hallway, pale and sweating, clutching her phone. "Something's wrong," she said. "Shula, something's wrong."

5
NIGHTFALL

"So," the boy said, "the name is both true and untrue."

FROM "THE GOOD GARDENER," AN ALUVOREAN STORY

✦

Nightfall caught up with them after less than a mile, carrying weapons for each of them. He had doubled back for the embig-genator, but it had fallen through the floor. He'd seen it near where Break Bones and Bezaed fought and decided it was too risky to try to get it. It was hard to believe Nightfall was a ten-year-old boy, the way he seriously handed out the weapons. He gave Jason a short knife, a quiver of arrows, and a bow. Jason was relieved to see that the bow had the design on the side that meant it could be used with magic. He had been practicing without magic at Baileya's insistence, but so far he had only managed to bruise his forearm by snapping it with the bowstring so many times. He could hit the target now, at least. If there was no wind. And if he stood relatively close and the target stood very, very still.

Eclipse received a short sword. She grinned when the pommel hit her palm. Shadow got a knife slightly larger than Jason's, despite being only six years old. Jason started to object, then had to admit that this was probably the wisest way to divide up the weapons. Nightfall had a small but heavy stone hatchet, with Scim markings up the handle and moving along the head toward the blade.

"Any sign of who was winning?" Jason asked.

Nightfall shook his head. "Break Bones was bleeding from cuts to his shoulder and arm, but he fought as fiercely as the Kakri warrior when last I saw them."

"And Bezaed? Had he been wounded too?"

Nightfall shrugged. "He was thrown from the top of the house by a unicorn. I suspect he has some bruises at the least."

Delightful Glitter Lady popped her head out of Jason's pocket and let loose a happy squeal. Jason patted her head. "Good girl. Way to smash the bad guy."

"I'm the one who bit him," Shadow said, arms crossed.

Jason slapped him on the shoulder. "First blood goes to Shadow!"

Shadow grinned.

Trying to cover their tracks was pointless. The Wasted Lands were dry, dreary plains, punctuated with the occasional brittle shrub or pile of refuse. Perpetual darkness was the norm, and a gloomy thickness hung in the air most days. If you could call them days at all. The dry, dusty ground beneath their feet left easy evidence of their passing, and the time it would take to erase their tracks would slow them so much it wouldn't matter.

"If we do not find Baileya," Eclipse said, brandishing her sword, "we should take Wu Song to the Aluvoreans."

Shadow spit on the ground. "Tree people."

"Better than the Kakri getting him," Eclipse said.

Jason didn't want the kids fighting, not when they were running for their lives. Well, his life, anyway. "We'll find Baileya. She always keeps tabs on me."

"Someone is coming," Nightfall said.

Jason twisted to look behind them. Was it Break Bones or Bezaed? But he couldn't see anyone. The Scim kids had better night vision than him.

"A rider," Nightfall said.

Jason looked at the kid. He was looking ahead, not behind.

"Take cover," Nightfall ordered, low and urgent. He and his siblings scattered, hiding behind the scrubby bushes. They had practice, clearly, because Jason couldn't see them even though he had watched them settle into their hiding places.

"It's Baileya," Jason said, even though he couldn't see her yet. He knew it was her. She was always keeping watch, for one thing, and for another, well . . . he just knew when she was nearby.

"What if it is someone else? Hide!" Nightfall hissed, but Jason knew it was her. She would be riding on her brucok, the giant ostrich-like creature she had stolen from her brother in the desert. That brother (yes, there were more than one trying to kill him) had been named Caramel Popcorn. Or something close to that. If he and Baileya really got married, he was going to have to work hard to remember all the names of her siblings.

He could see her now in the darkness. Maybe Nightfall couldn't tell, but Jason knew the way she moved, the easy way she rode on the brucok's back, casually holding her twin-bladed staff in the crook of her arm. Jason hated that bird. It had sat on him in the desert, tried to bite him any time he was close enough, and hissed at him when he got too close to Baileya. She had suggested that Jason give it a name so that "a natural affection will spring up between you two." He had gone through a long list of names: McNugget, Foster Farms, Drumstick (then Baileya had objected that calling it a food name would only create more tension), Birdy McBirdface, Less Delightful Glitter Bird, and Captain Emurica. The bird had slowly become Jason's worst enemy. Sure, the Elenil and the Scim and the Zhanin were trying to kill him, but this bird truly hated him. So Jason called it Moriarty, after Sherlock Holmes's nemesis.

Once the kids could see Baileya better, they appeared from their hiding places, but they still gathered around Jason at a slight distance, as if they were all his guards. Eclipse turned the hilt of her sword in her hand nervously, and Shadow held his blade straight ahead, as if waiting for someone to impale themselves on it.

Baileya wore the loose, flowing blue top she liked best. In battle she tied it down with her sash, but now the sash was wrapped around her waist, a likely sign that she hadn't run into trouble on patrol. Her dark hair was pulled back, and Jason's heart leapt into his throat at the sight of her golden skin and the spray of brown freckles across her cheeks. Her silver eyes flashed at the sight of him, and a wide smile spread across her face. She slid from the brucok and ran the few steps between them, wrapping him in a tight hug. Jason was always surprised by her excitement to see him. Something about her running to close the space between them made his heart sing.

"Wu Song," she said, "you come out to meet me."

They pulled apart, their hands on one another's forearms. Her arms were solid, layered in muscle, but graceful and smooth. He squeezed them. "I'm always glad to see you," he said, and Baileya beamed at him.

Moriarty made a honking sound, then hissed at Jason. "He doesn't like it when I'm close to you," Jason said.

"He's jealous," Baileya said, and gave Jason a peck on the cheek.

"We have been stopped too long," Eclipse said. "It is dangerous. We should move."

"He's not wrong," Jason said. "We need to run."

"Running is our life," Baileya said, "so we must take what small moments we can." She touched his cheek with the tips of her fingers. "You are clever, though," she said to Eclipse, "to see the coming trouble. A cohort of Elenil are scouring the Wasted Lands, headed this way. The captain of the guard, Rondelo, rides at their head upon the noble stag Evernu. Some dire change has come that the captain of the guard would leave Far Seeing and enter the Wasted Lands."

Eclipse looked up at her, hands on her hips. "Where will we go then, Baileya? What is our destination?"

Baileya's brow furrowed. "To the house, I think. We can defend it against a small cohort. They are moving fast, but not so fast that we could not reach home before them. It is even possible they are not seeking Wu Song."

"Possible but unlikely," Jason said, and Baileya smiled at him. Something about his outlaw renegade fugitive status was cute to her.

"Your brother is at the house," Nightfall said, "locked in battle with Break Bones."

Baileya's eyes widened. "You should have said this at once. There is no time to lose."

"I wanted to tell you when you hugged me," Jason said, "but honestly, the thought went clean out of my head."

She grinned at him. "You did not want to cut my embrace short. But my brother will be after us soon. I will go back to help Break Bones or, if he has already fallen, to slow Bezaed. Nightfall, you must ride with Wu Song. Eclipse and Shadow, you will come with me as sentinels."

The two younger Scim flanked her as soon as the words came out of her mouth, and Nightfall had already swung himself onto Moriarty's back. "The Elenil are to the north," Nightfall said, "your brother to the south. So we will ride southwest, toward the great trees. I think we can hide from them without leaving Scim territory."

"We may not be able to stay in the Wasted Lands," Baileya said, "not if the Elenil and my brother have found us. Go toward Aluvorea, and we will return as quickly as we can. If we have not returned to you by the time you reach the Aluvorean border, then I fear my brother has triumphed and will reach you before we do. So hide in the Wasted Lands or seek help in Aluvorea, whatever you think is wisest if such a thing comes to pass."

A wave of fear hit Jason like a wall. "Be careful, Baileya."

She boosted him onto Moriarty and patted his hand. "My brother will not harm me," she said. "It is you he must kill, not me."

"About that," Jason said. "He said he's trying to catch me so he can murder me in front of your relatives."

Baileya frowned. "This is to our advantage. He will not fill you with arrows, then. He will have to get close."

"I bit him," Shadow said. "Hard."

"Fierce warrior," Baileya said, no smile on her face. "Well done. You can tell me the tale as we travel."

"We must go," Eclipse said.

Baileya squeezed Jason's hand. "Fly swift and straight. I will see you again." With that, she turned and trotted toward the mansion, the two Scim children trailing behind her, one on each side.

Nightfall did not say good-bye. He put his heels to the brucok, and they sped away to the southwest.

"I should probably drive," Jason said.

Nightfall didn't even look over his shoulder. "Baileya never lets you."

"That's because she's good at it, and Moriarty always tries to bite me when I'm in charge. But I'm older than you. You probably can't even drive a car."

Nightfall shrugged. "I don't know what a car is."

"Exactly."

Nightfall pulled the reins so Moriarty would jog around a stone, and Jason nearly lost his grip. He snatched at the giant bird's feathers, and the bird squawked and ran faster. Jason fell one way, then counterbalanced and nearly fell off the other side, popping back and forth like a metronome more than once before getting his balance again. "You did that on purpose," Jason said. "Both of you."

Nightfall gave him a sly grin. "True."

Jason wondered what would happen when Baileya confronted her brother. She said he wouldn't want to hurt her. The law of the Kakri gave him permission—encouraged him, really—to kill Jason because he was Baileya's fiancé. The law gave no such protection to someone who killed his own siblings, a grave injustice in the Kakri system. Jason had asked Baileya if it happened sometimes—it seemed likely that when you were trying to murder your sister's fiancé you might accidentally harm your sister, instead. She laughed at him. "The Kakri do not miss," she said. In fact, she told him a story about a woman who had protected her fiancé without ever fighting her siblings by making it impossible for any of them to get a shot at her fiancé without harming her until their engagement year was up. It was a sort of Kakri comedy . . . the woman who protected her hapless fiancé from violence by putting herself in danger. Baileya had been generous to share the story with Jason, as the Kakri people considered a story like this to be of great value. "It is a family story," she'd said. "Soon we will be family." She had taken his hand at that point and squeezed it, and he had blushed. He still couldn't figure out a way to tell her that he had only accidentally asked her to marry him. He wasn't going to lie to her, but he couldn't bring himself to say it. He was convinced she would be angry or embarrassed enough to end their relationship, and he didn't want to risk that. He had stayed here in the Sunlit Lands because of her. Instead he had asked her why she didn't use the same strategy as the one in the story. Why not just keep herself positioned near him at all times so her brothers and sisters couldn't get a shot at him? She smiled and said, "I have many more siblings than the woman in the story."

"Wu Song," Nightfall said. "I have wanted to ask you a question. But not in front of the others. It is . . . personal."

"Um. Okay," Jason said. He couldn't imagine what possible question the kid could have.

"Why do you reveal your true name to us?"

Jason saw some bobbing lights off in the gloom to the far north. Probably a small Scim settlement. Or, knowing Jason's luck, it was the Elenil. But Nightfall didn't seem concerned, so Jason didn't mention it. "Humans aren't like Scim. We don't have war skins or war skin names." Names like Break Bones were war skin names. Like the war skins themselves, the names were designed to intimidate, and to protect the Scim. He had seen some Scim—like the kids—out of their war skins, but he had never seen Break Bones in anything but. It seemed to be a deeply personal thing, deciding who could see you without your war skin. But the names . . . well, he only knew war skin names. He hadn't learned any personal names of the Scim, except for Madeline's little friend Yenil.

"I thought Jason was your war skin name," Nightfall said.

"No," Jason said, but then he considered some more. "Sort of, I guess. You only share your true name with your family, right?"

"Or our closest friends. People who we trust with our lives."

"Where I come from, a lot of people have a hard time saying my name. So I have another name, a more common name, to help them be able to say it."

Nightfall nodded. "I see. Like the tame Scim. They take on a name the Elenil choose, so that they will not intimidate with their war skin name."

"Wait," Jason said. "That's sort of right, I guess. But it's not like that—Jason is my real name too. I've been called that since I was a kid."

"At home?"

"No, at school, and when I wasn't with other Chinese people. I—" He paused. Was it the same thing? He had his given name, his Chinese name, and he had another name that wasn't on his birth certificate, a nickname that let him move through American society, where many people didn't know Chinese and weren't willing to do the little bit of work required to learn to say his name.

"So why do you share your true name with us?"

Jason reflected for a minute, watching those distant lights. "I'm trying to be completely honest, Nightfall. I decided after my sister died that I would never lie again. Wu Song is my name, and I don't want to hide that. Jason is my name too, or at least it's something I've been called since I was a kid. I don't want to hide things about myself, not if I can help it."

Nightfall turned and looked at him. "Many of the Scim have taken an oath to kill you."

"Yeah, yeah, them and half the Sunlit Lands."

"I have not taken the oath."

Jason knocked the kid in the shoulder. "Aw, thanks, Nightfall."

Nightfall's war skin flowed off of him, dropping all the excess muscle, the intimidating face, the jutting tusks, and leaving only a wiry Scim kid who didn't look all that much different from the kids Jason had run around with when he was in middle school. "You have treated me like family. You have shared your true name. You have shown kindness and even weakness to me and to my brother and sister."

"I, uh, well, when you say it that way—"

"I am saying, Wu Song, that to me you are a brother. My name, my true name, is Nola."

"Nola," Jason said. "Thank you."

"You must say, 'I will keep it safe.'"

"I will keep it safe," Jason said.

"As I will keep yours safe," Nightfall said.

A lump formed in Jason's throat. This kid was related to Night's Breath. He had hoped to make a connection to Night's Breath's family, to his mother and wife and children, but they had rejected him. Now this boy, Night's Breath's nephew, had reached out to Jason. It didn't change what had happened in the past, but Jason felt strands of loyalty knit between him and Nightfall. Nola. They were brothers now, and what did that mean except that Eclipse was his sister and Shadow his brother? He thought of Jenny, and saw her for a brief moment the way he had seen her on that last and terrible day, upside down in a smashed car at the bottom of a cliff face. He closed his eyes tight, trying for the thousandth time to wash the picture from his mind.

When Jason opened his eyes again, he noticed the distant lights were closer. "Nightfall," he said, "did you notice those lights to the north?"

Nightfall twisted to get a better view. "Elenil," he said, as if the word was a curse. "They bring light for the hunt." His war skin flowed back onto him, and he snapped Moriarty's reins.

"I should have probably mentioned that sooner," Jason said.

6
THE PRINCIPAL'S OFFICE

You are more forest spirit than woman.

FROM "JELDA'S REVENGE," A SCIM LEGEND

✦

Shula's first thought was that Madeline's body had finally given up. Madeline's face was flushed and sweaty, and she stood half leaning against the wall, her phone in hand, a wide-eyed, open-mouthed look of panic on her face. Shula crossed to Madeline, ready to catch her if she should fall.

"Something's wrong," Madeline repeated.

Shula grabbed Madeline's forearms. "Hospital?"

"School," Madeline said. "The principal . . . called. Yenil."

"No," Shula said, pulled back to the day she had been called by her sister's school. They were sending all the children home because of a nearby bombing, they said, but they could not find Shula's parents. A bombing. That meant the Russians, who were dropping bombs on the city with little regard for who was in the buildings. As she had heard her father say more than once, "Russians above, ISIS below." The terrorists and rebels and their own government were all ravaging the city while people like Shula and her family just tried to get by, to find a safe place to buy groceries. She remembered the day her little sister had learned that the Russians were Orthodox Christian. Or at least, many of them were. "We should be safe from the Russians, then," Amira told their father, "since we are Christian too."

Baba said, "A bullet does not stop to ask if you are Muslim or Christian, habibti." Shula knew that was true. Bullets may not ask if you are Muslim or Christian, but people do, and it was people who directed the bullets, and dropped the bombs, and set the fires.

Shula's heart pounded in her chest, her breathing fast and shallow. Her first thought was guns, that someone had broken into Yenil's school, had shot the children. Her hands tightened on Madeline's forearms. Madeline sagged, and Shula scooped under her, directing her to the easy chair by the fireplace. Mrs. Oliver still lay on the couch. Although her breath came quiet and regular, her brow was furrowed and her mouth twisted in a frown.

"We have . . . to go," Madeline gasped, "get . . . Yenil."

Shula nodded. She knew the best thing in an emergency is to keep your head, to stay calm, and to be committed to your actions. She did not know the exact situation. She could try to call the school, but her English was uncertain. Mrs. Oliver was still in shock, and Madeline was in no shape to drive. Shula could drive. In the chaos of Syria, her father had needed her to have this skill, even though she hadn't been old enough at that time to get a license. She certainly didn't have an American driver's license. Sofía could drive too, but then who would stay with Mrs. Oliver? If Madeline went anywhere, Shula would be her shadow. Madeline wouldn't let Sofía go alone to get Yenil, and Shula wouldn't let Madeline leave without her, which would leave Mrs. Oliver alone.

Shula held her hand out to Sofía, who locked eyes with her, car keys in hand. It was Mrs. Oliver's car. She never let Sofía drive it by herself, not once since Shula had been here. But this was an emergency. Whatever had happened, Madeline was panicking, her breath coming more irregularly, and still she was trying to stand.

"You go," Sofía said. "I will take care of Madeline and Mrs. Oliver." She looked back at the two Oliver women.

"I'm . . . coming," Madeline said.

Shula put her hand on Madeline's forearm. "Sofía is right."

Madeline scowled. "I'm . . . coming," she repeated, her lip turning up in a half snarl.

Shula knew better than to argue with Madeline at a moment like this, and to be honest, a small feeling of relief flowed over her. If she was pulled over by the police, it would be helpful for Madeline to be there. Or if the school refused to release Yenil to her. They hadn't been sure if it was wise to put Shula's name on the "trusted adults" list, because what if, somehow, the immigration authorities found out about it? If Shula was deported to Syria, there was no guarantee she could get back to the US again. No guarantee, for that matter, that she could find her way back to the Sunlit Lands. She might be trapped there. Again.

Shula shivered. She blocked the memories of her last day in Syria. She did not think of that. Her parents, her sister, her brother. They were gone, and she had a new family now. Madeline. Yenil. Perhaps these others, who Madeline thought of as family . . . Mr. and Mrs. Oliver, Sofía.

Madeline was struggling to her feet.

"Do you want your wheelchair?"

Madeline nodded gratefully. She didn't like to ask for it, but she needed it. In a moment, Shula returned with it, and she backed out the front door, past the fallen groceries, and to the car. She opened the door, and Madeline carefully got in. Shula folded the chair again and wrangled it into the trunk, bashing her elbow hard. She rubbed it absently as she slid into the driver's seat.

The school was not far. Shula drove with the care of a new driver, making sure to follow every rule, to stop completely at the signs, to turn on her blinker. At the same time, though, she was distracted by Madeline's pained breathing and the uncertainty of what had happened to Yenil. "What has happened?" Shula asked.

Madeline tried to answer but was so upset that the words wouldn't come. She finally managed to say, "Fight. At school."

This made Shula feel slightly more settled, but only slightly. She saw Amira's panicked face that day in Syria. The crowd of people, parents and grandparents and siblings, descending on the school, then tumbling away like leaves in the wind, skittering off to their apartments, and Shula weaving among them to take her terrified little sister by the hand and make their way home. Checking her mobile to make sure her parents knew she had Amira. Boulos was with them that day. He had been wandering off into the city many days, which upset their father. But today he had been nearby somewhere and had arrived just as they walked out the school gates. Shula had almost melted with relief, and he had walked in front of them, turning his head to the left and right, and stayed with them all the way home. Some people were saying that the Russians wouldn't bomb again, not so close to the first site, but in this city of half-fallen apartment complexes and volunteers donning white helmets to pull innocent people from the wreckage of their homes, who wanted to risk their family based on what you thought the Russians might or might not do? It's not like they called before dropping their bombs, unless you counted the high whine of their distant engines.

Then Shula and Madeline were at Yenil's school.

The parking lot was too big, to make room for all the Americans and their cars. The path to the front office was too long, and the buildings had too much glass . . . far too much glass to be safe if someone came with intent to harm, or if an earthquake happened, or any number of other calamities. Shula kept telling herself that a fight meant something small. She needn't worry. It was much more likely that someone had upset Yenil, that she had put on her war skin and smashed something.

"Slower," Madeline said.

Shula had been pushing the wheelchair so fast it almost careened off the sidewalk. "Sorry."

Shula pressed the doorbell by the front door and leaned over so they could see her in the black eye of the camera. The door buzzed, and she pulled it open, trying to get Madeline turned around and through the door while holding it open. Madeline waved her off and wheeled herself through, coughing so hard she bent almost in half. Shula pulled a handkerchief from the zippered pouch on the back of the chair and gave it to Madeline. She wiped her mouth and nodded for Shula to get the next door.

The women behind the front desk were busy. A child was sitting next to one desk, his head tipped back, tissues and a bag of ice on his nose. Shula clenched her fist. *Oh please, don't let that be Yenil's doing.*

"We are here for Yenil," Shula said.

The women did not answer—one was on the phone and the other tending to the boy. Madeline took the flat of her hand and slammed it down on the counter, hard, twice. Both women looked up, their eyes wide. "Yenil," Madeline said, then held on to her armrests when the coughing took her.

The woman on the phone asked her caller to hold, and came over. "You're Yenil's . . . mother?" she asked, looking first at Shula and then at Madeline.

"No," Shula said. "Madeline is her—" She paused. Madeline had told her the word to say. It was a war word. A soldier's word, not a family word. Ah yes, she remembered it now. "She is her guardian."

"I'm glad you're here," the woman said. "These things happen from time to time, but I've never seen a girl get so . . . well, so violent. Yenil is in with the principal and the school counselor."

Shula moved Madeline's chair toward the swinging gate that led behind the counter, and the woman moved it aside for them. She gestured toward the back of the office, and Shula navigated between the desks and tables and chairs, coming uncomfortably close to the little boy who sat crying, the bag of ice pressed against his nose.

The principal was a middle-aged man with silver hair, wearing a loose suit. He sat behind a wide desk. To his left was the counselor, a kindly looking woman in professional clothes who was looking with concern at Yenil. The little Scim girl sat with her arms crossed, her pigtails askew, a scowl on her face, and—Shula nearly crumpled to the floor with gratitude—not in her war skin.

The principal's eyes flickered to Madeline's wheelchair, then to Shula, with that split-second judgment Shula knew so well. His glance was too quick, and he looked away too fast, a sure sign of someone who felt guilty about his own conclusions. *The crippled girl and the foreigner, here to take care of the violent schoolgirl.* Shula bit the inside of her lip to keep from saying anything.

"Mrs. Oliver?" the counselor asked, holding out her hand.

"Ms." Madeline shook the counselor's hand.

The counselor paused. "Of course. Ms. Oliver. I'm the school counselor, Mrs. Montgomery. This is Principal Clifton. And you are?" She looked at Shula.

"That's Ms. Bishara," Madeline said, sitting up straighter in her chair.

"A pleasure, Ms. Bishara. And how are you related to Yenil?"

Madeline cut her off. "What happened?"

Principal Clifton gave her a long, cold stare before answering. Shula knew his type too. Not used to having his authority ignored. Not by children or parents and certainly not by a teenage girl. "We were just asking Yenil that ourselves. She doesn't seem interested in telling us."

Yenil glared at the principal. Madeline held her hand out to the girl, but Yenil looked away. Too angry. Too scared. Shula could not imagine how she was keeping from putting her war skin on.

Mrs. Montgomery spoke to Yenil in a soft voice. "It's okay to tell us, Yenil. We're just trying to understand why you hurt those boys."

Yenil's dark eyes turned toward Mrs. Montgomery, but she didn't say anything.

"Boys? More than one?" Shula looked back into the office. "The boy with the bloody nose is one."

Mrs. Montgomery nodded. "She knocked a second boy down and punched a third in the stomach. Those two are back in class. I'm afraid Yenil did her best to hurt them."

Yenil dropped her chin and stared at Mrs. Montgomery again. "I did not try my best. I could have hurt them worse."

"We'll take her . . . home now," Madeline said.

Principal Clifton drummed his fingers on his desk. "Not until we've gotten answers from your child."

Shula stiffened. Was he threatening to keep Yenil from them? "Can he do this?" she asked, turning to Madeline for answers.

Madeline shook her head. "Not unless . . . he wants to hear . . . from my father's lawyer." She held her phone up. "He's on speed dial."

"Now, now," Mrs. Montgomery said. "There's no need to get contentious. We only want to hear Yenil's side of the story."

Yenil hunched over in her chair. Shula moved beside her, draping her arm over the Scim girl. She whispered in her ear, "It is okay to tell them."

The little girl glared at Shula, tears in her eyes. "They said mean words," Yenil said.

"Like what?" Madeline asked.

"That I am ugly," Yenil said through clenched teeth.

Shula gasped and pulled the girl close. Madeline put her hand on Yenil's forearm. "You're beautiful . . . Yenil . . . They shouldn't . . . have said it."

"That's no excuse to punch them in the face," the principal said.

Yenil's face contorted in fury, and she whipped her face toward Shula, an accusation in her eyes: *You said it was okay to tell them.*

Madeline glared at the principal, then spoke to the counselor. "You allow . . . this sort of . . . bullying?"

Mrs. Montgomery shifted uncomfortably. "Of course not, Ms. Oliver, but these are children, and schoolyard taunts are common. If Yenil had come to us—"

"Not talking . . . about kids. Talking about . . . Principal Clifton."

The principal's face turned bright red. "If you think for one—"

The counselor threw her hands up, as if she could get between Madeline and the principal's words and somehow keep them from getting to each other. "Mr. Clifton, please! Calm yourself! We are the adults here, let us set a good example." The counselor settled back in her chair. "We all need to take a deep breath."

A shadow flitted across Madeline's face. Mrs. Montgomery looked at her and winced. Shula said, "Another day this conversation would be better. We will go home now."

"We need the rest of the story," Principal Clifton said, "before you go."

"You can't . . . keep us . . . here," Madeline said.

"Of course not," Mrs. Montgomery said in a soothing voice. "It would be so helpful to know, though, from Yenil's point of view."

Shula squeezed Yenil's shoulder. Maybe if the girl could be convinced to tell her story, to tell it quickly, they could be on their way.

Yenil's jaw set. She crossed her arms tighter and dipped her chin to her chest.

"What other things did the boys say?" Shula asked. "I know you, Yenil. This is not enough to make you angry."

Yenil burst into tears, shaking her head.

"It's . . . okay . . . Yenil."

"They said my parents are dead!" Yenil shouted. "Then they kept touching me! Pulling my hair! I told them to stop!"

Madeline's face went red. "They . . . touched you?"

"One boy pushed me. The others pulled my hair."

"You should have told a teacher," the principal said.

"No, Yenil," Madeline said, her voice fierce. "You should . . . have punched them . . . in the nose."

"Ms. Oliver!" the counselor said.

Yenil jumped from her chair and stomped her feet. "I told the teachers before, but they don't stop the boys! They told me I should just stay away from those boys. One time they made them sit down part of recess. The teachers don't stop them though. They don't do anything."

"It's no wonder she's violent at school if she's being encouraged to be violent at home," Principal Clifton said.

"You're letting . . . boys . . . assault my little girl . . . and doing nothing," Madeline said. "This is . . . on you."

The principal's lips quirked upward. "But she's not *your* little girl, is she?"

"What does this mean?" Shula asked. "Madeline is Yenil's guard."

"Guardian," Madeline said.

Mrs. Montgomery clucked her tongue. "I'm sure that's true, dear. But I looked at your letter of guardianship and, well . . . it's irregular. We don't usually ask too many questions, but this one, on closer inspection, looks like it may have been forged."

"What is this . . . forged?" Shula asked.

"Fake," Madeline said.

Shula's face flushed hot. She didn't know anything about the paperwork. Madeline had done all that. Her mother had offered to help, but Madeline had waved her off. To get the right papers for an orphaned girl who had been adopted from a fantasyland and brought to the United States would have been challenging. No doubt Madeline had done what she needed to do.

"Checking on it is just a formality," Mrs. Montgomery said. "A letter signed by a judge saying Ms. Oliver is Yenil's guardian is sufficient, it really is. But the letter we have . . . it appears to be just a note from Yenil's parents saying they have put Yenil in Ms. Oliver's care for the year, that's all. We want to make sure Yenil has someone responsible for her. Legally." She emphasized the last word.

"You are threatening us," Shula said. "Why?"

"No threat," Principal Clifton said, holding up his palms. "We'll give you a week to put your hands on the documentation. We just want to make sure that everything is . . . well, legal."

"Or?" Madeline asked. "You will . . . suspend her? What?"

"If you don't have legal custody," the principal said, "we'll call Child Protective Services. They can figure out what would be best for Yenil."

Shula's hands tightened on the back of Yenil's chair. The girl crouched in front of the principal's desk, breathing heavily. Shula wasn't sure what they were saying. She thought she understood the basic idea, she got the words, but it sounded like something more was being implied. "You will take her from us?"

"She's ours," Madeline said, her words overlapping Shula's.

"But she's not *yours*, is she, Ms. Oliver?" The principal steepled his fingers together. "As for whether she would stay with you, that's not my decision. Child Protective Services would decide whether to take her away."

Yenil crouched lower, her breathing going ragged. "No one can take me away," she said in a half growl.

"Be calm," Shula begged.

"Let's go," Madeline said. "Yenil, let's go home."

"You can't take me!" Yenil screamed, pointing at the principal. "I am stronger!"

The principal stood. "Are you threatening me, young lady? I promise you I am the stronger one."

Yenil's war skin flowed onto her so quickly Shula could barely see it happen. Her skin thickened and hardened, turning an almost grey color. Her hair thinned, her muscles grew. Sturdy tusks jutted up from her teeth, pushing out her lips, and her brow protruded forward, forming a small shelf over her eyes.

"Yenil, no!"

The principal stumbled backward, and the counselor screamed.

Yenil placed both hands on the corner of the principal's desk, grunted, and threw it to the side like it was an empty cardboard box. It hit the wall, shattering the window. Glass fell in a sparkling curtain, bouncing off the desk and onto the floor.

"I am stronger," Yenil growled.

Madeline grabbed Yenil and yanked her into her lap on the wheelchair. "Shula," she said. "The car."

Before the adults could recover, Shula grabbed the wheelchair and steered them out. The two women in the reception area had jumped to their feet, moving toward the crash from the principal's office. When Shula wheeled past the kid with the bloody nose, his eyes fell on Yenil, and he scooted backward in his chair, almost knocking it over, making panicked sounds. Shula pushed faster.

Shula helped them both into the backseat of the car. Madeline stroked the girl's thin hair, shushing her, comforting her. Shula folded the wheelchair as quickly as she could, her hands shaking, shoved it in the trunk, and started the car. They drove away from the school in silence.

7

A CONFRONTATION

Two young lives who might have brought greater joy to the world,
cut off, destroyed, in a moment of power-drunk madness.

FROM "JELDA'S REVENGE," A SCIM LEGEND

✦

The Elenil war party thundered behind them, magic spheres of light hovering near, lighting the fierce faces of the Elenil and the beasts on which they rode: tigers, stags, and other things Jason had not seen before, some with willowy and graceful legs, others with too-long necks and thick hides.

Jason leaned forward, holding tight to Nightfall's waist as Moriarty bucked and swerved, his long legs stretching to the limit. "They're gaining," he shouted.

Nightfall didn't look back. "Why do you keep telling me this? It doesn't help."

Jason nodded. "I've never been particularly helpful in these situations." Up ahead, Jason could see a strange termination to the perpetual darkness of the Wasted Lands. It was still a good distance away. The land beyond that sudden cessation of darkness shone bright and fair. "Is that the end of the Wasted Lands? Maybe we should head for the light." Not that they would make it before the Elenil caught them. But the thought of getting into sunlight again cheered Jason. And who knew? Maybe it would be easier to ditch the Elenil in the sunlight. The darkness wasn't helping.

"There are rules in the darkness," Nightfall said. "Treaties and agreements between the Scim and the Elenil. Once we enter the light, we are unprotected. When we get near it, I will turn to the right or left and attempt to outrun them."

"You can't outrun them *now*," Jason pointed out. "We should take our chances in the light."

Nightfall grunted. "Are they still gaining on us?"

Jason frowned. He was clearly being dismissed. Delightful Glitter Lady rearranged herself where he had tucked her into his jacket against his chest. She let out a plaintive whine.

"What are you, ten years old?" Jason shook his head. "Maybe I should make the decisions."

"I'm holding the reins of the brucok," Nightfall said. "I get the final say. Now . . . are they still gaining on us?"

They were, of course.

But two dark shadows loomed over them now. Silent, or at least unheard over the thundering of the Elenil steeds, two enormous birds with impossibly long wingspans flew in the darkness just over the Elenil's orbs of light. "There's something else," Jason said, "in the shadows above them."

Nightfall risked a look. A grin spread across his wide Scim face, terrifying in his war skin. "It's the Black Skulls!"

Jason squinted. He could almost make out the details of the birds, and Nightfall was right. They were monstrous owls. A figure sat on each, wearing the black-painted skulls of horned animals. The Black Skulls were brutal Scim warriors, seemingly impervious to pain and impossible to wound, let alone kill. There were three of them, and as he had come to discover only a few short weeks ago, they were all humans . . . and the founder of the Skulls was Darius Walker, his own high school classmate. Darius wore the skull of an antelope and fought with skill magically donated by the Scim people themselves—and a passion that was 100 percent his own.

"There's only two of them," Jason said.

"I'm thankful for any," Nightfall said. "Tell me what they do."

As he said the words, the two Skulls dropped from their birds, landing on the two lead Elenil. Two lights went out as the Skulls dragged the Elenil to the ground. The other Elenil struggled to avoid trampling them, parting in a panic around their fallen comrades and the unexpected enemies from the sky.

"They jumped off their birds and took out two of the Elenil!"

"Good," Nightfall said. "Are the other Elenil turning back to help them?"

"Yes. We should make for the sunlight now, while they're distracted."

The Scim boy snorted. "I'm telling you, Wu Song, that's a terrible idea."

The Elenil were falling behind now, the thundering sound of their war party replaced with the sound of steel on steel and shouts from the warriors.

A dark shape slipped alongside the brucok. It was Darius, the original Black Skull himself, riding on a gigantic possum, its long nose quivering and its lips pulled back to reveal yellowed teeth as long as Jason's forearm.

"This way," the Black Skull said, taking hold of Moriarty's reins in one gloved hand and directing them to the right, away from the wall of sunlight. "Quickly," he said, leading them toward a cleverly concealed ramp in the desert floor. It took them into a small hollow, barely large enough for the three of them and their animals.

Moriarty snaked his long neck around and bit Jason in the arm.

"Ow!"

"Be silent," the Skull said, his voice deep and hoarse.

"Tell Chicken Dinner to stop biting me then!" Jason rubbed his bicep. The bird didn't have teeth, but his beak still left a red mark. Jason glared at the brucok. "People eat birds, not the other way around. Don't bite me, it's unnatural."

"You have to be quiet," Nightfall whispered.

"Is this study hall?" Jason asked, whispering back. He knew he should stop talking, but sometimes he got nervous. Or sometimes a giant bird bit him.

The Skull glared at him. "Jason. Silence."

"I never understood how that worked, telling someone to be quiet by making noise yourself. Like . . . shushing someone with a SHHHHH that's more distracting than someone quietly whispering."

Nightfall jabbed him in the side.

Jason sat down and took a deep breath. He hoped Baileya was okay. Usually about now she would come riding to his rescue, skewer the bad guys, and tell him, "Run, Wu Song!" It was their tradition. He hadn't heard from her, though, which made him nervous. He knew Break Bones wouldn't hurt her, and he hoped her brother wouldn't either, but who knew? The Kakri were unpredictable.

They sat in silence for a long time. Jason could hear the sounds of the skirmish above, but barely. In time, those faded, replaced with the sound of the Elenil riding again, moving away but seemingly still in pursuit of something. Darius held his hand up for a minute, signaling for them to keep silent.

"Our plan worked," he said at last. "We intended to distract them, hide you, and then draw them away."

"Thank you," Jason said.

The Skull knelt down in front of Nightfall. "As for you, child . . . Break Bones himself has trained you, and yet you run directly for the light? Don't you know that there are protections in the dark? We have agreements with the Elenil, bought at a great price. They cannot kill you without cause here. In the light there are no such guarantees."

Nightfall glared at Jason. "Yes, sir," he said. "I will do better next time."

The Black Skull laughed. "You did well enough, Nightfall. Especially carrying such a helpless load." He punched Jason in the shoulder.

Their friendship had grown in strange ways. Darius and Jason both loved Madeline Oliver in their individual way, which brought them together, sort of. But it was a weird kind of bond, to miss the same person. On the other hand, they also had the bond of shared history, being from the same town, the same school. Now, being two of the three people from their school to have traveled to and lived in the Sunlit Lands . . . well, they had a lot more in common than almost anyone else in the world. Still, Jason wasn't a hundred percent sure they would have been close friends on Earth.

"That was my idea, running for the light," Jason said.

"It was a terrible idea, and you're lucky you didn't actually make it there," Darius said. "Now, let's get you somewhere safer until we can take you back to the mansion."

"About that," Jason said. "A Kakri warrior found us and, well, it's not safe to go back there now."

Darius paused. "In that case . . . in that case, I'm not sure where to take you. We'll have to check with the elders. The Wasted Lands are getting more and more volatile after Madeline brought so much destruction to Far Seeing. The Elenil are angry and pushing the boundaries of our agreements. It's not safe at the mansion, it's not safe abroad, it's not safe in the villages. Maybe there is no safe place anymore."

"We need to find my brother and sister, and Break Bones, too," Nightfall said, a tinge of worry in his voice.

"And Baileya."

"We will," Darius said, guiding his possum up and out of their hiding place. "But first we find a safe place for Jason, since he's the one the Elenil are looking for."

"Me?"

"They want to kill you. The archon wants your head."

Jason put his hands on his neck. "But I like my head." He knew the Elenil were after him, of course, but hearing someone else say it brought a glitchy feeling that rose from the pit of his stomach. "I'm attached to it," he said weakly. They surfaced into the deep darkness of the Wasted Lands. A light breeze blew across them, and Delightful Glitter Lady whined.

"What is it, girl?"

"Hold," a voice called. "Do not move."

Jason turned at once to find a small collection of Elenil, their lights sheathed in some sort of shadowed film.

The lead Elenil gestured to his orb, and the darkening film fell away. Jason squinted in the light. "I said do not move."

"It's only natural," Jason said, holding his hand up to block the light. "When someone says 'don't move,' you want to turn and look at them and see who's talking and why they don't want you to move. Next time you should give more detail."

"Silence!"

"Like, 'Don't move, it's some Elenil warriors, and we have lots of arrows pointed at you, so don't even turn around.' That's the sort of information that would be helpful."

There were five of them. They wore the traditional Elenil finery. Long, brocaded sleeves covered their arms, and high collars protected their necks. Their loose hair flowed to their shoulders, and they were thin and almost willowy. The lead Elenil was dressed in pale yellow, with a purple thread winding through his clothing. He held a shining sword, and beside him stood a white stag. To his left stood an Elenil with a fierce scowl on his face. He had a short bow in his hand, an arrow nocked, and two more dangling from his hand. A tiger crouched beside him, growling softly. Jason knew them.

"Slowly place your weapons upon the ground," the first Elenil said.

The Black Skull did not move or speak. Nightfall followed his lead, standing in absolute stillness.

"Wait!" Jason stepped between the Elenil and his friends. "I know you both. You with the stag, you're Rondelo. Madeline's friend. And you with the tiger, you're the guard from Far Seeing. You chased me when I stole a durian. I remember your name, too. It's Soda Pop."

"Sochar," the Elenil guard growled, the tip of his arrow pointed at Jason's heart.

"Close enough," Jason said, satisfied with himself. "I can't believe I remembered your name. It's amazing, really."

The Black Skull shoved Jason roughly back. "Put down *your* weapons, Elenil," he said, his deep voice booming. "Our treaties make it clear you cannot harm us here, on our own land, when we have not made any attack against you."

"Except to maim our archon," Sochar snarled. "You lopped off his hand in the seat of his power, shamed him in front of the assembled messenger birds, made a mockery of the highest authority in the Sunlit Lands, and now you stand here in the accursed shadows and claim sanctuary because of ancient treaties sworn in brighter days?"

"To be fair," Jason said, "it wasn't us personally who did the lopping."

"Peace, peace," Rondelo said, letting the tip of his sword sag toward the ground. "We need not fight. Sir Black Skull, I know thou art a man of honor. Let us set aside our arms and discuss this like gentlefolk."

"He is no man," Sochar said, "but a boy. And not a Scim, neither, and thus not covered by the treaties. Let us fill him with arrows and be done."

Rondelo's eyes slid toward Sochar, but he didn't contradict him. As near as Jason could tell, Rondelo was in charge. The other Elenil looked ready to fight, though. Maybe Rondelo wouldn't be in charge for long, not if they had their way. They wanted blood, and the thin barrier of Rondelo's authority wouldn't keep them back for long. Jason became hyper-aware of his every move. He got the feeling they were looking for an excuse, a reason to act.

He knew exactly what to do.

Back home, back on Earth, his friend Josh Chen taught him that if the police pulled you over, you should have a pair of nerdy glasses in the car, because if you're Asian American, the police don't see *you*, they see the stereotypes they expect. Wear baggy jeans or gold chains, or have the wrong kind of tattoo or rap music playing, and they think "gangbanger." But quickly hit the pre-programmed button to turn your stereo to classical music and throw on a pair of nerdy glasses, and you're a harmless "Smart Asian." Jason had never tried it himself, but Josh swore by it. *If they're going to have stereotypes*, he'd said, *let's at least use them to our advantage.*

Of course, the Elenil didn't have stereotypes about Asian Americans. They probably had some about humans, but Jason wasn't clear what those would be. Thinking about this whole thing in the context of interacting with a police officer, though, helped Jason understand what he should do.

Carefully, slowly, he put his hands up, palms out, before lacing them behind his head.

"What are you doing?" Sochar said, intently following Jason's every move. His eyes flicked toward Nightfall.

"A magical incantation. What does it look like I'm doing? I'm showing you I'm no threat so we can put down our weapons and have a civilized conversation."

Jason could just see Darius's eyes in the recesses of the Black Skull mask. Darius said, "Rondelo, let the Scim child leave us. He has no part in this and was not party to the incident with your archon."

"*Our* archon," Rondelo said. "For is he not the ruler of the entire Sunlit Lands? Not only the Elenil but the Scim also are under his authority."

Nightfall couldn't stay silent for that. "He is not my archon, and if he were, I would cut off his other hand."

Sochar's face twisted into a mask of fury. The other Elenil, except Rondelo, looked nearly as angry as he. "Insolence," Sochar said, his voice shaking.

"Um, Nightfall?" Jason tried to get the kid's attention without moving his hands from behind his head. "Let's try to calm everyone down, not get everyone worked up."

"The archon is a fool," Nightfall said. "A fool and a tyrant."

"The archon gives you food and shelter. The archon brings light to the Sunlit Lands."

Nightfall let out a bitter laugh and stepped toward the Elenil warriors, his fists clenched. "Do you see any of those things here?"

What happened next, Jason didn't know exactly, even though he would later play it over and over in his mind. There was a skirmish on the Elenil side. Rondelo—he thought it was Rondelo—shouted "Peace!" There was a wordless shout. An arrow appeared in Nightfall's chest. The boy looked down at it, his eyes wide, as he sank to his knees. His hand hovered near it, didn't touch it. He fell sideways, rolling onto his back.

Then the world crashed in again, as the Black Skull launched himself into the small crowd of Elenil, slicing through Sochar's bow with a single swing of his scythe, his fists and feet swirling, connecting with Elenil faces and weapons, breaking them.

Jason cradled Nightfall's face. He was still breathing but with ragged, labored gasps. His eyes found Jason's, and he opened his mouth but no sound came out. He looked away again and closed his eyes. His breaths got farther and farther apart.

"No," Jason said. "Nightfall, no." Nightfall didn't respond. Jason leaned closer, whispered to him using his true name. "Nola, hang in there. We'll get help. Just—don't die."

Jason jumped to his feet. Two Elenil lay on the ground. Sochar's right arm hung limp. Rondelo fought one-on-one against the Black Skull, but Darius could not be wounded, not when the magic of the Scim came to him through his mask. The last Elenil—a particularly tall one—was coming up behind the Skull. Jason shouted a warning, running to Darius's aid, but Sochar grabbed Jason with his good arm, slinging him around so he couldn't get there in time.

The tall Elenil bashed the Black Skull in the back of the head, knocking his antlered face forward. Rondelo grabbed the antlers and, with a practiced kick, knocked Darius's feet out from under him. Jason struggled but couldn't get free. The tall Elenil pinned the Skull to the ground, and Rondelo tore the mask away, revealing Darius's sweat-covered, enraged face.

"You've broken the treaty," Darius shouted, his voice no longer the grating, deep voice of the Black Skull. "There are rules to be observed. You killed a defenseless boy."

"He's not dead," Sochar said dismissively.

"The human is not wrong," Rondelo said. "Sochar, you had no—"

Sochar raised his hands. "I feared for my life, Rondelo. You saw him move toward me!" He looked to the other Elenil. "You saw him. He advanced on me. He threatened me, and I defended myself. How does this break the treaty agreements?"

Jason jabbed Sochar in the wounded shoulder, and the Elenil cried out and released him. Jason ran back to Nightfall. "He's maybe—*maybe*—ten years old."

"Even an infant viper can bite," Sochar said.

How Sochar could think Nightfall was a threat in that moment, Jason didn't know. But he didn't seem to be lying. He had honestly thought Nightfall was going to hurt him.

"This must go to the elders of the Scim for reckoning," Darius said. "Let them decide if the treaty is broken, and let them decide the punishment."

Rondelo paused, as if considering this. "No. Archon Thenody desires Wu Song's presence at Far Seeing. Let him be the judge. I will not keep him waiting any longer."

Darius pushed against the Elenil who held him. "I have appealed to the elders! By treaty right you must take me to them. We are in Scim land—you must take me to the Scim authorities for judgment."

Rondelo regarded him coolly. "True enough," he said. He ran a long cord through the eyes of Darius's mask and tied it onto his belt. "If you were a Scim. But you are a human. The treaty has nothing to do with you."

"What about him?" Jason shouted, pointing at Nightfall. "Doesn't he get a say in this?"

Rondelo's eyes flicked toward the bleeding Scim boy. "Speak up, child, if you have an opinion."

Sochar rubbed his injured arm. "He made his choice when he attacked us."

Rondelo frowned at him. "Silence, Sochar. You have done enough for one day."

Sochar grunted, then came over to Jason and pushed him to the ground. He rolled him onto his chest, then held him while the other Elenil tied Jason's hands behind his back with a rough thong. "Archon Thenody will not care for the loss of one Scim if we bring back these two humans."

"He will care if the treaty is broken. Will he not?"

Sochar had nothing to say to that. The two Elenil on the ground began to stir. They got to their feet while Rondelo searched Darius for weapons and bound his arms. "What of the boy?" Sochar asked.

Rondelo considered this. "Leave him. Perhaps the other Black Skulls will return and find him, or one of the Scim. Whatever happens now is in the hands of the Majestic One."

Sochar walked over to Nightfall, leaving Jason on the ground, struggling to see what he was doing. "Leave him alone," Jason shouted.

The Elenil stalked back to him, kneeling down near Jason's head. "Don't worry," he said softly, "I cannot harm him now. Your little friend is already dead."

No.

Jason struggled against the leather thongs tying his arms. No!

His teeth clenched, and his blood pounded against his skull. This was his fault. The Elenil were after him, not Nightfall. He should have sent the boy away, should have taken the risk on his own. Now Nightfall was dead. Who would tell his sister and brother? Who would tell his family? Once again, Jason Wu had brought death and destruction to a Scim family. Once again, being near him had caused someone pain.

No. That wasn't true, not exactly.

Jason did not tell lies. Not anymore. It wasn't just being near him that had caused this. It was being near the Elenil. They would pay, he promised himself. Sochar first and foremost, and then Rondelo and all the rest of them. They would pay, wound for wound and blood for blood. He promised this to himself and to the memory of Nightfall. Whatever came, they would pay.

8

THE MOTH

He saw the sort of woman she must be
to overcome her sorrow and still live.

FROM "JELDA'S REVENGE," A SCIM LEGEND

✦

Shula could not sleep that night. She lay beside Yenil, listening to her breathe. The Scim girl had quieted soon enough after the incident with the principal, but Madeline was furious and Shula was agitated. Madeline kept making her way to the front door, looking out the window, then mumbling to herself about what would happen to the principal if he called the police. What she would do to him. What her father's lawyer would do to him. Madeline had told her parents about what had happened at the principal's office, minus the war skin. Her parents tried to take a conciliatory tone, suggesting there had been a misunderstanding, but Madeline, livid, kept at them until they had become nearly as enraged as she was. Mr. Oliver had gone into his study, and Shula had heard him talking to his lawyer on the phone, voice raised.

Shula found herself on the verge of tears several times that evening.

She knew why, knew it was the loss of her family. She had worked hard to keep that memory behind a wall, to keep her grief compartmentalized and isolated. *I am strong. I have power.* She snuck into the garden and went to the side of the house, where no one could see her. She let the magic of the Sunlit Lands rise from beneath her skin and watched the flames flow over her. She stood in the cool night, letting the reminder of her power comfort her. *No one can hurt me.* Not her body, in any case. Her emotions were another story, and so she must keep herself aloof from others. It was safer for her and them. She would be lonely, yes, but she wouldn't be reminded of her lost loved ones, and she could move on with life. The only emotion she would allow herself to feel with any regularity was anger.

Anger. It sat in the core of her chest like a fire, and if she ever felt it die down too much, she would give it more fuel, stoke the flames, remind herself not to set it aside, to let it grow. Losing her anger would make her vulnerable. Letting anyone get close would put her at risk. Madeline had been the lone exception. Something about the way she had walked into their shared room in the Sunlit Lands had disarmed Shula completely. But Shula had been shocked by how different Madeline was when her illness returned. Less patient, more angry. It made sense on reflection, but Shula couldn't help but think of the girl she had known in the Sunlit Lands as the "real" Madeline. There was something about Madeline that first day they met in Mrs. Raymond's home, something that made Shula want to protect her. Not because she was weak—she wasn't. But because she had an outlook on the world that was so kindhearted and loving that Shula couldn't help but think of both Madeline and her worldview as fragile. She didn't want that precious naiveté to break.

Maybe *naiveté* was the wrong word, because she had watched Madeline discover the truth of the Elenil magic system and the oppression of the Scim in record time, and Madeline had actually done something about it. She had made hard choices about herself and her life and had taken consequences that Shula couldn't even imagine. Shula rubbed the long scar on her face. Well. She could imagine it, but it was so different from her own experience. Even now, as her health failed, Madeline had arranged much of her life around taking care of Yenil and making sure Shula would be cared for when she was gone. Which left Shula with the uncomfortable possibility that Madeline was not naive at all and somehow still managed to be kind-hearted and focused on bringing justice to the rest of the world. Shula did not like this conclusion, because she feared what it might say about herself.

Then, of course, Yenil had come into Shula's life and stepped directly into the painful place where Amira had once been. Shula had tried to resist for a sum total of three minutes before giving in and adopting the little girl into her life. This had been a mistake. Their lives were too similar: both orphans, both casualties of war. Both strangers in this land, both navigating unimaginable loss. Yenil was too like Shula's sister, and too different from her. She was a reminder of what could have been, which was another way to say that she was a reminder of what was not, of who was lost.

So Shula could not sleep.

She padded around the house, barefoot in the luxurious carpet of her wealthy American family. She paused outside Madeline's room, listening to her tortured breathing. A sharp pang of hurt hit her as she realized how this little action—the restless wandering, checking in on Madeline—had become almost a ritual. She was losing Madeline, too.

In the darkened living room, she curled up on the couch, a soft blanket over her shoulders, and looked out at Mrs. Oliver's garden. Small lights lit the path, and the strange, out-of-season foxglove flowers bowed their heads in a gentle breeze.

"I can't sleep either."

Shula jumped to her feet.

A gentle laugh came from across the darkened room. "I didn't mean to startle you, Shula." It was Mrs. Oliver, sitting in the easy chair. Shula hadn't noticed her, hadn't expected her to be here in the middle of the night.

"I did not know you were there," Shula said. If she had been any more startled, it was entirely likely Shula might have used her magic and lit herself on fire. In addition to terrifying Mrs. Oliver, it would have ruined the couch. Not to mention the carpet. She could have caught the house on fire.

"She's getting worse," Mrs. Oliver said. "She's getting worse, and so I can't sleep."

Shula didn't know what to say to this. It was true. "Yes," she said.

"Have you ever lost someone you love?" Mrs. Oliver turned on a standing lamp next to the chair. She looked small and alone in the weak light.

Shula could not bring herself to answer the question. "Have you?"

Mrs. Oliver leaned back in her chair. She stared into the garden. "Is it very strange if I say that I don't remember, Shula?" She pushed her blonde hair back from her face and held it in both hands, a gesture that, for some reason, Madeline found endlessly infuriating. Shula, though, had a sudden jolt of emotion as she realized that she was sitting in the dark, talking to a mother. Not her mother, no—that could never happen again. But someone's mother. Talking about their feelings. Talking about important things. Shula did not care how this woman held her hair back when she was thinking.

"How can this be?" Shula asked.

"I don't know. I wish I did. I have this feeling that something is missing. That I have lost someone, but I can't remember who. Maybe more than one person? I feel sad, Shula, I feel sad all the time. I try to put on a happy face and do the little social events with the women in the neighborhood, play my racquetball and plan the parties, but it doesn't work. Of course I am sad about our Maddie, too." She began to cry.

Shula went down the hallway to the nearest bathroom and returned with some tissues. She sat on the floor by Mrs. Oliver's legs. She debated for a moment, almost afraid to do what she wanted, because Mrs. Oliver sometimes seemed so cold, but then she thought, *Isn't that the exact way I make myself seem to other people? I make myself cold so they won't come close, even though that's what I want.* So she leaned her shoulder against Mrs. Oliver's leg and laid her head on the older woman's knee. Mrs. Oliver stroked Shula's hair. Shula closed her eyes. Her own mother used to stroke her hair like this. It felt familiar and forgotten and impossible and wonderful all at once. A tear ran down her face.

"My mother is dead," Shula said, and it felt like an admission. She never spoke about this if she had the choice. It seemed that Mrs. Oliver didn't even know.

Mrs. Oliver's hand paused for a moment, then continued stroking her hair. "I'm sorry, Shula."

Shula could not say anything in response to this. If she spoke, she would sob. Either way, no words would come, so she stayed silent.

Mrs. Oliver slid from her chair and took Shula's face in her hands. "There is always a home for you here."

Shula sobbed now, and Mrs. Oliver took her into her arms. They sat there, crying together, for what seemed like a long time. A noise came from Madeline's room: the sound of coughing, and a painful wheeze, and then silence again, and Shula stopped crying immediately and moved to Madeline's door, checking to make sure she was still asleep. Madeline lay on her back, propped on a pile of pillows, her face contorted in pain, her mouth wide open, as if that would somehow allow more air into her lungs. As near as Shula could tell, she was still asleep.

As Shula walked back to the living room, she realized for the first time just how much Madeline had put her parents through. She had left them without warning and disappeared to the Sunlit Lands. There she had found a cure—and then rejected it—and fought a battle that was not her own. Madeline returned without explanation, sicker than ever, and with two strangers in tow: a Middle Eastern teenager and a little girl from another world. On top of that, Madeline had no patience for her parents' questions and refused to even try to answer them. She'd made it clear she wanted Shula and Yenil in the house, and that was the end of the conversation. It was a strange interaction. Shula didn't understand it, but maybe that's how families operated in the United States. But poor Mrs. Oliver: her daughter was dying, and she didn't know the truth about any of it, about anything.

Madeline was kind, loving, thoughtful. But not toward her parents. Her father was scarcely there at all. Madeline said he didn't deal well with illness and had been largely absent since her sickness set in. Her mother was cold and aloof and concerned about many of the wrong things, but Madeline treated her with a contempt that Shula found unsettling. She knew how families worked, knew that there was deep hurt, probably on both sides, and that Madeline didn't act this way for no reason. And yet . . . Shula did not want to treat Mrs. Oliver the same way. She wanted to treat her with respect, with kindness, with thankfulness for letting her live in her home. She wanted to be honest with her. She struggled with this, because to be honest meant to make a decision for Madeline, too. But to not be honest with her . . . Shula didn't want to treat Mrs. Oliver the same way Madeline did.

Mrs. Oliver was still sitting at the foot of the easy chair, her hair disheveled, wiping at her face with a tissue. Shula took her by the hand and led her to the couch, sitting beside her. "I have something to tell you," she said. "It is about a place called the Sunlit Lands."

A strange glimmer of recognition flared in Mrs. Oliver's eyes. "I know that place."

Shula's eyes widened. What did this mean? Maybe Mrs. Oliver had misunderstood and thought she was talking about something else. "You do?"

Mrs. Oliver nodded slowly. "I had a dream about it, I think. It's like . . . like Narnia?" She shivered. "I never liked those books."

So she did know something. Shula frowned. "The Sunlit Lands are another world. They are next to our world. It is . . . it is a place filled with magic and monsters and war."

Mrs. Oliver smiled dreamily. "Oh, Shula. Don't be ridiculous."

"There are people there, powerful people, called the Elenil."

The older woman's hand clenched hard against Shula's. "Don't talk about them. We don't talk about them, not here. Not in my house."

"Mrs. Oliver. I want to tell you what happened to Madeline. Where she was last year."

"Yes," Mrs. Oliver said, her eyes rising to meet Shula's. "I know something happened, but what was it? Where was she? Where did she find you? How did she come to be with Yenil?"

Shula took a deep breath. "An Elenil named Hanali came to her in the hospital. He offered to heal her with magic in exchange for a year's service to his people. Madeline agreed. That's why she was missing for so long. But she discovered that the reason she could breathe was that she had been linked to Yenil, who was giving her own breath to Madeline. Madeline couldn't stand this, so she broke her magical link, and we came home, here, to you. I came with her to help with Yenil, and to be with Madeline."

As Shula spoke, Mrs. Oliver's eyes had unfocused, as if she were staring far away. "Where was Madeline?" she asked. "Where did she go? Where did you come from? And Yenil?"

Shula leaned toward her. "Mrs. Oliver? I just told you. Hanali—"

Mrs. Oliver hissed. Hissed like an angry cat, her lips pulled back to show her teeth. Shula pulled away, and Mrs. Oliver's face slowly returned to normal, an almost placid, dreamlike look replacing the furious mask of a moment before. "I wish I knew, that's all. What happened to Madeline, where she went."

Shula shivered. She tried one more time. "There is a place called the Sunlit Lands—"

Mrs. Oliver's back arched, as if she had been hit with a jolt of electricity. Her hand jerked toward the ceiling, and for a moment Shula saw a flash of light from Mrs. Oliver's left wrist. A sure sign of magic, one that Shula had seen a thousand times before on her own wrist, on Madeline's, on nearly all the humans in the Sunlit Lands, but much brighter. An afterimage of a primitive tattoo burned in her eyes.

Mrs. Oliver wept softly, her face in her hands.

How could this be? Had Hanali done something to her? Was this part of the deal with Madeline? Somehow Shula didn't think so. The magic looked different, messier, more painful. "Mrs. Oliver? Have you ever been—somewhere like Narnia?"

Mrs. Oliver's face twisted with rage and regret. "Not like Narnia . . . oh, how I hate even the name of that place! They told me it would be all wonder and magic, but it wasn't, not at all. It's all loss and pain, pain and loss." She stood. "They told us they would come for our daughter one day, told us we wouldn't be able to stop them. But I know, Shula, I know." She was like a sleepwalker, rambling and nonsensical, her words slurring together.

"Maybe you should go to bed—"

"No!" Mrs. Oliver's eyes flew open. "No, I have to protect her. Especially at night. Especially when she's dreaming." She snatched Shula's hand and pulled her to her feet. "Come with me. Come, I'll show you."

She dragged Shula out the back door. The night air was bracing, frigid. The pale light from the moon shone down on the garden. Mrs. Oliver dragged her toward the small pond, where Yenil made her faerie houses—little huts made of flowers and sticks. Mrs. Oliver stepped on them, kicking the sticks and spreading them into random piles. "Every night I destroy them," she said.

But Shula had seen them many times when she played with Yenil in the garden. Madeline loved those little houses, and so did Yenil. They would be so sad to see them knocked down.

Mrs. Oliver grinned at her, a smile wild and desperate. Shula's heart beat faster, and she pulled her hand away.

"Then these flowers," Mrs. Oliver said, her lip curled up in disgust. She waved her hand over the patch of foxgloves. She snatched one of the stalks and crushed the bells between her fingers. "They come through the flowers," she said. "Have to pull them up by the roots, have to smash them all."

A sudden compassion came over Shula. Here was a woman who had lost her daughter—was still losing her daughter. She needed help, not for Shula to draw away from her. Shula wrapped her arms around the older woman. "Mrs. Oliver. Let's go inside. You should go to bed."

"The flowers!" she said, shaking Shula off and falling to her knees. "Have to get the roots." She was grabbing the stalks, low, and yanking them out of the ground. "Help me," she said, pleading. "Help me!"

Shula knelt beside her, and together they pulled all the flowers up, yanked them out like weeds. Shula shivered in the darkness, her hands and knees wet with dew. The plants came up easily enough, and soon a large mound lay between them.

Mrs. Oliver cried out and pounced on the pile, and her hands came away clasped together. "I caught one. Look!"

She opened her hands, and there, in her palms, was the crumpled form of an insect. Shula peered at it. "A moth?"

Disappointed, Mrs. Oliver shook her head. She slid the moth into one palm, and with her other hand pointed along the broken body. "Do you see its arms? The little legs. The tiny face. It's a faerie."

Shula leaned closer, and yes, it was dark here and hard to see. But she didn't see a faerie. She saw a moth. Crushed, dead, but ordinary. The dust from its wings rubbed off on Mrs. Oliver's hands.

"Good job," Shula said. "You did it. You protected Madeline." She stood and held out her hand to Mrs. Oliver. "Let's go to bed."

Still in her dreamlike state, Mrs. Oliver took Shula's hand. "I did it," she said. "I protected her, like a good mother. I did it." She kept mumbling this over and over, all the way into the house. Shula pointed her in the direction of her bedroom, and she wandered off, mumbling to herself.

Shula put Mrs. Oliver's teacup in the sink and folded the blanket she had put on the couch. She checked on Madeline . . . still restless, but breathing. She looked in on Yenil, who had thrown off her covers and was sprawled on the bed. She tucked her back in, then lay down beside her. Yenil usually struggled to fall asleep without Shula or Madeline nearby. Tonight, Shula didn't think she could sleep if she were too far from Yenil. She wanted to make sure she was safe. The house was quiet and still. She fell asleep easily.

She woke in the morning, late. Yenil had already gotten up, had somehow climbed over Shula without waking her. Mrs. Oliver was in the kitchen wearing her racquetball clothes, her blonde hair perfectly coifed, a steaming mug of coffee in her hand. Madeline sat looking out the window into the garden. Shula put her hand on Madeline's shoulder. Madeline looked up, smiled at her, turned back to the window.

The pile of uprooted flowers was gone. In fact, a new crop of foxgloves grew where they had been. The faerie houses stood intact on the shore of the pond. Astonished, Shula turned to Mrs. Oliver.

Mrs. Oliver smiled at her, took a sip of her coffee. "Did you sleep well, dear? As soon as my head hit the pillow last night, I dozed straight through. I saw your teacup in the sink, though. Trouble sleeping?"

Shula looked back to the flowers. Then to Mrs. Oliver again. "Yes," she said. "Yes. My sleep was . . . troubled . . . last night."

Mrs. Oliver pushed her lip into a pout. "Poor thing." She patted Shula's hand. She gave Madeline a kiss on the forehead. "I'm off to racquetball. Good-bye, darlings! See you this afternoon!"

Shula followed her to the front door, stood at the window and watched as she pulled the car from the driveway and turned down the street. She hadn't been dreaming. She was certain of it. No . . . the teacup was in the sink. So it wasn't a dream. What was happening?

9
IN CHAINS

Help me, dear friend, for I am trapped among the roots of this
prison tree, and when the water rises, I will surely drown.

FROM "JELDA'S REVENGE," A SCIM LEGEND

✛

The Elenil made camp along a river, well outside of the Wasted
Lands. They didn't pitch tents or start a fire. The glowing orbs that
had lit their way in the darkness of the Wasted Lands doubled as
heaters. They floated near the Elenil, exuding warmth. Not that it
was much necessary—the weather was pleasant enough that night.
The crystal stars of the Sunlit Lands had begun to slide over the horizon,
though the plentiful trees screened most of them from view.

Jason and Darius sat side by side, leaning against a tree trunk. Jason
was exhausted from shouting at the Elenil. The tears had dried on his face,
as his hands were tied behind his back. Baileya would come, he knew that.
Or Break Bones. Or possibly Delightful Glitter Lady. He had made sure
to release her when the Elenil were distracted. The little rhinoceros had
not been pleased to leave him, but she'd seemed to know what he needed.

"You have to calm down," Darius said. "If we're going to get out of this, we're going to need to be calm and think everything through. When the chance comes to run, you're going to take it."

"You mean *we're* going to take it," Jason said. "Together."

Darius shook his head. "They took my mask. I'm not leaving without it. And believe it or not, I'd love to see that little weasel the archon again. If they want to walk me straight into his presence, that's their mistake."

"Rondelo's coming over," Jason whispered, and they both fell silent.

Rondelo crouched down, bringing his face to their level. "You mourn your fallen comrade. You are angry."

This was such a colossally stupid observation that Jason couldn't find a strong enough response. He settled on, "You wear weird clothes and kill children."

Rondelo frowned. "Your feelings do you credit, Jason. It is right for you to be angry. The archon will hear this story presented fairly, I promise you that, and we will live by his pronouncement of justice."

Jason snorted. "You might remember that I was part of the whole thing where his hand got chopped off. I don't know that his ideas of justice and mine are going to overlap much."

"It may be so, but we are people under authority. We must trust that those above us have information we do not and are making decisions as best they are able. Perhaps in their place we would do the same."

Darius couldn't stay silent for that. "An easy position to take when it is your own people in power. You didn't submit to the Scim authorities when we were wronged in the Wasted Lands."

Rondelo said nothing to that, though he had the decency to look away. Jason thought he might actually be ashamed. After a moment Rondelo pulled two lengths of silver manacled chains from his belt. The chains were thin as twine, and they sparkled in the light from Rondelo's floating orb. "I fear I must put these on you. They are magic chains. They cannot be undone, save by the archon himself. We are in the open, and the journey is long. I cannot have you plotting to escape. The only way out of these chains is to face the archon himself and submit yourselves to his justice."

Darius turned to make his wrists more easily accessible. He wasn't one to fight the hopeless battles, not when there was a bigger problem to work on. "Pray that I don't have a sword in my hand on that day."

Rondelo smiled at that, cut the thongs tying Darius's wrists, let him put his hands in front of him, and latched on the chains. There was a flash of light as they closed over Darius's wrists. "Thou hast a warrior's spirit." He held the second set up to Jason.

"I hast that spirit where I don't wearest handcuffs. No offense to you and Darius. It's a conscious fashion decision I made some time ago. Not because of this current situation, I've just never liked the look. Makes my wrists look small." He gave Rondelo an appraising stare, taking in his brocade jacket and the intricate silk stitching on his clothing. "I mean, you wear that crazy getup to go camping and catch fugitives. Surely you understand."

"I'm afraid I must insist," Rondelo said, cutting Jason's bindings. He waited until Jason put his hands in front of him and snapped the cuffs on Jason's wrists. There was a flash of light and a shock of cold, as if the metal had been dipped in liquid nitrogen before being put on him. "Ow!"

"It stings," Rondelo said.

Jason shot an accusatory look at Darius. "Thanks for the warning. You didn't even flinch."

"They'll do worse than this to us, Jason. Be prepared."

Rondelo stood and walked away, but Jason called his name. The Elenil paused and looked back at them. "I gotta say, buddy, I'm a little disappointed you would break someone else's fashion norms, especially given you Elenil with all your gloves and high collars and weird hats."

"War and fashion are hard companions," Rondelo said.

"Exactly. That's why I want you to know that before this is all over, I'm gonna see you in jeans and a T-shirt and a baseball cap. It's not personal, it's just that this is war, and that's what's going to happen."

Rondelo smirked. "I shall take this warning into account. I have seen the strange fashions of the humans, and I do not wish to be humiliated in such a way." He walked off, stopping to talk to the other Elenil warriors.

"That guy is the worst," Darius said. "But you are one strange little dude."

"One, Sochar is the worst. But Rondelo is too pretty, and it makes you want to like him. Then he's all nice, which makes you want to like him more. But then it turns out he's also a bad guy." Jason paused. "He's a bad guy, right?"

"Clearly."

Right. Of course he was. He had captured them and stood by and done nothing while Nightfall had been killed. "So he's a bad guy, but I really want to like him. Madeline practically had a crush on him. She'd go all weak in the knees and have trouble talking straight when he was around."

Darius frowned. "We'll kill him soon enough."

Oh yeah. Darius was Madeline's boyfriend. Or had been once. Jason probably shouldn't have said that about the crush. On the other hand, he was committed to the truth and had to say what he thought. But killing a guy because your girlfriend had a crush on him was next level. "You're so dark, man. With all the killing and everything."

Darius looked uncomfortable. "Yeah, well. Only the people who deserve it."

"Who decides that?"

"The guy holding the sword." Darius shook his chains. They made an almost bell-like tinkling sound.

The guy holding the sword. Or the bow. Jason couldn't help but think of Nightfall, and how was that any different? Sochar had decided for some reason that the Scim kid was deserving of the death penalty. Some weird combination of fear and anger had driven him to feel threatened by a child. This wasn't the first time either, because he had done the same thing to Mud. If it hadn't been for Mrs. Raymond and Hanali taking Mud in and healing him, the kid probably wouldn't have survived. Jason's teeth ground together. Mrs. Raymond and Hanali hadn't been around this time, which meant Nightfall hadn't been so lucky. He had been murdered because Sochar was so afraid of the Scim that he would kill a kid.

It didn't look like there would be many consequences for that, unless Archon Thenody was way less terrible than Jason thought he was. Which seemed unlikely, because Jason knew the Elenil ruler, and he was the sort of guy to dangle you over a cliff and threaten you for no reason. Jason had to admit thinking about Darius stabbing Rondelo only gave him the barest tinge of bad feeling, nothing like the raging tidal wave of grief which kept threatening to engulf him because of what had happened to Nightfall.

He wasn't sure he could run Rondelo through with a sword himself, but if Sochar were here in front of him, Jason thought he could pretty happily choke him to death with the chains of his manacles.

Jason sat up straight. "Did you hear that?"

Darius shifted, his eyes searching the camp. "No. What was it?"

"There it is again. That chirping."

Darius leaned forward. "It sounds almost like . . . a cell phone."

Jason grinned. "Yeah! It's a cell phone bird."

Darius's brow wrinkled in consternation. "I knew there were messenger birds in the Sunlit Lands, but they don't usually ring like cell phones."

"No! Well, sorta." Messenger birds could speak and carry messages, which, according to the way Elenil magic worked, meant they must be getting those voices from someone else . . . a chilling idea Jason tried not to dwell on. But the cell phone bird was a bird whose chirp sounded just like a cell phone ring. When he and Baileya had been on the run in her homeland, the Kakri territories, he had heard them often. Baileya could do this spot-on impression of them. He hadn't heard one his entire time in the Wasted Lands. Which meant that it wasn't a Kakri bird but a Kakri warrior making that sound. Jason grinned. "Baileya's here."

The booming voice of Break Bones came bursting through the darkness and into the camp. "You have broken the treaty between the Elenil and the Scim! Return with us to the Wasted Lands or there will be blood. I have spoken, and my words are binding upon all who hear me."

Rondelo was already on his white stag, Evernu. "To arms, Elenil! Sochar, take the prisoners and make haste for Far Seeing. We will join you if we can."

Darius and Jason scrambled to their feet, standing with their backs to the tree. Sochar was heading toward them, his massive tiger close behind. "How will he fit three of us on a tiger?" Jason asked.

"Split up," Darius said. "It should slow him down for a minute. Every second gives us a chance that the Scim will recover us from the Elenil. Run toward Break Bones's voice."

"But where's Baileya?" Jason asked. "If I can find her, we'll be safe."

Breep-breep! The sound of a cell phone bird came again, this time directly above them. Through the branches he could see her, the beautiful

Kakri woman who had somehow become his fiancée, crouched near the trunk fifteen feet above them. Her dark hair fell around her face and to her shoulders, and he couldn't understand how she managed to avoid being seen in a tree while wearing the loose-fitting cream-colored pants and flowing blue blouse-thing that she favored. In one hand she carried her favorite weapon, a sort of spear with a curved knife on one end and a straight blade on the other. She grinned at him and gave a cute little wave with her fingers.

Sochar unsheathed a sword as he ran. "Do not move, either of you!"

A shower of leaves and branches poured down between them, and Baileya stood in the center of it, her weapon in hand. The startled Elenil didn't have time to slow before Baileya pivoted on one foot and brought the other up in a savage kick directly to his chin. His head went backward, his body still moving toward her. She sidestepped and set her foot on his chest, the point of her blade under his chin. "Do you yield?"

Sochar's tiger came flying into her, knocking her onto her back. The tiger's maw opened wide over her face, and she whacked it in the teeth with the shaft of her spear.

Jason jumped onto the tiger's back, throwing his chain around its face right as Baileya pulled her spear away. He got the chain under the animal's mouth and yanked back, hard. The gigantic cat bucked twice, rolled over onto its back—Jason nearly lost his breath—then scrambled up and ran into the forest, Jason still choking it as hard as he could.

They crashed through the bramble. The tiger knocked him against tree trunks and brushed him through branches. More than once it shook its back to try to dislodge him, but Jason, terrified, just tightened his grip around the tiger's neck. Between Jason's choking and its frantic behavior, the tiger passed out in less than a minute, though it seemed like a hundred million minutes to Jason. He lay beside it, arms still wrapped around its neck. At this angle it was hard work to get the animal's head up so he could unwrap himself from it. He finally got free and stood, legs shaking. There was blood on his face. He reached up, touched it with his fingers. They came away wet. The blood was getting in his eyes. Must have been from one of the branches.

Baileya came flying to him out of the trees and wrapped her arms around him in a colossal hug. He almost fell over. She grinned at him with that look in her eyes that always made him feel light-headed, but he really was feeling light-headed and started to pass out. She helped him gently onto the ground. "It is only a scratch," she said.

"I don't like the sight of blood," Jason said. "Well, not my blood, anyway."

"You bested a tiger!"

Jason looked at the sleeping giant. "On the other hand, he's not bleeding, and I still might faint."

She sat beside him and let him lean on her strong shoulder. "Rest a few moments, brave warrior. What a story you have made for us today! 'Wu Song Bests the Tiger'!"

"Hey, that's a famous story where I come from."

Baileya loved stories. For her people, stories were much more than entertainment. They were life, they were money, they were used in trade and matrimony and celebrations and passing on knowledge. A new story was worth a great deal. "You are a wealth of stories, and you have not told me this one yet."

"I'm actually named for a famous tiger slayer."

"You are full of unexpected wonders," Baileya said affectionately, patting him on the hand. "Now come. We brought many Scim, and the Elenil will be in retreat soon. We do not want them to come upon us in their exit."

"Where's your brother?" Jason asked, getting to his feet with a slow, careful effort.

"I tied him, unconscious, to his steed and gave the creature a hard slap. It will be a day or so before he is on our trail again, and by then we will be hidden deep in the heart of the Aluvorean forests. We are not far from them here, on the outer edge of the Wasted Lands."

Jason leaned on her as they stepped over a fallen log. "Did you beat him too badly?"

Baileya snorted. "There is a reason the Kakri women are the more highly regarded warriors."

She stopped, her hand on his forearm. He could hear it too. Shouts and the crashing movement of animals and people running forward through the undergrowth. The floating orbs of the Elenil sped ahead of them, casting strange shadows as their varied steeds leapt and ran behind.

Rondelo led the way, his white stag bounding out of the darkness. The remnants of his party came after him. Sochar rode with a second Elenil on a pearlescent horse.

A Scim war party followed close behind, stone axes at the ready, and their harsh battle cries filled Jason with delight. "They want to kill me, too, you know," Jason said. "But I'm glad to say they hate the Elenil more than they hate me."

The tiger flinched, and though they were a little bit away from it now, Jason couldn't help but flinch as well. Then, to Jason's amazement, the tiger shrank from gigantic-terrifying-tiger size to regular-tiger size. Baileya stiffened, and her hand tightened on his.

"Did you see that, Baileya? That tiger just shrank."

As he said it, the floating lights of the Elenil flickered and fell to the forest floor, dead. "Zhanin," Baileya whispered, then yanked on Jason's arm, hard. "We'll have to hope they inspect the Elenil first."

"Zhanin? Aren't they the murderous seafaring people who also want to kill me?"

"Yes," Baileya said, pulling him down a narrow track through the trees. "Some of them can negate magic. Only the fiercest of their people, though. The ones who are both judges and executioners."

"Wait," Jason said. They could barely see the Elenil and Scim through the dark.

"It is not wise, Wu Song."

"If they're coming after me, I should at least see them first."

The Zhanin came through the woods, four lean but muscled people with bare copper-colored arms and long pants and shirts that looked to be made from leather the color of seaweed. A pale phosphorescent light seemed to emanate from them. The Elenil were in disarray, their magical mounts gone feral. So many things about the Elenil required magic. Without it, they looked helpless. One of the Zhanin dragged an Elenil from a bucking horse, forced him to his knees, and shouted, "Where is the human boy?"

No one answered, and the Zhanin shoved a long knife into the Elenil's body. He fell to the side, motionless.

"Where is the boy?"

Jason's stomach turned over, and he felt faint. He was no fan of the Elenil soldiers, but to see one so casually tossed aside made him sick. These Zhanin might be more brutal in war than the Elenil. "On second thought," Jason said, "let's run away fast."

Baileya gripped his hand in hers and led the way.

10

UNDERWATER

He made good, sweet water to flow upon the land.

FROM "THE PLANTING OF ALUVOREA," AN ALUVOREAN CREATION TALE

✦

Madeline knew she was dreaming, because she was underwater, and she could breathe. It didn't feel quite right—there was a labor to it. She had to work hard to pull the water into her lungs and then almost shout to expel it. But she was breathing.

She could see the sunlight above, piercing the green-tinged water and sinking down to her. There was a glow coming from her. From her wrist. A bright green-white light that came from inside her skin, from a point of light the size of a sunflower seed, too bright to look at directly.

A school of silver fish swam toward her, then turned like they were one animal, disappearing into the murk beyond. She dove further down, toward the bottom of the ocean or lake or wherever she was. She tasted the water on her next breath. Salty. It didn't taste quite like the sea, though. But it must be . . . It wasn't fresh water, that much was certain.

There was a strange statue, about twice the size of a man, standing on the bottom. He had a thick, reptilian tail, like a crocodile, that dragged on the ground, trailing beside his stocky legs. She swam around front to get a better look at him. His hair was long and green, growing like ivy from his head. He had a thick beard made of leaves, which undulated lightly in the gentle movement of the water. His broad shoulders had something almost like scales on them, which ran down both his arms. Rising from his head like antlers were two great tree branches.

The statue was so lifelike, Madeline wanted to touch it. She reached out and touched his face, then jerked away from the supple texture of his cheek. His eyes opened in surprise. "How did you come to be here?" he asked.

"I'm dreaming," she said. Speaking was easier than she thought it would be.

"But you are not of my people," he said, studying her face. "You are made of dirt and wind and fire. I am of sticks and moss, leaves and branches, water and mud. But what's this?"

He reached for her arm, pulled her close. He studied the shining seed in her arm. "An Aluvorean put that in me," she said, "using a stone flower."

"It is not the seed of a stone flower," he said. When his face came close to her arm, she could smell a floral aroma coming from the moss growing on his antlers. "It is . . . the seed of a Queen's Tree." His face, so sad. "And you but a child."

"What does that mean?"

"It means that when you come to Aluvorea—"

"I'm not coming to Aluvorea. I'm staying home. I need to take care of Yenil, make sure she's safe. I need to figure out the thing with the principal and make sure she has a guardian, make sure Shula can stay with her."

The tree man did not look away from her, his eyes still sad. "It means that when you come to Aluvorea, you must ask for Patra Koja."

"Patra Koja," she repeated.

"What is your name, girl?"

Something about the way he asked her . . . she didn't want to say. "It's a dream. You should know."

"You are the annaginuk in waiting, the enalanok, the emes esutol. But you are not an Elenil." His eyes focused on her face. "You are not an Elenil, are you? What does this portend? Surely they would not turn to the humans again, not a second time. What strange times I have lived to see." He dropped his head. "These are times of great sorrow. Oh, annaginuk who is to come, what betrayal has brought you to this path? Or what noble intent of your own heart? You have agreed to help them, but have they warned you of the price?" He looked up, gazing at something over Madeline's head.

Madeline turned. A wooden crown floated in the water above them. It was intricately carved and carefully polished around the base . . . as if it were braided branches. But then, up from the base a series of living branches grew. Some of them stretched out, wild, while others massed together to hold what looked like shining jewels. It floated toward her, and there was a feeling of great power in it, but also heartbreaking loneliness and loss. Madeline instinctually swam backward, and into the wide chest of the antlered man.

"It is the Heartwood Crown," he whispered.

She screamed and sat up in her bed, gasping for air. Like always, gasping for air. Her chest ached, and she saw a glow coming from the seed in her arm, a light that lessened and then went away even as she noticed it. Tears streamed down her face.

It was then that she realized it had not been an ocean she had been in. It had not been the briny water of the sea. It had been a lake of tears . . . whether her own or Patra Koja's or someone else's, she did not know.

11
OLD FRIENDS

In those days the whole of the Sunlit Lands was covered in forest, and magic was everywhere.

FROM "THE PLANTING OF ALUVOREA," AN ALUVOREAN CREATION TALE

✦

They came to the edge of Aluvorea on the second night. Baileya kept them at a fast pace. Break Bones had found them, and Darius eventually caught up too, holding Delightful Glitter Lady in the crook of his arm. He had found her while looking for Jason. The terrible Zhanin warriors in their strange seaweed leather had harried the Elenil, chasing them toward Far Seeing. The arrival of the Scim had caused enough distraction for the Elenil to slip away, and the Zhanin had set out after them. It appeared the seafaring warriors thought Jason was still with the Elenil. Baileya had been cheered by the news, but she immediately demanded that they choose a destination and "make haste."

She and Break Bones had decided on Aluvorea. It was closer than the Southern Court, another place they had debated, but the people there were unpredictable. Jason and his friends had moved back into the Wasted Lands first, taking cover in the darkness, then waited for night to make a break for the great trees of Aluvorea. The Scim forces had split from them at the border and returned to patrol their own land. Jason was relieved, because even though they were theoretically on the same side, at least for now, several of the Scim warriors tightened their grip on their weapons whenever they came near him.

He and Darius were still in their chains. Break Bones had tried to sever them with his stone ax. Darius sat before a large stone and held his hands as far apart as he could, turned his head away and closed his eyes. Break Bones had swung his ax, shattering the stone beneath, but Darius's chains had been unharmed. Break Bones attacked the chains with a manic fervor, sending up sparks. Dissatisfied that his attempts to break Darius's chains had been unsuccessful, he looked for Jason, who had quietly hidden behind Baileya. She said the chains were almost certainly enchanted by the Elenil, and further experiments in breaking them were set aside.

Which meant two days of wearing the shackles for both Jason and Darius. It annoyed Jason but seemed to take a heavy toll on Darius. He grew increasingly sullen and frustrated, and more than once Jason saw him stop to knock the chains against a rock or tree. Jason didn't love the shackles, sure, and the thought of wearing them until they could find the right key among the Elenil made him nauseous, but the thing that weighed more heavily on him was the loss of Nightfall. He had insisted they try to find Nightfall's body to send back with the Scim warriors, but they could only find a small patch of bloody sand. Break Bones said it was possible one of the other warriors had taken his body to return to his family, but he wouldn't risk sending a message to find out. Instead he had given the Scim warriors strict instructions to send word—not via bird if they could help it—to the old dilapidated mansion. Break Bones was skeptical that Nightfall was truly dead. "Did you see his lifeless body? No? Then you are taking the word of the Elenil. I prefer to see that the light has gone from his eyes myself." Break Bones thought the boy might have gathered his strength and returned home. He would check in there when he could. Despite himself, Jason felt a small flutter of hope.

They could see the trees of Aluvorea as black shadows against the stars several hours before they got there. Jason thought at first they were mountains. By dawn they had just reached the entrance to the forest, and the golden morning light danced over the moss-covered boulders on either side of wooden steps that rose between two trees the size of towers. The trees were larger than any Jason had ever seen, and the wooden steps looked almost like they might be roots from those trees, cleverly grown in just the right way to make stairs. He couldn't see where the stairs went, exactly, only that they disappeared into the shaded recess of the forest. A chorus of birdsong came from the trees, and steam wafted from their trunks as the early sun warmed them. Jason couldn't help but notice that the sunlight didn't seem to penetrate far into those dark woods.

"The Sentinel Trees," Break Bones said, "or so the Scim call them. To walk between those two trees is to enter Aluvorean territory."

Delightful Glitter Lady shivered in Jason's arms. "I feel exactly the same way," Jason muttered.

"We must be cautious," Baileya said. "The Aluvoreans and the Elenil have a strained relationship, but they are still allies." Her eyes moved to Break Bones. "And they have no love for the Scim."

"Nor we for them," Break Bones said. "In truth, I should leave you here at this gate. I desire to speak to the archon of the Elenil about this recent breaking of our treaty. What say you, Darius?"

Darius looked at Break Bones, his face deadly serious. "If your plan is to speak with cold steel, brother, I'll ride with you."

Break Bones laughed. "I've never had much use for words."

"They've chained me like a slave and stolen my mask. I have much more than words to share with them." Darius's face clouded over even darker. "I will not forgive this."

"You're going to ditch us right before we meet the talking trees? I've seen this movie," Jason said. "The trees come to life and eat us."

"The trees of Aluvorea do not speak," Baileya said thoughtfully, "though some of the plants are carnivorous."

"Plants should be vegetarian," Jason said firmly. "I refuse to go near any that aren't."

Darius put one hand on Jason's shoulder, an awkward gesture when still in chains. "There are too many people after you, or we could all go to

Far Seeing together. But once we've had our say with the Elenil, we'll come back to find you."

"I've never been a 'storm the castle' kind of guy, anyway. The one big battle I was in I got my rib cage crushed in and accidentally killed someone."

"Come now," Baileya said. "You have been in many battles. Have you forgotten the battle of Westwind?"

"Yeah. That's the time I tried to shoot an arrow and instead I dropped it—and the bow—into a moat."

"But what of when we ran from my brothers in the Kakri territories?"

"As I recall, you dug a hole in the sand and had a giant bird sit on me."

Break Bones spoke up. "What of our battle upon the stairs of the tower with no doors?"

"Hmm. Let's see. I got wounded, and then Delightful Glitter Lady knocked you down the stairs."

"Yes," Break Bones said. "But it was you who thought to turn her loose upon me."

"Pretty sure that was Dee's idea. She hates you, you know."

Break Bones threw back his head and laughed loud enough to wake Dee, who gave an affectionate look around at all assembled and then made a contented sigh and snuggled back into Jason's lap.

Darius smiled for the first time in two days. "So battle is not your greatest contribution. Find another way to help, Jason. We'll meet again soon."

They said their farewells. Baileya was never one for long good-byes. She didn't try to dissuade them or suggest another plan. Jason and Baileya watched them go, Break Bones riding his great wolf and Darius on his enormous possum. "That's completely ludicrous," Jason said. "Riding on a possum, of all things. And in the middle of the day, too. Terrifying, but ludicrous." He turned to Baileya. "Why didn't you try to keep us together? Wouldn't it be better to have four of us instead of two?"

Baileya put an arm around him. "Wu Song, if it were the whole world against we two, I would not wager against us. You are not skilled in battle, but you are wise and honest. And I am more skilled in battle even than most Kakri. They must follow their story, and we must follow ours, and trust they will wind together again one day. Besides, when would I object to the two of us being alone?"

Then she gave him that smile, the one that made him feel like water was boiling in his feet and shooting steam through his entire body. He felt his face burning. "Delightful Glitter Lady is here too," he said.

Moriarty hissed. Baileya crossed to him and patted him on his wide, feathered side. "And don't forget our brucok."

Jason narrowed his eyes. "Oh, I haven't forgotten him." Under his breath he muttered, "My mouth waters just thinking about him."

Baileya stiffened, and her hands went to the two pieces of her spear. She quickly assembled it. "Someone comes down the stairs."

It was a man, or at least something in the shape of a man. He was lean and tall and wore a hood that covered his face. His cloak had green and yellow leaves woven into the shoulders and cascading down the sides, overlapping one another like feathers or scales. He carried a long knife in one hand, and he advanced toward them with some speed.

Baileya stood ready, and Jason pulled the knife from his own belt. It was awkward when his hands were still tied together, but better an awkward knife than an empty hand.

The stranger stood fifteen feet away but did not speak.

"We come in need of sanctuary," Baileya said.

The stranger didn't move or acknowledge her. He pointed at Jason but still did not speak.

Jason didn't really want to say anything. The creepy hooded figure just stood there pointing at him, which reminded him of a cartoon he knew. But hey, maybe this guy didn't even speak the same language as them.

"Um," Jason said. "O Ghost of Christmas Future, please show me how Scrooge McDuck is a terrible humbug, and make him feel bad so he will give a turkey to Tiny Tim the mouse. Which is kind of dark, seeing as how Scrooge is a duck and everything."

"Wu Song," Baileya said, a clear warning in her voice.

"Did I tell you this story? Scrooge is a duck, and he gives this mouse family a Christmas turkey. Or it might be a Christmas goose, I don't know. I guess it could be a Christmas duck for that matter!"

The man in the hooded cape lowered his knife. "Dude," he said. "I never thought about that. That's super messed up." He threw back his hood.

"David!"

Baileya laughed and put her spear away, and Delightful Glitter Lady wriggled from Jason's arms and ran to the newcomer. David Glenn had been Jason's roommate when he first came to the Sunlit Lands. They had split up six weeks ago in the midst of a big battle: the Knight of the Mirror had given each of them a different magical artifact to keep safe. For Jason it was the Mask of Passing, which he and Baileya had tried to hide in the Kakri territories, and David had gotten a key of some sort. The Disenthraller, something like that. They had given the mask back to the Knight of the Mirror after the fight with the archon, but David had been in Aluvorea, hiding the key there. Apparently he hadn't left.

Jason tackled him, and David threw him off easily enough. "What's with the handcuffs, bro? You try to get away from Baileya or something?"

"Har har," Jason said. "Elenil caught me, and when we escaped we forgot to ask for the keys."

David grinned. "That makes more sense. Baileya's not the type to lock someone up when she could just cut their feet off."

"She would never do that," Jason said, offended. He looked at Baileya. "You would never do that, right?"

"I never have," she said, as if that somehow answered the question.

David helped Jason to his feet. "Let's take a look at those cuffs." He produced a small key from his cloak. "This thing has come in handy more than once already. Seems to override any lock, even magic ones." The teeth of the key were too large to fit in the keyhole on Jason's cuffs, yet it slid in easily, turned, and the chains fell to the ground.

"Man, we should go get Darius," Jason said.

David looked off in the direction he had gone. "The Aluvoreans wouldn't let me come out until your Scim friend left. I can ask them to send word, but Darius will have to come back without the Scim. They don't use messenger birds here, so it would have to be someone who could ride fast enough to overtake them."

"That might be good," Jason said, "so he can get out of the chains at least."

"I'll send word, then," David said, throwing his arm over Jason's shoulders. "Now come on. I have one more surprise for you two."

Delightful Glitter Lady frolicked around David's feet as he led them up the stairs, his arm still around Jason. Baileya came behind them, leading Moriarty. The temperature dropped as they crossed into the shadow of the great trees. Passing underneath them, Jason shivered, and he stopped for a minute to take in the truly majestic height of them. He almost felt dizzy looking toward the top. "We're not in Aluvorea proper yet," David said. "They sent me out, thinking a familiar face might make the transition easier."

"The transition?" Jason asked, suddenly nervous. "Please tell me we're not turning into trees."

"You're not turning into trees," David said, laughing.

"Or bushes. Or like, flowers or grass. I mean in general turning into plants."

"Bro, am I a plant?"

Jason looked at him. "I don't think so. But they appear to have infected your cloak."

"Uh-huh." David stopped and pointed to a hedge of thorns twice as tall as Jason.

There was a small wooden door worked into the hedge, with a black iron knocker. The door was a friendly yellow and was the opposite of anything frightening. If anything, it looked charming and inviting for a door set into a hedge of thorns. You would much rather go through the door than the hedge, that's for sure. A rabbit peeked out from the hedge, then popped back into it.

"Go over to that door and go inside. You don't have to knock or anything—they know you're coming."

"Who?" Baileya asked.

"Don't worry," David said.

Baileya stepped forward to go with Jason, but David put out his arm. "Jason first. Just for a minute."

Jason hesitated. "It's okay, Baileya. We can trust David."

He walked toward the brambles. He could feel Baileya watching him, scanning for danger, looking for trouble. That made him feel a little more comfortable. He came to the door. The wood was rough, like it had never been worked by human hands, never been smoothed or sanded. Metal bands held it together, but they were polished and seemed almost cheerful.

Jason couldn't help but think that someone had worked hard to try to make this door look inviting, which was, it turned out, making him suspicious. He pushed on the door, and it swung open.

The room was formed by walls of hedge, and it appeared that hallways of hedge led elsewhere, as if he had entered a great hedge maze. There was no roof, and the floor was simple dirt with straw strewn over it. A rabbit ran across the room, popping into the far wall of the hedge. A blonde woman sat in the center of the room, a blanket over her legs. Her face was emaciated and her eyes tired, but she smiled when she saw him.

Jason had never crossed a room so quickly. He wrapped Madeline in his arms, and they both were laughing and crying and talking at once.

12
THE PRIEST'S TALE

The Elenil promised on his name
that no harm would come to her.
FROM "JELDA'S REVENGE," A SCIM LEGEND

+

The priest stood at the door again. Father Anthony. Shula could not believe he had come back and that he had waited until Mrs. Oliver was gone. Had he been watching them, waiting for this moment? She wouldn't let him in, of course, but she couldn't avoid the feeling that the old man knew something that might be important to them. The scars on his wrist looked suspiciously like some primitive version of Elenil magic, much like the light tattoo she had seen on Mrs. Oliver's wrist. He had known Hanali's name and recognized Mrs. Oliver. How could this be? Now he stood on Madeline's front porch, a sheepish look on his face.

"Marhaban, Shula," he said, leaning so she could see him more clearly through the glass panel beside the door.

She didn't open the door. "Go away."

"I need to speak to Madeline," he said, "about the Aluvoreans. I need to warn her."

Shula's hand drifted to the handle. Did he know something that would be helpful to them? She doubted it. She glanced at the scars on his wrist. She wasn't sure if they should make her trust him more or less.

"There were seven of us," he said, desperation creeping into his voice. "When we were teenagers—like you. We went to the Sunlit Lands too, with no one to guide us."

"A trick," Shula said. "You are lying. Or you are Elenil. We don't know you. We cannot trust you."

"My advice won't change any of that," the old priest said. "You are wise not to trust them, not to trust any of us. Shula, there were seven of us when we walked into the Sunlit Lands, but only four came back. Just listen to my story, that's all I ask."

"Let him . . . in," Madeline said, her voice barely strong enough to make it to Shula. She stood in the living room, leaning against the easy chair. Shula shot her a questioning look, but Madeline had already made her way to the front of the chair and was lowering herself into it.

The priest entered meekly. He didn't try to shake hands or say anything else to Shula. He went into the living room, sat on the couch, and quietly introduced himself to Madeline.

"Go on," Madeline said. As her disease progressed, she had lost the will for social niceties. She used the minimum number of words and went straight to the heart of a matter.

"We were seven," the priest said. "Only four of us returned. One was murdered by a people called the Zhanin." He waited, seeing if they recognized the name. "The shark people," he continued when they said nothing. "One chose to stay . . . in the service of the Elenil. He remains there today. Another died, eaten by the forest that is called Aluvorea."

"Eaten by the forest?" Shula wondered if her English was preventing her from understanding exactly what this meant.

"Yes. The people of the forest encouraged this. They trapped her, and against her will she was fed to the trees. We had been running from them—the forest people. The trees were working against us. Everywhere we turned, the path would disappear, or the trees would become too thick for us to walk between them. Finally we found a lake with an island in the middle. We thought we would have a chance there, away from the trees, so we swam for it. But some of them were waiting there, waiting for us. They had directed us to the island, this had been their plan all along. They took Allison and—" The priest pulled a handkerchief from his jacket and pressed it under his eyes. He couldn't say anything more.

Madeline's face was like stone. "And the rest of you?"

"Released," he said. "They only wanted Allison."

Yenil came running in, her hair loose and wild. She wore a dress Madeline's mom had recently bought her, but it was buttoned incorrectly and made her look more wild, more out of control than in her regular clothes. She didn't see the priest, just threw herself into Madeline's arms and said, "Maddie, can I play in the garden?"

Madeline's face lit up when she saw the girl. "Of course. Faerie village?"

"Yes! I found some rocks last night, and I'm going to make a new house."

"Wonderful."

Shula unlocked the back door, and the three of them watched her run through the sun-dappled garden until she came to the small pond where the faerie village stood. Shula noticed the priest's troubled expression as he watched the girl.

"You brought a Scim girl here?" he asked at last. "But how? And why?"

"She was . . . in need," Madeline said, then looked to Shula. She didn't have the strength to tell the story right now.

"The girl was Madeline's magic source," Shula said.

The priest's eyes grew wide. "You found her? The Elenil told you?"

"Another human found her and told Madeline. That's why she is back here. She broke her agreement with the Elenil."

His eyes wandered to the tattoo on Shula's wrist. "But you have not broken yours."

"No."

"I've never heard of someone defying them in this way. Madeline, they must be furious. Are they trying to kill you?"

Madeline laughed, actually laughed, at that, until the coughing stopped her. "No need," she said. "They only . . . have to . . . wait a little bit."

"Incredible. No one else has done this in a hundred years or more. Far Seeing must be in an uproar."

"Now," Madeline said, "tell me the rest."

"The rest? I've told you all I came to say. The Aluvoreans are dangerous and not to be trusted."

Madeline's face hardened. "Tell me the rest," she repeated.

His face fell. "You have to understand, we saw terrible things. It wasn't like we expected. It wasn't good times and beautiful animals and sunshine. It was war and terror, and things happened that . . . things happened that changed us. They were twisting us into something else, something worse. Broken, terrible people."

"Spare me," Madeline said. "That girl," she indicated Yenil, out playing in the garden. "Her parents were . . . murdered . . . because of me. I'm still . . . here."

Shula couldn't sit and watch this anymore. "You can give Madeline what she asks or leave. She does not have time to play games with you, priest. You priests claim to have power, to speak for God, but what help are you? Where were you when Madeline was taken to the Sunlit Lands? Where were you when my family needed help, before they were killed? You were in your church, preparing the wine and bread. You did not have time for us outside your walls. You were praying and not doing. We do not need you."

The priest raised his hands in surrender, leaning away from the onslaught of Shula's words. "You are right, Shula—everything you say is correct. I was at the hospital when Madeline was taken, and I couldn't stop it. I was in the hallway when your young friend Jason was searching for Hanali, stood there frozen while he struck a deal, and I could not stop it. But I am doing what I can now. I've found you both, and I've come to help."

Madeline's face contorted in anger. "So do something . . . helpful. Tell me . . . the rest."

The priest sighed, and his whole body seemed to collapse in on itself, as if revealing what he was about to say would be to remove a pillar that held his body up. "We were seven, as I said, when we entered the Sunlit Lands. Two were killed. One remained. Four returned home." He paused, shifting uncomfortably on the couch. "Of those four, three chose to have their memories . . . removed."

"How?" Shula asked.

"There is a fruit in the Sunlit Lands called the addleberry. It is sweet and purple, and it creates, in small doses, minor pleasure by removing unhappy memories. Small ones. An unkind word someone spoke to you or that you spoke to another. A minor loss. A small disappointment. But in larger doses it is used in magic for larger transformations. If you wish to change shape, for instance, to become another person, you must first forget who you are. Your history, your family and friendships and so on, must be removed. Three of us chose that. They thought that if they could forget what had happened in the Sunlit Lands, and if they could forget what we had done, that they could be happy again here, on Earth. So they drank a potion, an addleberry wine, until all was forgotten. They chose to forget those we had lost in the Sunlit Lands and one another and also . . . to forget me. Not that I blame them."

"But you remember?" Madeline leaned forward in her seat, looking at him intently.

"Yes, God forgive me, I remember it all. Everything we did, everything we said, the sacrifices we made and the sins we committed." He looked at his wrist, at the pattern of scars that looked uncomfortably like the tattoos that Shula had on her own wrist, or the complicated mass of scars that spread across Madeline's whole body. "With age, sometimes the others . . . their memories return in small bits here and there too. The Elenil told us this might happen. So someone who owed me a favor in the Sunlit Lands has given me a small bit of magic to reinforce their forgetfulness. When needed." He looked at Madeline for a long time. "It seems your trip to the Sunlit Lands has worked some memories loose for your mother."

Madeline fell back in her chair, her face white. "Of course," she said. "Of course."

"Wendy was with us. Your father, Kyle, was with us too. The Elenil couldn't understand how Wendy and Kyle remembered each other. No matter how much they forgot, they remembered that."

"That's why," Madeline said, "they've been so . . . strange. About me . . . being gone."

The priest ran his hand through his white hair, distressed. "Yes. They have to come up with another story. They can't come to the conclusion that you've been in a fantasy world, even if you were to say it to them outright. Even though you disappeared for months at a time and came home with a Scim child. They can't ask questions about those things, because they can't be allowed to remember their own time in the Sunlit Lands."

"Hanali," Madeline said. "Hanali did this."

Father Anthony closed his eyes, blinking back tears. "I can't deny it, Madeline. We knew him in our time there, so long ago."

"This happened . . . when you were . . . teenagers."

"Yes."

"And Hanali . . . didn't want . . . you to leave?"

The priest shook his head, unable to speak.

Shula asked, "What does this mean?"

Madeline was getting up out of her chair, painfully. Slowly. "It means . . . Hanali has been . . . responsible . . . for my messed-up family." She paused, angry, struggling for breath. She took a painful, deep inhalation and rushed her words out. "My mother absent because she can't be reminded. My father a workaholic because he can't be reminded. Because I remind them." She gripped the back of the chair. "They can't be around me because of Hanali."

"Your parents love you," the priest said.

"I know that!" Madeline yelled. Her shout rang against the walls of the living room. It held such fury that Shula immediately knew it was not purely in response to the priest—it was a distillation of everything that made her angry these days. Her illness, her past with her family, her separation from Darius, the injustice of the Elenil to her and to the other people of the Sunlit Lands. Anger that this man would enter her home and reveal a secret from her parents, then have the gall to follow it up seconds later with a reminder that they loved her. Shula felt her own anger rising. Who was this man to come into Madeline's home and create such anger in her? Why couldn't everyone leave her in peace, even for a day?

Shula moved next to her. She put Madeline's arm around her own shoulder and held her up. "It is time for you to leave, Father Anthony." When he did not leave, she glared at him, then at the door. "You know the way."

He paused halfway to the door. "Madeline, I tell you these things so you'll know . . . it's too dangerous. The Aluvoreans will kill you."

Madeline let loose a sharp bark of laughter. "The Elenil . . . already have."

"What do you mean?"

"I get sick, no family history." Her breathing was coming in short, staccato bursts. "Every transplant list I get on, something happens. They lose my place in line. Something falls through. No treatment works. All so I would be vulnerable. All so I would say yes to him when he came to the hospital."

The priest's head dropped to his chest. "I fear you are right. Hanali made you sick so he could bring you to the Sunlit Lands."

Shula stood beside her friend in mute horror. Hanali—the strange but kind Elenil who had invited both her and Madeline into the Sunlit Lands—had purposely made Madeline sick? And he was killing her with this disease? She thought back on her own situation and the murder of her family in the fire. Could Hanali have been involved in that as well? She shuddered.

"Good-bye," Madeline said, and motioned for Shula to help her get to her room.

They made their way down the hallway, Shula watching over her shoulder to make sure the priest let himself out. They passed out of sight of him before he made it through the door. Shula laid Madeline down on her bed, then helped her get elevated.

Madeline pointed to her closet. "Sturdy boots. Walking boots," she said. "Start with those."

Shula looked at the closet, confused, then back to Madeline. "What do you mean?"

"We're packing for my trip," she said. "Back to the Sunlit Lands."

"No," Shula said. Everyone she ever came close to, she lost. She knew she would lose Madeline in time, knew the disease would take her, but could not bear to lose her faster, to the Sunlit Lands. "We do not even have a way to get there."

"The Aluvoreans . . . want me to come," Madeline said.

"They will kill you," Shula said. "The priest, did you not hear the priest?"

"The Aluvoreans or the Elenil," Madeline said. "If I stay . . . Hanali kills me . . . with this sickness. Go there . . . maybe he can fix it. Or maybe I make him . . . pay. For this."

Shula stood at the closet and hesitated. She had lived in the Sunlit Lands long enough and knew the Elenil well enough to know that a healing was unlikely . . . and that even if it was possible, it would come at a price Madeline had already refused to pay. "Madeline, you have no strength. You cannot breathe. Maybe it is time to let this go."

Madeline coughed for a long time. When she could speak again, she said, "I was . . . settled . . . before. But I . . . know more . . . now. I told the . . . Aluvoreans . . . I would help them . . . once. I can't let . . . what happened to me . . . happen to someone . . . else. I am going . . . back."

"But—"

"Sturdy. Walking. Boots," Madeline repeated.

Shula found the boots, and then, following Madeline's instructions, she filled a backpack with water, rope, granola bars, a pocketknife, a spare inhaler, a change of clothes. She didn't understand what had set off Madeline. A chance at healing? Not much of a chance. She did not seem focused on revenge, no matter what she'd said. But something about the priest's words had given Madeline a new fire, had caused her to want to go back to the Sunlit Lands. Maybe Madeline didn't know herself. Shula checked on Yenil from time to time, playing in the garden. Would they take Yenil, too? Or leave her to be cared for here, in this house, by Mr. and Mrs. Oliver and the staff? It would not be a bad life, not at all. No doubt they could take care of the school problems, the principal and his threats, and the dubious nature of their guardianship better than Shula and Madeline could.

Yenil was crouched beside the faerie village, a grin on her face, happily talking to the make-believe creatures in her town of sticks and moss. Shula pulled the curtain back so they could see her as they packed, and it made Madeline smile, washing away her anger and even the stubborn look of resolve that had been on her face. Shula stopped packing and watched her. It was rare these days to see a moment of true happiness for her friend. But sadness crept across her face soon enough, and Madeline stole a guilty look at Shula.

Shula realized with a start that Madeline might have a different plan than she did. She wasn't wondering whether to bring Yenil, she had already decided to leave her. And maybe to leave Shula, too. "You have to let me come with you," she said, but Madeline didn't answer.

PART 2

*Sister, O sister, it is a dark night, but
I see trouble near the horizon.*

**FROM "MALGWIN AND THE WHALE,"
A TRADITIONAL ZHANIN STORY**

13
FAR SEEING

Now, fair lady, what three commands have you for your servant?
For you have saved me, and I must do as I have promised.

FROM "JELDA'S REVENGE," A SCIM LEGEND

+

The rain beat down on the bedraggled line of pack animals and people waiting outside the city gate. The rain was colder than it should have been—just this side of sleet. Since the archon's hand had been cut off, the weather in Elenil territories had been unpredictable.

Darius rearranged his hood, covering his face. Not that anyone in the security line knew what he looked like. His face wouldn't be the problem if they searched him. The Sword of Years was wrapped in oilcloth and stashed in his wide bag underneath a pile of filthy clothing in the hope that the guards wouldn't dig deep. The white robes he wore when he was a Black Skull were in his bag as well. And he still wore the handcuffs the Elenil captain, Rondelo, had put on him.

Most of the soldiers checking the line ahead were human. The Elenil almost always used human soldiers. Darius had no quarrel with them. They were pawns. It was the Elenil who were the problem, building their entire society on magic that required stealing from others. The Court of Far Seeing loomed ahead of them, grey in the sleet. Other than that one dark night of the Festival of the Turning, Darius had never seen it like this, never seen it any way other than shining white in the Elenil's bright dusk or practically glowing in the midday sun. The typical weather in Far Seeing was a stark difference from the Wasted Lands. When Far Seeing was at its darkest, the magical connection gave the Wasted Lands a few hours of almost dawn. Weak plants, nearly white from lack of sun, reached for the light. Grey-skinned children in their war skins came out of their hovels, laughing and turning their faces toward the dim brightening. Sometimes, watching the children of the Wasted Lands rejoice in their meager leftovers made Darius angrier than seeing the Elenil take their excesses for granted. It wasn't so much that the Scim children accepted their lot, it was that they didn't know anything better.

Darius had figured out the way Elenil magic worked almost the moment he arrived in the Sunlit Lands. He'd thought it was night when he arrived. Which is to say, he'd thought it was a normal **night.** On the third day of brightening which refused to give way to full dawn, he'd realized that there was no sunlight in the Wasted Lands. That was the day (night) that he walked into his first Scim village. The shabby houses made of mud and scraps, the meticulously cared for but ragged clothes on the monstrous creatures who lived in those houses, the way they worked hard in the meager fields: he recognized it immediately. He had been in these neighborhoods often enough in the United States. He knew poverty didn't just happen. There were forces at work—cultural and personal, historical and contemporary—that flowed around and through a place like this. And like it or not, once a place like this existed, there would always be people who benefited from making sure most of the impoverished people stayed that way. The magical tattoos like shackles, the occasional Elenil guards making their rounds through the Wasted Lands . . . Darius knew this world.

So it gave him a grim satisfaction to see the Elenil magic weakening and out of control. Sleet and cold here meant clear, mild skies in the Wasted Lands for once. When he felt uncertain, when he felt a prick of something that seemed like it might be conscience for his violent actions, for his leadership in the Scim rebellion, Darius steeled himself by thinking of the people he'd met in the Wasted Lands. He thought of Dread Teeth, who had sold his farming skill to an Elenil with a hobby farm in exchange for a warm piece of bread once a week. The poor soil of the Wasted Lands yielded less and less, and his family needed food. Darius thought of Rend Flesh, who had a terrifying war skin name but was only a child . . . four years old when his parents died in a skirmish with the Elenil. Rend Flesh called Darius uncle, and whenever Darius returned from battle, Rend Flesh wanted to hear every detail. "They killed my parents," he would say every night before he fell asleep. Darius thought of Wolf's Howl and Muzzle, two Scim cousins who lived on the edge of Elenil territory, where there was enough sunlight to grow food. They had to keep a constant eye out for Elenil patrols, who would arrest them or worse, but when harvesttime came, they pulled a cart throughout the Wasted Lands and handed the food out for nothing more than a thank you.

It had taken time for the Scim to trust him—this strange human who came into the Sunlit Lands through some back door. At that time the Scim were always fighting on the defensive, just trying to keep what little remained for them. Darius had seen the way they put on their war skins to appear dangerous. He told the elders over and over, "If you make yourself appear dangerous and are still attacked, still damaged, still taken advantage of, then it is time to stop appearing dangerous and to actually become dangerous." It was Darius who had encouraged the Scim toward open war. Darius who invented the Black Skulls, who saw a way to invert the Elenil magic system to make the Scim strong. It was Darius who found Break Bones and encouraged him to become something more than another angry Scim, to actually do something with that anger, to become a war chief, a leader. And it was Break Bones who had finally said, "We will take this battle to the gates of the Court of Far Seeing." Darius had gladly followed him there, sword in hand.

So when Darius looked at the main tower of Far Seeing through the sleet and saw that it was still damaged, he didn't feel conflicted about it for a moment. He didn't mourn the loss of the intricate Elenil architecture. The symbolic crescent-shaped stone which had once floated above the center of the city was still missing, and the tower itself had damage from when it fell, and Darius was glad. Proud, even. Madeline had done that. His girlfriend. Or ex-girlfriend. She had done from the inside what Darius and the Scim had been trying for months to do from the outside.

And she'd done it not through brute force but simply by refusing to participate in the Elenil system. The Elenil always set up the game so that if you didn't play, you lost. Madeline turned that on its head by embracing her loss and calling it a triumph. The messenger birds who had heard her speech and seen her decide that she would rather die than be an oppressor had spread the news, sparking a thousand conversations among the Elenil, among the Scim, among all the people of the Sunlit Lands. And of course, it was a Scim child, Yenil, who had picked up the sword and struck a true blow to the leader of the Elenil, the archon. Darius did feel conflicted about that. After all, it was the Elenil who had made Yenil who she was: stolen her breath and murdered her parents, taught her that she had to fight to live. They had forged the weapon that cut them off from their power. But she was still a child, and Darius felt a keen sorrow that she had not only had violence done to her but had done violence herself before she was even ten years old.

Unintended consequences. The Elenil oppressed the Scim until they were desperate. So desperate that they built an army bent on destroying the Elenil.

There had been unintended consequences in following Madeline to the Sunlit Lands, too. He had arrived before her—somehow (magically) more than a year before her. By the time he found her again, he had changed. He had embraced his anger, acted on it, become harder. Not toward her. Never toward her. But back home in the "real world" he could pretend sometimes not to see how broken things were. He could set it aside for a few minutes, pretend he wasn't angry. Now what few moments of peace he found felt dishonest. They felt undeserved, and he couldn't figure out a way to explain this to Madeline.

He had felt a distance growing between them, a distance he had always attributed to her illness. Now he realized that it was that, yes, but it was also the fact that she didn't notice things like how the Elenil magic worked. She had to have it spelled out for her. Even though she'd had all the pieces.

And yes, once he explained it, she was rightfully horrified and had removed herself from the system. She had stood up for herself and for the Scim in a way that Darius found brilliant, attractive, exceptional. But he was tired of explaining things, just like she was tired of trying to explain to him what it felt like to be dying. So their breakup, which he had always thought of as her thing, turned out to be about both of them.

They still loved each other. She didn't want him hanging around waiting for her to die. He didn't want her to see him so angry all the time. The most loving thing they could give each other was space. She had asked him to stay here, to fight for the Scim people and help them find freedom from the society that had trapped them in poverty and subservience. Which he had done. Was still doing. There was a purity to this calling, a clearness to it. Now, with her blessing, he could do this not only because he was angry, not only because there was injustice, but because his love wanted it done too. Love was all mixed in with the anger and the righteous fury. So he pushed forward, seeking justice.

The Scim had a real advantage after the maiming of the archon. For the first time they had found themselves with the upper hand in battle, and the Elenil were demoralized and on the defensive. Until everything fell apart as the Elenil and Zhanin and Kakri came looking for Jason Wu. Archon Thenody had recognized, rightly, that Jason and Madeline had become public figureheads. If the archon could kill or capture Jason, the Elenil would be assured that their power had not lessened. In fact, just the archon announcing the death penalty for Jason had invigorated the Elenil. Not their human army, though. Jason had a way of making friends wherever he went, and the human soldiers who served the Elenil were conflicted. More and more, the Elenil themselves were taking to battle and leaving the humans to deal with simple security, like this guard walking around the gates of Far Seeing, checking for troublemakers in the crowd.

Darius shuffled, giving him an excuse to rearrange his sleeves to cover the chains. They chafed, and not just against his skin. The psychological toll of the shackles was heavier than he would have expected. He couldn't stop thinking about handcuffs and his cousin Malik in the back of a police car. He couldn't stop thinking about a slave's chains. He didn't like to think that he, a twenty-first-century Black man, could so easily lose his freedom—one gesture from someone else, and here he was, in chains like his ancestors. Maybe if he still had his skull mask it would be different. When he was the Black Skull, he was stronger. When he was the Black Skull, he couldn't be hurt. When he was the Black Skull, he didn't have any questions. But now the Elenil had his mask, and he was trapped in these chains.

The line moved. One of the pack animals slipped in the mud and fell to its knees. General irritation flared along the line as a tall, sodden, hairy person shouted at the Maegrom merchant whose packs had spilled into the mud. A human guard intervened, waving everyone around the mess.

Darius rearranged the pack on his shoulder. The Sword of Years grew heavier every day and demanded more and more of his attention. The magic in the sword bent his will, pulled on him like stones in a backpack. It didn't actually speak to him—it just made him feel what it wanted, like a mental itch demanding to be scratched. Break Bones had brought the sword to him after the fight with the Elenil, as it was still his responsibility. Darius had returned it to the Scim elders, but they had refused it. A disagreement had broken out among them as to whether the sword was a blessing or a curse, and it was decided that either way they would allow this human, this friend of the Scim, to wield it. The sword thirsted for the blood of any Elenil who had benefited from the death of a Scim. Its wounds could not be healed by magic. When Darius held it in his hand, he could feel it lean toward the nearest Elenil. Even if they were miles away, the sword would lean. He could spend his whole life following it, bringing retribution for the past.

He had not decided if this was what he wanted.

Except for one person. The archon. Archon Thenody remained the ruler of the Elenil, and Darius hated him. Madeline had decided not to kill him and not to destroy the source of Elenil power, the Crescent Stone, choosing instead to destroy only the magic which she herself benefited from.

Darius respected Madeline's choice. But she had not lived among the Scim. She had not seen—or had seen only for a few moments—the mud-floor hovels, the paltry vegetables, the wounded and deformed Scim who sold the best parts of themselves for a mouthful of food.

Some of the Elenil might be unaware of their part in this. Not that it excused them. But Thenody knew, and worked hard to keep the status quo. Darius, as a representative and advocate for the Scim, had every intention of infiltrating the city and killing him. Just look at what the guard Sochar had done to Nightfall. In the presence of witnesses, and in Scim territory, he had killed a Scim boy and walked away without penalty. This was, in Darius's mind, a grave condemnation of the government of Far Seeing, of all their leaders. It made sense for the archon to pay the price.

"What race are you?" one of the guards asked, prodding Darius in the shoulder.

Darius kept his face low, his shackled hands hidden in the folds of his robe. It was a question he dreaded, even though he knew what the guard meant. "Human," he said.

The soldier nodded. "I thought so. How long until your service is through?"

Most humans came to the Sunlit Lands as indentured servants. A year or more of work for the Elenil in exchange for whatever deal they had managed to make. "Too long," Darius said.

"Tell me about it." The soldier laughed.

Darius nodded toward the city gate. "Why the holdup, buddy? The Elenil like to keep us waiting in the rain?"

The soldier shrugged. "Since the Scim attacked, we've had to tighten security. Nothing major. A quick scan to make sure you are who you say, a few questions. They're not letting Scim in anymore, just humans. They let a few others in, depending on their business. Saw a Zhanin last week."

"The shark people? Rare around here."

"Rare anywhere. Said he was hunting the people who had put magic out of balance in the attack. A few humans and some Scim."

Darius nodded, and a cascade of freezing water spilled from his hood. "Your boss is coming. Looks like trouble."

An Elenil strode down the line, his white-blond hair nearly shining in the grey rain. He wore armor, something that had been rare outside the battlefield just a few months ago, especially for the Elenil. He had a thin, angular face. Darius recognized him. Rondelo. Young for an Elenil, only a couple hundred years old, but dedicated to fighting face-to-face instead of sending humans to do his dirty work. Darius didn't like him, but he respected him. And, perhaps, feared him. He was fierce in battle, and so far as Darius knew, he still had possession of Darius's skull mask. He was also one of the only people in Far Seeing who would recognize Darius's face. Darius turned away, hoping Rondelo wouldn't notice.

Rondelo pulled the human guard a few steps away and spoke to him in a low, urgent whisper. The guard returned, and Rondelo continued down the line. "Closing the gates," the guard said. "Captain says the tool they're using to detect magic went off. Someone in line has a magical artifact with a lot of power. They're going to check everyone."

Darius winced. He should have expected this, but he hadn't. What could he do? Fight his way in? It would be a long fight from here to the archon's chamber, especially in chains. The sword would make it easier, maybe. It was excellent in battle against the Elenil, but even a magical sword had limitations. It hadn't been able to put a scratch on Darius's chains, for instance, and while it would happily skewer an Elenil, he doubted it would be able to take all these guards unless they waited patiently in line for their chance to fight him one-on-one. A frontal assault on the gate was impossible. On the other hand, Darius had never been one to shy away from doing the impossible.

The wiser course would be to walk away. To wait. To let the Elenil continue to oppress the Scim and bide his time until a more favorable, less risky opportunity came along. He felt the sword in his bag, calling to him. Begging him to pull it out so it could have a taste of Rondelo's blood. Darius flexed his fists. He reminded himself of his goal. To lose a shot at the archon just to kill Rondelo would be foolish. *But,* the sword seemed to whisper, *what if you killed them both?*

Yes, he could kill Rondelo, make his way through the city gates, and find the archon. Assuming he could beat Rondelo. The Elenil were fierce fighters. Not invulnerable, no, but difficult to kill. He had killed an Elenil once before, but only one, and he'd had certain advantages in that battle. But his rage was getting harder to fight down. He had changed so much since coming to the Sunlit Lands. He had never wanted to be an angry person, always kept his anger sedated and sleeping, but something about this place . . . He wasn't content to be powerless anymore.

"You want me to take a quick look through your bag, send you to the front of the line?"

The human guard. Trying to be friendly. Darius looked toward the front of the line, trying to calculate how far he was from the wall, how far from Rondelo and any other Elenil. Rondelo was too close. One shout from this guard would bring Rondelo charging back in about the time Darius could loose the sword and deal with the guard.

"I'll wait," Darius said. "Or maybe trek to the other side of the city, see if another gate has a shorter line."

"No worries," the guard said. "Us humans got to stick together. Just give me a quick glance, and I'll send you to the front. They said it's Scim magic, and you're no Scim. When we find the guy with the magical artifact, we'll confiscate it, arrest the Scim, and open the gates again."

"I don't want any special treatment."

The guard's eyes narrowed. For a second Darius thought he was noticing for the first time that Darius was Black, the way he was staring at him. Then he looked down and realized the real issue. Darius grimaced. His left sleeve had slipped aside, revealing his chains. And that he bore no Elenil tattoo on his left wrist. No brand showing his magical debt to the lords of the Sunlit Lands.

"Captain Rondelo," the guard called, trying to sound nonchalant. "Let's get this human to the front of the line."

Rondelo turned, annoyed.

"No need for that, sir," Darius called.

But the Elenil was headed their direction. He must have heard the underlying desperation in the guard's voice, must have seen the way his hand had shifted toward the sword at his waist.

The Sword of Years screamed to be unleashed. Darius could practically feel it bucking in the bag, begging him to put his hand on the hilt. He slung the bag around, reaching for the opening. He had begged Break Bones more than once to come into the line with him, to take off his war skin and try to get in through subterfuge instead of brute force. But the Scim had refused, saying he had another plan, which he wouldn't talk about. Darius had seen a handful of Scim without their war skins but never Break Bones.

It was another reminder that Darius, despite being a champion of the Scim army, was still an outsider.

A rock sailed into view, pinging harmlessly off the guard's helmet. The guard whipped out his sword.

Darius took several steps back, not wanting to be in reach of that blade, especially not before he had his own sword in hand.

"Unfair!" someone shouted from the line behind him. "That human is rushing another human to the front of the line!" Darius glanced over his shoulder.

It was a Maegrom. Short, grey-skinned, and apparently very accurate with stone throwing, the Maegrom lived in an underground kingdom, where they mined and provided precious resources to the various peoples of the Sunlit Lands . . . for a price. This one was furious. He wore a red cap pulled low over his dark eyes. He picked up another stone. Other people in the crowd started to shout, stepping up to the guard in front of Darius.

"Captain Rondelo!" The guard gestured wildly toward Darius. "That human there, in the hood!"

Darius froze. Rondelo changed direction, heading toward Darius instead of the guard. His white stag, Evernu, leapt past him, and Rondelo smoothly lifted himself onto the stag's back, pulling his sword free in one fluid motion.

Darius shook off his paralysis. One thing he could do was run. He had been in track and field in high school. On the other hand, he'd never had to outrun a magical stag, and he had never raced with his hands in chains or with a heavy bag slung over his shoulder. He reached into his duffle while he ran, splashing through puddles. He angled away from the city, knowing that more Elenil could come pouring out of those gates at a simple command from Rondelo. He knew Rondelo was a better warrior than him one-on-one. But with the Sword of Years in his hand . . . Darius had a chance, a good chance. If only it weren't for these chains!

The rain fell in thick curtains. Darius didn't dare waste a second to look behind him, and he couldn't hear the stag's hooves over the pounding rain. He grabbed hold of the Sword of Years and pulled it free.

Seemingly out of nowhere, a knee-high stone appeared in his path. Darius tripped, tried to regain his balance, and crashed to the ground, skidding on his chest through the sodden grass. He almost impaled himself with the sword but managed to twist so that he didn't cut himself. He rolled to a stop and got back to his feet all in one motion. He had dropped his bag.

"This way," a voice said. It wasn't a stone at all. It was a trapdoor covered with grass. Beneath it was a small Scim, holding the door up. "Quickly," he said.

Darius's bag was between him and Evernu. The white stag was bounding toward him, and there was no way Darius could get to the bag and back to the trapdoor. It wasn't possible.

The Scim grunted in frustration. "Do they have the word *quickly* in your world?"

Darius dove through the opening, and the Scim pulled the trapdoor shut. Everything went dark. "Down the passageway. Quickly. That means fast."

Darius didn't talk back. He couldn't stand up straight in the passageway, and he couldn't see at all, but he did what he was told, his sword held in front of him. A light flared from overhead. A grinding, tearing noise came from behind them. "The Elenil found the door," the Scim said. "Move farther down the tunnel. The Maegrom built emergency levers into this place."

The tunnel ceiling dropped lower as Darius moved farther in. "What are you going to—"

The Scim grabbed a stone rod that jutted from the wall. He yanked, the stone came free, and the tunnel behind them rumbled and collapsed. "Move to the next stone pin. We have to collapse the whole tunnel now that the Elenil know about it. Hurry."

Darius had lived among the Scim long enough to know their ways and to recognize them on sight. This Scim was little more than a child. Darius moved to the next pin, waited for the Scim to pull it out, and then they hurried along to the next. "You should have warned us you were coming," the boy said. "Sent a bird or sent word with the weekly messenger."

"I don't know who you are," Darius said. "And what weekly messenger?"

The boy closed his eyes, as if trying to overcome a deep pain or keep himself from lashing out at a stupid question. "The elders didn't tell you about us. They gave you the Sword of Years, but they didn't trust you enough to tell you." Darius felt a pang at that. Maybe he was even more of an outsider than he thought. The Scim boy opened his eyes. "They're keeping our secrets close. That's good, I guess."

The boy pulled a last pin, and a cloud of dirt plumed up around them. Darius coughed and wiped the dust from his eyes. "What secrets? Who are you?"

"This way," the Scim said. They had come into a natural stone tunnel. Darius followed him. "You *are* Darius Walker, right? The Black Skull?"

Darius nodded, then realized the Scim couldn't see him. "Yeah. Who are you?"

The boy stopped and looked up at him. "You came up with the idea for the Black Skulls. The magic involved and the guts it took to come up with it and then use that magic fighting the Elenil . . ." He shook his head. "I respect that, Darius. In some ways it inspired my work here in Far Seeing."

"I hate to keep asking this over and over," Darius said, "but who are you?"

The little Scim grinned. "My name is Mud. I'm the leader of the anti-Elenil resistance."

14
UNDERGROUND

She wandered like a deer, her path repeating over the days,
her feet making tracks through the woods.

FROM "JELDA'S REVENGE," A SCIM LEGEND

✦

Shula did not think this would work. It was nothing like the way she had entered the Sunlit Lands the first time, but Madeline insisted this was what they had to do. So they stood in the garden nearly three hours after nightfall. Madeline sat in her wheelchair, her backpack in her lap, and Shula stood behind her wearing hers. Madeline had put Yenil to bed herself, even telling her a story. Yenil adored Madeline's stories, but they had become increasingly rare as her breathing worsened. Shula felt a pang of worry at the thought of leaving Yenil behind. She had checked on her before coming out into the garden, had kissed her on the forehead and whispered good-bye, feeling foolish about the whole thing because she suspected she would only be standing in the dark garden with Madeline for a few hours, and then they would return inside and her friend would admit that there must be another way to get into the Sunlit

Lands. Something better than standing by a patch of flowers waiting for something to happen.

Shula tried to convince Madeline to leave a message for her parents—a note, a text, a voice mail, anything. But Madeline refused to say good-bye to her mother or even to tell her that she was leaving, despite Shula begging her to talk to the woman. Madeline felt it would be cruel, knowing what they knew now: that her mother had been to the Sunlit Lands and that her cracked memory and strange behaviors were in part because she had allowed those memories to be locked away, hidden. "I may not come back," Madeline had said.

All the more reason to say good-bye, Shula thought. But Madeline would not be swayed. A common theme with Madeline these days. She didn't have the capacity to discuss decisions when she had made up her mind. So now they stood in the garden, waiting to go to the Sunlit Lands. They weren't sure how it would happen. It wasn't as easy as snapping your fingers or putting on a magic ring. Madeline had followed a magical hummingbird into a sewer and had to squeeze her way through into an underground forest, which led to a door that required her to prove she had the permission of the Elenil to enter.

Shula's path to the Sunlit Lands had been even less pleasant. She still had nightmares from time to time about the passage. She, too, had been approached by Hanali. He had come up to her in an alley on the night her parents and brother and sister had died.

"Greetings, Shula Bishara." He spoke in Arabic. He was wearing a pale-green jacket and trousers, all silk. He had an ivory-colored shirt with ruffles on it and shiny black shoes with heavily polished golden buckles. His pale hair was loosely pulled into a ponytail.

Shula held a knife toward him, the blade shaking. "Who are you?"

He bowed. "I am Hanali, son of Vivi. I have come here from the Sunlit Lands." He actually called them 'aradi mada'atan binur alshams, "The Lands Illuminated by Sunlight."

He promised her revenge. In a city like hers, who could expect to get real revenge? And who would pay the price? The Russian bombers? The terrorists? The countries that armed them? The sympathizers and rebels, or the government that made alliances with Russians and created a society of such injustice that terrorists could gain a foothold? Also, she had been taught—at church as well as by her parents' example—that revenge was a lesser thing. That mercy and forgiveness were better for all involved . . . for the wronged as well as the oppressor. She knew that—had been taught it for years—but the raw wound in her heart rebelled against it.

Hanali produced a thin metal band, silver, about as big around as her wrist. He told her revenge could be had but only for a price.

When she agreed to take the bracelet, he held it out to her like a bone to a dog, but she didn't care. She snatched it from him, slipped it on her wrist. It tightened like a noose, and when it finished tearing into her skin, she felt them for the first time . . . the flames. The flames she had demanded, that she had bargained from this strange man. They rose from her own heart, as if it were a furnace stoking fire through her whole body. The fire lit the very air around her, but she herself—her clothes, her skin, her flesh—was untouched. Her hair flowed in shimmering waves of heat.

Then Hanali showed her the way to the Sunlit Lands. Down, down, down, through rubble and dust and darkness. She squeezed past a corpse, heard the voice of a survivor crying out that she was stuck, could someone please help her, please. Still she pushed forward, wedging herself into smaller and smaller and more difficult ways. Three days of crawling. At least, she thought it was three days. She slept twice. She arrived, broken and burning with fever, dehydrated and numb, at Hanali's feet. He crouched down beside her and said, "Oh, my dear. The Scim will fear you. Everyone will fear you."

He gave her over to Mrs. Raymond, who was in charge of new arrivals. She fretted over Shula, nursed her to health, washed her, put her in a clean room with a clean bed and clean sheets, but Shula did not trust her, not for a moment, because she knew better now. Trust led too often to love. Love led to loss, led to pain, led to where she was today. So she used her flame to harden herself, like a clay pot fired in a kiln. She set about becoming the best warrior for the Elenil that she could be, because being a soldier made her memories easier. Being a soldier meant that she had not murdered anyone, there had just been casualties. She hadn't caused the death of her parents' killers, she had eliminated a threat to the security of her city. She did not kill the Scim, she fought them for the greater good of the Sunlit Lands, and if some died, well, that was not her fault. They should not have gone to war if they didn't want to lose their lives.

But these old paths to the Sunlit Lands would not work for them. She and Madeline could not reduce a building to rubble and dig their way through it. Madeline said that the sewer she had previously crawled through had not worked for Darius. She and Madeline had both returned from the Sunlit Lands to Madeline's house through the hedge, led by the Garden Lady, but that path would not open for them now, even when Shula went and stood against it and tried to push into the bushes. Madeline spoke gently into the hedge and nothing changed, nothing happened.

"We need . . . a hummingbird," Madeline said, but there were no hummingbirds. Shula had never seen one at night, anyway.

"We should go back to bed, try again in the morning."

"No," Madeline said firmly.

But what was to be done if the Sunlit Lands didn't invite them back in? They couldn't follow a map or look it up online. They could only wait for an invitation. "Maybe the Garden Lady?"

Madeline pulled three buttons from her pocket. For some reason the Garden Lady liked small bits of trash and useless trinkets. Part of her magic, maybe. Madeline held the buttons out in her open palm. "Garden Lady? Are you . . . there?"

The garden remained the same. It wasn't silent, but there were no strange sounds, no magical lights or unexpected animals. Only the strange out-of-season flowers that kept growing no matter what. Shula moved the wheelchair closer to the flowers, but it didn't change anything.

"Maybe it's all . . . make-believe," Madeline said.

Shula knelt beside her. "What does this mean?"

"Pretend. I have been . . . sick . . . so long. Maybe . . . I made these stories up . . . for comfort."

"Am I pretend then too? Is Yenil?" Shula asked, sitting in the grass along the path. She lay back and looked at the stars. The city lights dimmed a lot of them, but a few bright ones stood out. "You walked in the Sunlit Lands. It is not pretend. This is a stupid thought."

Madeline twisted in her chair to glare at Shula. "I read all . . . fantasy novels . . . as a kid."

Shula laughed, a small joy flickering in her heart. "I read only love stories, and yet I have no love."

Madeline moved from the chair to the grass, lying beside her. "I . . . love you. Yenil . . . loves you."

Shula laughed again. "I did not read love stories about sisters and children."

Madeline folded her hands across her stomach. "I always . . . wanted a sister."

Shula winced. She thought of little Amira. She thought of how Amira would crawl into her lap and ask for stories, and how Shula would weave strange, rambling tales that were half Bible, half *Thousand and One Nights*, and Amira loved them. "A sister is good."

Madeline bent almost in half, giving out a strangled shriek, then fell back on the grass again. Shula's first thought was to check her breathing, but Madeline's breaths were coming fast and hard. She was wheezing, struggling, and kicking. Shula rolled toward her, and Madeline flailed one hand, waving at her other arm.

Her wrist—the one with the seed in it—was stuck to the ground. The seed was glowing fire bright. Brilliant green tendrils burst from Madeline's skin and struck into the ground. She screamed. More shining fingers of plant matter grew from her arm and dug into the ground, yanking Madeline around and pulling her face hard into the dirt. Shula snatched at the vines, breaking as many as she could, but more sprang up in their place. They were burrowing into the soil, digging a hole and yanking Madeline into it.

Her whole arm was underground now, and her shoulder was sinking. Shula grabbed hold of her other arm and pulled. Madeline cried out, then shouted, "My backpack, Shula!"

Shula lunged for it, knocking the wheelchair over. She grabbed the pack and headed back for Madeline. Her head was halfway in the hole now, her other arm pushing against the grass, her legs kicking, her feet trying to find a solid place to push back. What was in the backpack that might help? Shula wasn't sure. She put it by Madeline's hand, then grabbed her waist and tried to yank back again. She couldn't move her a single centimeter.

The ground moved like a wave and knocked Shula back. She leapt to her feet again. Madeline's entire upper body was in the ground now, and her feet weren't kicking anymore. Shula grabbed hold of her boots, leaning back and pulling with all her strength, but it wasn't working. She shouted for Mrs. Oliver, for anyone, to come and help, but no one came. No one heard.

"Madeline!"

No answer. Madeline's legs were gone up to her knees. Shula grabbed both of her boots and yanked as hard as she could, her feet on either side of the hole, her back arched as she struggled. One of Madeline's boots gave way, and with a sudden burst of speed, her feet disappeared completely. Shula was left holding one boot in her hand.

"No!"

The ground was already closing up, returning to normal. Shula swallowed hard, a horror of cramped dark places coming over her. But she had traveled through such places before, and she would not leave Madeline alone down there. Shula jumped into the hole headfirst, felt it closing around her waist. Ahead of her, she couldn't see anything in the darkness, but she could hear the ground moving, closing. She clawed with all her might, trying to keep the soil and dirt at bay. It was in her hair, falling into her face. She spit it out of her mouth, tried to keep it out of her eyes.

She pulled herself forward, felt her feet scrape into the hole as it closed behind her, plunging her into total darkness. She wiggled and pulled and fought and managed to get just ahead of the claustrophobic tunnel. It was still collapsing, but she was moving faster now. Not as fast as Madeline, though. The tunnel turned, and for an instant she caught sight of the green glow from the seed in her friend's arm.

Shula was on her hands and knees now, crawling as fast as she could, afraid to stop even though she was choking on dirt, even though she couldn't see anything ahead of her. The smell of wet, rich soil grew overpowering, making her cough. She could die here, she knew. She could struggle with all her might against the weight of the soil and be stuck here until Madeline's parents decided to excavate the garden.

She couldn't catch up with Madeline, try as she might. She paused to spit the dirt from her mouth, which she knew might be a mistake, but she couldn't keep going like this. She wiped mud and soil from her eyes. She wasn't going to be left behind, she wasn't.

"You're not going to stop me," she said, anger boiling up in her. "You aren't!"

She felt it then, the burning in her heart, and she didn't try to stop it. She let the flames come, bright and searing. The tunnel lit with flames, and the dirt clinging to her turned to ash. The dirt moved away from her as if it were afraid, and Shula stoked the flames with grim satisfaction. Soon she could crawl again. The darkness flickered ahead, trying to outpace her bright anger. They thought they could take Madeline away from her? They thought they could take anyone away from her ever again? No. Never. She shouted in defiance, and her flames stretched farther, and the soil drew away.

Soon she could crouch and then run. She shouted Madeline's name. Ahead of her, the tunnel forked into three paths. "Trying to trick me?" Shula yelled. "I'll burn every one of these tunnels if you try to keep her from me. I'll burn every centimeter, every millimeter if I have to."

"No need for that, dear." A voice floated down from the leftmost tunnel. "Come this way, young lady. I'll make sure you find what you need."

"What I need is my friend," Shula said, skeptical.

"I know that right enough, and I know where they took her." An old woman wearing a ridiculous straw hat appeared from the tunnel. Her grey hair shot out of the hat in all directions, and there were flowers all along the brim. "Shula Bishara. I told them not to try to bring Madeline without inviting you. I told them. I did! Ask them yourself! They said, oh no, it will be fine. Fine, fine." She raised her eyebrows. "Those addlepates shouldn't have involved Madeline in the first place."

Shula knew this woman, in a way. She had seen her more than once but only when Madeline was there. She thought of the woman as Madeline's guide, not her own, and she found that right now, with Madeline missing, she did not feel much affection for the old lady, who had done precious little to help them in the past.

"Other than bringing you home from the Sunlit Lands," the old lady said, raising an eyebrow.

Shula frowned, her flames flickering. "Don't read my thoughts," she said, and realized she was speaking fluently. Which meant they must be back in the Sunlit Lands, or almost back. In the Sunlit Lands everyone spoke the same language because of the Elenil magic.

"Not to worry, child. Sometimes old age is better than clairvoyance. I know what young people like you are thinking often enough. Nice to know my guesses are still good, ha! Come on, then, Madeline will be waiting for you. Did you bring her boot? The poor girl arrived with only one boot."

Shula looked down at her empty hands. "I had it for a minute."

"No problem, dear." The Garden Lady looked up at the ceiling of the tunnel. "Go get the poor girl's boot, you ninny." She leaned toward Shula despite the flames. "The dirt here is dumb as a rock." She laughed for a long time about that. "Dumb as a rock," she said, under her breath. Then said it again.

They came to a small dirt chamber. Madeline lay in the center, half buried, the green glow still coming from her arm. Shula doused her flame, fell beside Madeline and started brushing the soil from her face.

"Help me," Shula said.

"Bah." The old lady was digging through a large handbag. "Dirt won't hurt Madeline." She put on a pair of rickety bifocals that did not appear to be hers. She had to twist the frame to fit them on her face. "That was quite a sight, you lighting the whole underground on fire. I wasn't sure you were going to make it." She poked the side of the tunnel. "Go on, then, what are you waiting for? Open up!"

The tunnel didn't move. "We're trapped." Shula felt the flames coming again and leaned away from Madeline.

A boot popped out of the side wall. "Ah," the Garden Lady said. "That's the holdup. Just doing what I asked. Oh dear." She patted the wall. "Sorry, dear, sorry, I forget these things from time to time." She held the boot up. "Yes, I know I asked you to get it, Wallace. And yes, I know it's rude to call you a ninny." Smoke and the stench of burned leather rose from the boot, and it was caked with dirt. A small stream of dirt fell on the Garden Lady's head, and she shook her hat out in annoyance. "That's quite enough from you, Wallace. Peace! I won't call you a ninny, and you stop behaving like one. Fair enough? Fine then." The Garden Lady smacked Madeline's boot several times against the side of the wall, then handed it to Shula. "Still better than no shoes, I suppose."

The tunnel opened and a cool breeze wafted toward them, bringing fresh, pine-scented air. Moonlight brightened the tunnel. Shula could see trees ahead. "Welcome back," the old woman said, but she wasn't smiling.

Shula put Madeline's arm—the one without the seed—around her neck and lifted her friend. She carried her out of the ground, and together they came into the Sunlit Lands for the second time in their lives.

15

THE RESISTANCE

You will not let them wage war?

FROM "THE GOOD GARDENER," AN ALUVOREAN STORY

✦

The Scim child called Mud had been leading Darius through a network of tunnels for a half hour. "This tunnel is named Wilfred," he said. "He's been helping us for about two weeks now. A friend of the Maegrom, I'm told. Came here with his brother Wallace."

The people of the Sunlit Lands said strange things like this from time to time. "Why Wilfred?"

Mud shrugged. "Why are you Darius? Why am I Mud?"

Darius knew precisely why he had his name. "My father named me. Darius means 'kingly.' That's why." This topic was tied to one of Darius's most vivid memories of his father. Darius had been, what, eight? Some kids at school had called him "derriere," and Darius had been furious at his parents for giving him his name. His mom had said, "Talk to your father," so Darius called him. His dad had actually come over, sweeping into their place without knocking, which his mom hated, but she didn't say anything. Darius could tell he was angry. His dad took him outside, walked with him down the street. It was cold that day, raining, and his father just kept walking, smoking a cigarette, his eyes hard. Then he stopped suddenly in the middle of the sidewalk and made Darius look at him. "Kingly," he said. "That's what your name means. Some stupid kids want to make it French? Your name is from one of the oldest languages in the world. Persian. Your name existed before France. Those kids, they *call* you a name, but Darius *is* your name. Understand?" Darius didn't understand. He shook his head, mumbled something about the kids at school again, and his father crouched down, flicked his cigarette into the street. "You are a king—that's why me and Mom gave you that name. You don't get mad at those kids for calling you names. They jealous, that's all. When people come against you, when they try to make you feel small, when they say you're nothing, you remember they're commoners, Darius. But you. You're royalty." Then his dad stood up, said that a king should be treated like a king, took him to the 7-Eleven, gave him twenty bucks, and said to get whatever he wanted. Walking home with a gigantic Slurpee and his pockets full of candy bars, Darius had felt like a king. When the kids made fun of his name after that, he knew what to do. He gave them that look, the one he'd seen in his father's eyes that day. He learned to make his eyes hard. And those kids learned not to call him names anymore.

Mud sneered. "Kingly, huh? Humans have strange names."

Darius snorted. "So why Mud?"

Mud considered this. "Because mud means rain, and rain means crops. If there's mud, there's life. Mud does more for the commoner than a king does. That's what my mother said, anyway, before she died."

He said this so matter-of-factly that Darius thought it must have happened a long time ago, which seemed unlikely, given that this Scim was only a child. But such was the lot of a Scim in the Sunlit Lands. Tragedy piled on tragedy, but it was embraced with a sort of fatalistic understanding that this was ordinary, not something to derail your life.

"You'll have to crawl in this part," Mud said, ducking down into a shorter tunnel.

Darius got on his hands and knees. Crawling with shackles on and carrying a sword was difficult. He was surprised again by how much the chains themselves had been bothering him. Not just the inconvenience of them or the sores that were forming on his wrists, though he didn't like those. There was a sort of incipient panic as well. The thought that the chains were just the start of worse things to come. Imprisonment or slavery or both. He thought of his cousin Malik, who ended up in jail because of a corrupt system. He hadn't done anything wrong, but he had still been arrested and then convicted. The one time Darius had visited Malik, his face was drawn, more angular than Darius remembered, more angry, less expressive. "They're taking care of me," Malik had said. The taxpayers took care of your room and board, sure, but you gave them something in return. A feeling of security, or hard labor on a farm, or help in making license plates. The prisons' job was to keep you in chains, whether actual ones or through laws and iron bars. The job of the enslaved was to either shut up and work or try to find a way out or maybe both. Darius didn't have a stomach for any of it. He'd been taught his whole life not to let himself get in a place where someone would take away his freedom of movement, his freedom to choose his own life. These chains were eating away at his self-determination, and he was eager to get them off.

Mud led him into a small chamber which was cluttered with stones, roots, and piles of dirt. A small grey person—about the size of a human toddler—sat on a twisted root, his feet dangling. Darius could almost stand up straight in this room. "This is Oreg," Mud said.

"Nice to meet you. I'm Darius."

Oreg grunted. "Never met a Maegrom before, eh?"

"No."

"We don't take time for pleasantries. Too busy."

"Telling me that took more time than it would have to say hello."

"Yes, but now I never have to say it to you in the future. It's a long-term benefit."

"It seems rude," Darius said. He wouldn't usually push a point like this, but he was tired.

Oreg leapt down from his root and approached Darius, his tiny grey face poking upward like a mole's. "Hello. Good-bye. There, now I've said them. I hope you've had your fill, because I won't be saying them again."

"He's a human," Mud said, as if that explained everything.

"He certainly is," Oreg replied, and it seemed clear this was an insult. "Chains," he said, pointing impatiently at Darius's hands.

"Yeah," Darius said. "Rondelo put these on me."

"Chains," Oreg repeated unhappily, motioning with his hand for Darius to lean closer.

Darius crouched down, putting the chains within Oreg's reach. Oreg felt the chains lightly with his fingertips, then leaned forward and sniffed them. He flicked the shackles and turned his head sideways while he listened to the reverberations. Finally, he licked the link where the chains connected to the shackles, gave a small jump, and spit into the dirt. "Magic," he said. "Of course."

"We knew that," Mud said. "Can you get them off?"

Oreg gave him an impatient glare. "What's one more human in chains, more or less? Up there in Far Seeing they're lining up to do what the Elenil tell them. Why should this one be any different?"

"No tattoos," Mud said. "Go ahead and look."

"Hmm?" Oreg grabbed Darius's wrist, pushing the shackle back and forth to look at the skin underneath, scraping it over the ragged sores that came from the metal rubbing across his flesh. "How did he come here, then?"

"He made a way," Mud said.

Oreg stared at Darius in disbelief. "This one? Him?"

"Yes. He's also the one who came up with the idea for the Black Skulls. In fact, he's the first of them. He's well respected by the Scim elders."

Oreg narrowed his eyes. "This one did that."

Darius got the distinct impression he wasn't meant to speak during this exchange, so he kept his mouth shut. But he didn't much like being called "him" and "this one," and he didn't like Oreg poking and prodding him or the shackles.

"I can take off the chains," Oreg said.

Darius slumped in relief. "Thank you."

"Only the chains, not the shackles."

"Unacceptable," Mud said. "As leader of the anti-Elenil resist—"

"As leader of the anti-Elenil resistance," Oreg mimicked, mocking him. "As leader, you surely know that not all things are possible. Even though you're a child. These shackles," he flicked them with a finger, "are magic. I've seen this type maybe twice before. The archon himself forged them, and with rare exceptions, only he can open them. You'll have to ask Thenody to do it."

"What sort of exceptions?" Darius shook his chains.

"You have the Sword of Tears, I hear. You don't happen to have the Disenthraller, do you?"

"No," Darius said.

"Hmph. Well, that would do it. There may be other magical remedies, I don't know. But nothing I can do here. I can take off the chains at least, leaving you with a lovely pair of matching bracelets."

Mud pulled on Oreg's ear. Oreg swatted at him, but the Scim boy didn't let go. Oreg struck his arm, and Mud released the Maegrom. Mud rubbed his arm sullenly and said, "Any Elenil who sees those will know he's a criminal and report him to the palace guard."

Oreg picked up a piece of black stone. "Wear long sleeves." He touched the stone to the chains.

The chains hissed and moved away from the stone. Oreg grabbed them so they couldn't move, forcing them into contact with the black stone. The links in the chains gave way, and they fell, making a musical cacophony as they struck the floor. "That was easy," Darius said.

Oreg gave him a sour look. "If fifty years of experience in the Maegrom mines were easy to come by, you could have done it yourself."

He was right. Darius and Break Bones had tried everything they could think of to get the chains off, and nothing had worked. "I'm sorry," he said.

"Stop wasting my time," the Maegrom said. He picked up the links of the chain and shook them at Mud. "And I'm keeping these!"

"Fine, but we need a new bag for his sword. We can't be walking around Far Seeing with a Scim sword."

Oreg humphed and threw an empty sack at them. Darius put the sword inside, and Mud forced Oreg to give them some filthy rags, which made it look a little more like a sack of laundry, at least. It wasn't much of a disguise, but it was better than nothing. Darius pulled the mouth tight.

"Come on then," Mud said, ducking down a tunnel.

"Good-bye," Darius said, but the Maegrom didn't answer. Darius followed Mud. "Where are we going now?"

"I'm taking you into the heart of Far Seeing. You want to kill the archon, right?"

The sword practically jumped from the bag into Darius's hand. "Yes. I really do."

"So let's get you within striking distance. We can get you in the throne room easily enough just by showing someone your shackles. The trick is to get you in while you're holding the sword. I know just the person for it. He's not far from here."

"A friend of yours?"

"I wouldn't say that," Mud said.

The tunnel shook, and a shower of dirt covered them. "What was that?"

"The Elenil recently discovered Wilfred. They've been trying to get rid of him. If Elenil magic was working properly, we'd be having a hard time of it. But so far, so good."

"What happens if the Elenil figure out how to stop Wilfred?"

"We drown in dirt, I guess."

Darius didn't like the sound of that. He wished he had a shovel instead of a sword in his bag. Mud was moving fast, and Darius had to walk faster to keep up. They passed other Scim in the tunnels every once in a while, but they were all children: dirty, emaciated, grim-faced children. Then again, the tunnels were a little narrow for a human. It might be impossible for a full-size Scim to get in here in his or her war skin.

"We have to walk topside for a little bit," Mud said. "Try to look like you belong."

A cleverly disguised trapdoor—it looked like a bit of cobblestoned street on the top—opened into a side alley near the palace square. Darius pulled himself out of the tunnel. The Sword of Years was practically singing with a desire to be unleashed. So many Elenil were here, and the sword wanted to have done with them.

"Take your hood off, you look like a criminal."

"It's raining," Darius said sullenly. He slung his hood back. It was amazing how wearing a hood or not signified so much. Back home his mom wouldn't even buy him hoodies. Too dangerous, she said. People might be afraid of you, might shoot you or call the cops. But it wasn't the hoodie they were afraid of, Darius knew, because he saw plenty of white kids wearing hoodies. They were afraid of not being able to see his Black face. They'd been conditioned by television and movies and the news to see him as a criminal. He thought he had left that behind here. In the Sunlit Lands he was just human. But here in Far Seeing, he actually was a criminal. He was in greater danger if someone saw his face and recognized him. Not many here would know him by sight, though, so better not to look as if he had something to hide. He wiped the rain out of his face.

"Hold there." It was an Elenil, and just when they walked out of the alley. He held a stone device in his hand. It glowed faintly. "It says here you're carrying a magical item. Scim magic, it says. What are a human and a Scim child doing with Scim magic?"

Darius's hand flew toward the sword, but Mud grabbed his wrist and grinned up at the Elenil guard. "Oh, sir, I am so glad you asked. Do you see the bag that my friend here is holding?"

"I am not a fool, Scim. Of course I see it. That's where the magical artifact is."

Darius's heartbeat sped up. The sword was calling to him, telling him to pull it out, to keep them safe. He could make short work of this Elenil.

"Oh, not at all, sir. The magical artifact is not in the bag. It *is* the bag, sir." Darius was amazed by how quickly Mud changed his way of speaking. He went from sarcastic and impatient to obsequious and sub-servient without missing a beat. It was no different than Darius himself, he realized. One set of words for home with the family, another for the kids at his private school, another for the warriors of the Scim. He had learned to speak the language of the people he was speaking to. He had no language of his own.

Mud pulled the bag open, showing the filthy clothes Darius had shoved on top of the sword. The sword was begging Darius now, asking to be released to destroy this Elenil. Why had Mud brought them out so close to the palace? There were only a handful of Elenil guards anywhere else in the city. What was Mud thinking? The tower was crippled, broken. No doubt there were more Elenil guards than usual. Their previous reliance on human guards hadn't gone well for them.

"A magical bag that creates filthy laundry," the Elenil said.

"No, sir, my mother made it. It can take all the filthy laundry of all the Scim in our neighborhood. Then I can carry it to the wash."

The Elenil guard recoiled. Elenil did not wash their clothes—they placed them in magical compartments, closed the lid, and the next morning found the clothes clean and put away. Of course Darius had seen how the magic worked. The clothes were taken in by Scim launderers, who cleaned them and returned them when the Elenil were elsewhere. It was magic in the sense that they never needed to think about it. The Scim took care of all such distasteful things in their lives.

The Elenil gathered his courage and steeled himself. "Nevertheless, I'll need to see the contents poured out here. The archon commands that any magical artifacts be brought to him and their owners arrested."

"Not my mother's laundry bag!" Mud cried, falling on his knees in front of the guard.

Darius shifted his grip on the bag, getting ready to reach into it for the sword if need be, and immediately realized his mistake. The guard glanced toward him, his eye caught by the unmistakable flash of metal from the edge of Darius's sleeve.

The Elenil unsheathed his sword. "Why does this human wear Elenil shackles? He's an escaped prisoner!"

The sword practically leapt into Darius's hand. He lifted it, the point toward the Elenil. "This is the Sword of Years," Darius said calmly. He felt a spike of joy to have the hilt in his palm, the blade turning toward the heart of an enemy. "It comes to bring long overdue justice to those who oppress the Scim." The sword hummed in his hands. "It tells me that you have benefited from the pain and suffering of the Scim people. And the penalty for your crimes is death."

The Elenil stepped back, a horrified look on his thin face. "Who made you the harbinger of justice for the Scim? You are only a human boy."

Mud stepped to the side with the quickness of a feral cat, putting himself well outside the range of either weapon. "You're drawing too much attention," Mud said.

"I don't care," Darius said through gritted teeth. The sword made him feel strong and brave and convinced that no one could get in his way. It gave him a certainty, a confidence that he rarely enjoyed back on Earth. "New plan. I'll fight my way to the top of the tower, with or without your help."

Mud rolled his eyes. "Wilfred." The ground opened up, and the Elenil guard yelped as he fell inside. The cobblestones closed back over him with a grinding snap.

Darius stumbled backward, shocked. The sword, disappointed, sent its tip into the cobblestones, like a dog sniffing for a scent. "What did you do?"

"We have to move before anyone comes to investigate." Mud walked across the street, trying to look casual. "Put your sword away," he hissed.

Darius scooped up the bag, shoved the sword in, and covered it with laundry. He had a feeling of regret at not murdering the Elenil, a feeling he recognized at once. Every time he successfully fought the sword's urge to kill, Darius felt this same disappointment. What did that make him? He had killed before, of course, but it had always had a feeling of necessity, of being part of the war. This time . . . well, clearly, it had not been necessary. There had been other solutions. And he had jumped straight to killing in the first moment it seemed that another solution wasn't working. This, too, filled him with regret, but he had to admit that the larger regret, the one that was stronger and taking up the most emotional space, was that he hadn't plunged the sword into the Elenil's chest. So this was who he was. Was this who he had always been, or was it getting worse? He wasn't sure.

"Up these stairs," Mud said.

They weren't stairs so much as a grand entranceway. It was an Elenil home, complete with marble columns and plants hanging from the balconies, and two waterfalls that fell from the roof and washed down on either side of the entrance. The sword sang with delight. More Elenil within reach.

Two humans stood guard, but they let Mud through as if they hadn't seen him. One nodded at Darius, but the other said nothing. "Not very good guards," Darius said.

"They aren't guarding against the likes of you," Mud replied. He led Darius up a wide stairway, onto the second floor, and then past a room that appeared to be nothing more than a thousand suits of clothes hanging from hooks or thrown across furniture. "Fop," Mud said dismissively.

They entered an interior courtyard, the sunlight dazzling as it lit up the garden, the fountains, the shimmering pond that lay in the center of this mansion. An Elenil sat at a small, round table, his white-blond hair carefully braided into a crown with trailing plaits cascading down his back, his pale ivory clothes covering every inch of him in pleats, folds, cloth flowers, and embroidered patterns of golden birds eating silver fruits. He stood, and his cape dragged on the grass, and when he held up his gloved hand, lace nearly engulfed it. "Ah, the Black Skull himself, unless I miss my mark. I don't believe we've been properly introduced. I am Hanali, son of Vivi."

"I know you," Darius said. "The Elenil slave master who recruits humans to do your dirty work."

Hanali tipped his head. "I would not describe my work thus. Nevertheless, it is not wholly inaccurate. Do you think so, Mrs. Raymond?"

A middle-aged human woman sat at the table sipping a cup of tea. "I describe it nearly identically," she said.

"In that case, this is Mrs. Raymond. She houses and cares for the slaves."

"You're insufferable," she said, but she stood and took Darius's hand. "I know your name from Madeline. You are welcome here, Darius Walker. Don't mind Hanali, he's an acquired taste."

Mud spit on the floor, which made Hanali frown. "If anyone can get you in to the archon's presence, it's Hanali."

"Mud, be a dear, and fetch someone to clean up your spittle. Now. Why would I want to get you an audience with the archon?"

"So I can kill him." Darius set his bag down. The sword was calling to him, wanting to kill Hanali, too.

"Oh, I don't think I'll be doing that," Hanali said. "We went down that road before, and look where it has gotten us. Magic is half failing, unpredictable, going through fits and starts. We're actually having rainstorms! Did you see what it did to my flowers earlier today? Beat the poor little petals to the ground. I had to get a special dispensation to use the magic necessary to provide sunlight for the courtyard. No, I have a better plan for you."

Darius had seen Hanali's plan for Madeline and was not impressed. He crossed his arms. "And what might that be?"

"Oh! Lovely bracelets, Darius. I must get some similar ones made for one of the archon's parties. Wouldn't that be funny?" No one responded to this, so he looked at Mrs. Raymond. "That would be funny, wouldn't it, Mary?"

She twisted her face into a sour look and shook her head. "Stick to the topic at hand, Hanali."

"Ah yes. I am not going to help you kill the archon," Hanali said. "I am going to help you start a war between the Pastisians and the Elenil."

"The necromancers?"

Hanali flashed a devilish grin. "The same."

16
LAMISAP

I will let the people come into the forest, and perhaps these woods will become what the Sunlit Lands were meant to be: a refuge for those who have been harmed by the injustices of the world.

FROM "THE GOOD GARDENER," AN ALUVOREAN STORY

+

So this is Aluvorea," Jason said. "I don't like it."

He had been shocked to see Madeline. Also shocked by how tired she looked, and how thin. Her skin looked almost grey, and her eyes were sunken. Her cheekbones stuck out too far. He hadn't seen her for almost two months, but she looked like she had taken six months' worth of downhill movement with her health. Of course, time on Earth moved differently, so maybe it had been six months? He thought of his parents, and a pang of guilt hit him. He had barely thought about them the past weeks, what with all the training with the Scim and, honestly, the excitement of his relationship with Baileya.

Shula was here too. She had been happy enough to see them, but they had only talked to Madeline for a few minutes before Shula had interjected and said Madeline needed to rest. Madeline hadn't objected, so Jason and Baileya had quietly let themselves out of the little room in the hedge. Jason was excited to catch up with David, anyway.

David had been here in Aluvorea since he'd left the Knight of the Mirror's tower. He had made a few friends in the woods and had been spending some time getting to know the lay of the forest. He hadn't heard from Kekoa. Kekoa hadn't even sent any birds to David, which only reminded Jason that their old friend had sent word to him saying he needed help. Jason had hoped that maybe Kekoa had sent more details to David, but no luck.

"He can't send birds," David said. "Not here."

"Too hard to find you with all the trees or something?" So far this place reminded him of any forest in America, just with bigger trees. Like someone had never figured out you could chop them down or something. They were growing out of control, and even a lot of the paths between them were covered with vines or moss or other growing things. He couldn't help but imagine that there were wolves and other carnivorous beasts out among the trees. His imagination was not his friend, he knew that much.

David shook his head. "The Aluvoreans don't allow it. Because the messenger birds take their magic from Aluvorea."

"Wait, what?"

"See those little flitting things in the trees?"

Jason moved closer. There were hummingbirds buzzing around the higher branches, but looking again, he saw that there were other things—wingless but with the quick, almost blurred motions of the hummingbirds and about the same size—jumping around in the trees. They almost looked like . . . tiny people. "Tell me those aren't faeries," Jason said.

Baileya smiled. "Have you never seen a faerie?"

"We don't have those on Earth." He looked at David. "We don't have those, right?"

David shook his head. "Not many, no."

"We don't have many in the Kakri territories either. I've only seen them here and in the more heavily wooded sections of the mountains."

David held his hand over his head, palm up. "Hold on. Diwdrap, are you there?" He held his hand patiently and motioned for silence with his other hand when Jason started to question him. "Here she is!" He moved his hand gingerly down between them. "Thank you, sister, for coming down to meet my friend. This is Jason, from my homeland, and Baileya of the Kakri."

Standing in David's palm was a woman no larger than Jason's middle finger. She wore a simple dress that seemed to be made of moss and leaves, with a sword on her belt that looked to have been made from a long, rather savage-looking thistle spine. She had iridescent purple-and-green hair, not unlike the colors of a hummingbird's feathers, and a pinkish color to her skin. She bowed low to them, one arm across her waist. Baileya returned the gesture, and Jason tried to, but he somehow put his feet in the wrong place, lost his balance, and tripped.

David and Baileya laughed, and Diwdrap smiled, revealing perfect, tiny white teeth. "She doesn't have wings," Jason said once he had managed to get to his feet again.

Diwdrap held up a finger as if to say "wait just a minute," then let out a high-pitched chirp. A hummingbird descended from the branches above and hovered by David's palm. Diwdrap took a running leap and landed on the bird's back. It zipped up, to the left, and then buzzed at Jason's head, as if getting a closer look. Diwdrap gave him a nod, the bird hovering at his eye level, then sped away into the trees again.

"Not a big talker," Jason said.

David raised his eyebrows, as if waiting for Jason to figure something out. Jason turned to Baileya, who had the same expectant look on her face. It must be some Sunlit Lands faerie tale or something, because he had no idea what they were wanting him to put together. A quiet little faerie with no wings. Hummingbirds, the only birds he had ever seen in the Sunlit Lands who never talked. And the Aluvoreans didn't use messenger birds.

"Nope, I don't get it," Jason said.

David leaned against a tree trunk. "It will come to you."

"Seriously, dude. Give me a hint."

"Well, do birds talk back home?"

"Parrots do. Mynah birds. Big Bird does."

"In general?"

"No."

David shook his head. "Right. So it's . . . magic?"

"Yeah, Elenil magic." Uh-oh. It was starting to come together. Jason got a pudding cup every morning. But the pudding had to come from somewhere. Some hospital on Earth was losing a cup a day so it could appear to Jason in the Sunlit Lands. When Madeline had been able to breathe, it was because a Scim kid was giving Madeline her breath. So messenger birds . . . "Are you telling me the Elenil stole the voices of those cute little faeries so they could have messenger birds?"

"It's a sore spot with the Aluvoreans still," David said. "The hummingbirds refused to become messengers, which is why they can't talk, and the Aluvoreans won't allow messenger birds within the forest. The faeries and the hummingbirds consider themselves one tribe now."

Jason scratched his head. "Wait. How do you learn their names if they can't talk?"

David laughed. "You always ask interesting questions, bro. They point out things that are close to their name. Thistle, Sunlight, Flower, Dewdrop—like that. And they have a sort of sign language. I'm not fluent, but I can understand a good amount now."

It hit Jason that he had never once wondered about the messenger birds and how they were able to speak. If he had taken even five minutes to reflect on it, he would have realized that given the way Elenil magic worked, it had to be something like this. He probably would have guessed they used Scim prisoners of war or something, but this made more sense. Given the number of messenger birds, it had to be something on a larger scale. Of course it did. Which, honestly, far from making the forest seem friendlier made Jason more nervous about it.

"Is this place really safe for people like us? I feel like we might be, um, unwelcome here."

David was whittling at a stick with a large knife. "Nah. They know the Elenil are trying to kill you. They like you already. They're allied with the Elenil but sort of out of necessity. They're glad to help you if they can. And they're in the middle of something with Madeline, too."

Baileya put her hand on his shoulder. "It will be a difficult place for Bezaed to follow us, or at least to follow without our knowledge."

Jason smiled at her. "True. That's a good thing." He looked back at

David. "How do the faeries keep going, knowing about the Elenil stealing their voices? Why aren't they at constant war with them?"

David shrugged. "There's nothing to be done about it today, so they're living the best life they can in the meantime. If the chance to change things comes, believe me, they'll be there."

Delightful Glitter Lady was sniffing a large red flower at the edge of the clearing they were in. "Dee, keep away from that," Jason called. Who knew what the plants around here would do to a kitten-sized rhino?

The idea of the faeries simply living with the fact that their voices had been stolen didn't sit right with Jason. "I don't get it," he said to David. "Why aren't they fighting alongside the Scim, then?"

David glanced up from his whittling. "Okay, bro. You know how I grew up at the Crow Agency? On the rez?"

"Yeah." David was Apsáalooke. Crow tribe. He had grown up on the reservation in Montana.

"There's the memorial for the Battle of the Little Bighorn on the rez. You know that story?"

"Custer's Last Stand, right?"

Baileya leaned close. She loved stories of all kinds, and even history from Earth interested her. "It was a battle?" she asked.

David nodded. "We don't call it Custer's Last Stand, though. We call it the Battle of the Greasy Grass, or the Battle of the Little Bighorn. It gets complicated, this story, because my people, the Crow, they were on Custer's side as scouts. But Custer and his men, they come down on this settlement of Lakota, Cheyenne, and Arapaho. They have the element of surprise. They have superior firepower. But they lose the battle. Badly. Badly enough that it becomes famous. A monument is put up celebrating the lives the army lost. There's even a memorial for the horses that died."

Jason knew where this was going. "But not the Native people."

David raised his eyebrows. "Not at first, anyway. There's one now. It has a quote on it that says, 'In order to heal our grandmother earth we must unify through peace.' The names of the people who died from different tribes—the names we know, anyway—are there. It's a sacred place. People still bring prayer cloths to the battlefield and put them up when no one's looking. The memorial staff don't even try to take them down anymore, because they know more will show up."

"I know this is somehow answering my question about the faeries not fighting alongside the Scim."

"Yeah. So in World War II something like 25,000 tribal people fought. Which side do you think they fought on?"

The Allies. Obviously. "Yeah, but the Elenil are still taking advantage of the faeries. They're still doing harm to them today."

David just stared at him, as if he should be able to put the pieces together. Again. When Jason looked back at him helplessly, David said, "Buddy, you got to learn more about this stuff. Just . . . when you get home, do an Internet search on water rights, and missing indigenous women, and the American Indian boarding schools. Man, I already told you about my grandpa, didn't I? This isn't ancient history—there's stuff still happening. The Scim have been enemies of the Aluvoreans for a long time. They've invaded and clear-cut the forest in places. There's never been a peace treaty. The Aluvoreans aren't going to jump in and fight for the Scim any more than the Lakota were going to jump in and fight for the Germans in World War II."

David stood and showed Jason the carving he had done. It was a horse. Not intricate but definitely a horse. "Things aren't so simple, Jason. You have to pay attention, look for the complexities. There's still animosity between the Cheyenne and the Crow, especially with some of the older folks. There's still conflict between our tribes and the US government. But hey. We've got a memorial now, right? And it's better than the one for Custer's horses." He pushed the horse into Jason's hand.

A faerie flew up on a hummingbird, a different faerie than last time. He chirped twice, and David said, "What is it, Thastle?"

The tiny man on the hummingbird's back made several signs. David crossed his arms, then looked into the branches overhead. "Okay. Let's ask Diwdrap if she'll go." He turned to Jason and Baileya. "I sent Thastle to find Darius, but he said they've disappeared. Probably being careful no one sees them along the way. I'm going to ask Diwdrap to try to find him—she's one of our best trackers."

Diwdrap appeared beside David and made a few high-pitched chirps.

"Are they talking in bird language?"

"I don't know, bro, I don't speak bird. But I'm going to take Diwdrap to Madeline, see if she wants to send a personal message and if she has any idea how to find Darius."

"Okay," Jason said. "See you in a minute."

David walked off, three hummingbirds flying around him. Jason turned the horse over in his hand, then passed it to Baileya.

She didn't look away from him, though. "You are troubled."

"I just . . . if things are that complicated, if there are so many sides and different agendas and everything, how do we even know who the good guys are? And if we don't know that, if the lines aren't clear, then how do we keep ourselves safe?"

Baileya smiled. "I know you, Wu Song. You are not worried about protecting yourself. You are worried about your friend. About Madeline."

"I know I can't save her. But she's my friend, Bai. I have to watch out for her."

"I promised you I would protect her," Baileya said. "You know I am a person who keeps my word."

"Of course," Jason said.

"But it may be that to protect her might put you at risk, Wu Song. This is something we must discuss."

Baileya's golden brow was furrowed in concern, and her silver eyes were filled with worry.

"What's to discuss?" Jason said. "She's my friend. She's friends with both of us. Why wouldn't we risk everything for her?"

Baileya took his hand. "Wu Song. It is . . . different now. Do you see the sickness on her?"

"Sure. I mean, she doesn't look great. But she was sick before. She was sick last time we were here."

"You have always been one to embrace truth, Wu Song. I must say this to you, though it will be difficult. Your friend—our friend—Madeline has gone too far down the path toward death. She will not be walking back the other way, Wu Song. To protect her now is only to delay, not forestall."

"Then we delay it," he said, pulling his hand away. "Baileya, if it's a day or a week or two hours, we protect Madeline until the end. Agreed?"

Baileya stared out into the tangle of trees. "If the choice came to her or you, Wu Song, would it not be wiser to save you, who may have many years of life ahead?"

"Ha! I could get hit by a bus tomorrow!"

She raised an eyebrow. "A bus?"

He kept forgetting she had never been outside the Sunlit Lands. "Okay, not a bus, and probably not tomorrow. I could get hit by a runaway goat cart." Baileya's eyes sparkled with amusement. "Okay, fine, I could get hit by a falling tree. I'm just saying that yes, I'm healthy, but I could still die before her."

Baileya put her arm around Jason, and he felt her warm affection fill him completely. "Your love for your friend does you credit, Wu Song. I will do my best to protect her and you."

"And if the time comes, Baileya, you take care of her."

She put the horse in Jason's palm and kept her hand over his. "I will do my best in the moment. I will not make a promise I cannot keep."

That was probably the best he was going to get from her. He squeezed her hand. "Thank you, Baileya." She was staring out at the tangle of trees again. "What is it?" he asked. "Is someone out there?"

She locked eyes with him. Those eyes—so gentle but filled with a deep understanding that always frightened him—he could never look away from those eyes, even though he nearly always blushed when she held his gaze. "Wu Song," she said. "I have told you more than once that there is something important about you. You are honest but also kindhearted. You share your stories freely with the world."

"I can't fight, I'm a slob, I fall down a lot. I know, I know. Stop, you'll make me blush."

She leaned toward him, dropping her voice. "You turn away praise in a strange way, even when it is true. You answer with a joke, although I cannot deny the jokes are true as well. And while you share stories freely, you do not share yourself."

His eyes widened. He had told her the entire story of what had happened when he lost his sister, Jenny—how she had gone out on a secret date, and he had refused to tell their parents even when she had been missing for a long time. How she had been waiting, crushed inside her boyfriend's car at the bottom of a cliff. How he had come to her, and she had told him that she had been waiting all along for him to come. That it was his fault, as their father had never hesitated to make clear. Telling Baileya all that had helped him sort out his feelings about it. He had even said out loud that he knew it wasn't his fault. And he did. But that didn't change that he sometimes felt like he could have done something more, that he could have stopped it somehow. He had never shared all these details with anyone. Anyone but Baileya. "I told you the worst thing I've ever done."

"Yes," she said. "I am still considering your story. I have ten months yet to consider it."

Telling her his story had brought other benefits too. It was how they had gotten engaged, of course, but it also had made Baileya his closest friend. He hadn't stopped to think about it like that, almost as if she were in another category completely. But he knew he could tell her anything—his deepest, darkest thoughts—and she would only respond with love. "I just meant that I've told you things. I've been trying to share myself with you."

She looked like she wanted to continue the conversation, to say something more, but she held herself back. "I do not wish to argue," she said. "Only to say to you that I believe you are an important person. That you might change this world, Wu Song, if you embrace your role here."

He laughed. "Change the world? I doubt it."

She kissed him on the cheek and let go of his hand and walked away into the trees. "You have changed mine already, Wu Song."

Then she was gone, and Delightful Glitter Lady followed her, scampering at her feet, pleased to be leaving the clearing to explore. Jason watched the trees where she had disappeared for a few minutes, debating whether she meant for him to follow.

He pocketed David's carving and made his way back to the area just inside the border gate, where he had first seen Madeline.

Baileya and Jason had arrived within a few hours of Madeline and Shula. David had been sent to welcome Madeline and Shula, and then they had been encouraged to wait for Jason and Baileya. David said they had known Jason and friends were en route because of "sentinel plants" the Aluvoreans used. Though they were miles apart, they were connected to one another through a vast network of underground roots, none of them thicker than a piece of string. Together they formed a sort of networked brain system. They could communicate with one another about rainfall, soil conditions, and on and on. Jason didn't understand how it worked, exactly, which he blamed 100 percent on David, who got tired of trying to explain long before Jason's interest wore off (it still hadn't). Jason's current theory was that the plants could tell they were coming by the impacted soil created by their mounts, the way sunlight was blocked for a moment by their passage, or maybe even the way their conversation altered the airflow. Who knew? But however it worked, the Aluvoreans had known they were coming.

The Aluvoreans had been surprised when Break Bones and Darius went their separate way instead of coming with Jason and Baileya. Madeline was deeply disappointed she had missed Darius, and she asked David if there was someone who could try to catch him and Break Bones. But that hadn't worked. Now their best bet of getting in contact was another wordless tracker faerie. Jason wasn't sure how Diwdrap would give Darius the message even if she found him.

Jason found Madeline and the others in a small clearing near the door in the hedge. Madeline had a chair made from a stump. Shula sat on the ground to one side of Madeline, drawing in a small notebook. David stood nearby, and a woman in a brown robe stood in front of them. She had skin that was varied colors of green, like the light filtering through maple leaves in summer. Her hair was short and almost woolly and a darker green, like healthy moss. She was speaking to Madeline, who listened intently but did not seem to be saying much.

"Hello, friends and also green lady," Jason said, flopping onto the ground beside Madeline and leaning against her stump.

"Greetings, Wu Song," the green lady said. "The story of your adventures in the Kakri territories and Far Seeing are popular ones here in Aluvorea."

"No kidding. I would like to hear one of those. I wonder if it's much like the actual story." He waited for her to introduce herself, but she only watched him, as if expecting something more, so he asked, "What's your name?"

"I am called Lamisap, which in your language would mean 'the flower which blooms from the midst of the moss.'" She smiled, as if waiting for something.

"That's a beautiful name."

She smiled more broadly, and he noticed her teeth were as white as the bark of a birch tree. David cleared his throat. "She's welcoming you into the conversation, Jason. You sort of interrupted when you walked up. In Aluvorea there's an assumption that you must have something more important to say, so she's waiting for you to share your thing before she goes on with hers."

"Oh." Jason rearranged himself against the stump. "Madeline needs a more comfortable chair."

Madeline slapped him on the back of the head, but when he looked back at her, she was grinning, and so was Shula. David said, "We'll move into the forest proper soon. Things are a bit more luxurious there."

"The stump . . . is lovely," Madeline said, smiling at Lamisap.

Lamisap bowed her head, seeming pleased that Madeline was pleased. "With your permission, friend Wu Song, I will continue?"

"Um. Of course. Please, uh, carry on."

Lamisap turned her attention back to Madeline. "I did not think you would come, that day in Far Seeing."

"I made . . . a promise," Madeline said.

"Yes. But my sister and I both knew you were not well. We did not know what would happen in Far Seeing or even if you would survive. Aluvorea was not pleased with us, that we gave you the emes esutol."

Madeline raised her arm, showing Lamisap the small black seed in her forearm. "I assume that's this."

"Of course," Lamisap said. "Aluvorea said it would be dangerous to give it to you and that you had already sacrificed a great deal because of the Sunlit Lands, and it would be cruel to ask for more. My sister and I . . . we stole it. We took it without permission. It was not ours to give. And Aluvorea is right—it is much to ask of you."

"What exactly are you asking for?" Shula asked.

"No, I know this one," Jason said. "It's always the same. I've seen enough movies and cartoons to know how magic woods work. The magic of the woods is all twisted, and now there are terrible monsters, and things are getting all decayed and disgusting. There's, like, mushrooms growing into human-sized things and attacking people, and, like, carnivorous plants and stuff. Right?"

Lamisap blinked, confused. "There are plants which eat people, of course, but those are not new. They have always been a part of Aluvorea." She seemed distressed and went on to say, "Some plants have thorns, but that does not make them bad. A rosebush is not evil."

"But eating people, that's bad. We can agree on that."

"They are plants, Wu Song. What do they know about such things?"

There was a shaking sound from the forest behind Lamisap. An old wall covered in ivy was moving—or at least, the ivy was. A second woman stepped out of it. She had skin the color of a summer sky, long trailing vines of hair, and piercing green eyes. She carried some large leaves in one hand, blade shaped and as long as a machete. They looked almost tropical.

"Greetings, sister Lin. You are welcome here."

The new woman smiled and bowed to each of them in turn. "My sister Lamisap tells stories that are curled in on themselves." She looked at Jason. "Some plants grow well in the wild but become weeds in cultivated places."

Jason's mouth fell open. Was that a dig at him? He sort of thought it was, but he wasn't sure. He was trying to formulate a response, but Lin had already begun to talk again. "I will speak to you in the way of your people, who are more blunt and straightforward than our own. Aluvorea is not corrupted or dying. She is losing her magic. The trees which are magic are becoming only trees, like those on your Earth. The firethorns are spreading, threatening to burn the rest, but in a way that would bring destruction, not renewal, for there is no heir to the Heartwood Crown. The borders of the carnivorous forest have expanded, and the trees which bring magic to the Sunlit Lands are in danger."

"I just want to point out that the mushroom thing was maybe a step too far, but 'borders of carnivorous forest expanding' is very much in line with what I said."

David jumped in. "It takes a while to get the whole story, because the Aluvoreans see it all as connected. They haven't gotten to the main bit yet."

"By all means take us to the main bit," Jason said.

Lin and her sister exchanged looks. Lin said, "We—my sister and I and some other Aluvoreans like us—think Madeline may be the one we must grow alongside." They waited, as if this explained everything.

"I'm sorry, but we have no idea what that means." Jason looked at Madeline, to make sure he wasn't stupid. She shook her head. "No, we have no idea."

"David," Madeline said. "Can you . . . explain?"

David squeezed his eyes shut, as if he were following some internal map to a faraway destination. "Okay. I'll try. It's like this. There's a place called the Queen's Island, in the northern part of Aluvorea. No one has been there in years."

"Centuries," Lin said.

"That's a lot of years," Jason said.

"Right. There's a—a pond that used to be a river—"

"It's a lake," Lamisap said, "called Anukop."

David took a breath, trying not to get annoyed. "On the island, or so the legends say, is a throne carved into a tree. And on the seat of the throne there's a crown made of wood called the Heartwood Crown. Whoever wears the crown has a sort of—they can control the woods. They can alter the magic, edit it, change it."

"Grow alongside," Madeline said. "This is . . . what you mean?"

"Yes," Lin said. "We want you to help us grow into the next thing we will be."

Jason laughed. "Is that all? Why didn't you just say so?"

Lin and Lamisap exchanged looks. But before they could answer, a tall Elenil woman walked into the clearing, wearing a long silver dress that went from just below her chin all the way to the grassy floor.

"Gilenyia," Madeline said.

"They did not say so because the Heartwood Crown does not exist." Gilenyia gave each of the humans a hard stare. "If it did, the Elenil would destroy it."

"We are sorry," Lamisap said.

"Sorry for what?" Jason jumped to his feet.

Gilenyia gave Jason a pitying look. "For agreeing to turn you over to the Elenil, of course, Wu Song."

"We are sorry," Lin said. "But they promised that if we turned you over to them, Wu Song, they would leave the rest of the humans here in peace. We can continue with what needs to be done for Aluvorea. They will not harm the forest, and we are promised you will get a fair trial."

Elenil guards stepped out of the woods from all around them. They were surrounded.

"Um," Jason said. "Is this how fair trials usually start, in your experience?"

Gilenyia looked at him coldly. "You know us better than that by now, Wu Song. We are taking all of the humans back to Far Seeing. We'll return them when all have stood trial."

"You promised us the other humans would stay here!" Lamisap shouted.

"You did not tell me that my dear friend Madeline was one of them. What are you doing back here, I wonder?" Gilenyia stepped toward her.

David, Shula, and Jason put their backs to Madeline, keeping her protected behind them.

"I do not like plant people," Jason said, glaring at the two Aluvorean women.

"Put them in chains," Gilenyia said to her guards.

"Aw, man, I just got my chains off," Jason said, but by then the Elenil were on them.

17
A PROPHECY

Sometimes we think we have found truth, but
we have only found the beach in winter.

EXPOSITION ON A TRADITIONAL ZHANIN SAYING

✛

I want to make this clear," Darius said, advancing on Hanali. "I am here to see Archon Thenody. He sent his people into the Wasted Lands seeking my friends, and while there they killed a Scim boy. A harmless Scim boy."

Hanali tried to speak, but Darius snarled at him to be silent. Hanali lifted himself up straight, making himself taller.

The sword begged to be in Darius's hand, but he ignored it. It was not time. Not yet. He did not have his robe or his mask here, but that did not mean he was someone to be dismissed. He would be heard, and if that meant he needed to speak their language, then so be it. He didn't need a sword—he needed only the strength of his own presence. They weren't dealing with Darius Walker, teenage runaway, now. He was the Black Skull, champion of the Scim people. "I am not here to entreat the archon for his help. Nor to inconvenience him. Nor to dethrone him. I am here to put him to death for his crimes against the Scim people. I do not care about the Pastisians or their wars, and I do not care about your political squabbles or preferences."

Hanali tugged at the lace on his sleeves, doing his best to seem disinterested. "He's a fiery one," he said to Mrs. Raymond.

"I told you," she said. "He's not one to manipulate and influence, he's one to bring in on your plan."

Hanali threw his arms wide, as if for an embrace. "What more would I expect from the man who found his own path into the Sunlit Lands in search of his beloved? What more would I expect from the man who founded the Black Skulls and fought his way through the walls of Far Seeing, striking fear into the hearts of all Elenil?"

Darius clenched his fists. Rainwater was still dripping from his face, but he didn't pause to wipe it away. He didn't know this Elenil well, and he wasn't sure if he was being mocked or if Hanali was attempting to build a connection.

Mud sat on the floor. "Bah. He's fine for a human, but what use is he to me? Too recognizable."

Hanali laughed. "Oh, poor Mud. You are but a foot soldier, and I the leader of the resistance. Do not attempt to understand the complicated plans of your betters."

The Scim boy rolled his eyes. "You are not leader of the resistance, you're just another pretender to the throne. I'm the leader of the resistance." He crossed his arms and thrust his lower lip out. "I am! You just want to take over. I want all of the Elenil gone and the Scim put in control."

Hanali motioned for Darius to sit. "Come, brave sir. Let us discuss this. Why are you so determined to murder the archon? I daresay Madeline wouldn't be fond of the plan. Nor Jason, but he has always been a bit soft. What makes you so full of steel and determination? Why so quick to kill? I remind you that I am a friend to the Scim. I have been working here, quietly, behind the scenes, to make things better for them."

Darius watched Hanali motion to a delicate cup of tea as if Darius were a wild animal and Hanali were trying to gain his trust with a treat. Hanali's smile froze on his face, as if he were concentrating hard on looking harmless. The woman, Mrs. Raymond, watched with wry amusement. Darius was still unsure what the Elenil's game was. He had seen this type of person before. He stood in a place of authority and power, he promised help—maybe even gave help—but you could never be sure if he did this for you or for himself. You couldn't be sure if he was part of your community or not.

Hanali frowned. "Is it the tea?" He lifted the cup he had invited Darius to take. "You're right, of course. It's barely warm."

Mrs. Raymond took another sip of hers. "Don't play the clown, Hanali, the tea is perfectly hot. Nothing is wrong with it."

"Not good enough for a guest," he said dismissively, and waved at a human servant, who came over to take away the cup and the teapot. "Bring a new tea, if you please. Something specifically for our guest."

"Perhaps I did not make myself clear," Darius said. "I am not here for pleasantries."

"Yes, yes, you're here for murder. Perfectly clear, sir, perfectly. But is there any reason we can't have a hot cup of tea before the stabbing and beheading and so on? We can sit and be civilized, and you can tell me your plan to murder the archon, and I can tell you my plan to start a war, and we can compare notes."

Mrs. Raymond sighed. "Darius, I assure you he is quite serious. You may as well sit, he won't stop prattling on regardless."

The servant returned with the teapot and a fresh teacup. Hanali gestured to the chair. Darius sat reluctantly, and Hanali poured the tea. Darius picked up the tea, took a sip. It was warm, with a slight floral and berry taste. He felt rough after the days of travel, the journey through the tunnel, the battle with the Elenil. The tea was actually nice. Darius relented and sipped the hot beverage, feeling his muscles unwind a bit.

"Would you warm mine, too, please?" Mrs. Raymond asked, lifting her teacup.

Hanali gave her a look of disdain. "But my dear, your cup is perfectly hot. Perfectly hot, those were your exact words." He motioned to the servant again. "Take this teapot away. I will not have anything spoil Mrs. Raymond's perfect cup of tea." The servant bowed his head and stepped away from the table, still holding the teapot. He didn't move further away, just stood at attention with the teapot in his hands.

"You are a petty thing," Mrs. Raymond said. Hanali looked pleased. He steepled his fingers, turned his back on Mrs. Raymond, and gave his attention to Darius. "Now, my friend, tell us: why are you so set on killing the archon?"

Why was he so set on this path? It was the wrong question. "This isn't something new, Hanali. It has been my plan for some time." He took another sip, set the cup down. "I've been planning this since the moment I became a Black Skull. Break Bones has always known this, the Scim elders know. But I haven't told anyone else."

Hanali's eyebrows raised in mild surprise. "Not even Madeline?"

"Especially not her," Darius said, his voice rising. He put his hands flat on the table, willing himself to be calm. Madeline still believed there could be another way to bring peace. Something without all the bloodshed. She honestly thought somehow that all the people of the Sunlit Lands might have a change of heart, might discover they wanted to treat each other with kindness. It was one of the things he loved about her—that naiveté, that belief that somehow the best part of people would rise to the top and win over the worst. He wanted that flame of belief to stay alive in her, to burn strong. He wanted, if he was being really honest, to believe that for himself, but he'd seen too much evidence to the contrary. So he would fix the world himself, as he must, and if the blood of the archon was not enough to make the change, then he would still have his sword, wouldn't he? He didn't need Madeline's objections when he had already decided what must be done. It was a load he could carry alone. No need to weigh her conscience down with it too. "She wouldn't understand. You saw her up on that tower. You saw how she decided the archon's life was more important than her own."

"That's not what I saw," Mrs. Raymond said. "She decided it wasn't her place to decide for the Elenil and Scim what their future would be. But she wasn't going to be a part of the injustices herself. She removed herself from the equation. It was the Scim girl who made the choice to cut off the archon's hand. She's the one who brought us to where we are today."

"Oh, pish-posh," Hanali said. "You weren't even there, Mrs. Raymond."

"I saw it all through a messenger bird," she said. "Don't tell me that doesn't count."

"A little bird told you," Hanali said coldly. "Drink, drink," he said to Darius, sipping at his own tea.

Darius took another sip of the hot tea. He did feel more relaxed.

"Go on. You were saying that Madeline is wrong."

Darius sighed. Madeline wasn't *wrong*. She just wasn't practical. Sure, she could try to disconnect herself from the unjust system she benefited from, but could she ever fully do that? And would it change anything? And how long would it take? And would it be wrong of Darius to kill the archon when it would save countless Scim? Hanali was thinking in black and white, in two dimensions, something that surprised Darius, given how old the Elenil must be. "Don't be so simple minded, Hanali. Is this really about right or wrong?"

Hanali leaned back in surprise. "Is it not? I have found humans to think every little decision to be a moral event."

Darius tried to think of the right way to explain this and found himself staring into the swirl of loose leaves in his tea. The others waited patiently, though he didn't know why. A small question began to itch in the back of his mind: why did they need him so badly? He cleared his throat. "Madeline loves these fantasy novels called the Tales of Meselia. Do you know these books?"

Hanali gave him a small smile. "I haven't read them. But yes, I know them well. I daresay Mrs. Raymond knows them better than I. She has always had a soft spot for fantasy."

Mrs. Raymond narrowed her eyes, frowning at the Elenil. "I know them, Darius. Go on."

He lifted his hands, drawing their attention. "I'm Black. No doubt you know this already."

Hanali waved his gloved hands, as if this were a minor distraction. "I am unquestionably beautiful and stylish. Certain things go without saying. Please, go on."

"Fantasy novels . . . well, they're not always the most popular in my community. When I started reading them with Madeline—not just Meselia, but other books too—my mom told me to stop wasting my time. Told me it would give me the wrong idea about the world."

Hanali's eyes lit up with sudden interest. "The wrong idea about the world?"

"Yeah. See, in a lot of fantasy novels—especially the early stuff—the bad guys are always dark. Dark purposes, dark castles, dark skin. The Orcs in Tolkien. The Calormenes in Narnia. Stuff like that. When I read fantasy looking for someone who looked like me, they were always the bad guys."

"Aravis is Calormene in *The Horse and His Boy*," Mrs. Raymond said, though her face showed no excitement about the statement.

"Yes, and her son, who is half Calormene, becomes one of the greatest kings of Archenland," Darius said, trying to be patient. "I'm not saying there aren't a handful of people with dark skin who do something good in the books, but I am saying they are the exception rather than the rule. One 'noble savage' for every hundred, every thousand 'ordinary' dark-skinned warriors."

"Fascinating," Hanali said. "Such wonderful names and places. Archenland! Calormene! Aravis! It reminds me of other names I hear humans say from time to time. Minnesota! Colorado! Costa Rica! What strange and wonderful places you have in your world."

Darius couldn't tell if Hanali was joking. Not that it mattered much. "So one day I was reading *The Once and Future King* by T. H. White. It's all about King Arthur . . . how he grew up and became someone who changed the world for the better. And I was really resonating with it. It's all about doing away with national borders, the need for a better solution in the world than violence and bloodshed, a sort of pacifistic war book. Madeline had given it to me and said she knew I would love it, that it was a favorite of hers, even that it reminded her of me. She said I was like Arthur. I was the boy no one noticed who would be king, who would be the example that the whole civilized world would try to follow."

"High praise," Hanali said, sounding impressed.

Darius drank another gulp of tea. "She was my girlfriend, remember. She loved me and saw me in a different way than others did. Her affection for me clouded her vision."

Mrs. Raymond leaned forward. "Love sometimes reveals a thing in the beloved that others cannot see. Do not dismiss her words so lightly."

"It doesn't matter, that's not the point. The point is that there's this part of the story where Wart—that's King Arthur as a kid—gets turned into a falcon. He goes into the mews to hear all the stories these noble birds will share. That's how it's presented—these noble birds. But one of the birds, he's crazy. He starts spouting off about how the world is being destroyed by all these different groups of people, and one of the groups he mentions is Black people. Only he uses the n-word. The n-word!"

Hanali's brow crinkled in confusion. "This is not translating correctly."

"It's a slur in English," Mrs. Raymond said. "Used against Black people specifically."

"So, to be sure I am following all this . . . an insane bird in a work of fiction used a slur against your people."

Darius groaned in frustration. "You don't see? Madeline read right over that. She didn't notice it, or didn't remember it when she was telling me. For her it's a story about choosing to throw away the idea that 'might makes right' and instead embrace 'do what is right, whatever the cost.' It's about how power comes with corresponding responsibilities to the people you're in authority over. This is a message I believe. But at the same time she didn't see this issue, this underlying issue with it."

Hanali motioned to the servant to fill Darius's teacup. "You are becoming agitated, my friend. More tea."

"I'm saying that Madeline reads all those stories differently than me. She didn't understand that a throwaway slur about Black people—even though it's presented in the book as being something only a crazy person would say—ruined it for me. It made me more aware of the other things . . . like how Native Americans are constantly being run down as savages in the book for no reason. Basically any time archery comes up, the author has to say something about how savages don't do archery the same way as the Brits, that they're lesser. It doesn't matter for the person writing the book, because I wasn't part of the audience. He wasn't thinking about me and my response, or he wouldn't have included it. All these fantasies, all of them, come from this point of view of some Norse or Anglo-Saxon medievalism. The great god Aslan comes and puts the Calormenes in their place. The one true king returns and destroys the Orcs and the dark men with their elephants. The happy ending isn't happy for my people."

"You, however, are not an Orc." Hanali said this with a tentative tone, as if he weren't quite sure.

"I don't know, Hanali. I don't know. Maybe that's part of the problem. But see, Madeline knows these stories. Narnia and Middle-earth and King Arthur. She believes them, believes what they tell her. For her, she can just disengage from the system and trust that the Peasant King or the Majestic One or someone is going to come along and fix everything. Maybe she doesn't notice every little injustice, every slur in the story, maybe she thinks too highly of the people around her, that they want to do the right thing in their heart of hearts, and if she's wrong about them, well, that's okay because the new king will take the throne and he'll save us all. If we just live a quiet life and do the right thing in our little sphere of influence, it's all going to be okay. The new king will fix every wrong. Your plan is the story Madeline has believed her whole life: new king, new world. You become archon, you change things."

"Undeniable. Trust me, my friend, I have every intention of doing just that."

Darius walked to an ornate vase sitting on a small, oval table. It had gold paint showing some scene from an Elenil myth. Darius didn't recognize the story, but the picture was of a male and female Elenil holding a stone, and light was radiating out from it, and below them were the other peoples of the Sunlit Lands, some cowering before them, others with beatific smiles. "It's this story," Darius said. "This is the problem. In this story, I bet some Elenil comes along and saves the world and sets it up the way it is now, Elenil on top, everyone else scrambling for table scraps."

"More or less," Hanali admitted, taking the vase gingerly from his hands. "This vase has been in my family for several centuries. Please do not touch it again." Hanali set the vase on the table. "The question, however, my dear sir, is why you are determined to kill the archon and why, of all things, you have chosen to keep this secret from your friends."

"I didn't tell my friends because they don't understand. For them, the king comes and makes the world right again. They don't see that in their 'right' world, my people suffer. As slaves or working class or prisoners, disenfranchised and marginalized. The fantasy utopia requires my people to live in a postapocalypse. I look at those stories and realize that maybe, from my friends' point of view, I'm the bad guy. Look at it this way: a few days ago an Elenil soldier murdered a Scim kid named Nightfall. Just a child."

"I cannot follow your argument, Darius. You jump around. Hawks and kings and Minnesota, and now it's Scim children and the working-class apocalypse. Please, sir, please get to your point."

"If Madeline had killed the archon when she had the chance, Nightfall would be alive today."

Hanali considered this. "Perhaps."

"No, not perhaps. True. Madeline chose to spare the archon's life and do what she could do herself. She removed herself from benefiting from the system. Maybe that would work. Maybe. If everyone else benefiting from the system did the same thing, it could. But if she had killed the archon, those soldiers would have never been in the Wasted Lands. They would have never come across that child. By trusting that justice was coming tomorrow, she guaranteed more injustice today."

"How do you weigh this out?" Hanali asked. "The archon's guards would have killed her, as well as your friends, if she had harmed the archon. Most likely I would be archon in his place now."

"Would you have sent your people into the Wasted Lands to destroy the Scim?"

"Not at all. In fact, I had unofficially had several conversations with the Scim elders about how to move toward lasting peace."

"So. Nightfall would be alive. Madeline chose Nightfall's death. I chose his death, by standing by and letting her dictate that choice to the rest of us. Not that I wanted Madeline to die, of course. I would have grabbed her if I could, flown her away. I would have fought for her, protected her, until my final breath. Her plan, though, is to be righteous herself and trust that it will change an unrighteous society. I don't believe that. I believe we have to go beyond that. We have to fight the injustice. Destroy it. Not just in ourselves but in others, too."

Hanali moved to the other side of the courtyard. "But in this case, would it not make more sense to pressure the archon, as I intend to do, with an unexpected war, and for me to take his place when his inept leadership is brought to light?"

"No offense," Darius said, "but I don't trust you or any other Elenil to bring justice for the Scim. Why would you? I don't think we'll reach full equality until there's a day when a Scim can take the throne."

A slight smile came to Hanali's face. "As you know, Darius, we Elenil check in with various prophets and soothsayers and oracles. We like to know what is coming in the future." He picked up Darius's teacup and waved the servant over. He opened the teapot and poured the dregs of Darius's cup in before setting the lid firmly in place. Mrs. Raymond looked at him with incomprehension. "They're all quite clear on two things, Darius. One, that Archon Thenody will be killed by a human—a human using the Sword of Tears. And two, that I will take Thenody's place. As you can imagine, he is less than thrilled, and getting a human into his presence has become, well, problematic." His smile widened. "So teatime is over. I think you are our man, Darius Walker. I have every intention of helping you."

"I'm not interested in helping you," Darius snarled. He pointed at Mud. "I'd rather put that Scim kid in charge of the Sunlit Lands. I trust him more than I trust you."

Hanali laughed at that, and Mrs. Raymond studied the top of the table, a look of sad determination on her face. "Thus revealing your excellent judgment, sir. My apologies for Hanali's rudeness."

Darius wavered to his feet, feeling a wave of nausea rise up from his stomach. "You poisoned me."

"It is not poison as such," Hanali said, stepping toward him.

"Hanali!" Mrs. Raymond said sharply. "What have you done?"

"A sleeping potion only, Mrs. Raymond. When he wakes, he will be in the loving possession of the Pastisians."

Darius grabbed the vase, the one with the Elenil holding up their enlightened stone and cowing all the people of the Sunlit Lands. "The necromancers," Darius said, but his words came out impossibly slurred. He raised the vase over his head.

"Not the vase—" Hanali cried, but his words were cut off by the sound of pottery shattering.

Darius kicked the shards in grim satisfaction before toppling to the floor, still smiling.

18

AMBUSH!

As for me, I dive down deep, down to the roots of the world.

FROM "MALGWIN AND THE WHALE," A TRADITIONAL ZHANIN STORY

+

They were surrounded. The Elenil were advancing on Madeline and her friends: David, Shula, and Jason. David could fight, and he had weapons on him. Shula could fight too, and she could turn herself into a flaming torch. Madeline could barely breathe, and Jason, well, he was probably about as useful as Madeline in a fight. She counted six Elenil. Plus the two Aluvorean women, but they weren't fighters. If Darius were here, or Break Bones, they might have a chance. Or Baileya.

Where was Baileya?

Jason must have had the same thought, because he shouted, "Baileya! Hey, we're being kidnapped by bad guys!" One of the Elenil pushed Jason to his knees, wrenching his hands behind his back. "They are not as gentle as I would like!"

Madeline hadn't moved, was struggling just to stay sitting upright.

"Let him go." It was Baileya's voice.

She stood behind Gilenyia, having pulled the Elenil woman's arm behind her back, the spear blade of Baileya's weapon under Gilenyia's chin, resting on her neck. Everyone stopped moving. David slapped Jason on the shoulder. "Hey, bro, your girlfriend is saving us!"

"Fiancée," Jason said.

The Elenil holding Jason loosened his grip but didn't let go completely. "Gilenyia, what are your orders?" he asked.

Gilenyia sneered. "She can't harm me." She drove her free elbow backward into Baileya, spun to one side and broke free of the Kakri woman's hold. She pulled a silver knife from her sleeve, and before Madeline could shout a warning, drove the knife toward Baileya's neck.

Baileya plunged her spear into Gilenyia's heart.

The Elenil woman tried to stumble away, but Baileya pushed her to the ground using the haft of the spear. The silver knife fell to the forest floor. Baileya put her foot on the woman's chest and pulled her spear clear. Blood gushed from the wound, and Gilenyia's mouth went slack, her eyes focused on something in the far distance.

In the confusion, David pulled his own knife and, with a peculiar slashing motion Madeline had never seen before, managed to keep the nearest Elenil guard at bay. A wave of heat came from behind her—Shula lighting herself on fire.

"Stop, stop!" the two Aluvorean women cried. "You will set the woods aflame."

Shula said coolly, "If they put me in chains, I promise you I will burn more than the woods."

"Our deal is broken," one of the Aluvorean women said. Lamisap. "We made it with Gilenyia, and we were promised a peaceful transfer and that the woods would not be harmed."

The Elenil hesitated. "Yet our archon demands these humans be brought to him," one of them said.

"You will not all survive the fight to put us in chains," Baileya said. "Certainly Gilenyia will not. Unless I am much mistaken, you have no healer."

But that wasn't completely true, was it? "I'm a . . . healer," Madeline said.

"Madeline, what are you doing?" Jason asked.

"I am," she said. She locked eyes with one of the Elenil. She had no idea which was in charge now that Gilenyia was bleeding out. "Leave Aluvorea . . . and I'll . . . heal Gilenyia."

The guards did not look pleased about fighting Baileya, or about being killed or permanently damaged without a healer nearby. "We will wait outside the forest," one of them said. "We will wait a full handbreadth of the sun's movement for word from Gilenyia. If we do not receive word from her, we will enter the forest again but in greater numbers, and we will not rest until we have found you or burned Aluvorea to ash."

"It's . . . a deal," Madeline said.

The Elenil backed away slowly until they were out of David and Shula's range. Then they turned and moved swiftly toward the gate that Baileya and Jason had entered a short while ago. When they were out of sight, Madeline got straight to business. "Shula . . . get Gilenyia's . . . knife."

Baileya was wiping the gore from her spear, seemingly unconcerned about Madeline's decision to make a deal with the Elenil. But that was her way . . . she fought when needed but lived in the moment. If Madeline asked her opinion about the decision, no doubt she would tell her. "Baileya," Madeline said, "thank you."

Baileya inclined her head. "You are under my protection, friend Madeline. I would lay down my own life to protect yours." Baileya gave Jason a look after she said this.

"Could you . . . watch the . . . Aluvoreans? I want them . . . to stay here for . . . this."

Baileya's face stilled, her frown grim. "With pleasure." She moved beside the two sisters, who babbled excuses. Madeline didn't have time to listen.

"We have something that may help," one of the Aluvoreans said. Lin— the one who had just returned to the clearing.

"Yeah right," Jason said. "You've helped plenty."

Madeline ignored them. "David . . . lay Gilenyia . . . straight. Jason . . . help me."

David moved like a cat, with such confidence, as if he didn't need to think about what his body would do, he just did it. He had the Elenil woman laid out flat in a matter of seconds, before Jason had managed to get Madeline up from her stump.

She put her arm around Jason's shoulder. "I don't think this is a good idea," Jason said.

Madeline hugged his neck. "You're probably . . . right."

"Mads, you're not well."

She hated when people said this to her. As if she didn't know. They were the ones who didn't know. She thought of it every time she took a breath. Then her friends—well-meaning friends—wanted to warn her when she was doing too much. What did they know? "You . . . of all people . . . should understand." She tried to keep the venom out of her voice but wasn't completely successful.

"I do, I just . . ." Jason couldn't put words to it. Tears brimmed in his eyes. "Mads—"

And just like that she felt bad for lashing out at him. She put her forehead against his. "Jason . . . not much time . . . for me. Let me . . . choose how to . . . use it."

"Okay." He choked the word out, and she put almost all her weight on him. He took it without complaint, moving her beside Gilenyia. He helped her lower to the ground. He knew what she would need to do for the healing . . . put her "magic bracelet" next to Gilenyia's. Of course, hers was broken, and she wasn't sure this would work, but she had to try. Jason pulled Gilenyia's arm across her body and laid her left wrist on top of Madeline's.

"Please," Lin said. "Please, I may be able to help with the breathing."

Baileya sent a look to Madeline. Should she let the woman pass? Madeline knew it could be a trick, but she always found herself erring on the side of hope. "Okay," she said. "Send her . . . over."

Jason crossed his arms and stood between Lin and Madeline. "Okay, what is it?"

The blue woman held a sheaf of leaves in her hand. They were glossy green, like tropical plants. "This is called Queen's Breath. We use it to swim underwater for long distances. When it is wet and placed on the throat, it can—for a time—give someone breath."

"It can . . . heal me?"

The woman shook her head. "Only lessen the pain. Make the breath come easier."

Well, that was better than nothing. Madeline nodded to Jason, and Lin bent over her. She laid one leaf along the side of Madeline's neck, took a small canteen from inside her robe, and doused the leaf in water. A thousand pinpricks stabbed Madeline at once, and she cried out, then breathed deep. The oxygen flowed. Not like when she was well. More like when she breathed from an oxygen tank. Like she was doing the same amount of work but getting more out of it. "Thank you," Madeline said. She felt a moment of hopefulness. If this plant grew in the Sunlit Lands, who knew what else could be here? Maybe there was another way to be healed other than the deadly exchange required by the Elenil.

Lin put the leaves in Jason's hands. There was considerable embarrassment in her eyes. "We should not have betrayed you thus. Take these leaves. They will have to be changed often, laid on the neck and then wetted. They do not last long. An hour each, at most. So use them wisely."

"Fine," Jason said. "But next time you're tempted to sell me out, please don't."

A noisy gasp came from Gilenyia. Madeline had nearly forgotten her in the momentary euphoria of getting a bit more life from her breathing.

"Jason," Madeline said, "we're losing her."

"Okay," he said. "We'll keep watch—you do your thing."

Madeline closed her eyes, trying to find the connection to Gilenyia's magic tattoo. She couldn't help but think that she had done this last with Gilenyia's help, when she was healing Shula. Gilenyia had taught her everything she knew about this, from the first day when she had forced Madeline to make a choice between healing a stranger or saving Jason's life. Now she was reaching out with her own magic, trying to find the network of mystical passageways that would let her access the wounds in Gilenyia's body. But Madeline's magic bracelet wasn't connecting to Gilenyia's tattoos. She continued to quest out, seeking to find it. Strangely, although she couldn't find Gilenyia at all, she could sense Jason's magic near her. "Is she breathing?" she asked without opening her eyes.

A moment while Jason checked. "Yeah. Not great, but yeah." Another pause. "Mads, if you take her wounds, you're not going to make it. I'm not sure *she's* going to make it, even if you do."

"I have to try something." She could feel his magical connection burning bright beside her. Maybe because they were close friends. She didn't know. But she could actually see Gilenyia's magic through Jason's. And—she thought—maybe a glimpse of Gilenyia's connection through his.

She took another deep breath, feeling the cold bite of the magic on her neck, and then she reached out and entered through Jason's magic tattoo. "Oh whoa, hey!" Jason said. They were standing together next to Gilenyia's body. Not her actual body but a vision of it. "That was weird," Jason said. "Also—pretty sure my real body just fell down. A little warning next time?"

This was the psychic space she entered when healing someone. She didn't know if it was real or mental, she only knew that now she and Jason were connected in another space they had somehow constructed together—it looked almost identical to the Aluvorean forest clearing their physical bodies were in. They looked, more or less, like themselves. Gilenyia still lay on the ground.

Madeline knelt beside Gilenyia. She could see the magic in her, pulsing and powerful, coursing through her whole body. "I'm not sure what's happening. I couldn't see her magic except through your connection."

"Maybe my magic is still hooked up to you, since my deal was to do whatever you say in exchange for pudding cups."

"Okay," Madeline said. "I'm going to try to look inside her body now. You remember what this is like?"

"Not really."

Jason had been healed once before, but he had been almost dead. For Madeline, this mental space was a strange rush of emotion and symbolic visuals. She would see a wall or feel the reality of a body. She could alter things, take things on herself, move wounds from one person to another. "I don't know what will happen with both of us in here, Jason, or what you'll see or feel. Try not to get in the way, and don't be scared."

"Too late," Jason said. "On maybe both things."

She put her (not physical) hand on Gilenyia's (not physical) wrist and concentrated. It worked. She had encountered Gilenyia in someone else's mind once, and she had been a cold, silent force. It had terrified Madeline then. Gilenyia was silent now, too, but in a different way. Before she had felt cold and calculating, like a predator watching its prey. Now she was cold and empty, like a house with all evidence of life removed.

Blood was still pumping out of Gilenyia's chest. "I hope someone's working on that in the real world," Jason said. "Instead of relying on the magic healing."

Madeline ignored him and tried to take some of Gilenyia's wound onto herself, but it wouldn't come to her. She remembered that when she had healed Shula, she had taken the wounds into herself and then passed them on to a Scim healer who was there for that purpose. Gilenyia had been there, watching over the whole process that day. Maybe, since she was connected through Jason, she had to move the wounds through him. "Jason," she said, "this may hurt."

"Okay," he said. "Let me sit down then." He took Madeline's hand in his and sat cross-legged next to Gilenyia. "Ready."

He was a good man. She was so thankful for him, and sorry this next thing had to happen. She started with the internal wound, where the spear had pierced through a lung, near to the heart. No doubt Baileya had purposely missed. Madeline held onto the wound with her mind and *moved* it into Jason, just as Gilenyia had taught her.

Jason groaned, and his hand loosened in hers. She squeezed, and prepared to move the wound from him, now, to her. Except that it wouldn't move. She couldn't get it from him. "Jason," she said, "I can't get the wound through you to me."

He raised his eyes to her, his forehead drenched in sweat. "I know, right?"

"Because you're not releasing it," she said.

"Uh-huh," Jason said. "Not going to either."

"I need to heal her."

"Do it with my body," Jason said, pausing as a wave of pain hit him, "not yours."

"Of all the infuriating—"

"Charming," he grunted. "I really prefer charming."

"Jason, she'll die."

"Don't much care," he said.

Madeline let the wound pass back into Gilenyia, and Jason slumped to the ground, exhausted. She brushed the hair back from his forehead and patted him on the shoulder. He was annoying but sweet. But also annoying. Sweet once, annoying twice. She turned her attention back to Gilenyia, wondering if there was something else she could do if she went deeper into Gilenyia's mind and body. She concentrated, trying to see where else she could go.

She felt herself moving into Gilenyia's mental space. Madeline stood in an empty mansion now. She walked past staircases that were wide enough for two cars to drive up. She passed an empty ballroom and a series of drawing rooms and sitting rooms that were likewise empty. She found Gilenyia near the back door, sitting on a small chair. At least, she thought it was Gilenyia.

In the physical world, Gilenyia had blonde, almost white hair and was significantly taller than Madeline. *Statuesque* would be a good word to describe her. She was slim but had full hips and a curvy form and flawless skin. She could walk into any modeling firm on Earth and be hired instantly.

This woman in the vision house was smaller, with dirty-blonde hair and a plain face that was somehow still unmistakably Gilenyia's. She glanced at Madeline when she came toward her. "So the Kakri girl managed to kill me," Gilenyia said.

"Not yet." Madeline studied her. Gilenyia looked almost human . . . like a simpler, plainer version of herself. Madeline reached out with her mind and touched her. Yes. This was Gilenyia if she had been human rather than Elenil. Strange.

"Would you like to see yourself as an Elenil?" Gilenyia asked. "In our minds such things are possible. I can show you what it would be like." She looked Madeline up and down. "It's not too late for such a thing, you know."

Madeline started. "You can't have children," she said. It was a realization that came of exploring the woman's physiology for the healing. It was one of the laundry list of things about Gilenyia's body that Madeline could choose to alter.

"No," Gilenyia said. "This is not the Elenil way. You must have noticed how few young Elenil there are."

She had, in fact, noticed. Hanali, Gilenyia, and Rondelo were all considered young, despite being hundreds of years old. "You are sad about it," Madeline said.

Gilenyia sighed. "Not that it matters now, Ms. Oliver, since I am at death's door, but yes, I am sad about it. Why do you think I have taken such keen interest in Hanali's pets?"

"Um, sorry to interrupt." Jason stood in the doorway, looking terrified. "Uh, hi, Gilenyia. Best wishes for your health and everything, but also you probably shouldn't fight my fiancée, so this is on you a little."

"Are you okay, Jason?" Madeline asked. "You look . . . frightened."

"You have a visitor," Jason said. "He's asking for you. Inside our minds, you know. Which creeps me right out. He said he can't go this deep, so he sent me and, well, I don't like it. At all."

Madeline put her hand on Gilenyia's shoulder. "I'm going to do my best to save you."

"Why, child? I was taking you to prison and your likely death. Why spare a moment of energy on me?"

"Because I still can," Madeline said. She knew other people thought it was stupid, but right now that really was her whole motivation. She was going to do a good thing for someone else because she had the ability to do so. That's it.

She followed Jason through the strange mind-house, and they found themselves in the clearing again, standing over Gilenyia's body. The whole thing made her feel nauseous and disoriented.

Standing beyond them, halfway in the woods, was the tree man from her vision—Patra Koja. His beard of leaves rustled in the wind, and the moss on his antler branches swayed. His small eyes, like dark-red berries, swiveled to follow her movements. She could see in this better light that his skin was covered in fine green scales, and his thick tail dragged on the ground behind him.

"We meet again," she said.

"Child." He looked at Jason, then at Gilenyia. "Why are you using Elenil magic for healing?"

"She's hurt," Madeline said.

Patra Koja grunted. A bird landed in his branches, but it didn't seem to bother him. "The Elenil magic is predicated on a limited system. It is artificial. There is only so much magic, so if I want benefit, someone else must receive detriment."

"Yeah!" Jason said. "And Madeline doesn't have the strength to take on Gilenyia's wounds. Tell her, tree dude!" He paused and looked at Patra Koja's tail. "Or alligator dude. Whatever."

"Nor does anyone have strength enough to heal her," the strange man replied. "Unless they wish to give their life for her. Not that it isn't noble, but is it necessary?"

"What do you mean?" Madeline asked. "You can heal her without hurting someone else?"

"Of course," Patra Koja said. "Magic is not a closed system. That is a myth of the Elenil, designed to give them power. Magic is like a forest. Magic is like water, like wind, like fruit from a tree. If I take an apple from a tree, do I lessen it?"

"No," Madeline said.

"No," he repeated. "In fact, it may benefit the tree, for its seeds will travel and perhaps make another tree, which will have apples of its own. Elenil magic says you must chop down the tree and burn it for fuel. Aluvorean magic says there are enough apples for all."

"Please, then," Madeline said, "heal her."

"Not here," the plant man said. "You must bring her to me. When last we met in this space, I told you to come to me when you arrived in Aluvorea. But you did not. Bring her to me, and I will heal her."

"Okay," Madeline said. "I hope she can survive the journey."

"I hope you both will survive it," Patra Koja said. He studied Jason. "You have another path to travel."

"Uhhh, I don't think so," Jason said. "I stick with Madeline. It's a rule of ours." He scratched his head. "More or less."

"You must travel to Arakam," the plant man said, "the great dragon of Aluvorea. He will tell you the cost of helping Aluvorea. He will give you wisdom in what must be accomplished." He paused. "He will tell you how to save the Sunlit Lands."

"Yeah, but I don't care about saving the Sunlit Lands if it puts Madeline at risk."

"You come to me," Patra Koja said to Madeline. "The boy goes to Arakam. If he comes with you, I will not heal this woman. The greater good must be served. If Madeline does not save Aluvorea, then magic will go the way of the Elenil, and it will grow stagnant, and then it will die." With that he walked into the forest, disappearing into the shadow of the trees.

"No way," Jason said.

"Jason," Madeline said. "What if Patra Koja—"

"Arakam," Jason said. "The dragon's name is Arakam."

"The plant guy is named Patra Koja."

"He never said his name."

Madeline blushed. "He might have said something in the last vision I had."

"Oh." Jason put his hands on his hips. "We have to find a better system for sharing information here."

"What if there's another way of healing? What if he can heal me without someone else suffering?"

What if there was a way to change everything? For her to go home? She looked at Jason, begging him to understand her. And whether it was because they had become such good friends or because they were in this psychic space and could understand each other more easily, Jason did seem to get it. Another avenue of possible healing for her changed the equation.

"So I'm going to go learn how to save Aluvorea. And you're going to go save the Elenil who was trying to enslave and probably kill us."

She grinned. Relief washed over her. "That's right."

"Sounds like old times," he said. "Let's go."

19
KIDNAPPED

They have forgotten that they are one people.
There is anger. There is murder. There is even war.

FROM "THE GOOD GARDENER," AN ALUVOREAN STORY

✦

Darius woke in a room scarcely larger than a coffin, on a narrow, uncomfortable bed. The Elenil would never allow a room like this in one of their homes, so he knew immediately that he was in a prison, or worse. His head felt thick and his stomach uneasy. He couldn't believe Hanali had poisoned him. He put his hand on the wall as he sat up, and he felt a heavy rumbling on the other side.

"The engine," a deep voice said. "Our room is beside the engine."

"Break Bones!"

The great Scim warrior sat hunched in the corner, like some sort of terrifying gargoyle brought to life. "They captured me outside the city. They knew precisely where I was and picked me up with little trouble. I blame our little friend Mud."

Darius rubbed his head. "Could be. He took me straight to Hanali."

"The boy has always shown more cunning than courage."

Darius swung his legs over the side of the bed. "Future leader."

"Probably," Break Bones admitted. "There is a small window at that end of the room."

The window was round, half the size of a basketball. Darius turned his neck so he could get his face close to the glass. They were in the air. Far up in the air. The ground below couldn't be seen, only massive clouds. "Headed to Pastisia," Darius said.

Break Bones shrugged. "Unless this vessel counts as Pastisian territory, in which case, we're there already."

"What do we do?"

Break Bones pointed to the door. "Unlocked. Whatever we want, I suppose. Throw ourselves overboard, puncture the dirigible. Light a fire. Fight to the death."

"I won't be fighting to the death unless I have Archon Thenody in front of me. I have words for him before I die."

Break Bones grinned. "I have promises to keep myself. Why, I promised your friend Wu Song that I would kill him, for that matter. He has made this a difficult promise to attend to, or indeed, to desire to attend to."

Darius laughed. This was a promise Break Bones liked to bring up occasionally just to harass him. Break Bones knew that if he ever came after Jason or Madeline, Darius would be standing in his way, no matter what.

"Oh, and to deliver Madeline's lifeless body into his arms, I seem to recall."

The grin widened, revealing Break Bones's big yellow teeth. "I hate to die leaving promises unkept."

Darius grinned back, then looked under his bunk. "They've taken the Sword of Years."

Break Bones frowned. "I assumed so the moment I saw you unconscious on the bed."

"We should go see what is what," Darius said.

"Agreed."

Break Bones stood as Darius moved toward the door, but he was too big for the two of them to come to the door at the same time. "After you," the monstrous warrior said, bowing low, his long fingernails pointing toward the door, his tusks protruding into the path. Darius had never seen him out of his war skin. But then again, they had been at war since Darius arrived.

Darius inclined his head and stepped past the Scim, opening the door a crack. No guards. He supposed there was no reason to guard them when they were flying so high. What was he going to do, take a bedsheet and try to parachute?

The hallway was narrow and paneled with polished wood. Luxurious but tight. "Servants' quarters," Break Bones said. That was probably correct. At least, there was no way the Elenil would stay in a room like this themselves. But this was not an Elenil airship, he reminded himself. The Elenil didn't enjoy air travel. They had the ability to create airships or grow birds large enough to ride, but they never did.

They came to a split staircase and had to make a choice: up or down. "Up," Darius said. "Servants are usually below decks, yes?"

Break Bones shrugged. Such things were outside his experience and below his interest. "Up or down, left or right, wake me when we find the enemy."

So up they went. Then up again. The stairs led into a large, bright room, full of dining tables and windows. In fact, the whole front wall was window, revealing the full vista of the clouded sky. Hanali stood with his back to them, watching the clouds, his gloved hands clasped behind him. Without his sword, Darius would have to throttle Hanali with his bare hands, but so be it.

He had taken only three steps when Hanali turned, a smile on his face. "Ah! You've awakened. Pleasant dreams, no doubt." He gestured to a table laden with food and drink. "Sit! Eat!"

They did neither. Hanali's face fell in disappointment. He clapped his hands, and a human servant appeared. "Bring a larger chair for our Scim companion." He looked pained. "I should have thought of that before you woke, Master Break Bones. It will be here in a moment, though."

"I'm going to kill you," Darius said.

"So dramatic! Come now, we have some time before we arrive in Pastisia—let's not sully it with murder. Sit, please. Ah yes, there you go." He lifted a teapot, one eyebrow raised. "Tea?"

"No," Darius said sullenly. The idea that Hanali had drugged him earlier made him angry, but he realized that Hanali offering him a drink now was meant to do just that. Hanali wanted him angry, wanted him off balance. Darius choked down his rage.

Hanali poured himself a cup. "Now, now, it's perfectly safe, I promise you." He took a sip, then set the cup near Darius. "No hard feelings, Darius." Darius didn't move toward the cup. "Well, I must say there are some hard feelings about breaking the vase. A family heirloom, you know. Hardly seems a fair price in exchange for a small loss of consciousness."

"Maybe you should have put away your breakables before poisoning me."

"Touché."

The chair came for Break Bones, and he sat in it immediately, loaded his plate, and began to eat. "Why the Pastisians?" he asked. "Have you sunk so low that the necromancers are a safe wager? None of the people of the Sunlit Lands are allied with them."

"Because none are so bold," Hanali said. "Once Thenody is deposed, we shall be allied with them. What a power we shall be! All our enemies will be crushed."

Break Bones wiped the grease from his mouth with the back of his hand. "The Scim, you mean."

Hanali waved this comment away. "Scim, the Southern Court, the Aluvoreans, it doesn't matter who."

"It matters quite a lot to the Scim."

"Bah. You're the ones who want to bring a century of darkness to the Elenil."

"A millennium," Break Bones corrected.

"This is why you are here," Hanali said. "I wish to be allied with the Scim as well, Break Bones. But this will be tricky. It will require the forgiving of old debts. We will have to set aside our bloody history to build a bloodless future."

Darius grunted. "Is that why you took the Sword of Years from me? Afraid it will work its revenge magic on you?"

"In a way," Hanali admitted. "I feared it would be used before you had a chance to hear the plan. My desire is to build an alliance between the Scim, the Elenil, and the Pastisians. We will storm Far Seeing together and remove the corrupted leadership. Darius, you can kill Thenody or do whatever you think is just. Then we will melt down the sword and start again. Let the past be past."

"You get to decide that, do you?" Break Bones asked. "You feel sorry for your past injustices, so now we don't bring up centuries of abuse at your hands?"

"At *my* hands?" Hanali looked at him in shock. "Surely not."

Break Bones tore off a leg of chicken. "Come now. Let us not begin our friendship with lies and half-truths."

"Are we friends, then?"

"Doubtful," Break Bones said. "Doubtful indeed."

They were interrupted by the arrival of Mrs. Raymond, who wore her plain dress and the long sleeves and gloves preferred by the Elenil. She went directly to Darius, ignoring Hanali's greetings. "I did not know about the tea," she said. "Hanali had told me only that he intended to convince you to join us on this trip, not that he would drug or kidnap you."

Darius believed her. He didn't know why. The relationship between her and the Elenil was strange: formal yet familiar. He had not seen such a relationship between many humans and Elenil.

"I have a question," she said, "if I may."

Hanali nodded. "I have said my piece, and there is time to consider before we arrive. Perhaps some other topic will help keep our minds from difficult decisions."

Mrs. Raymond took Darius's hand. "We were talking of fantasy worlds, and you mentioned Meselia when you spoke of not telling Madeline of your plan to kill the archon. You didn't quite finish your thought, and I would very much like to know what you had to say."

"Oh." His face burned. His speech seemed foolish now that he knew it had all been to allow the poison to do its work, that Hanali had merely been waiting for him to fall over. "Have you read *The Gold Firethorns?*"

She nodded. "I know it well."

Hanali barked a laugh. "It is so delightful listening to humans discuss their literature."

"Because you are illiterate," Mrs. Raymond snapped.

Hanali, chastened, took a sip of his tea and moved a small roasted bird onto his plate. "Reading and writing are impractical when I can dictate my words to a messenger bird."

"Indeed," Mrs. Raymond said, purposely turning away from him to make it clear he wasn't welcome in the conversation. "*The Gold Firethorns*," she said. "When Lily becomes a traitor to the Eagle King and is banished."

"Yes," Darius said. "And you remember Prince Ian?"

"Of course. Lily's love, and the reason for her banishment. A noble soul."

"'The noblest soul in Meselia.' And *Black*," Darius said. "Black and a hero. For the first time, as I read, I saw someone filling a space in a book that might conceivably be my space. I tried to explain this to Madeline—Madeline, who I love and who loves me—and she didn't understand. She started to tell me all about Ged in the Earthsea books and how he was a person of color too."

Mrs. Raymond looked down at her hands. "No. I suppose she wouldn't understand. Not at first."

A mounting excitement came over Darius. He had tried to explain this so often and never found someone who quite got it, who understood both the joy of fantasy worlds and the feeling of being cast as the villain in every single one of them. "Meselia felt real to me in a way that other places hadn't. I love Narnia and Middle-earth and Earthsea and all the rest, but it was work for me to come to them. I had to learn to see things from their point of view, to turn my head to the side to understand. But in *The Gold Firethorns*, for the first time I could see without all the work. And not just the characters, not just Prince Ian, but the profound sadness at the end of the book, with Ian missing and Lily banished, never to return to Meselia. Then, when I picked up the fourth book, I knew it would all be undone. That some old British woman wouldn't understand that you can't wash away all the tragedy in a few sentences in the next book, that Ian can't appear in chapter one and bring Lily back from exile and start a new adventure. There had to be consequences—there had to be an acknowledgment that the world is broken and it doesn't magically get repaired just because we wish it to be. But that's the way these books are, and I prepared myself for some magical cure, knowing the author didn't understand."

"And then?"

"And then I started book four, *The Skull and the Rose*, and Lily didn't return. Ian wasn't found. And in book five, *Graceful Lily's Kingdom*, she does return, only to discover that Ian has married someone else, and they both know it can never be between them. Even though his marriage was for the politics of Meselia and he doesn't love his wife. Even though he and Lily have pledged their lives to one another in a hundred different ways, they can't be married. It's sad, tragic. But it's real. Madeline loved all the Meselia books, but her favorite was always the last one, the last published one, anyway—*The Azure World*—where all evil is defeated and heroes from across time unite to destroy Kotuluk. But my favorite is Madeline's least favorite—*The Skull and the Rose*. The book that remembers that the world is broken, where hard choices are made and heroes are so close to villains that more than once I wasn't sure what the right decision would be."

"You see the world through different eyes," Mrs. Raymond said. "You fear Madeline will not understand."

"I fear she'll teach me to see it through her eyes," Darius said. "I fear she'll douse my anger. She'll prevent revenge and thus justice. I love her too much to make her party to what I plan to do. It will destroy her picture of me. She sees me as King Arthur on the path to victory, the white knight who brings right instead of might."

"She may know you better than you think," Mrs. Raymond said. "I suspect you stopped reading too early in *The Once and Future King*. That great king Arthur, who united the kingdom and created the Round Table, also ordered the death of many infants to cover up an old transgression of his own."

Darius's eyes went wide. "What?!"

"Even the great among us make mistakes, Darius. Madeline surely knows this. Do not think she is not angry, just because she chooses a different solution. And do not do her the disservice of dismissing her. You are twined together. Anyone can see it. Why make a decision without your soul companion? Why not get her insight, even if you reject it? Would she advise you to walk this violent path? Or find another?"

A shadow flickered across Hanali's face so quickly that Darius thought he might have imagined it, because suddenly the Elenil was laughing heartily and pounding the table. Once all eyes were on him, he wiped his own eyes with a lavender handkerchief, as if dabbing away tears. "I have to tell him," Hanali said. "I am sorry, Mary, I cannot hold back any longer."

"Do not call me Mary. How many times must I say it to you?"

His dazzling smile widened. "But in this case, it's important. Darius Walker, allow me to introduce you to Mary Patricia Wall, the author of the Meselia books."

"What?!"

Mary Patricia Wall had been missing for years. She was one of Darius's favorite authors, and Madeline's favorite by far. They had talked more than once about where she could be, what could have happened. Madeline had dreamed about finding the legendary final book in the series. Darius had bought Madeline a signed copy of the first Meselia book because Mads loved it so much, and he loved her so much. It had been hard to find, because it wasn't like new ones were coming to the market. It had been a surprising triumph to find that book, and now here he was, having found the missing author herself.

So she had been missing because . . . because she had been here, in the Sunlit Lands? So much fell into place. The books had that ring of truth to them because they were partly based on real events, no doubt. A hidden history of the Sunlit Lands, maybe, or Mary Patricia Wall's written wishes for how life in the Sunlit Lands could have been, instead of the complicated thing it was. And this woman had been at the core of it. The first human to greet Madeline when she entered the Sunlit Lands. Darius couldn't believe it. He stared at her. He knew it was rude, but he couldn't stop staring at her face, as if it would reveal more details. The only thing her face revealed, though, was extreme annoyance at Hanali for sharing her story. Darius tried to think of something more to say, but the words didn't come. He was in shock. Finally he managed to say, "But she's been missing for decades."

Hanali dismissed this with a wave. "Missing to you, perhaps. She has been right here all along. The poor woman wrote the Meselia books while she was in exile from the Sunlit Lands—long story—and she came sprinting back the moment I opened the door, no questions asked."

"Like Lily," Darius said. Mrs. Raymond stared daggers at Hanali.

"Precisely like Lily, from what I know of it," Hanali said.

"But why? Why 'Mrs. Raymond'?"

"It is my married name," she said. "My husband, and the father of our child, is Ian Raymond, king of Pastisia. I am Mary Raymond now and have been for some years."

"Her Majesty, Queen Mary Raymond," Hanali said, not even trying to disguise his glee.

She looked away. "Or so I should have been, if things had been different." She looked back to Darius, her gaze softening. "Perhaps I did not understand some things, like your Madeline."

Darius leaned back in his chair, struck mute with wonder. Not only was Mrs. Raymond Mary Patricia Wall, she was married to the necromancer king of Pastisia. He couldn't have been more surprised if Hanali had announced that he was going to wear only simple brown robes from now on. It went against everything he thought he knew about this woman. He had assumed her to be merely a sort of servant, doing a drudge job in the Sunlit Lands because of some deal she had made years before. But that was not the case at all. She had some other reason to be here, and Darius had no idea what it could be.

Mrs. Raymond stood, moving out of the dining room before Darius could say another word. "We will dock in Pastisia soon," she said over her shoulder. "I will send servants to dress you appropriately."

"Wait, *your* servants?" Darius asked, his voice full of wonder.

"You should have seen the ceremony when they welcomed us aboard," Hanali said, delighted.

"A good woman," Break Bones said, licking his fingers. "Strong. Forthright in her opinions. And it appears she also hates Hanali. I say again, a good woman. A pity she is married to a necromancer."

20
FELES EX MACHINA

I will teach them about the fruits that are good to eat,
and I will show them where the wild berries grow.
I will show them the cool places to lie on hot days, and
the shady spots in the river that are best for catching fish.

FROM "THE GOOD GARDENER," AN ALUVOREAN STORY

✛

Okay, David, spill," Jason said. "You seem pretty chummy with the Alu-whatever-eans, so did you know they were about to betray us and turn me over to the Elenil?"

"Whoa," David said. "You know me better than that, bro. I was fighting them right alongside you. Or I should say, I was fighting them while you were sitting nearby, not doing much."

"He speaks truth," Baileya said, "yet does not answer the question."

David took a deep breath. "No, man, I had no idea. You know I wouldn't send you off to your doom without fighting every single soldier along the way."

"Good enough for me," Jason said. It was, too. David had been a good friend to him back in Far Seeing, and Jason had never known him to be anything other than honest.

The Aluvoreans Lin and Lamisap had been suddenly eager to help them with various things, as if they hadn't just tried to turn them over to the Elenil. Lin had called for two urudap—animals that looked like a cross between a yak and a shrub—to pull Gilenyia through the forest, and a third that Madeline could ride on. Even with the Queen's Breath on her neck, she was weak. She could breathe better, could talk better, but she was tired. Slow. Jason was reminded that she was sick whenever he looked at her. No, not sick. Dying.

The urudap were slow-moving, intensely stupid animals. One of them had walked face-first into a tree and then stood there, unable to figure out where to go, until Lin grabbed it by the scruff and turned its head away from the trunk. You would have thought she'd made the tree disappear by the shocked expression on the urudap's face.

Lin had offered to lead them to Patra Koja. "No," Madeline said. "After you tried to turn us over to the Elenil? We will find the way ourselves."

"Please," Lin had begged. "Your presence here . . . Lamisap and I have risked much to bring you. Please let us help you, please."

Madeline had never been as hard as she needed to be in moments like this. Her anger wavered, and she agreed to let Lin join them. "You move ahead as our scout, though," she said.

Jason and Baileya had purposely cornered David and fallen back from the others so they could have this conversation. Jason regretted it a little now, because of course David wouldn't betray him like that. But he had needed to hear it said aloud.

David said, "I should catch up with Madeline. She and Shula are going to have to move Gilenyia, and . . . and it looks like they might need help."

Jason had hurt David's feelings. Of course he had. Jason awkwardly grabbed David's wrist, preventing him from leaving just yet. "David. Hey, I didn't—"

David grinned, then hugged him. "We're all good, Jason. Go slay that dragon or whatever."

"Slay? I'm pretty sure I'm just supposed to talk to him. Which is good, because I'm more of a talker than a slayer."

"The Elenil will be coming to look for Gilenyia soon," David said. "You'll want to get moving."

"Thanks," Jason said. They clasped forearms.

"War Party, to war!" David said.

"Three Musketeers, unite!" Jason said, laughing.

David disappeared down the track made by the urudap. "I still don't know why Kekoa wanted us to pretend to be French dudes!"

Jason watched him go. The reminder of Kekoa made him feel bad. They hadn't even tried to connect with him yet. And it wasn't just Kekoa, who could more or less take care of himself—Ruth was with him too, and she was all of nine years old or something. And Kekoa had sent word asking for help, which had to mean he was in pretty serious trouble. Jason felt torn that they hadn't found a way to get out there and bring Kekoa and Ruth back. Not that they hadn't been busy, but still. Something about the whole thing reminded him of Nightfall, and it stuck him in the gut like a knife. That poor Scim kid, killed by the Elenil right in front of him, and he couldn't do anything to stop it. He shook himself. He hoped Kekoa and Ruth were okay.

Baileya squeezed his shoulder. He looked up at her, still amazed that this tall, powerful woman was his fiancée. "The Elenil," she said.

"Yeah, yeah, 'Faster, Wu Song.' It's time to run," he said. She laughed.

"Delightful Glitter Lady has strayed into the underbrush. I will retrieve her."

"Thank you."

She flashed a glorious smile at him. "This will be a story of great value, Wu Song."

Sure. If they managed to survive it. Of course, among Baileya's people, that just meant all her stories would go to her people. The story of her death would care for the people of her family by buying them food and shelter. None of which changed the fact that he had no idea where they were going. Unlike Madeline, he didn't have mystical knowledge, or even a very good sense of direction.

Lamisap came to him, hesitating, then running her hand through her mossy hair. "Can I be of service, friend?"

Friend. Ha! And after she had just tried to turn him over to the Elenil.

"How does one find a dragon?" he asked, taking on the exact mannerisms of his history teacher back home. "Yes. Does one look for smoke in the woods? Or merely cry out, 'O dragon, where are you?'" He raised his eyebrows at Lamisap, as if expecting an answer.

"I do not know this word, *dragon*," she said.

"I thought the magic of the Sunlit Lands translated everything for everyone."

"For the Aluvoreans, it is different. We must learn the Elenil language."

"Oh yeah." He had forgotten that the magic of the Sunlit Lands made him speak flawless Elenil. He wondered if there were words he couldn't say. Like in Chinese, words like *guanxi* or *lihai* didn't really translate. He wanted to experiment. Even though this wasn't the time. "Effervescent," he said. Hmmm. Of course they had a word for effervescent. "Fop." Nope, that seemed to work fine. "Antidisestablishmentarianism." He looked at the Aluvorean woman. She had no idea what he was saying, but he definitely felt like the right words were coming. "Never mind. The question, Llama Nap—"

"Lamisap."

"That's what I said. The question, L-person, is how we find this Arakam."

"Arakam? Oh, that is easy enough. You need only decide if you would rather brave the kaska shram or the raskan . . . for Arakam lives near the great allae to the north."

"Ah," Jason said. "I have no idea what you're saying, but I am going to guess that you mean whether we want to go through a lollipop forest or a grove of money trees, and that the dragon lives near an amusement park to the north. Does that sound about right?"

"I do not know these words," Lamisap said.

"Yeah, I didn't think so." He called for Baileya. "Do you want to brave the kaska shram or the raskan?"

She emerged from the forest holding Delightful Glitter Lady in her arms. "I like the sound of the kaska shram. It is more poetic. 'Baileya, Wu Song, and the Kaska Shram.' Yes. It is a fine name for a story."

Jason nodded, turned back to Lamisap. "So. What does the kaska shram entail?"

"The carnivorous forest, which devours all who enter."

"Huh. Baileya, we're gonna go with the raskan. What is the raskan?"

"The fields of the firethorns," Lamisap said. "The thorns catch upon your flesh, then they roast you with their flames so that your body may be used as fertilizer for new growth."

"Well, it's no lollipop forest, I'll give you that," Jason said. "You better give me directions to both of them, just in case."

"You have but to walk north to enter the carnivorous forest. Or if you prefer the firethorns, turn to the east when you reach the carnivorous forest, and when you find the firethorns, pass north. Whichever way you—"

"Wait. How will I know I've found the firethorns?"

"When you see the fires," she said simply.

"Maybe I should be taking notes," Jason said. "Okay, so after I get eaten and/or burned to death, where do I go from there?"

"Follow the river north until you come to a great waterfall. Arakam lives beneath it."

"Got all that?" he asked Baileya.

But Baileya was watching the woods again. The last time she had done that, they were being secretly surrounded by the Elenil. She put Dee on the ground, and the miniature rhino came running to Jason. He scooped her up.

"What is it, Baileya?"

"Not the Elenil," she said. She narrowed her eyes. "Nor my brother."

Lamisap froze. "Roots and stone," she said. "It is a Zhanin. But how did he get past the sentinel plants?"

Baileya spun the two halves of her spear and connected them into one. "Wu Song. Take Delightful Glitter Lady and run to the north. I will come for you."

He didn't doubt that. She always had. "Okay, carnivorous forest it is," he said. She didn't answer, a sure sign that she had given her full attention to whatever was coming toward them. "I'll take the plant lady with me."

Lamisap didn't look well. Her green color was fading, and she had fallen to her knees. What was going on? He grabbed her by the arm, yanked her to her feet. Delightful Glitter Lady started twisting in his arms, fighting him. "Dee, calm down," he said, but then she was on the ground, running away from him and toward a new, crashing sound coming from the woods.

Two Zhanin warriors strode from the woods, dressed in their strange green leather, their hair tied and knotted at the back of their heads. As Dee ran toward them, the magic that kept her small wore off, and she rolled over one of the warriors like a boulder.

"C'mon, c'mon," Jason said, trying to get the Aluvorean moving. He felt bad not staying to fight, but we all need to be aware of what we do best.

The rough voice of the Zhanin soldier filled the entire clearing. "I come seeking Wu Song and Madeline Oliver. The Zhanin have found them guilty of creating an imbalance in magic. They must pay with their lives."

The Aluvorean woman had collapsed. Jason pulled her behind a large log. The green had almost completely faded from her skin, leaving her an increasingly pale, sickly white, like a plant without sunlight. The moss that made up her hair began to fall out in clumps. The Zhanin could turn off magic. That's why Dee was the size of an Earth rhino, and it must be why Lamisap was struggling to stay upright.

"They are not here," Baileya said, holding her weapon across her chest.

"Do not lie to me, Kakri woman. We track them by the residue of their magic. The boy has a binding agreement with the Elenil, and we can see it. The girl has broken hers, but there is still a scent of her magic on her."

Baileya raised her voice, making Jason flinch. "Do not think I am some magic-empowered coward like the Elenil. My skills as a warrior are hand won and honed daily. I will not fall before your blade merely because you remove all magic from the area."

"I have no quarrel with you."

"Yet you attempt to murder my betrothed."

The weather-beaten face of the warrior went suddenly impassive. "It is the law, Kakri woman. I am not judge but only the one who metes out the penalties the judge demands."

"Can I appeal to the Supreme Court?" Jason called, immediately regretting it. The Zhanin man looked his way, and so did Baileya, a look of exasperated anger on her face.

"So he is here," the Zhanin said, and stepped toward him, a massive cutlass in one muscled hand.

Baileya moved to intercept him. "Run, Wu Song, why are you still here? Run!" The Zhanin tried to bully past her, but she planted one end of her spear and used it as a mini pole vault, slamming both feet into his chest and knocking him backward. She landed easily on her feet. "I warned you, Zhanin. It has been many years since I was bested in one-on-one combat."

Lamisap groaned, her eyelids fluttering. Jason pulled her arm over his shoulder. "I think we should run. Do you think we should run? Yes? Okay." He dragged her into the woods. He wasn't sure how far he could carry her, and he wasn't making much headway. The path he was forging would be easy to follow, too. A massive crashing came from beyond the meadow, followed by enraged bellowing from an out-of-control rhino. He snickered at the thought of one Zhanin warrior trying to stop Dee.

About thirty yards into their journey, Lamisap started to regain consciousness. By fifty her color started to return. Another ten feet and she was standing on her own. She rested a hand against a tree trunk, gathering herself. "You stopped to help me when I betrayed you," she said.

"My dad always said I was a big dummy. Plus, I've got a weak spot for green people. The Green Giant. The Hulk. The Green Power Ranger. Uh . . . the Grinch. I don't know, all the green people."

"I will help you pass the kaska shram," she said.

"Oooh, I almost forgot the Teenage Mutant Ninja Turtles."

"I do not know many of these words."

"How do the Elenil have words for Teenage Mutant Ninja Turtles? I'm gonna have to ask Hanali about this." A shout and the clash of steel came from behind them. "Okay, we better get moving."

"This way," Lamisap said, and started racing through the trees.

Jason tried to keep up, but the branches kept whipping him in the face, and the ground was uneven. He was nowhere near as fast as Lamisap. She seemed to move as easily as a deer, leaping and weaving through the narrow spaces between trees without a moment's thought. Soon he had completely lost her.

She noticed that he couldn't keep up and waited for him. "I will go ahead and make sure the way is safe. Follow me as quickly as you are able." She disappeared into the trees.

In less than three minutes he had no idea which way to go anymore. He had followed in the direction she had gone, but there was no path, and she didn't leave any evidence of her passing. He tried looking for broken stems and footprints and all the stuff he had seen in movies, but it didn't work. "No bread crumbs, either," he muttered to himself. He decided shouting was probably not a good idea, and he was out of breath anyway. He put his hands on his head and tried to get his breath back, while walking vaguely in the direction Lamisap had gone.

"I wouldn't go any farther that way if I were you," a voice said.

Jason looked around. He didn't see anyone. "Oh yeah? Why's that?"

"There's a Zhanin just out of earshot there. There were three of them, you know. One is fighting your unicorn, and another is fighting the Kakri woman. A third one is just ahead, waiting for you. He already has your Aluvorean friend."

"I barely know her," Jason said. "Although I have to admit I know what she looks like, unlike my present company. For all I know, you could be an invisible Zhanin warrior trying to trick me."

"How would that trick you? If I were invisible and already standing beside you, would I not kill you and be done?"

"I don't know. Maybe you're the dumbest of the three Zhanin. Ever think of that?"

"Hmm," said the voice. "Getting bored now."

"Wait, where are you?"

"Humans," the voice said disdainfully. "Never looking up."

Jason looked into the branches of the tree above him. A tortoiseshell cat lounged on a sun-dappled branch. The tip of her tail twitched gently, and her eyes were closed in that I-might-be-napping sort of mystery face cats put on sometime.

"Are you the cat, or should I keep looking?"

The cat's eyes opened halfway. "Excuse you. I am not a cat."

Um. Jason looked around again. Nothing but trees. "I can see your mouth moving when you talk, though."

"Yes, yes, I'm the one talking, but I am not a cat."

"Oh." Okay. Well, the Elenil were notoriously bad at animal classifications. They called Delightful Glitter Lady a unicorn, and they called unicorns rhinoceroses. "So you're a . . . tiger? Lion?"

The cat moved her eyes to look at him with such a slow, deliberate intensity that he could feel exactly how annoyed she was to have to explain this to him. "Are lions cats?"

"Big cats. Yeah, I guess."

"Tigers?"

"Sure."

"I am not a cat. Therefore I cannot be a lion or a tiger. QED."

"QED?"

"Quod erat demonstrandum."

"I know, I know. From math class."

"From Latin," the cat said dismissively.

Oh hey! The Elenil magic hadn't translated the Latin.

"So what are you?"

"Rude," the cat said. "Where I come from it is considered polite to ask someone only *who* they are, not *what* they are."

"Okay, who then?" Jason asked.

"I am Remi."

"I'm Wu Song. Jason."

The cat closed her eyes. Her tail kept twitching.

Jason waited for her to say something more. "So I shouldn't go that way?"

"I wouldn't."

"Should I go back the way I came?"

"I wouldn't do that, either."

"What would you do?"

The cat opened her eyes again. "It seems likely I would sit in a tree and take a short nap."

"But if you weren't a cat, I mean."

"I'm not a cat."

Oh, right. "If you were a human, I mean."

The cat grunted. "Don't be gauche."

Jason leaned against a tree trunk. "What would you do, if you were me? That's what I'm trying to ask."

"I would ask someone for help, probably. Because I would recognize that I was a helpless baby lost in the woods."

"Remi?"

"Yes?"

"Could you help me out here?"

Remi sighed and stood on the branch. She put her back half up in the air and stretched her front paws out as far as she could, her claws kneading the bark of the tree. "I don't suppose I'll get any rest until I do." Then she unfurled her wings and flew to the ground, lighting at Jason's feet.

The wings folded up again, tucking tight against her back. They were covered in feathers that were the same color as her fur: a patchwork collection of white and brown and tan. Jason had to admit it was surprising. The Sunlit Lands always threw a new twist at you right when you thought you had it all figured out. "You have wings," Jason said. He found that restating the ridiculous things happening around him made them feel more real.

"All my life," Remi replied.

"So you're a flying cat."

"I am not a cat," she said crossly.

"A winged cat, I mean. I'm just saying, a cat with wings, not an ordinary cat."

Remi sat up straight, her green eyes piercing. "Do cats have wings?"

"No."

"Do I have wings?"

"Yeah, you sure do."

"Then I am not a cat. QED."

"I can't argue with that logic."

"No. You certainly cannot." Remi licked her front paw for a minute. Jason waited patiently. "Let us free your green friend from the Zhanin. Then we will get you on your way, and I will take a nap."

"Great," Jason said. "Thanks."

Then he followed the flying not-a-cat into the deeper darkness of the trees.

21

PASTISIA

Stay away from Pastisia. Necromancers, dark wizards, reprobates, scoundrels, liars, and thieves. And those are just the children.

LENIA OF THE SOUTHERN COURT

+

arius and Break Bones stood at the bank of windows in the airship's dining hall, looking down on the city as they came ever closer. The city was impressive. Tall, thin towers stood at multiple places. Unlike the white towers of Far Seeing, these were many different colors—lacquered red, blue, green, and yellow. They reminded Darius of the onion domes of Russia, but taller and more slender. A few had wide platforms built at the top. People glided between the towers in fantastical machines, hang gliders, and even suits with gliding material stitched between the arms and legs. Hanali had explained that the towers were for the airships to dock. Airships did not ever land—they moored at the towers. Passengers had to descend to the city below.

"I thought necromancers would have more lava, skulls, and smoke,"

Darius said. Darkness and lightning and evil caves were typical for necro-mancers in novels.

"Corrupted hearts can appear even in such an idyllic setting," Break Bones said. "We may yet see lava and skulls before the day is done."

Perhaps the strangest part of the city, however, was the arc of a gleaming crystal dome which stood behind it, rising over the city and disappearing into the heavens. Darius tried to get a clear look, but his mind rebelled at the sheer enormity of the thing. "What is that dome?" he asked Break Bones. "Is that part of the magic here?"

Break Bones looked at him sideways. "They are the crystal spheres," he said. "Surely you know of them."

"No." Darius looked at the way the sunlight seemed to strike the crystal at a strange angle. The dome went as far as he could see, disappearing in the distance.

"They are the sky of the Sunlit Lands. The nearest is the sphere of the sun. Then comes the moon. The stars are on another sphere, and then the four planets on increasingly thin and distant spheres. They each move in their own way and at their own speed."

"I thought all that talk of spheres and crystals was metaphorical."

"Not at all," Break Bones said. "Have you not noticed the way the stars move when they rise?"

He had, in fact, noticed that the stars—rather than the brightest appear-ing in all different places in the sky like back home—rose into the night sky like a blanket of lights being pulled over the roof of the Earth. "So this place is on the edge of the world. That crystal dome rises over the whole thing?"

"Indeed," Break Bones said. "Do not get too close to the edge. You do not want to fall into the gears of the world."

One of the strange side effects of life in the Sunlit Lands was that Darius was never certain when people were joking. But it was wise to be on the safe side. Darius would be sure to give the edge a wide berth.

Darius looked over his shoulder, making certain they were alone. "Break Bones. They have taken the Sword of Years and not made any offer to return it. My mask was taken by Rondelo and his people. Now we're wrapped up in someone else's schemes. I'm not here to put Hanali on the throne of the Elenil. What do you say?"

"I am with you, heart and soul," Break Bones said. "Whatever comes, the Scim people are crying out for freedom, not another Elenil ruler. Which means that even if we must secure our own freedom first, from Elenil or Pastisian or human or Aluvorean or whatever people may come, then so be it. I will not rest until there is justice for my people."

Darius studied the city below, looking for any information that might be of use. "I don't know their plans for us. I do know that necromancers are magicians who are in touch with the dead, and I can't help but think that's a bad idea."

"Hanali seems unwise to bargain with them. Yet he has always been a canny planner."

Darius stroked his chin. "War between the Pastisians and the Elenil might be to our advantage. But if we decide it isn't, then we leave here and go back to Far Seeing. Maybe we can still get face-to-face with the archon."

Break Bones let out a long sigh. "Ah, to battle into the heart of that tower was a joy I cannot bear to repeat. Would the terror in the eyes of the Elenil be the same as then, when they realized that for the first time in their history a Scim in war skin stood upon the stairs to the seat of their power? Ah, I think of it often. If Madeline and Wu Song had not been there, perhaps I would have already killed Archon Thenody."

Darius smiled at his friend. These rapturous remembrances of past battles always made him laugh, even if it wasn't how he remembered them. More than once he had awoken in the night, terrified by some nightmare of his battles against the armies of the Elenil. It might not be so bad if the Elenil didn't use human soldiers, but Darius felt an internal struggle that Break Bones didn't seem to. It wasn't something unique to the Sunlit Lands, either. Back on Earth he had often tried to set aside his anger about injustices he saw, but he struggled to do it. The injustices, even if you fought against them, might change, but they didn't disappear. In Madeline he had found peace. When he was with her, he felt like he was in some sort of bubble where injustice wasn't done to him. It was the strangest thing. She believed in him, and while she didn't understand all of his experiences, she didn't contribute to making them worse, ever. In fact, she seemed to not only see who he was, but to see him as someone better than he was. How could he not fall in love with someone like that?

They drifted closer to the city. There were shouts and cries from the airmen as they prepared to connect the airship to the slender wire of the tower. The airmen wore tight black clothing, with heavy coats and boots, silver masks which covered their mouths, and thick goggles over their eyes. Darius hadn't seen a single one without them, and he had only seen the airmen climbing on the outside rigging of the ship. On the inside the ship had been largely empty since he and Break Bones had left their room, with the exception of when they were fitted for their uniforms.

"You look dashing," Hanali said, carefully entering the room. Hanali had to be careful, because he wore a cape with gigantic epaulets that swept up on either side of his head like ocean waves. It ended in a long, full train that dragged behind him. Darius could not imagine how Hanali had managed to get through the narrow passageways elsewhere on the ship. The Elenil turned slightly to each side, inviting a comment on his own clothing.

"You look . . . ornate," Darius said at last.

Hanali's face brightened. "Ornate! That is a new description." He looked Break Bones up and down. "And you, sir Scim. You look—"

"Uncomfortable?" Break Bones gave him a sour look. "Then your eyes have revealed reality to you."

Mrs. Raymond's servants had dressed Darius and Break Bones in crimson uniforms, the livery of the Queen's Guard. Darius had objected to this, not having aligned with her as a ruler, but she had assured him it was the only way he would be accepted in Pastisia—where he had not wanted to go in the first place. Nevertheless, he now wore heavy black boots that came nearly to his knees, with slim pants that tapered into the boots. A white shirt with silver buttons and a high grandfather collar, open at the front, was covered by a crimson jacket with gold trim and tails that fell midthigh behind him. The cuffs of the coat had been cut wide to make room for his shackles, so they fell easily behind the cloth, which covered them completely. He had to admit that "dashing" was likely the best word to describe him. He liked it. After he'd gotten dressed, he had found himself grinning in the mirror, and then he practiced several serious looks. He'd like Madeline to see him like this. He stood taller at the thought of it and grinned again. He looked like royalty, like someone in charge. Who knew uniforms would be such a good look for him?

Break Bones wore a similar uniform, which was less than flattering on the enormous Scim. He looked like someone had forced a pet to wear a Halloween costume. He strained and pulled and rearranged every few seconds. Darius had no doubt he would be tearing himself out of the uniform at the first opportunity.

"You have noticed, no doubt, that we are docking," Hanali said. "In a few minutes we shall disembark together with Mrs. Raymond. There are a few minor aspects of genteel behavior I wish to impress upon you, as humans are often ignorant of such things, and Scim often ignore them."

"Then ignore them I shall," Break Bones said.

Hanali frowned at him and then continued. "The king is to be treated with respect. He is not one to trifle with or to make flippant comments to. Thank the Majestic One that Wu Song is not with us, as that boy's mouth would be our end. Remember, these are necromancers—people of dark magic. They speak across years, across worlds, and across the barrier of death itself. They listen to the advice and ideas of the dead. They are a savage people, willing to cross any line for power. As such, they see death in a different way than others and will not think twice before killing you or, more importantly, me.

"But without their help, we will continue as we are: the Scim locked forever in their parasitic arrangement with the Elenil, living in darkness and poverty—at war, but afraid to strike a decisive blow. The Elenil, who could sweep over the Scim as a wave, will be unable to bring either justice or destruction to the Scim for fear of losing all. If the Pastisians intervene on the side of right, they could tip this whole war into our hands."

"*Our* hands?" Darius asked, skeptical.

"The Scim, of course," Hanali said. "Or close enough. Surely we can agree that the Scim would be better served with an open-minded Elenil such as myself on the throne?"

Mrs. Raymond entered, wearing a bright-red dress, fitted in the bodice and flaring slightly as it descended from her hips. She wore a simple, understated silver band on her forehead, which Darius took to be a crown. There was a black band on her left bicep. She was flanked on each side by a human teenager wearing the same crimson uniform as Darius and Break Bones. Hanali tried to turn toward her, but his train was too long and his shoulders too wide. "Forgive me, Your Majesty, I am not able to turn," he said.

"Keep your foolish titles to yourself, Hanali," she said, her voice severe. To Darius she said, "Has Hanali warned you to be respectful?"

"Yes."

"Then come with me, and we will make our arrival known. Darius and Break Bones, you will walk on my left and on my right. Do not speak unless spoken to. Hanali, once you manage to extricate your outfit from the airship you may join us. Remember that you are all here as my guests, but it has been years since I have come here. We have heard rumors the Pastisians are preparing for war, or Hanali would not be here. Things may not be as they once were, and I cannot promise you protection, only a fair hearing."

Hanali clapped his hands together in glee. "So exciting!"

"Come along," she said, pulling on long white gloves. She led them down a long passageway, then down several flights of stairs.

"Should we have weapons?" Darius asked, doing his best to stay close to her in the narrow passages.

"They would not save you," she said. But as they came to the door which appeared to be the exit, Darius saw the Sword of Years sitting upon a table, unsheathed, beside Break Bones's great stone ax. "Put it upon your belt," she said.

Darius did, noticing a narrow loop in the leather for the first time. He could not sheathe the sword. It would not be sheathed again until it had drunk the blood of all Elenil who had brought injustice upon the Scim. The moment he put his hand on the pommel a weight descended on him, nearly driving him to his knees. The sword was thirsty. It twitched against his hand, desperate to make its way backward through Mrs. Raymond's attendants, to where Hanali stood alone, his outfit touching both walls and the ceiling. Darius slid the thing into the loop of his belt and felt a small relief.

A wide, oval door—like an enormous egg set on its side—loomed before them. One airman stood inside, his silver mask expressionless. Through a glass porthole Darius could see another airman leaning forward, one hand on the hull of the ship, the other holding a long rope. To his left yet another airman, mirroring the second. The wind whipped the ship hard enough that it shuddered. Then the two airmen on the outside of the ship leapt toward the tower in unison. They grabbed hold of a long, flexible pole attached to the tower. It had holes in it—they threaded the ropes through them and pulled tight. Then other airmen did the same, tying the ship to the tower in fifteen or so places.

"May I open the door, lady?" the airman inside asked, bowing his head toward Mrs. Raymond.

She nodded, and he threw several locks and swung the door wide. The wind whipped into the cabin, fierce and cold. The two airmen at the tower reached long-handled hooks to loops in the metalwork alongside the door, then slid a long plank up the hooks and into the side of the ship. It fell into place with a thump. The airman beside them asked permission to be the first to disembark, which Mrs. Raymond granted. He ran down the plank, connecting cleverly concealed cables from the bottom of the plank onto the long hooks, which now served as handrails. Once he was on the tower itself, he bowed and gestured to Mrs. Raymond.

She looked to Darius. "My guards must precede me."

Darius did not hesitate. Heights didn't scare him, and neither did necromancers or swords or death, for that matter. He strode down the plank. The city was a long way down . . . he guessed forty stories or so. Okay, he might be a little scared of heights. This was definitely far enough up that he'd have time to regret his poor decisions before he hit the ground. The wind caused the plank to sway, and he nearly lost his footing. He grabbed for the rails and held them the rest of the way down. He wondered if he died here, if the necromancers would talk to him about it afterward, or if he'd be in their power in some way. He didn't want to find out. When his boots hit the platform, Darius nearly sagged in relief.

Break Bones came after, but slower, more careful. They stood at either side of the plank and waited for Mrs. Raymond. She walked down without a single look below, and when the wind blew the plank, she did not touch the rails, merely shifted her weight and continued walking with the practiced confidence of one who has done the same many times.

The top of the tower had no walls or barriers to keep one from the edge, the only barrier being one's fear or good sense. A trapdoor opened onto a set of stairs. Mrs. Raymond pointed to it, and Darius led the way. The moment he stepped into the stairway he shivered in thankfulness for the end of the monstrous wind. He followed the stairs down, one hand on the hilt of his sword. They led to a wide receiving room, which was empty of furniture but had windows all along one edge, each of them facing toward the city, as if the most important thing to know when you arrived was whatever was happening in the streets below. They were on the very edge of the city now, which stretched from this tower to the end of the world, the crystal sphere of the sky.

When they had all descended the tower, Mrs. Raymond arranged them. "The king will greet us here," she said. "He will decide who will continue into Pastisia and who will be sent away. If not the king himself, then certainly one of his advisors. Hanali, stand there. Darius, Break Bones, here on my right." When all were arranged to her satisfaction, facing two wide, black doors, she held her hands together at her waist. "Now be silent," she said.

Everyone stood still. There was not so much as the whisper of cloth. Darius could hear his own heartbeat, his own breathing. The double doors opened, and they did not make a sound either. There was only darkness beyond. Even with the light of the windows behind them, he couldn't see anything beyond the threshold of those doors.

Then a golden face appeared. A mask. The man who wore it was tall, at least six and a half feet, and the mask moved toward them with a smooth and sinister gliding. As the man stepped into the room, the shadows seemed to cling to him. It took Darius a moment to realize it was not shadows at all but black robes which covered him head to toe. As he moved, Darius saw flashes of the man's arms and legs, also clad in black, from his boots to his gloves. Darius's hand went without thinking to the hilt of his sword, and his hand clenched it, ready to pull it free, to cut through his belt if need be to get it into the air quickly enough to strike down this monster.

Mrs. Raymond curtsied low and did not rise again. Around Darius, all the soldiers took a knee. Break Bones, too. Even Hanali managed to lower himself to one knee. Darius could not do it. The vulnerability it would require . . . This man, this necromancer, would be able to tower over Darius and destroy him. The man was close enough now that he could see the black eyes behind the golden mask. They turned toward him, but only for a moment, then returned to Mrs. Raymond.

"Rise, my queen. How often I have told you to be like this boy, and to bow to no one, not even to me." His voice was powerful, almost hypnotic.

She stood to her feet. "Husband. How I have longed to see your face." She smiled. "And still I am unsatisfied."

"How I have longed for you to ascend the stairs of my throne and take your rightful place by my side. And yet you linger in the lands of the Elenil and play matron to human children."

"I am no queen," she said. "I cannot pay the proper price."

"In time," the necromancer said. "In time." To those assembled he said, "You may rise." He turned to study Darius. He did not speak, only held his eyes for a long minute. Mrs. Raymond watched him but did not say anything.

"He is all you have described," the man said. "Should I do him the favor of a quick death or let him suffer in this world?"

Darius held his tongue, but his grip on the sword tightened. He would not die here. Not when there was so much still to be done.

Mrs. Raymond clucked her tongue disapprovingly. "You know my answer to this."

"Indeed, my love, I do. Very well. Let him suffer." He looked at those assembled behind her. "I dismiss all but the Scim, the Elenil, and this one here, this Darius. All others may go about their business, but know that the eyes of the king are upon you, and do no injustice upon my people lest you pay the price."

It was as if every person in the place had been holding their breath. They exhaled and moved quickly to whatever their next task was. Darius didn't know what each of them would do but imagined some would be needed to unload, some to bear messages to the city below, some to make the ship ready for its next journey. "Come with me to my chambers," the king said, and led them along the windows to a cleverly disguised door, which led to another room much like this one, also windowed, but facing the world beyond the city. There were plush red chairs there and a high-backed chair like a throne. "Close the door," the king said to Darius. When it was closed a series of locks spun into place, and Darius could not see the way to open them. "Sit."

They each sat, Hanali by himself because no one could get near him with his voluminous outfit, Mrs. Raymond beside the necromancer, and Break Bones and Darius across from them. "I must ask you each one question," the necromancer said. "I will know if you lie, and you will not enter my city. I cannot abide a liar. I will kill you with my own two hands. Will you agree to answer my question honestly?"

"Of course," Hanali said, as if he had never told a lie in his entire life. Break Bones only nodded.

"Yes," Darius said.

"Very well," the necromancer said. "The question is a simple one. Who is the last person you killed? And what is their name, if you know it? You first, Elenil."

Hanali nodded, his lips pursed. "I believe, if you must know, that it was a human child, about a year ago. Her name was, I think, Saanvi. I had brought her from a horrific situation into the Sunlit Lands. She had learned some things about me she found distasteful and threatened to take them to the archon. I told her that if she insisted, I would need to send her back to the human world, and she attacked me with a knife. So I killed her."

"You were in danger from the knife," the necromancer said, clearly not believing that to be the case.

"No particular danger," Hanali said. "But there are certain standards which must be upheld."

"You are aware of the great grief you have caused in the taking of a life?"

"At the time I did not think much of it, Majesty. But in the recent past I have lost my own father, whose name was Vivi, son of Gelintel. In my mourning I have become more aware of what this great loss must feel like to others. I have always been a sensitive soul."

The necromancer king did not respond to this but turned his attention to Break Bones. "And you, brave warrior? Was it upon the battlefield?"

"It was, and I do not know his name. He fought with resolve, and there was a strong spirit to him. He was a good adversary. I crushed his skull. It was no great honor for him or for me, as it was a regular skirmish between the Scim and the Elenil. No great victory was won nor any great loss dealt to either side. I do not know but he may have been healed by Elenil magics. But I think not."

"Have you grieved him?"

"No more than is seemly. A moment's remembrance in a time such as this."

"I see." He turned his attention to Darius. "And you, child, have you killed?"

Darius clenched his teeth. He was more man than many others he had met in the Sunlit Lands, and he knew that he looked it today in his uniform. It rankled to be called a child. He had not killed before coming to the Sunlit Lands. But in his fight against the Elenil he had killed more than once. Often it was in battle, and the humans he had wounded were likely healed by the Elenil. There may have been one here or there who succumbed to their wounds, but if so he did not know of it. He knew that many of the soldiers he fought were as much victims as the Scim themselves, but on the other hand, they had stood on the battlefield with swords in their hands. There were days when he felt guilt over their deaths, but again, he wasn't sure they had died. He didn't hold himself responsible. And, he reminded himself, this was war. There would be casualties.

But one death he couldn't get out of his mind had happened on a night only a couple months ago, during the Festival of the Turning, when he had taken on the mantle of the Black Skull and led the Scim into the midst of the Elenil. Their magics were silent for a night, no healing available, and he had killed one of the long-lived Elenil. He'd run him through with his sword, and the Elenil's allies had swept him away into the castle, a castle called Westwind. Darius knew that this particular Elenil had not survived. He had been one of the few casualties, and the Elenil had mourned him and shouted his name as a rallying cry in their fight against the Scim.

"I have killed," Darius said. "I am not haunted by guilt for it either." Not much, he told himself. "The one I killed deserved his death, for he stood in the path of justice."

"Know you his name?"

"I do."

"Then say it, and let us remember this villain whom you dispatched with such stoicism."

Darius hesitated, glancing at Hanali and Break Bones. The Scim nodded. "His name was Vivi, son of Gelintel."

Mrs. Raymond's face fell, and Hanali leapt to his feet. Hanali was shouting something, enraged, trying to make his way to Darius, calling for blood. Break Bones jumped between them and held the Elenil back easily enough. Darius did not move but looked straight ahead, into the eyes of the necromancer. Hanali fell to the floor, and Break Bones stood over him, making sure he did not make a move for Darius. The Elenil was weeping. Darius had never seen an Elenil do such a thing, and it chilled him to the bone. He felt bad for Hanali, but there was nothing to be done. Vivi had stood between Darius and Madeline. It had been war.

The necromancer reached out, losing interest in Hanali's emotional outburst almost immediately, and took Mrs. Raymond's gloved hands in his own. "And you, my queen?"

"You know the answer to this question," she said. "Will you make me say it again?"

"Yes," he said. "I must ask, and you must answer."

She took a deep breath, her face turning toward the window and the wide world beyond. "It was many years ago. Her name was Rebecca Raymond. She was our daughter."

22
PATRA KOJA

The Good Gardener said, "I shall call you Patra Koja."
(Patra Koja means, in the language of that day, "Bringer of Peace.")

FROM "THE GOOD GARDENER," AN ALUVOREAN STORY

✛

They had fallen into an easy rhythm. The yak-like urudap pulled Gilenyia, who remained alive but unconscious. They had bound her wound as best they could and laid her on a litter that Lin had made of branches and vines. The Aluvorean woman stayed ahead of them, guiding the urudap gently through the trees, for the creatures required a great deal of direction.

Madeline rode on the third urudap, and Shula noticed how ragged her breathing had become. No doubt she would need to use another leaf of Queen's Breath soon, but Madeline wanted to spread them out as far as possible so she wouldn't be caught without any in a moment of crisis. Shula walked alongside her, giving her encouragement and pushing her back up when necessary. David trailed somewhere behind, keeping an eye out for any who followed them.

"Patra Koja," Lin had said, "lives in the swamp in the eastern part of Aluvorea. Few of us go there. The Elenil do not like us to wander too far from the safest parts of the forest."

Shula wondered about this. It sounded suspiciously like the words of the occupiers in her own home city. "Who are the Elenil to decide where you can and cannot go?" she asked.

"It is for our protection," Lin said. "Their people patrol these woods often enough. Too often, I think. But these woods are the source of magic, and the Elenil fear their destruction. So they send their people to protect us."

Shula was not so certain, but she was new here as well. They had been walking for about an hour. She called to David, asking if there was any sign of pursuit. "Not yet," he called back.

Madeline needed to rest. There was a small clearing ahead, with a sheltering tree and some fresh water running alongside. Shula suggested a break.

"Gilenyia . . . needs help . . . soon," Madeline said.

"If you faint, we'll only go slower," Shula said. "I could run ahead to this Patra Koja if Lin can give clear enough instruction. Or you could wait here so we can move faster. Or you could use another leaf of Queen's Breath."

"Fine," Madeline said. "Fine, we'll . . . rest."

Shula, satisfied, helped get Madeline settled against the trunk of a large tree. David said he would keep watch. He didn't need a break, not yet. Lin climbed a tree with easy grace, disappearing into the leaves. She returned with a large, orange-yellow fruit, which she broke in half and offered to Shula. It was creamy and tart. Madeline ate a few bites but then refused to take more.

"Tell us . . . about the Heartwood . . . Crown," Madeline said.

Lin took a leaf of the Queen's Breath from Shula and wet it, then pressed it against Madeline's neck. She resisted putting it on, but such relief came onto her face when she took it. She relaxed, and Lin said, "I cannot bear to speak to you when you are in such pain. Use the leaves. I will find more if we need them."

"Thank you," Madeline said. "Now will you tell us about the crown?"

Lin crossed her legs and sat across from them. "Do you know what heartwood is?"

"No," Shula said.

Lin thought about this, then walked around the meadow, carefully examining each tree. She found two close together and beckoned Shula over. "Do you see this tree? Feel its trunk."

It was a sapling with silver bark. Shula put her hand on it. It was smooth and felt strong. Lin motioned to another tree, a larger one, which had a gaping cavity in the trunk. There was a space that Shula could probably crawl into. She touched the outer trunk. It still felt strong to her, but she could see it was thin, maybe only fifteen centimeters thick.

"Heartwood is the center of the tree. The strength of the tree."

"The core of the trunk," Shula said.

"Yes. It is the dead part of the tree."

"The dead part?"

"Yes. It does not grow anymore—it is dead. It is the hardest part of the tree. If the heartwood is damaged or eaten away, the tree can still grow for a time, but it is weakened. It is vulnerable." She grabbed the lip of the hollow tree and yanked on it, and a large chunk of the outer bark came away in her hand.

"The dead parts of the tree make it strong," Shula said, sitting next to Madeline and studying the other trees around them.

"Yes," Lin said. "Now, there is a crown called the Heartwood Crown. It is the heart of these woods. Of Aluvorea."

"It's the dead part of the woods? I don't understand."

Lin knocked on the hollow tree. "No, no, it is the heart of the woods. It is the strength of the woods—it creates the woods, makes them what they are. In centuries past, every hundred years a new forest person would take the crown and remake the woods. New trees, new plants, new magic."

Madeline sat up, listening closely. "So all the plants in Aluvorea are from different eras of the forest?"

"Yes, yes. There are addleberries—those are very old magic, from nearly the beginning of the Sunlit Lands. Firethorns—those are from the last crowning. The stone flowers are newer too. Of course, there are also plants from your world. Ash and spruce, maples and roses and bluebells and such. They are the oldest of all, from before the welling up of magic in these woods. I suppose only Patra Koja lived here in those days."

Madeline looked at the Aluvorean with careful attention. "New crownings. Does that mean . . . new magic?"

Shula noticed how much better Madeline spoke while using the Queen's Breath. She felt thankful to see her friend have a moment of relief.

"Yes! New magic for all of the Sunlit Lands! Until the Elenil made their pact and took control of the woods."

There was a crash from the woods behind them. Shula stood partway, looking that direction. They waited for more than a minute, but no other sounds came. Shula called out to David, and he called back the all clear. Shula sat down slowly, still listening.

"So the Elenil . . . control the forest now?"

Lin nodded, her face sad. "This is why my sister and I agreed to turn your friend Jason over to them. We had no choice. We had hoped to bring you without their knowledge, but we failed. They threatened to take you all if we refused to give them Jason, and you alone have the Queen's Seed. We could not risk losing you. We did not know the Elenil would betray us and take you anyway." Lin shivered. "We cannot lose you, not when you have the only Queen's Seed planted in you."

Madeline held up her forearm, looking at the black speck there. Shula noted that it had moved farther up her arm, toward her shoulder. "Which means . . . what?"

Lin's eyes lightened. "You can grow new heartwood! You can wear the crown. You have but to cross the river—or what was once the river—and go to the island where the throne sits—Inyulap Anyar—and take the crown upon your brow, and then you will choose how magic will work in these woods for the next hundred years. The magic that flows from here goes to all the Sunlit Lands. You will be the one we grow alongside."

A butterfly, orange and bright yellow, moved through the meadow. A rabbit dashed past them and into the undergrowth, followed by three faeries riding on hummingbirds. Shula said, "So who was the last one to wear the crown?"

"Another human," Lin said. "Many, many years ago. But the Elenil manage the forest now, and they keep it from taking on a new form. They have made . . . they have made a sort of dam for magic, and they keep reusing it over and over. It has grown stagnant."

"What do you mean?" Shula asked. "You mean how if Madeline needs to breathe, someone else would have to give their breath for it?"

Lin nodded, then climbed another tree, a smile on her face. "A corrupt view of magic, thinking it is limited. If you eat an apple, must a tree die? That is what Patra Koja says. If you drink from a stream, must it dry up? Does a tree die for every tree planted, or do more and more trees grow and the forest spread?" She threw down a heavy pod, and it landed with a thud. The Aluvorean slid down the tree and landed beside it. "The Elenil have crippled the woods. They have kept it from being reborn so that they can control the magic. They are the people who put a fence around an apple tree and say, 'There are not enough' instead of counting the apples and the people and sharing alike. In time such people find the fruit they hoarded has gone rotten. They cannot consume it fast enough."

"I want to make sure I'm understanding," Shula said. "You're suggesting that if the Elenil didn't babysit this forest, there would be a sort of reset of magic?"

"Yes, it would flow and be easily accessed by all." Lin held up the pod and smashed it against a rock, but it didn't seem to even leave a scratch on the pod. "If there is water in a lake, the sun evaporates it. The water is in the clouds. It goes away, far from the lake. Oh no, we have lost the water! But then it snows in the mountains, and in the summer the water returns through the river, having traveled many places. The Elenil say, no, we will keep the water in tanks of our own devising. We will not let it go to the people of the mountains, nor to the people beside the river. And so they create a new system, a closed system, where they are the givers of water, where only they control it or access it."

"How?" Shula asked. "How did they do this?"

Lin looked at her like she was a child. "By stopping death," she said. "By removing the heartwood. There is no more death for the Elenil, but also no more life. Do you see?"

Shula wasn't sure she did see. She knew the Elenil were long lived. In fact, people like Hanali and Rondelo and Gilenyia were considered children even though they were hundreds of years old. She wondered about that, though. Why were they the youngest of the Elenil? Why weren't there any actual children? "So the long lives of the Elenil are tied to Aluvorea?"

"Of course. The magic comes from the well beneath the world. The trees bring it up through their roots." She held up the pod. "The magic comes in many forms, like this seed. The Elenil have trapped it here, instead of letting the seeds grow where they will. No new magic sprouts. No old magic dies. It is weak. Vulnerable. It has no core."

Madeline held out her hand for the pod, turned it over in her palm. "My dad used to take me hiking, and we would see pods like this sometimes. He said this kind only opened when there was a fire. The rangers had discovered they needed to do controlled burns sometimes or the forest wouldn't be healthy. Forests—the kind with this sort of seed pod, anyway—need fire."

Lin's eyebrows rose. "Yes. But the Elenil keep the firethorns carefully in their territory. The firethorns should move through the woods from time to time, setting flame to the old and opening the seeds of the new. The Elenil make sure this cannot happen."

Madeline pulled at the Queen's Breath on her neck, resettling it slightly. "So if I put on the Heartwood Crown I'll be able to, what? Restart the forest?"

"Yes, yes! These old things will come to life again. There will be new magic. It will heal the Wasted Lands and spread the forest. Then the firethorns will burn the woods, making space for the new plants, the new magic."

Shula took the pod and cracked it against the stone. Nothing. Madeline said it would open with fire. Shula let her hands warm and get hotter and hotter until flames rippled alongside her fingers. The pod got hotter in her hand. Its skin started to blister, then to split open, and when it popped, a bright geyser of light shot out of it straight into the air, and sparkling seeds like glitter fell into the trees around them. Madeline gasped and actually clapped her hands. Shula smiled. It was like a firework. She wished Yenil had been here to see it. She wanted to use her fire to set off more of them.

"It will heal the Wasted Lands," Madeline said, her voice almost dreamy.

"But the Elenil will lose their immortality," Shula said, looking at the burned husk of the seedpod in her hand.

Lin's eyes lit up. "All magic will burn away for a few days, to be reborn for another century. No, the Elenil will not have so much of it, but such is the way of the trees."

David came running into the camp. He had a knife in his hand, and he looked around, confused. "I saw an explosion of light," he said. "I thought you were being attacked."

"It was a seed," Shula said. "Magic."

David glared at her. "I've been working pretty hard to cover our trail, Shula. Then you send up a flare?"

"Sorry," Shula said. "Honestly, I didn't know it would do that."

David frowned, then seemed to relax. "Okay," he said. "How could you know in a place like the Sunlit Lands? You could smell a flower and turn into an ogre. The rules here take some getting used to."

"I am sorry, really," Shula said. David had an earnestness to him that she found endearing, and when he saw work to be done, he stepped up and did it without asking permission or wondering aloud if it would be useful. If you didn't know where he was, you could assume he was doing something helpful.

"No harm done," he said and smiled at her. "It was about time to get moving again, anyway."

Madeline groaned. "Just ten more minutes!"

Shula took Madeline's hand and helped her to her feet. "David's right. We have to assume the Elenil saw that magical explosion." Shula thought about the whole forest alight with such explosions, as the magic renewed itself for another hundred years. It would be an incredible sight. But there were Elenil patrolling these woods, people whose job was to protect the forest from the flames. "Unless . . . I could set the whole forest ablaze," Shula said. "Jump-start the magic again, break the dam. Then it won't matter that there was one flare of magic—there will be hundreds of them."

Lin put a hand on her wrist. "It will not matter if there is no one to wear the Heartwood Crown. She who wears the crown shapes the character of the magic. Without a Queen's Seed planted in someone, they cannot wear the crown. Without the crown, they cannot shape the magic. The magic, unshaped, grows wild and dangerous. Unpredictable. Swayed by whim and folly. Those would be dark times. The forest must not burn until someone wears the crown."

David helped Madeline onto her urudap. "It will be dark times if the Elenil come across us here. Me and Shula can't hold off many of them." Shula noted again how quick he was to help, how slow to complain, and felt bad that she had been the one to wrestle a moment of annoyance from him.

They moved the rest of the day largely in silence. Lin occasionally pointed out the special berries and plants of the forest. Addleberries and faerie's bell were the most common—faerie's bell looked identical to the plant that Madeline called foxglove. There were also lightweed and silk-flower. By late afternoon, the temperature was falling, and they had come to the edge of a wide swamp. There was no longer a place they could walk without being ankle deep in water.

"I can go no farther than this, nor can these beasts," Lin said. "We are forest beings, and this is Patra Koja."

Madeline's brow wrinkled. "Patra Koja is a person."

"He is a person and a place. He is the swamp, and the swamp is him," Lin said. "I hope you find what you are looking for. I will go around the swamp and meet you on the northern side. After you are done here, when you are ready, I will guide you to Inyulap Anyar." She said a word to the urudap, and they pulled Gilenyia's litter from their backs. Lin moved away from the water and into the forest without another word, the urudap trailing behind.

"I'll carry her," David said, and he lifted Gilenyia. "She's cold," he said. "I don't think she has long."

Shula helped Madeline wade into the swamp. Without their guide they weren't sure where to go, and Madeline only said, "Where the water is deeper." Shula wondered how Madeline would know this, but she said it with certainty, like she had been here before. So David did his best to take them the most treacherous way, into the deepest paths, carrying Gilenyia with him. Shula did her best to help Madeline follow. A snake slithered by on the surface of the water. Fish sometimes brushed against her submerged legs—at least, she hoped they were fish. The mournful calls of strange birds vibrated against the water.

Madeline had more than exhausted her strength. She walked in a strange half-dreaming, calling for help even while Shula had her arm around her, even when there was nothing more to be done to help. Shula slipped on an underwater log, and she and Madeline both went under. She lost her grip on Madeline, and when Shula surfaced, her friend did not.

Shula screamed for David, who was already on his way toward them, having heard the splash of their fall. Shula thrashed in the water, looking for Madeline and unable to find her. They couldn't lose Madeline this way. Not like this.

There was nowhere for David to lay Gilenyia so he could help. He dragged the mud with his feet, trying to find Madeline, trying to calm Shula. "It's going to be okay," he said, but she could hear the panic in his voice. It had been too long. She wasn't sure if it had been ten seconds or two minutes, but she kept saying to herself over and over, *It's been too long, it's been too long, we have to find her.*

Then a strange creature rose from the water, branches like antlers on his head, his skin green with scales, his hair and beard made from moss and leaves. He was broad shouldered and heavily built. There were claws on his fingertips and webs between his fingers. Madeline was in his arms, unconscious, water dripping from her limp body, like something from a 1950s horror movie. Shula lit on fire without thinking, and David stumbled backward—whether from the monster or her heat, she didn't know. He managed not to fall, though. Shula stepped toward the swamp thing. "Let her go," she said.

The creature didn't step back or seem alarmed at all. He had eyes like red berries, and they turned slowly toward her. His head hung too low in the front, and his back rose in a hunch behind it. She couldn't help but think this was caused by the rack of antlers on his head, which, as she looked at them more closely, she could see were branches. Wisps of moss hung from the points, and a few yellow leaves still clung to the twigs.

"I will not harm you," the thing said, and when he spoke, his voice sounded strangely like crumpled leaves.

"Shula," David said, "put your flames out."

"But he—"

"I can't come close to you while you're on fire."

She put out the flame, reluctantly. David came alongside her. "Who are you?" he asked the creature.

"I am Patra Koja, of course. It was not my intention to frighten you." He lifted Madeline's body, as if this was evidence. "But to help."

"Promise," Shula said. "Promise you won't hurt her."

Patra Koja tilted his head, and the moss that he had instead of hair swayed with the motion. "Who can make such a promise? For often we harm one another without meaning to do so. But I promise that it is not my intent to harm her, or you."

Shula and David exchanged looks. "Okay," Shula said. "But if you hurt her, I'll burn this place down to the water."

The strange plant man smiled at that. "I do not doubt you would try. Now. I am concerned that your friend has lost consciousness, and while wearing Queen's Breath, too. So come quickly."

He turned and walked with a rapid stride, the water eddying behind him. They followed him through chest-deep water. Shula tried to help David, but he said it was easier now, with some of Gilenyia's weight carried by the water. She could see in his face that he was tired, and sweat rolled down from his hairline, but she took him at his word.

Patra Koja stopped at a raft tied to a tree stump. The raft was huge, easily the size of the bottom floor of a house. He laid Madeline gently on it. He took Gilenyia from David and laid her on the raft as well. Shula gratefully pulled herself out of the water and then gave a hand to David.

Shula found a mattress of sorts made from old leaves. She and David put Madeline on it, then worked together to get Gilenyia on another. Patra Koja piled dead leaves and small dry sticks between the two women.

"Would you please start a fire here?" he asked Shula.

"Okay," she said, and lit it with her hands. She and David came close to it, working to get dry.

Patra Koja laid one enormous green hand on Gilenyia's forehead and the other on Madeline's. "Both are unwell," he said. "The Elenil is almost beyond the reach of my magic."

Shula crowded close to him. "What about Madeline?"

"What about her, child?"

"Can you heal her?"

His face crumpled. The leaves in his beard made a crackling sound. "No, child, no. She is not sick in the same way as your Elenil friend. She has been made sick by one of the Elenil. There is a curse of sorts upon her, and I cannot heal her unless that curse is lifted."

Shula felt the small torch of hope she had been carrying flicker and die. "Of course you can't," she sighed. She should have known better than to think it was a possibility. Everyone she loved died, and she loved Madeline.

The plant creature studied Madeline carefully, then lifted her arm, tracing the network of magical scars. "Though I think it may be that I can use my magic to bring those who cursed her here. There were two of them—or three?—many years ago."

"Wait," David said. "You're saying that Madeline's sickness isn't . . . natural?"

"What sickness is natural?" Patra Koja asked, his eyes wide. He seemed to be asking with complete seriousness.

Shula felt like she had stepped backward off an unexpected cliff. She was falling, flailing, trying to make sense of what was happening. "You're saying someone did this to her," Shula said. "Someone *chose to make her sick.*"

"Yes."

"And you can bring them here?"

"Yes."

There was a sudden jolt of hatred in her, like hitting the ground after that long fall. "Then do it. Please." She would very much like to know who had cursed her friend.

Patra Koja sat cross-legged at Madeline's feet. "The Elenil woman first, or she will be beyond my skills. But for both I must make preparations." Vines began to grow from his arms and legs, wrapping around the logs beneath them and stretching into the water. "Please keep me from catching on fire." Then he closed his eyes and sat very still. A slight breeze blew over him, and the leaves on his head rustled. Vines grew up from the water and covered Madeline. Shula's first instinct was to tear them off, cut them, burn them. But David quietly put his hand on hers and gave a firm squeeze. She took a deep breath. She would trust Patra Koja. Because she didn't have another choice.

Then more vines grew up, like snakes, and covered Gilenyia.

23

THE ZHANIN

The wind is not love
The breath of the world is not love
That is only shared life
FROM "THE OCEAN," A ZHANIN SONG

✛

Jason crouched behind a log, watching the Zhanin warrior. He was a hulking brute of a man, his face a network of scars. Lamisap lay on the ground beside him, unconscious and no longer green. The Zhanin had turned off the magic again, and since Lamisap was a person deeply connected to magic, it had shut her down too.

Remi, the flying cat who was not a cat, perched in a tree beyond the warrior. She was watching him with her yellow eyes, the tip of her tail flicking back and forth, as if waiting for a special sign or signal from Jason. He didn't have one though. He had told her repeatedly that he barely knew Lamisap and that he needed to head toward the carnivorous forest and find his fiancée and his unicorn and also a dragon so he could find out the price of saving the Sunlit Lands.

He hadn't heard anything from Baileya. No sign of Delightful Glitter Lady, either. So now he was here, watching this shark warrior who had set a trap for him, trying to figure out how to save his guide. He had no weapons. He had very little experience.

He mentally listed his assets. Unicorn (absent). Warrior fiancée (absent). Various friends who could light on fire, fight like crazy, ride horses, shoot arrows, and so on (all absent). Ability to receive one room-temperature chocolate pudding per day via magic (present). Commitment to telling the truth no matter what comes (present). A big mouth (also present).

Well, this was crazy, but what else was he going to do? He stood up and waved at the Zhanin warrior. "Hi! I'm over here."

Remi stood up on her branch, her eyes round in disbelief. Her claws dug into the wood.

The warrior took three steps toward Jason, a massive scimitar in his hand. He hesitated. "You have received a death penalty," he said.

"I'd like to talk with you about that," Jason said. "Doesn't seem like a fair trial, what with the fact that no one ever talked to me. All this talk about the imbalance of magic? I don't think I had anything to do with that."

"I have neutralized all magic near here."

Jason shrugged. "The only magic I have is pudding cup deliveries. I mean, I like them and everything, but they're not much help in a fight."

The warrior seemed confused about this. "Pudding cups?"

"Unless I was fighting someone with really bad eyesight who wore glasses or goggles or something. Then I could sling pudding at their glasses. That might be an advantage. Or if there was a bad guy with a dairy allergy. An extreme dairy allergy."

"Come to me or I will kill your friend."

"Are you going to kill her after you kill me?"

"I would have no reason to do so."

"And are you going to kill me if I come over there?"

"Yes."

"I respect that honesty," Jason said. "I'm a little disappointed in your answer, but at least you told the truth."

The warrior stepped toward him. "If you will not come to me, I will come to you."

"I was afraid you were going to say that."

Remi rolled her eyes, spread her wings, and glided down to land gently beside Jason. She looked up at the Zhanin warrior and said in a cold, emotionless voice, "If you come closer, you will regret it."

The Zhanin gaped at her. "I have turned off all magic in this area."

"I am not using any magic."

"You are a flying cat," he said.

"I am not a cat," she replied, an edge coming into her voice.

"You are a talking cat."

"I fly, and I talk, but I am not a cat," she said, a clear warning in her tone. He stepped toward her, and Remi gave a weary sigh. "I warned you," she said. She glanced at Jason. "Hold on to something."

"Hold on to—?"

Remi's claws extended into the log she stood on, and she began to flap her wings. They went faster and faster, and wind whipped around her. Jason grabbed a tree trunk. He tried to shout at Remi, but he doubted she could hear him over the wind.

The warrior moved forward, a look of grim determination on his face. The wind loosened his ponytail, and it flew behind him in a raging storm of hair. He leaned forward, hard, his arm holding his scimitar over his head. The wind grew stronger. Jason dug his fingernails into the tree. He had chosen the right place, because the wind was pushing him into the trunk. He wrapped his arms around it and gave it the biggest hug he had ever given a tree. He loved this tree.

The Zhanin, however, was not loving the trees. As he pressed closer to Remi, the not-quite-a-cat beat her wings harder. Branches snapped from the trees, whipping the Zhanin in the face. He still stepped forward. A harsh meowing sound (probably not actually a meow, though, Jason knew, because Remi was not a cat) ripped through the wind, and a branch as big around as Jason's thigh broke off a tree and whirled away. The Zhanin took another step, lifting his scimitar to strike, and Remi jumped into the whirlwind, zipped around the warrior, grabbed him by the hair, and yowling, sent him spinning off into the maelstrom. He flew up over the trees and disappeared into the distance.

Remi spun around in the savage wind for a moment, then lighted gently on the ground. The wind had caused her hair to puff out into a gigantic fur ball. She casually licked her paws, putting her fur down bit by bit.

"You are not a cat," Jason said, shakily releasing the tree that had saved his life.

"Clearly," Remi said, without looking up from her licking. "I am a Guardian of the Wind."

"I have never heard of those," Jason said.

The cat paused her bath to glare at him. "Offensive."

"But I like them. I like them a lot."

"Naturally."

Jason stumbled over to the Aluvorean woman. Her green color was returning, and she had somehow remained on the ground during the windstorm. "Did you make the wind go around her?" Jason asked.

"Did you want me to make her fly away?" Remi seemed genuinely interested in this question.

"No, of course not."

Looking disappointed, Remi returned to licking her fur down, focusing on a stubborn bit on her shoulder. Jason felt a sting from his tattoo. The magic of his pudding cups must have been restored.

"Stop looking at me," Remi said, "until my fur is back in place."

Jason tried not to snicker. It was funny seeing a "cat" who was so powerful but who also looked like she had licked an electrical outlet. Remi huffed. "I'll be back after I've cleaned up." She glided away into the forest, like a cotton ball with wings.

Once Remi had left, Jason worked on getting Lamisap back on her feet. The forest had been radically altered by the windstorm: pinecones and seedpods were everywhere, and leaves had been stripped from many of the trees. There was a mess of broken branches all around them. When Lamisap was able to stand again, Jason helped her move around a bit.

"When the magic leaves," she said, "I am all but helpless. This is what will happen when the queen comes again."

"What do you mean?" Jason asked. He decided they should get going, so he broke the smaller twigs off a fallen branch and gave it to Lamisap as a staff. Together they moved in the direction she told him—toward the carnivorous forest.

"When the new queen comes, she will reset the magic of the world. We Aluvoreans have been living in the presence of magic so long, it has become a part of us. Some of us are more forest than people. The magic lives in us in a different way than others in the Sunlit Lands . . . except maybe the Southern Court. When our magic is gone, we will hibernate for a time. When we wake, we will be new beings, having grown alongside the new queen."

Grown alongside? He had heard them say this about Madeline. "Are you saying that Madeline is going to be the new queen?"

"If she so chooses. I hope she will. Lin and I . . . we did not ask permission to take the Queen's Seed to her. The Eldest among us was angry, even though we thought we did a good thing."

Jason wondered about that. There had been strange prophecies that Hanali said were about Madeline, but they had discovered that he said that about everyone—it was a way for him to get power in Elenil culture. So far as they knew, those supposed prophecies had been completely invented. But it was weird to him that Hanali had chosen Madeline to come to the Sunlit Lands, and then the Aluvoreans had chosen her to get this Queen's Seed. "Why Madeline?" Jason asked. "Why her?" It wasn't fair, really. She should have been allowed to go home, to live the rest of her life, but they had drawn her back.

Lamisap leaned on the staff Jason had made for her. Her eyes were a deep green with black in the center, like stones in a pond. The green skin was unsettling if you looked at it too long. He was sure he would get used to it. She looked up at him when she spoke. "In your friend Madeline we see hope to move beyond what we have become. We are all grown into ourselves—old ways of thought, and old hurts, and old revenges—and we have lived too long with these things. We have not let the next thing come but have created a cycle of life that does not cycle. It continues ever thinner, ever more encrusted with age, and it has become too heavy, like a tree branch coated in layer after layer of ice in the winter. The branch can only break. Soon the tree is in danger. Soon many trees are in danger. The forest suffers. We need a new queen."

"But why Madeline? Why her specifically?"

Lamisap looked away into the trees. "You will think us foolish."

"Yeah, well, if so, I will definitely tell you."

"My sister and I watched her when she came here, you know. To the Sunlit Lands. We saw that she was—" Lamisap paused, a look of something like shame on her green face. Or maybe embarrassment.

"Go on. Say it."

"We saw that she was kind. Troubled, but kind."

Hmm. Jason thought on that for a moment. "You knew that you would be growing alongside her, so you wanted someone kind."

"Yes."

Okay. That made sense. It wasn't some earth-shattering prophecy of the future or anything like that, but Jason could understand it, at least. "I don't think that's foolish."

"Once the idea took root, Lin and I could not put it out of our heads."

He helped her over a fallen tree. "You really like plant metaphors."

"Yes," she said. "They are the simplest. A seed must die and be buried to grow. A tree must, in time, give itself back to the forest. An eternal forest becomes a forest of ghosts and shades. There is life in it, but not healthy life. Aluvorea has become such a place. The Elenil have become such a people."

"You mean because they live so long?"

"Do you not know the story of the Elenil and how they became so long-lived?"

Jason grabbed a stick from alongside their path and whipped it at the top of some grass. "Nope."

"Long ago, an archon of the Elenil decided he would make his people live forever. He studied the magic necessary. He found that if they were willing to take a life for a life, they could live long indeed. Every time they grew old, they could use their magic to steal the life of another person in the Sunlit Lands. He began to enact this plan."

"Sounds like a terrible guy."

"Indeed. We do not speak his name in Aluvorea. But there was a Zhanin prince who learned of the archon's evil, for the Elenil had taken the life of one of his servants. Being people of the sea, the Zhanin have always been sensitive to the changes and currents of magic. This prince, who we now call the Prince of the Open Sea, brought the Zhanin together and told them that this practice of the Elenil could not be allowed. He dived down to the bottom of the world and seized control of the world's magic. He altered it so the Elenil could no longer steal the years of another. Instead he presented them with a choice—they could choose to live longer than others in the Sunlit Lands, but they must pay a terrible price. A price which they agreed to pay."

Jason didn't always love stories, but Baileya did. He wondered if she knew this one. He figured she would be along soon, because she always did manage to show up, but on the other hand, it had been a while. He was starting to get nervous. But he could at least get this story and tell it to Baileya if she didn't already know it. "What was the price?"

"If they chose to live for centuries, then they could no longer have children."

Jason almost missed a step, he was so startled by this revelation. That made sense. The Elenil didn't have any kids running around in Far Seeing. "What about Hanali, though? He's younger than the other Elenil. Gilenyia, too, I think."

Lamisap did not answer. She held up a finger for quiet. "No," she said, and the color began to drain from her. She fell to the ground. Which could only mean that there was a Zhanin near them again. Jason wanted to drag her to safety, but he knew he might only have seconds before the warrior came upon them. He jumped and grabbed a sturdy branch in the tree above him and clambered up several more branches. He could still see Lamisap, but he thought if he held still he might be hard to notice.

It took less than a minute for the Zhanin to arrive. It wasn't the same one that Remi had taken care of, which could only mean he had beaten either Baileya or Delightful Glitter Lady in battle. Jason clenched his fists, filled with a sudden rage. He knew it had been taking too long.

The Zhanin knelt down, studying the Aluvorean woman on the forest floor.

If Jason did this just right, it might work. He angled himself off to the side. He didn't want to hit any branches on the way down. He edged out onto the branch. He held a branch above him for balance. On the count of three. One. Two. THREE!

Jason cannonballed from the tree, landing directly on the Zhanin's shoulders, knocking his neck forward and slamming him to the ground. Jason sprawled on top of him, the Zhanin face down, Jason lying face up.

They both groaned. Jason felt certain he had broken something. He hoped that something was the Zhanin.

The warrior rolled to the side, spilling Jason onto the ground. Jason got to his feet quickly enough, but the Zhanin was faster. He gripped Jason by the throat. He didn't have a sword, which Jason was glad for—he would already be dead if he had. Baileya must have disarmed him, but if so, where was she?

Jason choked. His vision blurred. He didn't want to go out like this. Didn't want his final sight to be the sun-damaged face of an ocean-going assassin. He didn't want his last words to be . . . wait, what had his last words been? Something in his conversation with Lamisap, probably. No! He wouldn't allow that. He managed to get his fingers wedged in beneath the Zhanin's fingers and snatch a gasp of air. "Sorry," he croaked. "Sorry to drop in on you unannounced."

There. That was better. Those were respectable last words. His vision was definitely going now.

The Zhanin stumbled, losing his grip. A blur of motion hit the man in the head, punched him in the chest, kicked his knee backward, and sent the warrior tumbling to the ground.

"This man is my brother, and mine to kill." The Kakri warrior stood over the Zhanin, panting, a small, curved knife in his hand. It was Baileya's brother.

"Bezaed," Jason said, his throat still raw, his back aching from the fall, his elbows probably bruised. "Boy, am I glad to see you."

Bezaed turned toward him, the knife catching a glint of sunlight. "And I you, Wu Song. I have been tracking you for some time."

"You didn't happen to see Baileya back there, did you?"

Bezaed hesitated, then looked swiftly over his shoulder. "No."

"Would you mind terribly if, before you kill me, we went to check on her? Just to make sure she's okay?"

"She can take care of herself," Bezaed said. He was moving toward Jason now, with careful steps. "Besides, I don't want to kill you until I have taken you home to the Kakri territories."

Jason scrambled backward. "Any chance I could introduce you to my cat before we go?" He got to his feet and took a step backward, and then another. "Is that a no? Bezaed?"

24

THE PLACE OF KNOWLEDGE

Know who I am.

FROM "JELDA'S REVENGE," A SCIM LEGEND

✦

arius paced the long room he had been placed in. They had been brought to the base of the tower one by one—Hanali first, then Break Bones, then him. They let him keep the sword. "The Pastisians have nothing to fear from a sword such as that one," King Ian said.

King Ian. The necromancer and lord of the Pastisians. Ian Raymond. Such an ordinary name. And his wife was Mary Patricia Wall, the author of the Meselia books, which included a Prince Ian who fell in love with Lily. No doubt in reality Lily had been Mary Patricia, now Mary Raymond. The dorm hostess for new arrivals to the Sunlit Lands was also the queen of the necromancers and a well-regarded novelist from Earth.

A door opened, and the necromancer king strode in. "Walk with me," he said, his voice amplified by the golden mask. Time alone with the necromancer made Darius wary. The man had a presence that left little room for noticing anything else around you. He filled a room. Darius couldn't help but feel like it was an honor to get some of his time, but then he remembered that one of the first things King Ian had done when he met Darius was to ask Mrs. Raymond whether Darius should be killed. That seemed like something important to remember.

The king led Darius out of the tower and into the bustling city street. Unlike Far Seeing, which had people of many different descriptions, Pastisia seemed to have only humans. Most of them, like Darius, were Black. As if sensing Darius's observation, King Ian said, "All people are welcome in Pastisia, so long as they abide by my rules."

They walked among the people. The crowd was no problem—the people of Pastisia made way for their king. No one came up to speak to him or interrupt them. There were no guards so far as Darius could see. It was strange to see signs again, with words on them. The Scim and the Elenil used magic to communicate—there was no need for writing or reading when one could speak to a bird and have it fly your message to the recipient. Birds could keep track of your schedule, or tell you a recipe, or even tell a story—almost anything books could do, without the inconvenience of learning to read.

People made their way through the streets of Pastisia on bicycles and cars with great coal ovens on the front, belching out black smoke. Above them there were dirigibles and gliders, and people moving between high towers on hanging bridges. It was different from anything Darius had seen in the Sunlit Lands. More wealthy by far than the broken-down wastes of the Scim, and more scientifically advanced than the Elenil. The Elenil had an almost medieval culture. Here Darius didn't see a single horse or beast of burden—the industrial revolution was in full swing, though along different lines than back home on Earth.

A clockwork bird buzzed past their heads. King Ian must have seen the look of wonder on Darius's face, because he said, "The Elenil live in a world frozen in time. A magical mirror of Earth's medieval culture, preserved by necessity and by magic. They cannot read and thus cannot achieve a highly technological society, which requires a transference of knowledge they cannot sustain with their messenger birds. Technological advancement requires writing. It is the first technology of a scientific society."

"You think of writing as a technology?"

"Of course. Invented by humanity, it allows us to preserve knowledge beyond a human life span . . . to hear the insights and musings of the dead. It lets us hear from those who are far beyond our senses in the shape of letters and notes and books. And while it does present certain challenges—the difficulty of true interaction, the shortening of human memory, the educational burden to achieve proficiency—the benefits are vast, and they change the shape of human societies."

"Can we talk about the whole necromancy thing?"

King Ian turned his golden mask toward Darius. "Of course. Let us go to the Place of Knowledge, where we commune with the dead." He turned down a wide avenue. Darius noticed that some of the vehicles driving along it appeared to be electric rather than steam powered. "As we walk, Darius, tell me of your friend Hanali. Do you trust him?"

"No," Darius said plainly. "I think my girlfriend, Madeline, does, and I trust her. But Hanali? Not at all. He gave me drugged tea the last time I drank with him."

"He is sly and manipulative and a maker of intricate plans. I am examining his offer to me, looking for the trap, but it is too cunningly devised. I cannot see how he will take advantage of my people if I agree to it, and yet I feel certain that he would."

It was true. Darius thought back to the Elenil's response to the news that Darius had killed his father. Hanali almost certainly had suspected it had been Darius. There were only three Black Skulls, and it was well known that one of them had killed Vivi, and Hanali had known since practically that same day that Darius was the leader of the Skulls. The raging, tear-filled weeping had the feeling of a performance, an act for a reason Darius did not understand. Hanali was unpredictable. "He's complicated," Darius admitted.

The king did not pause, but Darius could feel the king's attention center more closely on him, even though he didn't turn toward him. "So are all people, it seems to me. Like you, Darius Walker. A man caught between many worlds yet truly belonging to none of them."

"What do you mean by that?"

"You have no one culture. You are Black at home and blend in as something else at your school. Here you are Scim but still human. You are angry and seeking justice, and struggle to keep your more merciful instincts in check. You have not decided who you are, that is all."

Darius's face burned. "I know who I am," he said, but the king's words cut. He strengthened his resolve to follow through on his plan. "Where is Hanali now?"

He felt the king's interest in the conversation lessen. How could this man so intensely communicate such things without even looking at you? The king said, "I have sent him to meet with my generals to discuss his plan for war."

"Shouldn't you be there?"

"I trust my generals," the king said simply. "They will advise me on this matter, and it is important that Hanali know his presence here is not the most significant event in my kingdom at this time."

"Meaning you think my presence *is*?" He had been flattered just a few minutes ago to think that the king would make so much time to spend with him, but now he felt unsettled. What was the king's plan for him, that he would skip a meeting between his generals and the potential future archon?

The king laughed. "Not at all, young man. But it is a diverting entertainment to spend some time with you, and I have hopes you will join my people here. You are well known as a warrior, but the way you twisted the connection of Elenil and Scim magic to create the Black Skulls shows an innovation I respect."

Darius thought of his skull mask, in the hands of the Elenil even now. It made him furious to think of them possessing the source of his invulnerability in war, and rather than making him feel nervous or vulnerable, it gave him a burning commitment to take it back and punish them for every way they had crossed him. "Majesty, if you go to war with the Elenil, I hope you will allow me to be among your fighters."

"It is not a matter of if but when. A separate question is whether to ally with Hanali and his Scim rebels." The king regarded Darius as they walked. "I am interested in the prophecy Hanali has shared with me."

"The one about the human who will kill the archon with the Sword of Years?"

"Yes. He thinks it is you."

"It makes sense," Darius said. "I want to kill him. My sword wants to kill him."

"I do not think you truly wish to kill him," King Ian said. "It seems to me that you wish you had the desire to kill him, but you are not so bloodthirsty as it would appear."

Darius frowned. The king was not completely wrong, but it stung to hear the words spoken aloud. Darius felt he should be used to this, the world conspiring to give him an ever-shrinking series of choices. Every solution to his problems threatened to make him someone he personally disliked. He could kill the archon, solve his problems through violence. He didn't care for that solution, not really. But the other choice was to do nothing, to abandon the Sunlit Lands, to go back to high school and leave the Scim in their current situation. That was the act of a coward, and it left people he cared about in danger.

These weren't new choices either. It happened in small things too. He remembered being in a math class and his teacher asking him who had done his homework for him. Not because he was a jock or because he was a guy. And he knew because when he finally convinced the teacher he had done it himself, the teacher had said, "That's impressive for someone like you." *Someone like me.* Of course Darius knew exactly what that meant. He meant most Black people are stupid and Darius had exceeded his expectations. So what could Darius do? Get angry, yell at his teacher? Report it, which would involve trying to explain to the principal why exactly that precise comment was racist ("It was a compliment, stop overreacting!")? Or swallow the insult, try to ignore it. And if he swallowed this insult, he would have to swallow another and another, and if he stood up to the man, he would have to do it again and again, and no matter what Darius chose, he was either the "angry Black man" or the subjugated, harmless, invisible kind. And he hated, more than all of that, the fact that he kept being surprised by it. That he felt so helpless, so overwhelmed by it, so certain there wasn't a way out. It reminded him of the shackles on his wrists. He could twist them and fight them or ignore them or hide them or stuff padding beneath them, but the shackles were still there, and he kept being told the only person who could take them off was his enemy. He could release his rage or swallow it, but either way the rage shook him, filled him, made his skin feel tight with the anger—at himself, at the system, at the injustice of the world.

And the choices kept getting smaller. The space of his freedom kept shrinking. And there was this feeling that once he chose a path, someone would block the other, making sure his choices boiled away to nothing. It was hard to explain, even to himself. It was like the world itself made him claustrophobic. The sky was falling, and he couldn't hold it up, and all the people walked around him, acting like he was a fool, telling him to stand up straight and take it. Telling him it was his choice to make and stop complaining.

And whichever choice he made, he would have to make it a hundred more times when the clerk at the store followed him for no reason, when his friends assumed he loved rap, when someone asked him where they could buy drugs. Even playing sports didn't feel like the release it should be because there was always someone who saw him as the beast, the machine, the "naturally stronger Black body." There were always people assuming sports was his "only way out of the hood" when they knew nothing about him, had never seen his home, didn't know his family.

Which was part of what he loved about being with Madeline. She loved him as a person. She loved Darius Walker, the man. Loved his story, his culture, wanted to get to know his world and his interests. He wanted to know hers, too. It was a relief to lie beside her in the grass and read fantasy novels out loud to each other. He liked listening to her bubblegum pop music and laughing at her when she sang along. And sure, okay, there were times when racism intersected with their relationship—he still remembered the "prom speech" from her dad, which seemed to be designed to say that he knew that Black kids were super sexual ("Not with my daughter")—but even then Darius didn't have to go through the complicated calculus of whether to be mad, because *Madeline* got mad, and Darius could take the role of the reasonable one calming her down. *It's not that big a deal, Mads. I'm sure he didn't mean it that way.* And for once he could be the magnanimous, forgiving type, not the angry man and not the guy who would let himself be walked on.

And Madeline backed him up. When he was angry, she told him, "You're right to be mad." When he was scared to speak up, she told him,

"Maybe it's wise to keep quiet just this once." She didn't think he was a terrible person, and she didn't let his responses in those moments define him. He had asked her about it once, and she told him about how she had been in a car accident when she was learning to drive. Her mom had been with her, and Madeline had a sort of nervous breakdown. She couldn't get out of the car. Her hands were shaking so bad she could barely get her learner's permit out. Afterward she had told her mom, "I'm sorry I'm such a wimp." Her mom had said to her, "Madeline, you are one of the bravest people I know. You were in a car accident, and you were scared for a few minutes. That's not who you are—that's something that happened to you." Darius didn't understand what this meant for him at first, until Madeline had kissed him and said, "Dealing with racism is like being in a car accident every day. It's not who you are, it's something that keeps happening to you." Darius wasn't sure he agreed with her, but the kindness, the generosity of that thought stuck with him.

So when it came to the question of whether to kill the archon or not, Darius felt like there was no good solution. Either way he became someone he did not want to be. But he couldn't deny that when the Sword of Years was in his hand, his desire to kill Archon Thenody and the Elenil who were like him only increased. "Perhaps you will be the one to fulfill the prophecy, Majesty. Maybe you will take my sword and use it to kill the archon."

The king paused, thinking about this. "No, dear friend, for the words of the Elenil prophets are clear. They say a human will kill him, and I am a Pastisian, born and reared in the Sunlit Lands."

"But you're human," Darius said.

"We reserve that term for those who were born on Earth," King Ian said. "People like yourself, or even those who were brought here as children. Many in my city were born here. I am third generation Pastisian myself, grandson of one of the founding members of this city. It is not I who will kill the archon."

As they neared the center of the city, the Place of Knowledge came into view. It had the look of a squat temple, built in the style of a ziggurat, and Darius had the unpleasant sensation that it crouched among the other buildings like a spider, its legs bent in preparation to leap upon its prey. The Place of Knowledge itself was encrusted with sculptures of skulls and skeletons, many of them dressed in hooded robes and nearly all of them going about their everyday life: shopping in the market, sitting at a desk writing by candlelight, embracing one another. It was a terrifying building, full of ominous portent.

"Do not let fear fill your heart," the king said, "for this is a place all must come to in time, even the Elenil. It is a place of truth. No illusion can survive here for long."

The king led him up the bone-white stairs. The doors yawned open as they approached, and they entered a small chamber with thick red carpets and white walls. The door closed behind them. A closet opened in the side of the wall. King Ian took off his gloves, then his mask. He removed his robe and hung it in the closet. His hair was close cropped and silver on the sides but black and full on top. His eyes were nearly as black as his robes had been, his skin smooth and black as midnight. The wrinkles around his eyes gave him a look of rested kindness, as if he were someone who laughed often, though Darius had seen precious little evidence of this.

"You may leave your sword here too," the king said, but the way he said it made it clear it was the wish of the sovereign monarch, not a simple invitation. When Darius hesitated, Ian said, "It clouds your truth with its own desires. You may take it up again when we leave here, if you wish."

Darius set his sword beside the king's mask. Masks and weapons. So much of his time in the Sunlit Lands came to this. Hiding his identity and visiting violence on the unjust. Strangely, he found that in the anonymity of the mask he had fewer questions about what his response to injustice should be. Putting on the mask of the Black Skull was a declaration of war. He would not shrink back, he would not apologize, he would not wait for justice to come—he would take it. Back home he had taken abuse, insults, hateful comments, all so he could go about his life without interruption. But here no one commented on him being Black, because here it was all about humans and Elenil and Scim and so on. If they hated him here, it was because he was a human being or because he had chosen to champion the Scim. Which wasn't much better, honestly, but at least it was a change of pace. He had to admit it was a relief to have someone else to champion. He was tired of standing up for himself.

"It is hard to lay it down," King Ian said. "Harder still to leave it."

It took Darius a moment to realize the king was talking about the sword. He was right—Darius was nervous to enter this necromancer's temple without it. Who knew what they might try to make him do? "I won't speak to the dead," Darius said. "It seems wrong to me."

Ian laughed and clapped him on the back. "Perhaps you will listen to the dead then." He pushed open a door, and they stepped through.

It was the largest library Darius had ever seen. Every surface was jammed with shelves which were weighted with books and scrolls and maps and folios and papers. Darius spun around, taking in the entire place. "These are magic books? Dark magic? Necromancy?"

King Ian laughed, pure joy bursting from him. "The look on your face, Darius! No, I doubt you would describe them as such, being a necromancer yourself."

"I don't understand." Darius picked up a book. A copy of Aristotle's *Poetics*.

The king took it from him, beaming, and turned it over in his hands. "My old friend Aristotle. 'The essence of a riddle is to express true facts under impossible combinations.' He died in 322 BC, thousands of years ago. And yet, here, he still speaks. I have had long dialogues with him in my mind, have fought his great philosophical intellect, have wrestled to find holes in his logic, have debated and raged against him, and still he speaks, implacable, unchanged. Yes, I speak to the dead. And they speak to me, and their wisdom—which might otherwise be lost to the world—takes root in my own life."

"Your necromancy—the thing that terrifies the rest of the Sunlit Lands—is that you can read?" So they didn't speak to the dead here, not really. Darius was stunned. Stunned and confused. How were the rest of the Sunlit Lands terrified of the Pastisians just because they could read?

Ian ascended a wide stairway, browsing the books. There must have been thousands of them. "Think of it, Darius. The Elenil are illiterate. The Scim, the Maegrom, the Aluvoreans, the Kakri, the Southern Court, the Zhanin—all of them are unable to read. To them this is a sort of magic, an inexplicable way to preserve knowledge, to communicate. You and I can know the words of a person who lived thousands of years ago. I can send a message to you that is indecipherable to a Scim, that is nonsense to an Elenil. Time and distance are no barrier to us. The others pass down their stories, elder to child, mother to daughter, grandfather to son. You and I overhear such stories once and take them as our own, free to all who have our peculiar skill." He held up a book, showed Darius the title. It was hand-bound in leather, the title scored into the cover: *Stories and Legends of the Elenil.*

"You're not necromancers. You're literate." Darius shook his head. He picked up another book, put it back on the shelf. "The entire world is afraid of you because you know how to read."

"It's a technology, Darius, and one that gives us vast advantages. In this place, this temple of knowledge, we keep only books from those who have already left us. It is truly where we hear the words of the dead. The words of the living we keep elsewhere in the city. Those are people we can still speak to, should we wish, and should we find the time and space to do so. But here . . . here we find our lost humanity." He led Darius to a wide room with smaller books, like journals. "Here we keep the reflections of the Pastisians, those who have lived in the Sunlit Lands. Here are my father's poems. There my grandmother's war journals. My brother's letters to his children."

Darius looked at the books, amazed at their collection. "Some of these must be unique. One of a kind."

"Nearly all of them," Ian said. He picked up a tiny book, about twice the size of a wallet. "A new arrival, written by one of my long-term spies in the Court of Far Seeing."

The cover of this one was paper, and the words were written in a confident, flowing hand. *The Words and Acts of Vivi, Son of Gelintel.* "Hanali's father?"

"Yes, kept here in this room because it was written by a Pastisian. But it is a work about Vivi. We collect the words of influential people, usually without their knowledge. There are words in this book that Hanali has not heard, I am certain. If you choose to take it, there will be some advantages for you in that relationship, I think. Though he is dead, Vivi can give you insights into his son."

Darius's brow wrinkled in confusion. "Take it? Shouldn't it stay here for others who need to read it?"

"Vivi has shared his words with me already. The loss of this book would be a significant one, but the potential benefit is more significant. I wish for you to take it and read it, and, should you choose, read it to Hanali as well."

"I can't take this," Darius said. "You can just tell me what it says."

Ian put his hand on Darius's shoulder. "My words and his may say different things, son." Usually Darius didn't like being called *son* by anyone but his father, but this time he didn't flinch. He was not offended. He was honored that Ian would speak to him like that. "Now," the king said. "Let me show you one more book before we leave this place. Let me introduce you to a man long dead who is held in great reverence by me and all Pastisians."

They did not have to leave the room. It was a Pastisian, then. Or so Darius thought. The book lay open on a stand. It was old, the pages yellow leaning toward brown, and brittle. "These are the words of Nikolas Pastis."

"The founder of Pastisia?"

"In a sense. He was a man who lived on Earth centuries ago. Greek by heritage, but he lived in the United States in the 1700s. He had a plantation, and he owned many slaves."

Darius's stomach clenched. How could Ian say a slave owner had been a great man? And why would they name this place after him?

Ian flipped through the pages with gentle reverence, moving toward the beginning of the book. "Listen to his words, Darius. He writes, 'I have come to an inescapable conclusion, though the Good Lord knows I have fought to escape it, like a man in a prison informed of his impending execution. I have paced out the limits of this cell, have raged against the bars, have cried and wept for release but discovered no relief. I cannot say these men I have enslaved are less than I. They watch over their children with the same tender care. Their prayers are as impassioned, the depth of their affection for their wives as touched by heaven as my own. I am no more their superior than I am inferior to a Frenchman. For are not the Greeks, despite our swarthy skin, the originators of all that is good in art and culture, which the European claims for his own? So I have freed them all, every one, though it shall be my ruin and I a pauper. For I am convinced of this: a great harm to me means little if it shall create a greater benefit to many others.'"

"He set his slaves free," Darius said.

"Yes. And six of them—my own ancestors among them—found their way to the Sunlit Lands. They made this place, and they named it for their old master. It is said they invited him to come with them, saying, 'Master, come with us to a place of safety for those who have been wronged. It is called the Sunlit Lands.' He wept and said, 'Call me not your master, for I shall forevermore be your servant. Who am I to accept your generous offer?' He would not go with them but remained on his land, which became a place of refuge for runaways and freed slaves . . . indeed, it is said he made a sort of Sunlit Lands upon the Earth for a time, and he was well regarded by victims of injustice."

Darius crossed his arms. "So he gave up his slaves. That's nothing more than what he should have done."

Ian put his hands on Darius's shoulders. "Do not underestimate the nobility of doing only what should be done. It is more than most accomplish in their lives." He closed the book. "He was a good man, by the end." He pressed the tiny book of Vivi's words into Darius's hand. "Will you hear the words of the man you killed?"

Heat came into Darius's face at those words. "Okay," he said. "Yes."

Ian smiled at that, but there was sadness behind his eyes. "Come, friend. We have spent enough time among the dead, even for necromancers such as we. Let us see what the living have to say."

Darius hesitated, the book in his hand much heavier than it should be, given its size. But the king had exited already, and Darius hurried to catch him.

25

THE HEALING

"This seed is full of magic," he said.
"It will bring blessing to the people of the Sunlit Lands."
FROM "THE PLANTING OF ALUVOREA," AN ALUVOREAN CREATION TALE

✦

Madeline woke to find herself still asleep. That's how it felt, coming to this strange in-between space, where her mind— her soul? her self?—interacted with other people, completely apart from her body. It had happened before, back when the Garden Lady had disconnected her from her suffering body long enough to let her say good-bye to Jason and Darius in visions before she left the Sunlit Lands. Something like it happened every time she connected to someone to try to heal them. She knew she wasn't truly disconnected from her body. She wasn't traveling anywhere, she was just connecting with others near her. Someone had said to her once, "Maybe the human soul is bigger than the body." It felt more like that. She was still tethered to the blood and bones and flesh of her failing body, but she was somehow free of its constraints, too.

Patra Koja was with her in this liminal space. He inclined his head to her when she became aware of him. He had placed Gilenyia's body (or an image of that body?) on a long white table. The Elenil woman looked peaceful. "She is far gone down a difficult path," he said. "I cannot wake her here. At least, not until we have worked some small healing."

"Why did you want me to come here? Couldn't you have done this yourself? Couldn't you have done it from a distance?" Madeline was reminded of the first time she had seen him, in her dreams, when he had been deep in salt water.

He grunted. "I brought you here to learn, just as I sent your friend to Arakam to learn. But first we must save your Elenil friend."

She wasn't sure she would describe Gilenyia as a friend, but she knew what he meant. "How does this work?"

Patra Koja gestured at the prone Elenil. "How does a plant grow? The sun, the water, the minerals in the soil. So it is with magic. We take what is present and use it to create growth, to bear fruit, to make life." He put his hand over Gilenyia's wound, and a green light came from beneath his hand. Gilenyia began to breathe more easily, and the flesh closed up over her wound.

Amazing. Patra Koja did not seem weaker or even tired after this. "Why would the Elenil do any other kind of healing? Is this harder to do?"

"Not at all. But like any resource, it must be used in moderation, not for every whim. The Elenil, rather than respecting magic and using its resources for all people, continually steal from one another and create a new status quo. They keep Aluvorea from its regular cycle of renewal so they can keep control. Magic has been corrupted. It must be flushed out of the Sunlit Lands and reborn."

Madeline put her hand on Gilenyia and felt the magical interface necessary for healing the way the Elenil did it. She could also feel what Patra Koja had done, could see the places where he had knit together the muscles and flesh, had repaired broken veins, had even created an increase of blood production. She recognized the green power at once. "This is the same thing the Queen's Seed is trying to do in my body." She opened her eyes and looked at the strange plant man. The branches on his head quivered. "Has the seed been trying to heal me?"

Patra Koja nodded. "It has been extending your life, but it cannot heal you. The magic that is killing you is moving too fast."

"What? The magic that's killing me?"

"Yes. Elenil magic is the source of your illness." He studied her. "I see its mark on you from an early age. I do not know why it took so long to begin to corrupt your health. Perhaps something about the agreement that brought it into place."

"Agreement?" What did this mean? Surely he wasn't suggesting that she had somehow made a deal that allowed her to be sick. If she had, she had been tricked, and she wanted to talk to someone about changing that. She couldn't imagine what she had possibly been given that would be worth this. "I didn't agree to this."

"No, no. I should have said that more clearly. This is an agreement that was made when you were young . . . perhaps even before you were born. It is not uncommon in some magical circles to do such things. It was an agreement made between two or perhaps three people, that much is clear. I have sent out my magic to identify them and bring them here. It is a massive amount of magic, but if you are truly the annaginuk, then what little magic we have managed to save will soon be returned to the sea."

Madeline tried to follow all that and didn't quite manage it. "If it was before I was born . . . who would have had the right to speak for me?"

Several leaves fell from Patra Koja's face. His eyes were sad. "A parent, I would say."

A parent. Of course. Madeline wanted to feel rage, anger, or even surprise, but she felt only a tired acceptance. She had barely seen her dad since the sickness started, and her mom vacillated between intense overinvolvement and happy-faced denial. "Why are you bringing them here?"

The plant man crouched down so his face was even with hers. "For closure. So you can speak to them of this agreement they have made, and perhaps discover its origin."

Her face flushed. "For closure." Those two words filled her with anger, which was ironic, given that realizing her own parents were responsible for her illness did not. "Because I'm dying," she said, her voice flat.

He put his green hand over hers. "I do not see a way that will not be true, Madeline Oliver. Death comes for all. Today or tomorrow or years from now. You have walked far down that path already. Would you wish to walk it again?"

This was true. As her breath waned, everything became more difficult. Just sitting somewhere. Walking was the most painful thing she had done in her life. She could scarcely eat anymore. She was tired. More than tired, even with the Queen's Breath. In moments like this, when her mind could act in the near absence of her body, she had a brief memory of what it was like to live.

"No," she said honestly. "But I'm not ready to go, either."

"That is the way of it," Patra Koja said.

The magical interface with Gilenyia drew Madeline's attention. This Elenil woman would live for hundreds of years . . . had already lived so many years more than Madeline. She could feel the connection and knew that Gilenyia could do nothing to stop her from changing it . . . from using Elenil magic to take what she wished, much in the way the Elenil had done for centuries. She could take Gilenyia's health as her own if she wanted.

"It is not wise to use Elenil magic in this way," Patra Koja warned.

"Will you try to stop me?"

"No," Patra Koja said. "Do as you must. I will only bear witness."

She knew in that moment that she could do it. She could take a hundred years from Gilenyia. She could, for that matter, simply take Gilenyia's breath. Gilenyia was not conscious, not able to stop Madeline. She explored Gilenyia's lungs, marveled at the way they expanded, that the branching passageways delivered air so effortlessly. She could take that. She could make herself well, at least for a time, and no one would stop her. She knew already that if Gilenyia died while Madeline had her breath, Madeline would keep it forever. There was no one to see what Madeline chose, no one to tell her that this would be an evil action. A life for a life. And didn't Gilenyia, the Elenil healer, make choices like this all the time, letting Scim die so Elenil could live? Wouldn't this be a sort of justice? She could move her curse, let it settle into Gilenyia's body. She could leave then, leave this all behind. She would have no obligation to continue here in the Sunlit Lands, no need to help the Aluvoreans with their broken magic system, no need to fight, no need to think about these things at all. She could go home, finish high school, be normal, maybe even be with Darius again if he would take her back.

This was the choice she had made her whole life, she realized. That simple question, What would it take to be normal? To be normal meant certain sacrifices had to be made. You had to keep your mouth shut. Don't bring up hard things or questions that make people uncomfortable. Don't worry so much about how exactly you got your beautiful life, just take it. Don't think about who else might have paid the price. She could be forgiven for doing the same thing everyone else was doing.

Not that everyone else was stealing their breath from another person. But it wasn't her fault that she had been cursed with this breathing problem. It wasn't her fault, and she didn't deserve it. She was a better person than Gilenyia. She was! She was certain of this. She felt the change in Gilenyia's breathing, saw her convulse, her body straining for breath. She felt her own body, far away, take a deep breath, pure oxygen entering her system. It was luxurious.

But where did it end? If she took Gilenyia's health, why not take it from others, too? How long until she had some other physical malady she didn't want to live with? She knew that if she took Gilenyia's breath it would not be the end. Two choices stood before her now: to live or to die. To take a life or lose her own. To become someone else, someone unrecognizable, so she could continue to live, or to be herself and cease to be.

Patra Koja said nothing. He stood, watching, still and quiet as a tree. She turned her back so he could not see her face. She thought of her parents. She did not, in this moment, blame them. Maybe they had faced a choice as difficult as this one. She knew in a flash of insight that it was her mother who had made this deal, who had allowed Madeline to be cursed. She didn't know how or why, but she could feel it in the moments of strange grief and defensiveness in her mother's interactions with her over the years. Little comments that made sense now. "I've done so much for you" and "you should be thankful" and even, sometimes, strange moments when she said "I'm sorry" when she had done nothing wrong, and Madeline's father would bustle her off to another room, another chore, another activity.

But this had never been Madeline's way, to take things from others. To steal, to harm, to kill. She thought of the painful decision she'd made to save Jason's life by killing a Scim. She had tried to keep from thinking about it, and with everything else going on—Shula coming home with her, and trouble with Yenil and school, and, of course, *dying*—she had managed to keep it stuffed down, hidden away. The Scim had a name, she knew. Night's Breath. Gilenyia had forced her into the decision, but Madeline had made it. She had chosen to let that Scim die so Jason could live. She had killed him, and she might as well say it plainly. She did it for the right reason, though, even if Jason didn't see it that way. So she wanted to say it wasn't her way to steal or harm or kill, but when it came down to it, she had done all those things. Had done all of them and had managed to avoid feeling bad about it, mostly.

She was in that place again.

Gilenyia was going to die. If Madeline did nothing, she was done. Why should she let the Elenil's breath go to waste? If Jason were here, she thought he would encourage her, tell her that he wanted her to live, and that was more important than what happened to Gilenyia.

No. That wasn't true. And if she could do nothing else for Jason, she could show him the respect of being honest. Jason didn't like the fact that she had killed Night's Breath to save him. He wouldn't be on board with killing Gilenyia to save Madeline, and she knew that for a fact because he had told her how proud he was that she had chosen not to take Yenil's breath. It would break his heart, but he would tell her not to kill Gilenyia. And Darius, she knew Darius would tell her to do it . . . but this was exactly the sort of thought she kept telling him he should lay aside, that he was better than that, gentler, kinder, more righteous.

She couldn't go back and change things with Night's Breath (and she wasn't sure she would want to). But she could make the right choice now. In fact, if she was dying (and she knew she was, there was no mistaking it these days) then she should see if there was something she could leave for Gilenyia. Some little gift. An apology of sorts, for considering murdering her.

But first she had to give Gilenyia back her breath. Back in her body, Madeline took a deep inhalation of fresh air, savored it. She was thankful for it. Gilenyia writhed, gasping for air. Madeline gave it back to her and watched Gilenyia's breathing go panicked for a moment, then gradually relax.

A weight of sorrow pressed down on Madeline. She shouldered it. This was a burden she would not have to carry long. It was her friends, her family, her loved ones, who would carry it soon, and this both added to her sorrow and lessened it. She reached out into Gilenyia's body again, looking for some small blessing she could leave her, and found it almost immediately. Gilenyia had lost the ability to have children. Perhaps had never had it. But Madeline could see this was not the result of some physical issue but a magical one. There were knots of power in place to prevent Gilenyia from having a child. Madeline's body, even breaking down as it was, still held the potential to birth a child—a potential she would never have a chance to use. So with the skills of Elenil magic that Gilenyia herself had taught her, Madeline took the knotted mess of magic inside Gilenyia into herself. She looked at what remained in Gilenyia, and confident that it had worked, she broke contact with the Elenil.

She stumbled, and Patra Koja caught her, lowering her to the ground. She had never felt so weak in this dream state, this mental space, before. She could not imagine it was a good sign. "I do not know if this thing you have done is a kindness or a cruelty," Patra Koja said. "Though I can see in all your heart you meant only kindness toward the Elenil."

She did not have the strength to answer this. "Patra Koja," she said. "If I enter your mind, can I see the state of Aluvorea? Can I see why I am needed, and what I may be able to give to this place?"

"Indeed," he said gently, and he showed her.

She could see it all. The many trees and plants that came from Earth—maples and redwoods and plum trees and dogwoods and evergreens—as well as the distinctly Aluvorean plants: stone flowers, faerie's bells, addle-berries, firethorns, and many others. She could see an island—the Queen's Island—and upon it a throne, and upon the throne a desiccated corpse from long ago, so old that it should have turned to bones and dust by now, and upon the brow of the corpse, a crown, polished and nut brown, and branches growing from the crown. It had woven branches at the bottom and then a profusion of wild growth at the top, reaching upward, and there were gems and strange images and reflections somehow set in the branches. One oval gem seemed more mirror than stone, and Madeline could see herself in it, she thought, cloudy and distant. The water around the island was a brackish, silent lake, and this felt wrong. It had once been a river, she knew, that flowed south through all of Aluvorea. The carnivorous forest was wrong. It should have never grown so large. The firethorns burned too hot to the east. They should not have been isolated and corralled as they had been, should have been allowed to thin themselves through the rest of the forest, to burn down the dead trees and underbrush and create rich soil for those which remained. The dragon, Arakam, stirred beneath the waterfalls to the north. She could see it all, that the healthy parts of the forest were smaller, that Aluvorea was shrinking. It had been, once, a great primeval thing that spread all the way through the Wasted Lands and went to the doorstep of Far Seeing. Now it retreated from encroaching desert.

"I see," she said, and she did. For now she saw the way the magic had been cut off, prevented from doing what it was meant to do. Aluvorea drew her magic from the deep places of the land. Madeline saw it like an orb, with the land in the center and chaotic water beneath. From that came the magic, which the trees brought up through their roots and spread through the land. Then the magic returned to the sea, in time, and was renewed and then came again. But the Elenil and the Scim had broken this cycle. They had stopped it, built a sort of magical dam, and now it had gone stagnant and strange.

She could get it started again. She saw how to do it. She would go to the island and take the Heartwood Crown and put it upon her own head, and she would reset the magic of the world. Not as punishment. Not for justice. As a gift. An extravagant gift.

She opened her eyes. Her physical eyes. Tried to breathe.

"Patra . . . Koja." She was covered in vines.

He was chest deep in the water. He came to the edge of the makeshift raft he had made. "Annaginuk. What do you bid of me?"

"The two . . . your magic . . . seeks. Have you . . . found them?"

"Yes. I know their names."

"Is one . . . my mother?"

"Yes."

She thought about that for a moment, but it was so hard to think now, so hard to do anything but push through the pain. "And my father?"

He shook his head. "It is an Elenil."

"Can you . . . bring my . . . mother?"

"I have enough magic to bring two people here," he said. She noticed that his leaves, which had been bright green when they arrived, were brown and yellow and orange now.

"My mother . . . and Yenil," she said.

"What of the Elenil?"

"Name?" she asked.

"His name is Hanali, son of Vivi."

Madeline closed her eyes. She had thought it might be him. She didn't understand what this meant, but it was too late now. She didn't want to see him. Not now. Not this minute. "Leave him . . . be," she said. "Bring Yenil . . . instead."

"So be it, my queen," Patra Koja said.

Shula was at her side, stroking her brow. David came near and, with her permission, began to cut away the vines holding her down with his knife. When she was free, David helped prop her up against Shula, her head elevated so she could get the best breath she was able. David, always a kind soul, sat beside them, his legs crossed, his knife in hand. Gilenyia slept. Patra Koja waded through the water.

They sat like this nearly until nightfall, when Patra Koja lunged forward into the swamp, as if catching a fish, and pulled Madeline's mother and Yenil from the water.

26

THE CARNIVOROUS FOREST

This place is safe.

FROM "THE PLANTING OF ALUVOREA," AN ALUVOREAN CREATION TALE

✚

Jason had managed to get away from Bezaed in the most ridiculous way possible. He had thought about distracting him by shouting, "Look over there! More Zhanin warriors!" but he had made a promise not to lie, and so he couldn't. So he just started saying things like, "Bezaed. There's not a Zhanin warrior hiding behind us. There's not. Don't even bother looking for one. I don't hear anything, do you hear anything?" After about ten minutes of this, Bezaed became convinced there was someone following them. Jason tried hard to dissuade him, which only made him more certain. Then Bezaed said, "Wait here," and Jason said, "I will definitely run as soon as you are out of sight," and he did. He had been running ever since, and he was thankful Baileya had made him run every day he was in the Wasted Lands because it had kept him just barely out of Bezaed's reach.

Jason had been running so hard from Bezaed that he hadn't even noticed when he arrived in the carnivorous part of the forest until a flower tried to sting him. He had promptly, with a great deal of screaming and swatting, run as fast as he could up a hollow log stuck at an angle into the forest floor. The flowers, which had long tentacle-like stalks, had swarmed around the base of the log and reached experimentally toward the surface of the log, as if deciding whether or not to make the climb. He had no idea why they didn't want to get on the log, but he was thankful. He had a vague memory that the things grew on dead logs, but also they were called stone flowers, so maybe not. He was having a hard time remembering the little things he had heard about this place, which was unfortunate, given that he apparently lived here on this log now.

A wonderful side effect of life among the meat-eating flowers was that Bezaed had wisely chosen to stay in the regular part of the forest, still in sight of Jason and, in fact, close enough to hear. Bezaed was far enough away, however, that he had fallen to "second most distressing thing trying to kill me" status. A close second, yes, but as Jason recalled, these flowers would sting someone, paralyze them, and then devour them slowly over the course of a week or so. That gave them an edge over Bezaed, who would just cut him with a knife.

"You know, we've never had a chance to sit and talk," Jason said. "What with you wanting to murder me since the first time we met."

Bezaed laughed at that. "You wish to exchange words instead of receiving my blade? Coward! You are not worthy of my sister!"

"I agree. Baileya is amazing."

Bezaed's golden face twisted in fury. "She should not be betrothed to a human."

Jason rearranged himself, letting his legs dangle on either side of the log. Could those flowers jump? He didn't think so. "Is that what this is all about?"

"It is our tradition, as a people, that we attempt to kill those who become betrothed to our sisters. To show the strength of our families and to make sure the suitor is worthy."

Jason crossed his arms. "I've been thinking about this—and believe me, I have plenty of reason to think a lot about this—and I think you're lying."

"I am not lying. I am going to gut you like a hare and leave your body to dry in the desert sun."

"Poetic," Jason said. "But I don't think the Kakri need to prove they're strong. Everyone is terrified of them. I'm duly terrified of all of your people except Baileya. I'm scared of her, too, but at least I know she'll only break me in half if I deserve it. As to whether I'm worthy of Baileya . . . I'm not. Killing me won't change that. Meanwhile, I hardly see her because she's busy trying to keep you from sticking me with a knife. Right now she's off handling one of those Zhanin. Besides, Baileya says that even if I were to break off the engagement, you would still kill me."

"Not so," Bezaed said. "If your betrothal ends, I will leave you in peace."

Mother Crow had told Jason that if you broke an engagement, the family continued to hunt you, just without the protection of your fiancée. On the other hand, Jason couldn't imagine Baileya leaving him to fend for himself, even if he broke up with her. "Leaving me in a weird place, because I don't want to die, and I don't want to end our engagement."

"I give you my word," Bezaed said. "Leave her and I will leave you be."

It would be nice to have one less person chasing him. There would still be the Elenil, of course, and the Zhanin and some of the Scim to deal with. Not much would change, and the things that did change would be for the worse. He hadn't meant to get engaged, but now he could not imagine life without the statuesque Kakri woman at his side. Or, him at her side, whichever the case happened to be. "I'm never going to leave her," Jason said. "I know I'm not worthy of her, but she's stuck with me."

"If you cared about her, you would give her the chance to find someone of her own people. Someone who could be her equal in marriage, not a mewling infant requiring constant care. Look at you now: trapped upon a rotting log, trying not to be killed by stone flowers or a Kakri warrior."

Jason pulled his legs back up on the log and rearranged himself, lying back against the rough bark and crossing his arms behind his head. "You're the one who's trapped," he said. "You have to stay there for the next year hoping I'll move. But I'm pretty patient when it comes to not getting killed."

Bezaed said nothing to that, but he disappeared into the woods. That made Jason nervous, but what was Bezaed going to do? Pole-vault onto the rotten log? Set a fire? Besides, every minute that passed was a minute that might turn things in Jason's favor. Baileya could show up. Or Delightful Glitter Lady. Break Bones. Or, for that matter, Darius or Madeline or Shula or pretty much anyone.

Meanwhile, more stone flowers were gathering around his log. They must smell blood or something, because while there had been maybe a hundred at first, there were easily five or six hundred now, and they seemed to be gathering more. He wondered if that meant there was a safe path somewhere else. The stone flowers didn't move as fast as, say, a squirrel. So if you could find a path with fewer of them, you might be able to run through this part of the forest without being killed. Which he would need to figure out if he was going to make it to see the dragon, Arakam. He was starting to have his doubts. He needed to put all of this in order and see if there was a way out.

So. What did he know?

Baileya and Dee were somewhere nearby, he hoped. So were a number of Zhanin warriors. At this point there should also be a force of Elenil moving through the forest, since they hadn't sent Gilenyia back out. Shula, Madeline, and Gilenyia were off meeting with the guy who had branches growing out of his head. Jason needed to go find this dragon to learn the price of helping the Aluvoreans. The two Aluvoreans he had met were spectacularly unhelpful, but supposedly this was all mixed in with the magic of the Sunlit Lands.

Darius was in Far Seeing, seeking justice for the Scim and especially for Nightfall. Break Bones was with him. They wouldn't be showing up to help, as nice as that might be. Bezaed was after him, purely because Jason was with Baileya, and he claimed he would go away if Jason left his sister alone. Jason had his doubts.

"You need to change your story," Bezaed said.

Jason sat up. There he was, back on the edge of the forest. "Couldn't find a pogo stick, huh?"

"I do not know what this means."

"Or a hang glider or jet pack or anything? Oh well." Jason lay down again and looked at the branches hanging above him. They were a little high for him to jump to. Maybe if he had a rope. "So you're going to tell me a story? I'd appreciate it, I'm super bored."

The Kakri loved stories. They treated them like money, and they didn't give them away for no reason.

"I am not here to tell you a story but to say you must change the story you are in."

"Now I don't know what *you* mean."

The warrior made a sound of obvious disdain. "The story you are in now ends with your death."

"Bah. Everyone's story ends there," Jason said. "'Happily ever after' is just where you stop telling the story if you want it to sound happy."

"Your story now, Wu Song, is this: a young human becomes betrothed to a Kakri woman. He is pursued and finally killed by her family."

"Or, you know, he is pursued and runs up a log and starves to death." He glanced over at Bezaed, who had a look of pure frustration on his face. "I'm just saying there are choices here. It's not 'get killed by Bezaed or nothing.' I really have my pick of people who want to kill me. It's a luxury, I know."

"I am saying, you can change this story, human. It could be the story of the human who broke an engagement and lived."

"And he was sad the rest of his life, the end."

"But it would be a much longer life."

"And he was sad for about twenty minutes until he got stung by a stone flower, paralyzed, and eaten."

"I will save you from the flowers."

"Well, there's a sentence you don't hear every day." Jason closed his eyes. "You're willing to risk your life to keep me safe if I don't marry your sister. It's a weird sort of insult, really. I gotta say, Christmas dinner is going to be awkward after Baileya and I are married."

"We do not celebrate this . . . Christmas," Bezaed said.

"Oh, Bai loves Christmas. Lots of food and stories. We celebrated at Far Seeing, and—"

Bezaed threw a rock, which hit Jason in the shin. Jason sat up. A bruise had already formed. He rubbed his shin, his irritation at the Kakri rising. "Hey, not cool, man. Don't try to annoy me into falling into that vicious mob of flowers."

"I am not here to listen to you prattle on about your Earth holidays. What is the best story to come of your choices so far, Wu Song? Do not they all end in your death? Again I say, change your story."

"My best story, huh? Let's see. I get out of this mess somehow. Baileya knocks you out, I guess. She probably has Dee with her. We figure out how to get through the carnivorous forest—I'm thinking stilts?—and we find the dragon. We ask the dragon the price of fixing Aluvorea, and he says, 'One pudding cup a day for the rest of your life.' After some initial complaining and uncertainty, I agree to these terms, making me a hero and giving the dragon a complete monopoly on chocolate pudding in the Sunlit Lands. Madeline saves the world. We are heroes. I get a castle, and Baileya and I get married. We figure out how to import comic books and American movies to the Sunlit Lands. Oh, and I introduce indoor plumbing to everyone, so we get filthy rich. Oh yeah, and Mads and Darius get together, I'm sure."

"This story is full of impossibilities."

"It's like you've never seen a Star Wars film," Jason said.

"Why do you insist on speaking nonsense to me?"

"Or James Bond. That guy can jump out of a moving plane onto a motorcycle falling off a cliff while wearing a parachute. Why can't I walk through the forest on stilts without someone saying I'm being ridiculous?"

"Your best story will never happen. But your worst could. You fall from your log. You escape the stone flowers, but I kill you. These things are far more likely than your story. You must change your story, Wu Song."

"Say that again," Jason said.

"You will die a terrible—"

"Not that part!"

"Change your story?"

"Yes!" Jason sat up straight. Of course. It all made sense now. He had told Madeline before she left the Sunlit Lands that he was searching for a story . . . a way to make the Sunlit Lands understand their situation and discover a way out of it. He had to be honest, he hadn't done much in this direction. But what if it wasn't about finding a story, it was about *creating* a story? Writing a new one? Changing the world through the way he spoke about it?

Bezaed, delighted by Jason's "yes," said, "So you agree to break your betrothal? If you swear it to me, I will leave you in peace."

"Nope," Jason said. "I've got a different story to tell you, so hold on to your hat."

"I have no hat," Bezaed said.

"Further evidence you should have held on. Do you remember at the festival for the Meeting of the Spheres? I was there."

"It was the night you became engaged to my sister. We celebrated the festival, and she came to us at the end to say you had told her your secret story, and she was considering its worth. Then you both ran into the desert, and I followed."

Yes. They had been in the desert. Baileya had taken him to a Kakri festival—something few outsiders had seen. They had sung songs and told stories and danced. Jason had told Baileya what happened to his sister, not realizing that this sort of storytelling was considered an invitation to marriage among the Kakri people. This night, of all nights, is where Jason had found his new story.

"That night I learned the story of how the Kakri came to be . . . how Mother Crow came to the people and invited them to come and live in the desert. They had to leave everything behind, but they followed her and became the mighty Kakri."

"What of it?"

Jason grinned. "So the old lady, Mother Crow? She invited me to come learn from her in the desert."

Bezaed frowned. "She is the elder of our people, but she is not Mother Crow herself. Besides, you are here, not there."

"You're not connecting the dots, my future brother-in-law. What I'm telling you is that I have been invited to become a Kakri by Mother Crow. Your eldest elder. Or however you want to say it. You say you don't want your sister to marry a human? I give you my word today that I will not marry your sister until I go into the desert with Mother Crow, just like your ancestors did, and become Kakri myself. You know I don't tell lies. I will do this."

Bezaed shifted from one foot to the other, clearly uncomfortable. "Among my people, we try to kill even the Kakri suitors for our sisters."

"Then shouldn't you wait until I'm Kakri?"

Bezaed leaned against the tree beside him. "Did Mother Crow truly say this to you?"

"Yes. She said to leave everything and come to the desert to learn."

"I will leave you then," Bezaed said, and started walking away.

"Hey, where are you going?"

"To wait for you in the desert. If you survive becoming a Kakri, then you and I will have words." Then Bezaed left, disappearing into the trees.

Jason almost fell off the log he was so surprised. "Hey, that worked. That worked!" He bounced in his excitement, and the log creaked beneath him. "Yikes." He carefully rearranged himself and then whispered a cheer and said, as quietly as he could, "That worked, yaaay."

When Remi found him three hours later, he already had a new plan.

"You are trapped on a log," Remi said, landing lightly beside him.

"I know, right?"

"No doubt you wish you had wings."

"One of several solutions I would accept." He scratched Remi's head, and she began to purr. "I have a favor to ask."

She had her eyes closed. "You wish me to take messages to your loved ones after the stone flowers eat you," she said. "I will do this for you."

"No, something else. See, I'm supposed to go find the dragon, Arakam."

She opened one eye. "You wish me to take a message to Arakam after you die."

"Getting warmer. Look, this is how the story is supposed to go: I trudge through the carnivorous forest. It is scary. Maybe we come across the fire-thorns, I don't know. Also scary. We come to the waterfalls where Arakam lives. Turns out he's not a dragon, he's like a, I don't know, a giant salaman-der or something because people in the Sunlit Lands do not know anything about animals. The giant salamander tells me whatever it is he's supposed to say, I slog back to find Madeline, et cetera. But I was thinking, what if we changed the story? What if, um, you flew to Arakam, he told you the stuff, and you came back and told me?"

"I cannot help but notice that in your story I do all the work."

"This is a natural side effect to me not having wings," Jason said, scratching behind her ears.

"Fine," she said. "I will do it. But not because I like you—I don't. Rather because I have been wanting to see Arakam and give him a good swat on the nose for several years now. He has been telling the Aluvoreans to call me a feline, knowing full well that they will not realize this is another way to say *cat*. It has been a great inconvenience."

"Offensive! Arakam should show more respect for a Guardian of the Wind,"

"Indeed."

"Would you like to blow all these stone flowers away before you go?"

She turned her green eyes on him. "Cleverly asked. But they do not move in the wind so easily. Observe." She set her wings to flapping, and a great wind burst through the forest. Jason clutched onto the log, trying not to get blown off. The stone flowers wrapped their little tentacles into one another, the ground, stones, grass, whatever, and none of them were blown away.

The log began to break. "Wait, wait, stop!"

Remi stopped. "You see?"

"I had to try," he said.

"Death by stone flower is a painful way to go," Remi admitted.

"I've just been trying to change the story, you know?"

"Indeed."

"It's amazing that you could blow that Zhanin warrior into the forest, but those stone flowers won't budge."

"They are quite strong."

Then it came to him again. Another way to change the story. "Before you go, do you think you could blow me off this log and into the forest?" Remi's tail twitched. "Not deeper into the carnivorous part," Jason added quickly.

Remi flew into the air and circled him a few times. "Let go of the log," she said, "and stand up."

Jason got carefully to his feet, balancing on the edge of the log. It creaked under his weight. Remi started bringing the wind, and he crouched down. The log was cracking. The wind getting stronger. He could feel the skin on his face pressing back in the wind.

Then the log broke, and he was screaming, falling toward the flowers below, and then the wind pushed him backward, and he was flying, soaring, tumbling above the forest. The tallest trees were far below him. He glanced back and could see Remi, no longer flapping her wings but gliding north. The wind lessened. He had not thought about this part. He was falling, still screaming. He spread his arms wide, hoping to catch a branch. A thick branch broke his fall, and he crashed through that one and into the next and then the next. He had been whipped in the face, legs, and arms, and now hung like a piece of laundry from a tree. It was a long drop to the ground still.

He checked himself for broken bones, but he was fine. Unless you counted all the bruises and cuts. Which he did. Twenty-seven. Twenty-eight if you counted the bruise on his shin. He pulled himself slowly, painfully to the trunk and started the downward climb. It was time to find Baileya.

27

THE GEARS OF THE WORLD

War is when two groups of people kill each other until one group says "enough." Then that group—the one who says "enough"—they are said to have lost the war.

FROM "THE GOOD GARDENER," AN ALUVOREAN STORY

✦

The Pastisians were preparing for war. Every person on the streets walked with purpose. In the sky overhead the towers were swarmed with airships. King Ian strode the streets, once again behind his golden mask, barking orders to those who moved too slowly, conferring with his advisors, making snap decisions about snags in the preparation. Darius and Break Bones still wore their crimson uniforms. Hanali had traded his ridiculous outfit for a tailored cream-and-gold suit with a crimson cape and a circlet of gold on his brow. Darius couldn't help but think he was trying to look regal . . . no doubt for when he took the role of archon for his own. Mrs. Raymond walked beside the king in a black dress. She would not wear the crown they had brought her, or the golden half mask. King Ian had frowned when she turned them aside but said nothing.

Keeping close to Ian was difficult in the midst of all this, but he demanded their presence. One moment they could scarcely keep up with him as his long legs ate up the streets. The next he stood in a knot of his subjects, speaking earnestly to them, and there was no room to be near him. The only one who seemed to anticipate his moves and be nearby at all times was Mrs. Raymond. She'd said back in the tower that she had killed her own daughter. Darius couldn't imagine it. He wondered what the story was there but knew it was far too sensitive a question to ask.

Ian called Darius and Break Bones to his side. "You, envoys of the Scim. Will the Scim take our side in the fight to come?"

"The Elenil are our eternal enemy," Break Bones said. "I only worry you will be too kind to them in your occupation. But in the battle? We will always fight alongside those who fight the Elenil."

"And you, Black Skull? Will you stand beside me, come what may?"

"I will," Darius said. "You have my word. I long to stand in the archon's presence and retrieve my mask, and my sword cries out for his blood. Not to mention these shackles."

"I know you are men of your word, and I will hold you to it. Now where is the Elenil?"

Hanali stepped forward with a smooth grace. "Here, sir."

"What plans are you hatching, I wonder?"

Hanali raised his eyebrows. "Me, sire? Only to bring justice to the Elenil. Archon Thenody has lost his ability to rule well. It is time to replace him."

"You wish to replace him, of course."

"Prophets and seers have said I will be his successor, more than once. They say a human will kill him, and I shall take the throne in Far Seeing. Thenody knows this—has known for some time. No doubt he is terrified by my absence."

The king removed his mask, as if he were trying to get a clearer view of Hanali. "Tell me again what benefit there will be in allying with you, Hanali, son of Vivi."

Hanali winced at the mention of his father's name and glanced furtively toward Darius. It was impossible to tell with Hanali if the wince was real or affected, a fact that put Darius off balance, feeling both guilt for the pain he had caused and annoyance at the Elenil. "I am glad to reassure you,

Majesty. The Scim resistance within the city knows and trusts me. Ask your own wife—she will acknowledge it. We have also a sentient tunnel who has networked himself beneath the city. When Thenody has fallen, my presence will make it clear that this is a coup, not a Pastisian invasion. The Elenil people will fight you to their dying breath if they think you are going against the will of the Majestic One to try to put Pastisians in charge of the Sunlit Lands. But if I take the throne, there will be those who are angry, but why fight if their new archon commands peace?"

The king held Hanali's eyes for a long moment before he said, "What need have the noble Pastisians of tunnels? We are people of technology. We will fly over your medieval walls, not burrow beneath them like rodents."

Hanali bowed his head slightly, then said, "I forgot to mention my keen fashion sense, Majesty. I am sure this would be of use as well. I could certainly help Mrs. Raymond find something more . . . elaborate to wear."

The king scowled but did not answer this. It was Mrs. Raymond who spoke. "Show respect, Hanali, or you'll find yourself a prisoner of the Pastisians, not a guest."

Hanali had the gall to laugh at this. "The Pastisians could not hold me long, Mrs. Raymond, as you know." He paused. "With respect."

"I hope we do not have need to try those words," King Ian said. "When the battle begins, you and Mrs. Raymond will be with me in the command ship. Break Bones, will your brothers join us?"

"I have sent word for them to meet us at the walls. We shall worry their forces from outside the wall while yours attack from within."

"Excellent. Where will you fight, sir?"

"Where the battle is thickest, Majesty, and the blood the deepest."

The king nodded, a business-like acknowledgment of a true warrior. "And you, Darius?"

A wave of excitement swelled within Darius's chest, battering at his ribs from inside. "In the front, Your Majesty. With whoever will be there first and fastest. I want to be the first person the archon sees break down his door."

The king watched him with solemn eyes. "Then we must take you immediately to the Gears of the World. The advance force prepares even now for departure." The king motioned to one of his people, and in less than a minute a sort of car pulled up beside them. More truck, perhaps, than car, with long benches in the back for people to sit on. The king and Mrs. Raymond got into the front, and the rest of them piled onto the benches. Except Hanali, of course, who could not "pile" anywhere but instead lit upon a bench like a dainty bird.

Darius couldn't get a read on Hanali. He didn't know if the Elenil was a fool or a genius playing the fool. He suspected genius, because he had plans within plans, secrets wrapped in seeming openness. Darius didn't trust him, but Hanali's entire persona—the extravagant outfits, the upper-crust way of speech, the feigned surprise when his plans were revealed, his supposed concern for the well-being of the Wasted Lands—all seemed designed to paint him as harmless. Even the way he was sitting on the bench said Hanali was a delicate little thing, no trouble at all. Darius felt lost in his interactions with Hanali, uncertain if he was reading the Elenil's intentions correctly.

Darius had the book about Hanali's father tucked into his jacket pocket. He hadn't had a chance to look at it yet, but he suspected King Ian had read the entire thing already. He wondered about the king's words about the book being useful in his interactions with Hanali. Darius didn't know what the book would reveal and could not imagine something that would be of use. But maybe it would provide some sort of road map for understanding the Elenil who might be the next archon. Hanali could be an important person in the future of the Scim people.

As they approached the section of the city called the Gears of the World, the buildings grew shorter, and the sparkling crystal sky grew closer. There was something strange about the sky above them . . . there appeared to be holes in it. Or possibly places where the crystal sphere above them wasn't polished or had grown dull. "Are those holes?" Darius asked.

Hanali glanced at the sky. "So it appears. Our astronomers have noticed them in the past. There are a variety of theories to explain it. Some believe them to be natural—holes created by debris from beyond the Sunlit Lands. Others think they have always been there, and still others believe them to be purposely made."

"What do you think?"

"I can say with all honesty that I have not spent a moment's thought on holes—whether in the sky, the ground, or even, should such a thing come to be, in the ocean. I am more concerned about things that exist, not studying a phenomenon that is nothing more than the absence of something else. It would be like worrying about who has failed to murder your mother instead of who has succeeded in killing your father." He glanced at Darius, an inscrutable look on his face.

"It was war," Darius said. "A battle." Hanali making comments about this directly and in this moment took Darius off guard. And maybe that's what it was meant to do.

"A battle that took place on a night that has historically been a truce observed by all people in the Sunlit Lands."

Darius's face flushed. "A truce day chosen because it is the one day of the year the Elenil are vulnerable. It was foolish of your enemies to allow that day to be one of peace."

"For precisely this reason: the Elenil are meant to live for millennia, not to die after a paltry few centuries. Yet you put your sword through my father and killed him."

Darius shuffled on the bench, uncomfortable. But Hanali was conveniently avoiding his own involvement in the whole scenario. "You are the one who gave the Scim—including me and the other Black Skulls—entrance to the city that night."

"You weren't meant to try to take it over," Hanali said angrily. "You did more than we agreed to! When I was archon, I would have returned the Scim artifacts to you, yet you and your people seized the moment and tried to take the city."

"You gambled and lost," Darius said. "You wanted power and didn't get it, and lost your father. That's not on me." The words poured out, almost without thought. Because the death of Vivi *was* on him, like it or not. The sword had not been in Hanali's hand. Hanali could not have known his father would pay with his life and could not have known that the Scim—at Darius's insistence—would alter the agreement with him in midbattle. But Darius needed to seek out Madeline at that time despite any consequences. And he didn't trust Hanali or his plan. If he and the Scim could take the city in that moment, then he thought they should, and not risk relying on Hanali. They had been so close to succeeding, too! Yes, Darius had made the choice to abandon their plan with the Elenil faction led by Hanali.

The death of Hanali's father was one of the consequences of that decision, and so be it.

Their vehicle stopped, and Darius jumped off first, putting distance between himself and the Elenil. Once everyone had disembarked, King Ian led them between two squat buildings to a narrow field. Men and women worked in the grassy plain, attaching a series of cables to large blue compartments. Each looked big enough to hold as many as ten soldiers. Every strand of eight cables came together in a single enormous hook made of black metal, large enough it would take three or four people to move it.

A soldier came racing across the field on a steam-powered motorbike. He leapt off and bowed low, holding out a sealed envelope. A tiny bird, maybe three inches tall, perched on his shoulder. King Ian tore the envelope open, his eyes scanning the words. "The Elenil are massing their armies near Far Seeing . . . humans as well as Elenil prepare for war."

"Surely this is no surprise, my lord," Hanali said. "Perhaps the Scim are testing the weaknesses of the wall again."

"No, my sources say this is different. They are preparing to travel. It is said they march on Aluvorea."

"Aluvorea?" Hanali asked. His pale brow furrowed. "Aluvorea."

Mrs. Raymond made an exasperated noise. "Do not play the fool, Hanali, not today. If you know why the Elenil would make war on those toothless pacifists, speak now."

Hanali faced her, mild annoyance on his face. "The only possible reason is to protect the Queen's Throne. If someone in Aluvorea has sent word that agitators are seeking to enter the heart of the forest and rebirth magic—if someone seeks the Heartwood Crown—then the archon would be a fool not to send all his resources: every used-up soldier, every wooden sword, every lame steed in his command, and every dry crust of bread to provision them. But I have heard no such news."

The king turned back to the messenger. "And the bird? Does it bring tidings for me as well?"

"No, sir, but for one of your guests. May I deliver it?"

The king assented, and the messenger nodded to the bird, which zipped to Darius and hovered in front of him. He was shocked to see a tiny woman sitting on the bird's back. She pointed to Darius's face and held her hand out flat, palm up. He had heard of the fae, of course, but never seen one. They did not get on well with the Scim.

The bird chirped loudly, drawing his attention back to the faerie, who jabbed a finger at Darius and then held her palm out flat. Uncertain what she was doing, he lifted his own palm flat. The hummingbird zipped over him, and the woman leapt off its back and landed in Darius's hand. She started a flurry of hand gestures, but Darius had no idea what he was meant to get out of it.

The messenger cleared his throat. "She asks if you are Darius, the one who walks."

King Ian leaned close. "Is that Fae Sign? Fascinating. I have not seen it before."

"Yes, Majesty. I studied among the Aluvoreans to write my coming-of-age book."

Darius studied the small woman, who seemed to be agitated that they were not speaking to her. She wore an acorn helmet and clothing made of woven moss. "What does that mean, coming-of-age book?" Darius asked.

"Each Pastisian must write a book of original knowledge when they reach adulthood," Mrs. Raymond said. "Observations, fiction, scholarly pursuits, or poetry."

King Ian said, "To be a productive member of society requires that one produce."

"OW!" Without thinking, Darius moved his hand. A sharp pain had come from his palm. The little woman jumped from his hand, and her bird slipped under her. She flew up to his eye level again and started signing.

The messenger looked uncomfortable. "She says to pay attention or she will stab you again."

The faerie held a slender thistle in her hand like a sword. She pointed at Darius again and held her palm out straight. Darius reluctantly mirrored her, and she leapt into his hand again. Whatever she was signing, it was clear she was being a bit sarcastic. She rolled her eyes and lifted her eyebrows.

"She asked if you are Darius, the one who walks, and wants to know if you're paying attention. She says she can come back after the war if we're too busy playing with knives."

"I'm Darius Walker, yeah." He leaned in close to her again. "Who are you?"

The messenger shifted to direct translation. "I'm Diwdrap of Aluvorea. Here's your message: 'Darius. You have just left Aluvorea, and we have just arrived. Come back to me as quickly as you can. Shula is with me as well, and Jason and David, too. Love, Madeline.'"

Darius stared at the faerie, as if this would somehow cause her message to make more sense. Madeline was back in the Sunlit Lands! Back, and he had missed her because he had left Jason too early on the outskirts of Aluvorea. "Is . . . is she okay?"

The faerie shrugged. "She's dying."

No doubt Madeline had sent this message immediately, but Darius and Break Bones had been so cautious to avoid being seen by anything or anyone.

"Perhaps," Hanali said, "Archon Thenody has learned of Madeline's presence among the great trees. Since the loss of his hand he has had a singular focus where that girl is involved."

"I have to go to her," Darius said.

King Ian searched Darius's face with his eyes, as if he could see straight into his soul. "The place of my warriors will be to take Far Seeing. The absence of the majority of Thenody's soldiers will only be to our advantage. To choose between love and duty is painful. I have never regretted choosing love." Mrs. Raymond put her hand on his arm. "I have regretted choosing duty over love more than once."

Darius thought about that. In a few days, if all went according to plan, the Elenil would be defeated, Hanali on the throne, the danger past, and he could seek Madeline out. On the other hand, if he went to her now, he could help her, protect her. Knowing Maddie, she was probably the reason the Elenil were marching on Aluvorea, and likely because she was doing something to change the world. Change it in a way she thought was for the better. No doubt the Elenil disagreed. He could be there with her. "Majesty, would you give me a way to get to her?"

King Ian closed his eyes, and Mrs. Raymond squeezed his arm. She said, "Husband. Some things are more important than swords and steel."

The king's dark eyes found Darius's. "We need every soldier for Far

Seeing. But who knows? If the Elenil are so worried about whatever is happening in Aluvorea, it might be best to send a group of my own there to work toward our interests. I will send a section of my people, Darius. You can join them there, or us in Far Seeing, as you see fit."

Darius bowed his head. "Thank you, Your Majesty."

Break Bones put a hand on his shoulder. "You go to her, Darius. I will find and kill the archon. Put the Sword of Years into my hand, and I will fetch his head."

Darius hesitated. "The prophecy says it will be a human." He held the sword out to the king.

"I have told you already, I am Pastisian. And I will not carry that sword. I will not wield a tool that seeks to sway my actions."

The sword wanted battle, that much was clear. But wouldn't there be Elenil to fight in Aluvorea? Perhaps Mrs. Raymond would carry it? But she shook her head before he could even hold out the sword to her. The prophecy had been clear, and Hanali thought it was about Darius. "The prophecy," Darius said. "What happens if I don't go to Far Seeing?"

"A prophecy can wait," Break Bones said. "The Scim have waited these many years for justice, what is a few days more?"

"You must decide quickly," King Ian said. "I am commanding my soldiers to speed their departure."

Hanali had been quiet. Uncharacteristically quiet.

"What do you think?" Darius asked him.

Hanali's eyes fell on the faerie. "She's lying. The Aluvoreans have been allied with the Elenil for hundreds of years. The archon sent a hundred of these little things out to find you, no doubt, hoping to distract you."

The faerie started signing like mad to the messenger, who held his hands up and told her she was going too fast.

"Think," Hanali said. "When last you saw Madeline, was she well enough to journey to the Sunlit Lands? How long has it been? She would be worse now, not better. It is too fantastic, too unlikely, that she would have returned at just this moment. It is not like her. She has said her good-byes, she is done with this place."

But Darius knew, somehow, that Hanali was wrong. This was exactly like Maddie. It wouldn't matter that she had said good-bye. It definitely wouldn't matter that her health was failing. Once Madeline made a decision, there was nothing to be done. It was one of the things he loved about her, one of the reasons he knew that when they broke up he wouldn't be able to convince her to get back together: she had broken up with him because she loved him, and there was no way she could be persuaded to change that.

He remembered a time at school when one of the kids on the track team said something about how Darius could run so fast because he was Black, and Madeline took it to heart. She had gone to the coach and said she was going to sit out of every meet until the coach agreed to have a conversation about it in a team meeting. The coach said no. Madeline started convincing other kids they should sit the next meet out. Darius said no. He was still going to run. It wasn't like he hadn't heard the comment before, or a thousand things like it. But she convinced eleven other kids to sit out, and finally the coach folded, because the upcoming meet was a big one. He told Madeline he would let her lead a conversation, or bring someone in to lead one, but she had to agree to sit out the next meet anyway. Or she could drop it for now and they'd have a conversation at the end of the season—no need for all the drama when they should be running.

Darius still remembered the grin on Maddie's face as she sat in the stands at that meet, and how she cheered for him even louder than usual. He remembered how she ran down to him after his race and threw her arms around him. And he remembered how she waited until the coach let her start the conversation with the team (which had gone surprisingly well—way better than Darius had expected) and then reported the whole thing, including the weird suspension, to the principal and told him that her next call would be to the newspaper unless "something was done," and suddenly the coach was missing a meet himself because he was off at a mandatory training of some sort. Coach was scrupulously fair to Madeline—and Darius—after that. Darius told her she shouldn't have gone to all that trouble, shouldn't have put herself on the line like that for a dumb throwaway comment someone else had made, and she had looked at him with real shock and said, "Darius, *that was wrong* what he said to you." As if when you saw something wrong, what else could you do? You had to fix it, right? Even if it cost you.

So yeah. It was exactly like Madeline to be in the Sunlit Lands again. And it was exactly why, if she were here, she would tell him to do the right thing. Sure, she wouldn't want him to kill the archon, but she would want him to help the Scim. If he saw Madeline before he killed the archon, he wasn't sure he would ever do it. She would convince him there was another way. So maybe it was now or never.

"The time of decision has come," King Ian said. "Hanali?"

"I, for one, will head to Far Seeing," Hanali said, but he seemed distracted.

"And you, friend Scim?"

"Yes," Break Bones said slowly. "I will go to Far Seeing. Brother Darius. You need not join us. With the Pastisians behind me and the Elenil here at my side, it seems likely we will overcome any barrier through brute strength or Hanali's guile."

Darius wanted to go to Maddie, so badly he thought he would be torn in two. But there was an issue of justice here. Darius had a responsibility. He had promised to confront Thenody about the murdered Scim child, Nightfall, too. Then there was the blood of the Scim shed over centuries to be atoned for. He thought of what Madeline would say to him if he chose to come to her and lost an opportunity to move the Sunlit Lands toward justice. She would be angry. She would want him to do the right thing, and come to her after if he could. Surely she could wait a few days. This wasn't an either/or decision. He'd kill the archon and leave immediately for Aluvorea. Far Seeing would be a detour, nothing more. His spirits lifted at the idea of seeing her again, and having done his duty, too.

He spoke to Diwdrap. "Can you take a message back to Madeline?"

"Of course," she said.

"Tell her that I love her and that I'll come for her after we take Far Seeing." He paused. What else should he say? "Tell her . . . tell her she has always been my something better." Those last words echoed a line from Madeline's favorite books, the Meselia novels. The same books that Mrs. Raymond had written, once upon a time.

The faerie gave him a skeptical look, then signed something to the translator. "I'll tell her," he translated. "But that's the sort of message that should be delivered in person."

With that she jumped off Darius's hand, landed on her hummingbird, and flew away, her hands speeding a message to the Pastisian messenger as she departed.

The messenger's face flushed. "She also has a message for the Elenil."

Hanali raised his eyebrows. "Oh? What did she say?"

"I'm afraid it's not repeatable, sir."

Hanali clicked his tongue in annoyance but said nothing. He seemed to be lost in thought. He watched the hummingbird speed out of sight.

The bird flew up, toward the taller buildings of the city, then in widening circles, as if looking for a path in the air, before it flew to the south. Darius looked at the king. "I go to Far Seeing, so long as Archon Thenody is there."

The king raised an eyebrow, then spoke to his attendants. "We walk toward the Gears of the World now. I would have a moment of private conversation with Darius."

Mrs. Raymond slipped her hand from the king's arm and immediately began giving instructions to some of the soldiers nearby. The guards made sure there was a wide berth around the king and Darius. Hanali didn't even make a comment, a testament to how distracted he had become.

The king put his large hand on Darius's shoulder as they walked. "You have made a warrior's choice, Darius Walker. I pray you do not regret it. Now I must offer you one more thing before you depart with my soldiers."

"What is that, Your Majesty?"

"Let me take that sword from you. The magic weighs you down, and it changes the way you think, the way you move in battle. It draws you toward blood, and you fight against it. It slows you."

Darius frowned. "I offered it to you a few minutes ago, and you didn't want it."

"I have no desire to use it. But I would gladly free you from it." He walked in silence for a moment, gathering his thoughts. Then he said, "Why do you want to bring justice to the Scim so badly, Darius Walker?"

It was a crazy question. "It's the right thing to do."

"Ah. But people such as you and I know that injustice fills the world like water. You cannot drink it all, Darius. So why have you chosen to empty this particular cup?"

Darius opened his mouth to speak. Then he realized that he didn't know the answer. The Scim had befriended him when he arrived in the Sunlit Lands. He had lived among them. He *knew* them. "They're my friends," he said at last. "And I want them to be treated well."

The king made a low rumbling sound in his chest, a sound of affirmation. "And did you have friends in your homeland who were mistreated? And did you throw everything away to help them? Did you abandon your time, your home, your loved ones, potentially your life to fight for them?"

No. He hadn't. He . . . he didn't know why. He didn't understand why he fought for the Scim with such intense certainty. He decided at last that there was only one answer that was honest. "I don't know why I fight for the Scim," he said. "Or at least, why I fight for them when I've never fought this way for someone else before this."

"I have a theory, if you would hear it," the king said. "A thought to consider."

"Okay."

The king stopped walking, turning his whole attention to Darius. His gaze felt as heavy as a lead apron. Darius couldn't have moved away if he had wanted. "As king, I cannot right every wrong. But I have come to realize that some wrongs are dependent on others. If I can find the core injustice and destroy it, many of the others are destroyed in time. Do you understand?"

"Yeah. That makes sense."

"In your world, in your country, there are many injustices. Some are visited on the people who look like you and me . . . black-skinned people like us, like many of the Pastisians. This is why my people first came here, as you know. Slavery, racism, socially constructed poverty—these things are not the core injustice. It is something deeper: the belief that some people are inferior to others. They are not to be treated well, because they are less worthy than other people. They are not able to break free, because they are not as strong as their oppressors."

"But we did break free!"

"You broke free of slavery, as did we. But you, Darius . . . Not every person in your country, not Black people, *you*. You have not broken free of this message that has been shouted to you by the world around you your whole life. You have not broken free of this core injustice, this oppressive lie which has been ingrained in you: you still believe you are inferior. You believe you are not worth fighting for. You believe you cannot have justice for yourself."

"I—"

"Yet in the Scim's situation you see a reflection, a strange reflection, of yourself. So although you have never fought for yourself with the same passion, the same ferocity, you fight for the Scim to prove that it can be done. You fight for the Scim as you wish someone had fought for you. You fight to make yourself worthy so that perhaps you can free yourself at last."

Darius trembled at these words. They sank into him. He wasn't sure they were true. He didn't want them to be true. But he couldn't deny that they fit the facts. They even fit things Madeline had said to him more than once—that he stood up for other people but would never stand up for himself. He couldn't talk about this anymore. He didn't want to think about this. "Your Majesty," Darius said, "we are running out of time to prepare for our battle."

"Ah," the king said. "Of course. One more thing. The sword. It has a powerful need for revenge. It whispers to you of justice but disguises the cost."

"Justice is cheap at any cost," Darius said.

"I do not disagree. And yet . . . you are so quick to sacrifice, Darius. You take the weight on yourself alone, when the community would gladly lift with you." The king held his hand out, and one of his attendants approached and gave him a sword. It had a strange box soldered above the hilt. The king pointed his finger at it. "This is a battery pack. It runs an electrical current into the blade. It has no magic in it—no will but yours guides it. It would be your blade, not a blade soaked in centuries of accumulated Scim blood. Use it here or in Far Seeing or in Aluvorea. My offer to send you there stands." He handed the sword to Darius.

Darius turned the blade over in his hand, studied it. "Your Majesty. I thank you for your generosity. But I must follow where the Sword of Years takes me."

King Ian took the electric sword back and handed it to his attendant, who backed away again. "I expected no other answer, but it is the role of kings to offer wellness to their people. So be it."

A buzzing excitement came from the Sword of Years. It could feel that it would be loosed upon the Elenil soon. Darius wasn't certain how he felt about everything the king had said, but there was something about Ian's confidence, his kindness, that amazed Darius. Not only that, but he also seemed aware of the injustices of the world. His kindness wasn't the result of blindness or naiveté. Ian had said that his role was to offer wellness to his people. Darius's heart swelled at the thought that the king saw Darius as one of his own. Maybe after the battle, after he had gone to Madeline, he could come back here again. "How soon will we board the airships?"

"I will speak to you once more before you fly from here," the king said. Apparently this ended his audience. Ian spoke loud enough to include everyone nearby. "Walk with me," the king said, "all of you. Come see the Gears of the World." He led them away from the buildings and toward the edge of the world.

There was a gap of about a foot between where the ground ended and the massive crystal sphere moved past. It was turning fast, and Darius put his hand out to touch it, feeling the smooth movement of the sky. The gap looked down into darkness and empty space. Darius shuddered at the thought of what might happen if someone were to fall into it. "Where do these holes come from?" he asked. Up close he could see that they were fairly large, about the size of a soccer ball.

"We drill those," the king said. "For our gondola lifts."

Hanali leaned close. "I see no gears in these so-called Gears of the World."

Mrs. Raymond snorted. "You're so literal minded sometimes, Hanali."

The king pointed out the giant hooks and cables still in the field behind them. "We connect these hooks into the sphere, and then the gondola is lifted into the sky. We can be anywhere in the Sunlit Lands in a day, in the amount of time it takes the sun to rise and set again. Once we're over the area where we wish to be, my people drop from the gondolas with gliders."

"How do you get the gondolas back?"

"We don't. They go into the sea on the other side of the world. They've never come up again on this side."

Break Bones said, "I have never seen a thing like this, nor imagined it in the world. It is no wonder the Pastisians keep their technology secret."

"Is it dangerous to the environment?" Darius asked. "Drilling holes in the sky seems dangerous."

"Every technology has an environmental cost. The Pastisians have purposely curtailed our technology for environmental reasons and because I will not allow the use of slaves or underpaid workers. This limits some of our options. But this particular cost is a small one for the strategic advantage it gives us."

"I'm ready," Darius said. "Which gondola will I board?"

"They are readying the first one now," the king said. "I will take you there. Say your farewells now." This was a smooth way of letting Darius know that he would be walking with the king alone, not with the others.

Darius clasped arms with Break Bones. "I will see you in Far Seeing."

Break Bones grinned. "We shall meet in the archon's chambers, our enemies defeated in our wake." Darius glanced at Hanali but did not speak to him. The Elenil had turned his back, feigning interest in the rising wall of crystal.

Mrs. Raymond, to his surprise, hugged him. While she was near him, she whispered, "The Elenil have done many things that are evil. Do not let your search for revenge corrupt you, too. Do not let them add the destruction of your soul to the list of their wrongs, Darius." She held his eyes for a moment, then released him to her king.

Darius walked alongside the king, mulling over her words. Ian said, "She has a way of saying things that haunt you in battle."

Darius laughed. "You both do. You should let your warriors focus on the fighting."

"You may die today," the king said solemnly. "It would be a disservice to leave you in ignorance of yourself."

"It's hard work, being a Pastisian," Darius said.

"Yes," King Ian said. "Did she speak to you of forgiveness?"

Not exactly. "No, she spoke against revenge. Or at least, what revenge can do to a person."

They had come to a gondola that had been laid out facing the sphere. Three men carried the hook, positioning it near the shining wall that rose endlessly over the Sunlit Lands. The gondola was upright, and soldiers moved in and out of it, making preparations. "She is a wise woman," the king said, "but we always come to a place of disagreement here. She thinks one can forgive injustice and show mercy and be done. I say you cannot forgive someone for the past if they continue their behavior into the future. Or rather, it is not true forgiveness. For if I truly forgave them, would I not then desire what is best for them? And do not the perpetrators of injustice harm themselves as well as others?" He shook his head. "No. It is *because* I have forgiven the Elenil that I must help them find another way. It is because I have forgiven them that I must tear down the unjust works of their hands. I cannot allow them to destroy themselves in their selfishness."

"I haven't forgiven them," Darius said. "I have no intention of doing so."

"Then you must beware, for you give the Elenil power over you. You are driven by them still if they loom so large in your world." The king clapped Darius on the back. "Words to consider as you journey to Far Seeing." He called to one of his people, "Get this man fitted with a glider suit. He's to be on the first gondola."

Within twenty minutes Darius was wearing a suit with long, flexible wings that extended beneath his arms, connected to his ankles. It was uncomfortable but, he was assured, more comfortable than riding the gondola to its termination in the Ginian Sea. He was given a brief training for the glider suit and assured it would be natural enough once he was in the air. There was a hook connected to his suit, which was fastened to the gondola as he and the soldiers boarded. The captain of the gondola shouted instructions to the soldiers who were positioning the main hook.

"Prepare yourselves," the captain said. She had a strong jawline and a fierce, determined look on her face. Then she shouted to the hook crew, "All is ready."

"Hook in three," one of them called back. "Three, two, one!"

The hook made the crystal ring as it clanged into place. It ascended faster even than Darius had expected, and the cable rose up behind it, the sound like a monstrous snake hissing. Then the gondola caught and jerked into the air. It swung and hit the wall with an enormous gong. Darius was knocked into the side of the gondola, not expecting the sudden jolt, and the other soldiers laughed and teased him in a good-natured way. "Normal on a first outing," one of them said. They were rising over the Sunlit Lands, with a speed unlike any Darius had experienced before.

"We will be there in a short time," the captain said. "Prepare yourselves."

To Darius's surprise, each of the soldiers took out a book and began to read. Maybe it made sense, in a hyperliterate culture, that the best way to center oneself for battle was to practice one's little necromancies. He felt in his own pocket and pulled out the book about Vivi. Perhaps there would be some helpful information about the Elenil that Darius didn't know, and it would keep him from thinking about everything King Ian and Mrs. Raymond had said to him. He opened to the first page and began to read.

28

NOT FAR NOW

All is not yet lost, for there are several hours until sunrise.
FROM "MALGWIN AND THE WHALE," A TRADITIONAL ZHANIN STORY

✦

It took them nearly an hour to calm Madeline's mother. Night had fallen, deep and black, but Patra Koja had called for something he called marsh lights . . . pale, floating orbs that lodged in the branches of the trees above them and washed everything as if in cool moonlight. Yenil was fine. She had been, in fact, overjoyed to see Shula and Madeline and had run into their arms, sopping wet and happy. Now that they were in the Sunlit Lands, she and Shula could speak the same language without trouble, and words tumbled from her in an unending stream. Patra Koja steered the raft toward land, and they found Lin waiting for them there. Shula happily took Yenil aside once they made landfall, and the two sat on the ground talking with one another about every topic that came into their heads. Yenil made a faerie house and danced with delight when a few actual faeries dropped by to inspect it. Gilenyia remained in a deep sleep, and did not stir or wake.

Madeline's mother, though, had panicked, asking over and over where they were, how they got here. Madeline tried to calm her, kept reminding her she was here too, that it was going to be okay, but nothing worked.

"Someone has damaged her memories," Patra Koja said. "I see a vast space that was blockaded many years ago."

"Can you fix it?" Madeline had put a fresh leaf of Queen's Breath on her neck, hoping that being able to breathe better would make it easier to help her mom.

"Not knowing the way the spell is structured and what provisions may have been included, I do not wish to take the chance. There could be a punishment to be paid if it is removed, but I know not what. It is intricate work, of Elenil make, that much is certain."

"Someone is coming," David said. "Everyone get ready."

The urgency in David's voice made it clear he thought it could be an enemy. Yenil came to Madeline and settled in her arms. David and Shula moved toward the place the intruder would enter, ready to fight. Lin stood behind them, and even Madeline's mother quieted, though her panicked gasping was still louder than Madeline would have liked.

There was a crashing in the woods, something or someone large moving toward them. It also sounded like it was dragging something. Whatever it was, it wasn't trying to be quiet, a sign it wasn't afraid of whatever it might come across in these dangerous woods.

Baileya emerged from the woods, coming to the edge of the swamp. She dragged a Zhanin warrior behind her, tied with vines and unconscious. Delightful Glitter Lady frolicked at her feet. "Is Jason here?" she asked, her eyes scanning the group. "I cannot find him."

"No," Madeline said. "We last saw him with you."

"You are all well?" Baileya took in who was there. She recognized Yenil, but her gaze lingered on Madeline's mother. "She has a sickness caused by magic," she said.

"The Kakri have always seen the negative works of magic more easily than the positive," Patra Koja said.

Baileya dropped the Zhanin warrior at Madeline's feet. "It is easier to see for those not addicted to it," she said. "The Zhanin are able to stop magic for a time. Madeline . . . do you desire me to wake this one up?"

Madeline reached for her mother's hand. She was staring into the distance, breathing in and out too quickly, not responding to Madeline's voice. "It's worth a try."

Baileya bent down over the fallen warrior and slapped him gently in the face. To Shula she said, "Bring me water," and to David, "Cut him free of the vines."

As the Zhanin began to stir, Madeline could only think what she would say to her mother if her memories returned. Madeline had to know what had happened, had to understand what had brought her to this place. "We are going to get you free of this spell," she said, squeezing her mother's hand.

"No," her mother said, weeping. "No, please no."

✛

Jason backtracked through the woods, picking twigs out of his hair and periodically checking his scrapes and cuts. Flying through the trees was surprisingly painful when one did not have wings. Well, maybe not surprisingly painful, just painful. He couldn't find Baileya anywhere, or the Zhanin warriors, or Delightful Glitter Lady. He had found an Elenil war party, but that had been before he got out of the tree. They passed beneath him, and he sat as silent and still as he was able. He debated doing a bird call but realized in the same moment that this would be ridiculous. Not that being ridiculous often stopped him.

"Are you lost?"

It was Remi again. She was in a tree ahead of him, her tail whipping contentedly as it hung off a branch. "You got back fast," Jason said.

"I'm not some wingless thing who can't make good time. Besides, Arakam was hunting south of the falls. He was easy to find."

The dragon! Jason felt a twinge of disappointment not to have seen it. "Was it amazing?"

"Arakam? Hmph. Nothing so spectacular as a Guardian of the Wind, I'll tell you that much. Just a great dumb beast."

"Did he answer my question about the cost of saving Aluvorea?"

"He did, in his great dumb beast sort of way."

"Well, go on, what did he say?"

"He talks mostly in poems and riddles, you know. But what he said was that there used to be a river that flowed around the Queen's Island, but it has been cut off and is little more than a brackish lake now. The last queen, centuries ago, was crowned against her will, so the magic she made is double edged. The firethorns, those are hers: designed to burn down the forest and renew it. The stone flowers, also hers: a punishment for those who took her. They are pure spite and no benefit. She wanted to hasten the day another queen would come, because the people would want to renew the magic, to do away with what she had put in place. But a curse was also put upon the water around the island, I know not whether by the queen or someone else. Whoever is first to cross from shore to the island, whether by boat or swimming or whatever way they may come, that person must take the queen's place and die upon the island."

Jason put his hand on a tree trunk and leaned hard against it. The first to cross the water would die. He knew it would be something like this. He knew Madeline intended to pay that price, he had felt for so long that she was heading toward something like this. He couldn't allow that. He needed to find her, to convince her that she didn't need to do it. Then he thought of his new skill that had worked so well: changing the story. "What else did he say? What were his exact words?"

"Oh, just the usual prophetic poems. They're never good poems, have you noticed? They're too busy trying to say something. Doggerel verse, emphasis on the dog. It was something like:

The first to cross the waters, dead.
The island now their final bed.
Let all who see them cry and wail,
To see their face all still and pale.

Or words to that effect, in any case. I don't think those were the exact words, but something like that . . . no rhythm and far too much rhyme."

Jason winced. He should have maybe gone to the dragon himself. Not that he would have remembered the whole poem, but maybe he would have heard something in it that caught his attention. A loophole. A way out. "Think, Remi, did he say anything else?"

She licked her front paw, meditating. "Oh yes! He said that the island would protect the corpse of the dead one so she couldn't be buried. The island likes to keep its queens. He said that is a cost too, that once someone sets off across the water, they will die, and their body will not be easily recovered."

"Well, which is it, that the body can't be recovered or just can't be easily recovered?"

She thought about this. "Not easily recovered, I think. One thing was clear, though: the first to cross the waters dies."

✦

Darius stood on top of the gondola. It was open, and two Pastisian warriors balanced at the lip as well, holding the cables which went straight up into the sky, watching the ground. It was cold here, and the wind blew fierce and strong, but the world below was beautiful. Madeline was down there somewhere. If he rode this thing all the way to the end, he might pass over her. But he would see her soon enough. When they first rose from the east, where they had connected the gondola, they could see the great airships and dirigibles of the Pastisians setting out for war, like an armada of monstrous birds.

They had passed clear views of the Kakri territories and the terrible mountain range to their west. He had caught a glimpse of the ruins of an old city, complete with broken-down statues, or so the Pastisians told him. "We fly much closer in the airships," they said. "But slower, too."

Approaching noon, Darius could begin to make out the Ginian Sea in the distance, and an island hazed in mist. "What is that place?"

The Pastisians exchanged looks. "We don't speak of it."

"Look there," one of them said. "The Court of Far Seeing!" The city shone in the sun, a white and gleaming promise that Darius knew had been broken far too often. The two Pastisians went below to tell the others to prepare for battle. Darius remained on top of the gondola and watched as the city drew near. This was a moment he had waited for, had worked toward, for far too long.

✦

Shula held Yenil close, so thankful the girl had come back to her. She stroked her hair and kissed her cheek. The girl reminded her so much of

Amira, especially now that they could speak again! It was a flood of words, as if a great dam had been broken and they could say all the things they had wanted to say in the time they had spent together. Yenil spoke of the faerie village in Mrs. Oliver's back garden, and of what had been said and done at school (some of those stories made Shula furious), and of how much she loved cats and other small animals, and flowers. She did not speak of the loss of her parents, though Shula knew from experience she must think of it at times. She was, mostly, happy to be reunited with Shula and Madeline. Shula realized that her battle to keep distance between herself and Yenil had been lost . . . had likely been lost long ago. The child was in her heart, and nothing Shula did now could remove her. She felt content but also a thrill of fear.

Mrs. Oliver had mostly calmed now, since Baileya had come with the Zhanin. She still seemed frightened but in a different way. When she'd first arrived it was a panic, a driving fear that could be neither named nor reasoned away. Now Mrs. Oliver named her fear: she did not want to remember. She knew she was forgetting something, seemed to have some understanding that it was caused by magic, and she did not want it undone. Madeline and Baileya continued working to wake the Zhanin. Mrs. Oliver seemed to understand that this was connected, and she trembled at the thought.

Patra Koja came to Shula, who stood on the firmer ground near the woods. Yenil was in the nearby trees, looking for leaves and sticks to make more faerie houses. Shula kept an eye on her as she waded through the underbrush, climbed trees, and dug under bushes. Hummingbirds zipped around her, and faeries pointed out flowers, sticks, and stones they fancied. Shula had wanted to get her a little farther away from the fearful monologue of Mrs. Oliver, and David said he would patrol the woods just beyond them and make sure to warn them long before any surprises could come their way.

"She is your sister," Patra Koja said.

Shula looked at Yenil, who was hunched over a flower, counting the petals. "She is like her, yes."

He shook his antlered head slowly. "The Scim girl, she is more daughter than sister to you. I mean Madeline."

Daughter? Shula examined this statement and discovered it to be true. Maybe she had missed it because of Amira, but even with her she had been more mother than sister, really. And yes, Madeline was closer than a friend. She could not imagine abandoning her, ever. Shula had been so determined not to bond with anyone else after what had happened to her family, and Madeline had come into the Sunlit Lands and destroyed that determination.

She watched Madeline, who even now was talking quietly with her mother on the raft that Patra Koja had made. Baileya had managed to wake the Zhanin and was speaking to him in low tones. "I would do anything for her," Shula said, with pure honesty.

"Death comes in many ways," Patra Koja said, "and so rarely with any meaning."

Shula remembered her apartment building on fire, her friends and neighbors watching the blaze. "There is always a meaning," she said. "Sometimes it means only that there are evil people in the world."

"Madeline will not be healed," Patra Koja said. "I do not see an unraveling to her curse. You know this already, I think."

"I hope you're wrong," Shula said. "But she won't accept a cure that hurts someone else. I'm not sure there's another way."

"There is a sort of life that comes with being the queen of Aluvorea."

"She turns into a tree or something like that," Shula said, skepticism dripping from her voice.

"Nothing so simple. The woods reflect her, they take on her character."

"So she dies, but the woods remind us of her? This is no different from death, Patra Koja. Everything I see reminds me of my parents and my brother and sister. Even these woods as they are now."

"She will die in any case," Patra Koja reminded her. "It would be a good thing for her to choose to spend her death in a noble cause."

"Why are you saying this to me? This is Madeline's choice, not mine, and I will always support her decision. If you're trying to convince someone, talk to Madeline. If she says to burn this place to the ground and take her back to Earth, I'll do that in a moment. If she wants to find this Heartwood Crown, then I will go with her."

Patra Koja put a green hand in his beard of leaves and stroked it slowly.

"I am saying this to you, Shula Bishara, so that when the time comes, you can help Madeline make her choice."

✛

"Mom?"

Mrs. Oliver's eyes had cleared. Lin had moved away, sitting some distance from the raft. Patra Koja had wandered off after Shula and Yenil. The Zhanin had agreed to suspend magic in this area after whatever Baileya had said to him. Probably told him that Madeline was near death anyway and that this would speed things along. Madeline doubted Baileya was wrong about that. That meant, unfortunately, that the Queen's Breath had stopped working too. Madeline had hoped otherwise, but the moment magic snuffed out, so did her breathing.

"Maddie," her mom said. She looked at Baileya and the Zhanin. "We're in the Sunlit Lands?" She looked at the strange swamp they were in, taking in the trees with their hanging moss, the strange plant man with the branches for antlers, the green woman, and Shula and Yenil on the shore.

Delightful Glitter Lady had wandered off somewhere, which was probably for the best. Madeline didn't know how her mother would do seeing a rhinoceros standing nearby. Not that it would be worse than seeing a green woman and Patra Koja.

"Allison?" her mom asked, confused. "Is Allison here?"

"I don't know . . . who that . . . is, Mom."

Her mom's face creased with worry. "Oh, honey. Your breathing. I'm so sorry." A tear rolled down her cheek, but Madeline didn't feel much sympathy for her. Not now.

"Did you . . . give me . . . to the Elenil?" Her mother reached for her, but Madeline pulled away. "Answer," she said.

"Madeline, it . . . it wasn't like that. There were seven of us. Your father and I. Allison. Tony. Lee. Gabrielle." She looked down, then away. Madeline noticed that was only six names, but she didn't say anything about it. "You don't understand this place, Maddie. Have you . . . have you been here long?"

"Long enough," she said. "I do understand."

"Madeline, we didn't all survive our time in the Sunlit Lands. They told us that making the deal was the only way home. One of the Elenil, he wanted me to stay. He wouldn't release me. He said the only way was if I would let one of my children come back someday. I told him never, never. He finally agreed that if we had any children, he wouldn't take them until they were sixteen. We could have their entire childhood, he said. I could be free if I agreed to that. I didn't want to, but . . . your father and Tony and I, we talked about it, and we agreed we would each take the deal, and then none of us would have children, ever. I added to the deal. I told him I wanted to forget everything. The Sunlit Lands, the Elenil, everything. He fought against that part of the bargain, but in the end he agreed. Your dad did that too. Tony decided to remember, and—well, Tony did better than us, I guess."

"You sold me . . . for your freedom."

"I didn't know you, honey. I didn't plan to ever have kids. When we went home, I barely remembered your dad or Tony or any of them. But your dad and I fell in love. Neither of us wanted children—that had survived the loss of our memories—but when I found out I was pregnant with you . . . oh, sweetie, I realized there was nothing I wanted more."

"You didn't warn me," Madeline said.

"I didn't *remember*."

"You always hated . . . my Meselia books."

"Narnia, Middle-earth, Meselia, I hated them all. I didn't know why, but I knew they were wrong, they were dangerous." Her face hardened. "They want you to believe these other places are so wonderful, but they will kill you. Allison is dead. My boyfriend, Lee—what they did to him I can't even say. The others, too. Only four of us escaped, only four."

"Not counting . . . me," Madeline said.

Her mother reached for her hand, and Madeline yanked it away. "Not counting you, Maddie."

"Dad?"

"He doesn't remember anything. He's been working so hard since you got sick, I think because the magic has been failing for both of us. We've been starting to remember, but neither of us want to, but we knew you were in danger, so we were trying, and it just—we should have done better, Maddie, I know we should have, but we did our best."

"I'm sick . . . because of . . . an Elenil . . . named Hanali. He recruited me. He . . . made me sick . . . so he could offer . . . me a deal."

Her mother's face twisted in rage and grief at the mention of his name. "Why won't he leave us in peace? He came to us on your sixteenth birthday. We told them . . . told them they couldn't have you. They could take us instead. We tried to back out of the deal. Hanali was with him. Then he said . . . that there would be a punishment for failing to follow the deal." Madeline felt sick. She remembered her sixteenth birthday. Remembered taking a ragged breath before blowing out her candles and thinking, *Well, that's weird, I can't seem to get a full breath.* She thought she was excited because of the party and the romantic date she knew Darius had planned for that night. But it only got worse.

Her mother reached for Madeline's hand, and Madeline pulled it away again. This time her mother moved closer, snatched Madeline's hand, and wouldn't let it go. "But our memories disappeared when they did. Your sickness started soon after. When Hanali came to you, did you take his deal? If he made you sick, he can make you well."

"Yenil," she said. "Was the plan . . . for my cure."

Madeline's mother went very still. A tear fell on her cheek, and she took a deep breath, as if steeling herself. As if she were about to do something painful, but there was no other choice. "You should take it," she said, almost a whisper. A sob choked off her words, but she waited a moment and then forced herself to continue. "What sort of life can Yenil have? Her parents are dead, and she's not doing well on Earth. She'll never really fit in. And you have so much more to do in life, so much more to see."

Madeline scowled at her, unbelieving. "But then . . . I would be . . . like you. Wouldn't I?"

"Oh, Maddie, no, don't say that." Her mother was weeping now, the tears flowing copiously down her cheeks. Her usually perfect hair was wet and tousled, plastered to her face. "Maddie, please forgive me. I'm sorry, forgive me. I didn't know! I didn't know what I was doing!"

Something about seeing her mother broken and crying knocked loose a small compassion in Madeline. It reminded her of her own terror when she had discovered that Yenil was suffering so she could breathe. Madeline had already done the same thing as her mother. Not just once, but twice.

Once with Yenil, not knowing the cost. Once with Night's Breath, knowing exactly what she was doing. Not only that, but Yenil's parents had died because of her, and who knew how many others in the Sunlit Lands? Her mother had a sort of amnesia that prevented her from seeing what she had done, that allowed her to keep living her perfect little life. It was a strange luxury. But it didn't absolve her of her wrongs against Madeline, not at all. In fact, Madeline thought it might make it worse, because she had chosen not to see what she was doing to her own daughter, how she was making her life better by making someone else's worse.

Madeline looked at Baileya. "Turn the . . . magic back on."

"No!" Her mother screamed the word, clawing at her daughter. "No, Maddie, no, not before we've talked, not before you understand."

"Mother," she said, calmly. "I am going . . . to reset the magic . . . of the Sunlit Lands. I'm not coming . . . back."

"I love you," her mother said, clutching at her. "I'm sorry. I'm so sorry. Let me go. Let *me* reset the magic." For a moment Madeline wished that could be. The idea of her mom protecting her at last, sacrificing herself so her daughter could live a few months more, filled her with longing. But it didn't make sense. Madeline's breathing wouldn't get any better. She would still die. She couldn't let her mother do that, no matter what she had done in the past.

"I know you . . . love me," Madeline said. "I'm still . . . angry. But I . . . understand."

"Madeline, please, let me come with you," she said. "Let me make it up to you, please."

Madeline grabbed her mom's shoulders, held her tight, forced her to look into her eyes. "Then take care . . . of Shula . . . and Yenil."

"I will," she said. "I love them, too, Maddie. I do, I promise. I didn't mean what I said before about Yenil. But these are terrible decisions, Maddie. How are we supposed to make these choices? Don't leave me, not like this."

"Mom. Tell me . . . how the Elenil . . . made you forget."

"They gave us addleberry wine until we forgot it all. Then Hanali sealed it with magic."

"Baileya," Madeline said, and the Zhanin let the magic flow back in.

Her mother's face smoothed out, and for a moment she was at peace. Then her eyes moved back and forth, confused, and a look of fear came over her again. "What is this place? Where am I? Maddie, what's happening?"

Madeline kissed her mother on the forehead. She stood and asked Patra Koja if he would take her mother and Yenil somewhere safe. The rush of oxygen from the Queen's Breath now that magic was restored made her light headed.

"David," she said. "Can I talk to you for a minute?"

"Sure." They walked away from the others.

She put her hand on his arm. "I want to ask you a favor. We're going to find the Heartwood Crown, and I . . . I won't be coming back. Shula won't leave me, I know. I don't think Baileya will either, not when Jason is out there somewhere. But would you . . . could you go with Yenil and my mother and make sure they're safe?"

David crossed his arms. "Of course." He gazed at her steadily.

Madeline couldn't avoid the feeling that he had something more to say. "What?"

"Your mom. She doesn't deserve the way you talk to her."

"How can you say that? Do you even know what she did? She *sold* me, David. I'm dying because of her."

He shrugged. "You're alive because of her too. Not saying she did right, just saying she did her best. I've seen a lot of trauma, Madeline, and this is someone who was forced to do what she did. She's a victim too."

"Yeah, well, she's not dying," Madeline snapped.

David didn't look away. "Nah. She's not. But you seem to think that dying has given you a pass to treat people poorly and do whatever you want. I hear the way Jason and Shula go on about you. How wonderful you are. How kind, how focused on others. I don't know you very well, but I don't see much of that. I see anger, and I see you expecting people to do whatever you decide is best."

"I'm dying," she repeated. "I'm sorry my emotional journey has been hard for you."

"You're not dead yet," David said simply. "I believe Jason and Shula. I believe you're a kind, exceptional person. Don't let the process of death take that away from you. Don't let it change your core self."

Madeline wanted to snap at him again, but as she opened her mouth, she realized that David was right. As her pain increased, it had been harder and harder to be honest about that and still think of others . . . something she had always done as long as she could remember. It took more energy, more strength than she had. David was right. She had let herself become a distorted version of herself, and people who didn't know her well might think she was someone completely different.

David put a hand on her shoulder. "I say these things because I am your friend. You are a good woman, Madeline. I'm only saying I hope you'll remain one in the time you have left."

Madeline let herself collapse against him, and he put his arms around her. She barely knew David, but he had proven himself to be her friend, and this conversation was another sign of it. "I don't know how to forgive my mother," she said.

"Sometimes we think we have to deal with our anger before we forgive someone. But I think that there are times when we have to forgive *before* we're able to deal with our anger. It's like breaking a dam . . . it lets the anger drain away."

"I'll think about that," she said.

"And I'll keep your mom and Yenil safe," David said.

She looked up at him. "Thank you, David."

He grinned. "Ah, there's the sweet and kind Madeline Oliver I've heard so much about."

She punched him in the arm. "I'm still angry," she said.

"You should be," he replied seriously. Then he trotted over to Yenil and bent down to talk to her.

Madeline went to Shula and Baileya next. "Will you . . . come with me?"

Baileya nodded once, simply. Shula hugged her and said, "Of course, Madeline. Wherever you go, I will go." She crossed her arms and looked to the trussed-up Zhanin warrior, and Gilenyia, still asleep on the raft. "I will speak to Patra Koja and ask him to take care of the Zhanin and the Elenil until such a time as it is safe to release them."

"Thank you," Madeline said, and she was overwhelmed by these small kindnesses, by the clear love of these friends she had made in the Sunlit Lands.

Saying good-bye to Yenil was hard. Madeline didn't know how to explain, but Yenil seemed to understand somehow. "I will take care of your mother," Yenil said, as if this were the most important thing in the world. "I am glad you were my benefactor." That's what they had called it when Yenil had given her breath to Madeline. Madeline had been the benefactor of Yenil and her family—when she and Yenil had been connected by magic, Yenil's family had received money and other benefits in exchange for Yenil's breathing. Madeline hadn't known about this deal, but it had been made nonetheless. She would have never met this Scim family if it hadn't been for her connection to Yenil. Madeline hugged Yenil for a long time, until the girl started to squirm. She kissed Yenil's cheek, and they said good-bye.

Delightful Glitter Lady came up then, squealing for attention and leaning against Madeline. She patted the little rhino on the head. "I'll miss you, too, Dee." Madeline grabbed Yenil's hand. "Do you think you could look after Delightful Glitter Lady until Jason gets back? Just for a little while?" Yenil nodded seriously, then picked Dee up, holding her to her chest like a stuffed animal. The tiny rhino let out a contented sigh.

Then there was her mother. She was sitting on a rock, staring out into the swamp. Madeline came and put her arms around her. Her mother patted her arms. "I love you," Madeline said.

"I love you, too," her mother replied, and there was nothing more to say. Madeline kissed her mother on the cheek and moved toward Shula and Baileya.

Lin intercepted her and took her hand, then knelt before her. "You truly are the annaginuk. We have waited for you these many years. Bid me any service, my queen, and I will gladly do it."

Queen? Once Madeline would have thought a title like that to be an honor, but now it only felt like a heavy burden. She put her hand on the Aluvorean woman's shoulder. "Take care of my loved ones. Keep them safe."

Lin looked toward Yenil, then back to Madeline. She stood and bowed, quickly, as if she could not trust herself to stay much longer in Madeline's presence without bursting into tears. She swept away toward the others.

"Let's go," Madeline said to Shula and Baileya, and her two friends came on either side of her. She put her arms around their shoulders, and they helped her walk, headed north, toward the Queen's Island.

She only looked back once. David was kneeling near her mother, talking to her. Yenil was showing Patra Koja and Lin a faerie house. It almost looked like something she might see at home, in her mother's garden. *They are safe*, Madeline thought, *and that is all that matters.*

✚

"Stand ready," the Pastisian captain said. They were all inside the gondola. They were nearly over the city. "When I pull this lever, the floor will fall away, and we will descend together to war."

Then the floor was gone. Darius fell straight down. He was in the center of the group, and the others peeled away with practiced simplicity, then spread their arms to release the gliding wings. Darius did the same, remembering his brief training, and they fell into formation as they moved toward the center of the city. He was surprised by how intuitive the gliding suit was, and he enjoyed the rush of the wind on his face. There was no sound other than the wind and the occasional flap of glider fabric. No one below had seen them yet.

The captain had perfectly planned their release—they were high above the city but just outside the walls. They were still out of arrow range as they crossed the wall. This small force had been tasked with taking one of the gates and holding it until the Scim arrived and the invasion began in earnest. They descended rapidly once they were over the wall, with the intention of doubling back and removing the most obvious of the nearby guards on their way to the gate. Darius nodded to the Pastisian soldiers as they descended. His goal lay elsewhere.

With a major portion of the Elenil army headed to Aluvorea and another sizable chunk distracted by the assault on the gate, Darius hoped to slip into the archon's tower and find Thenody, guarded or not. There had been uncertainty about the precise place they would drop, and the original plan had been that he would hide among the humans in a nearby market—if he could land without being noticed—and then slip in when the Elenil were distracted by the attack at the gate. It wasn't much of a plan, but it had been made quickly, and as King Ian said, "Our plan is to rely on your courage and see what comes of it."

Darius considered what he had learned from the small book about

Hanali's father and wondered if he could use it to his advantage. Or rather, how best to use it to his advantage. He was still astonished by what he had learned, and he couldn't help but think of Madeline and what it meant for her. His heart sank at the thought. He had to finish the archon quickly so he could go to her. A group of Scim street kids saw him fly overhead, shouted something, and ran another direction. Not to warn the authorities, he was sure. Maybe they were part of Mud's hidden army, and they had gone to get their commander.

He was high enough, he realized, to land inside the tower. He looked at the distance, calculating. Yes. He thought he could do it, if he planned it just right. Not toward the top, which was unfortunate, since the archon was most often in the highest sections. Still, to fight his way from the inside instead of from the outside would be an advantage. He banked toward the tower. He was low enough now that he was drawing attention. There was a long balcony about a third of the way up the tower he thought he could hit.

Elenil guards in the tower saw him now, and one loosed an arrow that whizzed to his left. He was no longer out of range, just distant enough that it was an unlikely shot. A gust of wind caught him sideways, and he drifted from his target. He tugged to one side and started losing altitude . . . too fast. He crashed into the side of the balcony, just high enough to flip over and land, crooked, on his feet.

His ankle twisted under him. He fell to his knees. His ankle hurt. But he had done enough training on his track team to be able to run in spite of it. He felt the ankle, didn't think it was broken. He pulled the tab that released him from the glider suit and rose to his feet.

An Elenil guard stood at the wide door into the tower. "Hanali told us to expect you," he said.

Of course he did. Of course. Darius loosed the Sword of Years and felt its fierce joy flood him. His lips pulled back from his teeth. "Drink your fill." He stepped forward, the sword eager to lead him to the top of the tower.

✠

Baileya wrapped Jason in a bear hug. "I knew you would be well! Did the Zhanin find you? Where is your Aluvorean friend?"

"I lost track of her. I did get away from a Zhanin, though."

Baileya's beautiful smile widened, and Jason felt the blood rush to his face. "How did you do this?" she asked.

"I made friends with a flying cat, and she blew him away with magical wind." Shula and Madeline both laughed at this, Mads hanging on Shula's shoulder. "No, really!"

Baileya became suddenly serious. "A Guardian of the Wind?"

"Yes! She flew off when we heard you all."

"You are an exceptional man," Baileya said. "I am glad to be at your side again."

"Where are we headed?"

"North," Shula said. "Either through the carnivorous forest—"

"Bad idea!" Jason said.

"—or the firethorns."

"I vote firethorns," Jason said. "And then across the lake to the Heartwood Crown?"

"What did . . . the dragon . . . say?"

Jason grinned, embarrassed. He scooped himself under Madeline's other arm and helped her as they walked north. "I sort of sent the flying cat to talk to him. She said that he said that the lake is cursed, and the first person to cross it will die."

Madeline didn't say anything to that. Shula looked to Baileya, who looked away. So they all knew this already somehow. "So," Jason said. "That dude with the tree growing out of his head just sent me away to keep me out of his hair. His moss. Whatever. So, what's the plan? You're going to just go sacrifice yourself? I thought Papa Tree was going to heal you."

"He can't," Madeline said.

"Why are you doing this? What if there's another way? Another magical potion? Or even a treatment back home."

"Jason. There's nothing." He could see the distress in her face. "There's not a . . . cure, Jason. So here's a chance . . . for me to . . . do something good. To really save . . . the Sunlit Lands. It's better than . . . waiting . . . in a hospital . . . bed."

Jason didn't know what to say to that. If they kept talking more, he would end up telling her his own thoughts—his plan to swim across before her and save the Sunlit Lands himself. And maybe, just maybe, somehow Madeline could be healed. It would be worth it to sacrifice himself for that chance.

Baileya was looking back at him, as if she could see exactly what he was thinking. He needed to distract her. "Oh! And I saw your brother!"

Baileya's eyes widened. Distraction: accomplished! "Bezaed?"

"Yeah. While I was in the carnivorous forest. He didn't want to come in there, so I was sort of hanging out in there so he wouldn't kill me. We had a long talk, and he's agreed not to kill me for a while."

Baileya stopped walking so she could give him her full attention. "Bezaed? My brother? The bloody prince of the Kakri agreed not to kill you?"

"Yeah. He said he didn't want me to marry you because I wasn't a Kakri, and I told him how Mother Crow invited me to come into the desert and learn from her. I told him I was going to do that, and then I would be Kakri, and then there wouldn't be a problem. He said he would wait to kill me until after that. I promised not to marry you until I had gone into the desert, and then he left me alone in the carnivorous forest, and then I came to find you, and here we are."

Baileya grabbed him by the back of the head, yanked him close, and kissed him full on the lips. Jason went weak at the knees and had to reach for her shoulders to keep from falling over. It was their first kiss. He felt like someone had shoveled a pound of hot coals into his belly. She pulled away, and he tried to stand up, but his whole body felt like jelly. He tried to think of something to say, something profound or at least suave, but all he managed was a weak "More, please."

Baileya laughed heartily and rapped on his chest with the back of her fist. "In time, Wu Song, in time."

He went back to Madeline, still shaky on his legs, and put her arm over his shoulder. Baileya gave him a smoldering look as she led them northward again, and he almost stumbled. Madeline laughed, her voice raspy. She squeezed her arm around his shoulder. "Smooth, buddy. So . . . smooth."

"You think so?" Jason asked. "No, really, was that smooth?"

Madeline and Shula both laughed, and Madeline squeezed him again.

✦

They hiked through the darkness and on into morning. When they reached the firethorns, they stopped for a break. Shula crouched down near the strange plants, studying them. Jason had told them there were Elenil in the forest, so they didn't want to wait long, but it was slow going with Madeline.

The plants stuck out of the ground like thin pipes. They had the look of old-world roses, with too many thorns and not enough leaves, and small cuts and holes along the stalk, almost like some sort of flute. From time to time the stalks let loose a pungent gas, which caught flame and shot out of the holes. The stalks were almost like canes, hard and blackened near the holes. There was no doubt that to walk through them would mean catching on fire occasionally. Shula could see why the Elenil were so meticulous about keeping them from spreading through Aluvorea.

She used her magic and let the familiar feeling of the flames come into her hands. She held them up close to the nearest firethorn and turned the heat up as high as she could. When the thorn lit its own flame, it wilted under hers. She must have burned something in the stalk that prevented it from catching itself aflame, because it collapsed on itself. It fell to ash.

Shula saved them from the firethorns, but it was Jason who came up with the plan. He said he had been working on "changing his story" and that fire might be seen as an inconvenience, but maybe it could also be a strength. He sent Shula ahead of them, because when she was aflame she couldn't be hurt by the firethorns, and she burned a firebreak for them. Baileya and Jason followed, holding Madeline between them.

They made decent time, though Shula's friends had to be careful to wait a short time before following her, because the ground was hot enough to burn their feet. She learned that if she burned the firebreak wider, they wouldn't be so hot as they followed behind her. Shula was thankful Baileya was with them—the Kakri woman was stronger than Shula or Jason and had more stamina. Shula didn't know if they would have gotten Madeline this far without Baileya's muscle.

A hummingbird circled them in the late afternoon. It looked as exhausted as their entire party, and Shula didn't know how it could see them through the smoke, but it descended and landed on Madeline's shoulder. A faerie rode on its back. Madeline asked the others to give her some space. She needed a break in any case, so Shula burned a larger space than usual, big enough to set Madeline down in the relative coolness of the center.

Madeline played a game of charades with the faerie for a long time, and when she was done, it chirped twice, then flew over the firethorns to the east. Madeline gave Shula a sad smile and then raised her arms to Baileya and Jason. They helped her to her feet. "A message from Darius," she said, and they continued on their way. Shula frowned at this. Darius should be here, not sending messages. She didn't understand how he could choose not to be with Madeline at this time—didn't understand how he had chosen, for that matter, to stay in the Sunlit Lands instead of coming home with them. He had left Madeline to Shula, and she was thankful for their time together. But Darius should be here. But there was no time to think about such things. She had work to do—they could not move through the firethorns without her leading the way.

Shula was thankful to be at the front of their small party. Thankful for a few minutes alone to put her thoughts in order. She knew the feeling of loss, knew it more intimately than almost any other feeling she could think of. She felt it pushing in now, taking up more and more space in her heart. She was thankful her back was to Madeline, so her friend could not see the hot tears streaking her face.

✦

Darius had climbed two stories, and there were many more to go. Messenger birds flew in and out of the tower in a flurry, which meant the gate must have fallen to the Pastisians. The Sword sang in his hands, though he doubted he had dealt a single fatal wound, given the healing magic of the Elenil. Still. They could not stop him.

He kicked a guard in the knee, parried his blade, grabbed him by the wrist, and flung him into the empty center of the tower. He didn't stop to watch the guard fall, instead using the spare moment to glance out the window. He could just see the airships in the distance. Soon he would be in the archon's chambers, and then he could set out to find Madeline.

Madeline wanted to rest. She knew she couldn't say that to the others. She couldn't let them know just how little strength she had left. How much the smoke from the firethorns further agitated her breathing.

She didn't have regrets, not really. She wished she had seen Darius again, somehow, here in the Sunlit Lands, but she had said good-bye to him once before. It was a strange thing, saying good-bye, because you never knew when it would be the last time. And how strange to have some deep conversation and farewell and then to see each other again a few days later.

She wished she had seen more of her dad. Wished she had been able to forgive her mother. David's words were weighing on her, but she couldn't see the way through to it. Wished things had been different, wished they had never been to the Sunlit Lands, had never met Hanali, had never made their infernal deal that left her gasping for breath and dragging herself through the blistering heat and sulfurous air of the firethorns.

She would have liked to have seen Hanali one more time so she could give him a piece of her mind. Would have liked to have read, somehow, the last, unpublished book from the Meselia series. It was strange, these small losses. She wanted to know what would happen in her favorite book series. She wanted to see the movies coming out next summer.

But she was thankful, too. Darius had been her rock. Jason had been the most loyal friend she had ever met, unless Shula surpassed him. Little Yenil. Baileya. She had an embarrassment of riches when it came to friends. She was thankful for her parents, too. The realization surprised her, but it was true. She didn't know that she needed to forgive them for all of this, because they had given her so many other things. She felt like maybe she had always known, somehow, what her mom had done. She felt she had forgiven her long ago, had forgiven her and forgotten about it, just like her mother had made the deal with the Elenil and forgotten.

On one of their breaks, she fell asleep. Only for a moment. Her breathing was so bad, it was a sort of fever dream. Hanali came to her in it. Here in the Sunlit Lands, she wasn't sure if it was real or imagined, if they were making a true connection or if it was only a dream. But Hanali came to her, all in cream and gold with a long crimson cape, a strange sadness in his eyes. "Madeline!" he said. "Why? Why have you come to Aluvorea?"

"Why did you curse me?" she shot back at him. "Just so you could get me to the Sunlit Lands?"

He recoiled in shock. "My dear girl. I brought you to the Sunlit Lands to *heal* you."

"But you made me sick in the first place, stole my breath, prevented me from getting treatments at the hospital."

"No! Never. That was my father, Vivi. Your mother had promised you to him. You were meant to come into our family . . . He said you would be my adopted sister. When your mother told him that he couldn't have you, he was furious. He put the curse on you. He said it was because of something your mother had done many years ago. I have always had . . . an affection for your parents. I do not properly know why. I argued with my father, begged him to reconsider. He always thought I was too lenient with the humans. He agreed, finally, that if you came to the Sunlit Lands for a year and followed the traditional ways of our magic, then you could be healed by those means. I could use my authority as the recruiter for the Sunlit Lands to heal you." A sad, puzzled look crossed his face. "But you rejected that."

"So you can lift the curse," Madeline said. "Patra Koja said the agreement was between you and my mother."

"No," Hanali said, crestfallen. "Patra Koja said the agreement was between your mother and me? This I do not understand. My father crafted both the original agreement and the curse, not I. And he crafted it so the only way to heal you was for someone else to give you their breath. A stranger . . . that is woven into the curse as well. So the only bargain I can offer is the same bargain as before. But to heal you in that way, we need to keep magic as it is. You must not go to the Heartwood Crown, must not reset magic. We will find another to give you their breath, and you can be whole again."

Even in this dream state, she wasn't tempted by that. Not much. A single thought of Yenil sent the possibility bounding away from her. Hanali was fading. She was waking up. "Why did you come to Aluvorea?" he asked again, mournful.

"Because they need me," she said. "Because I promised them." The seed glowed in her arm. Or rather, her shoulder. The green light flared bright, and she and Hanali both winced. She didn't know how to say the rest. How this was going to cost her everything, but she had less everything than the others. She was going to die—it might as well be to save her friends, to save this beautiful place and make it something better.

She felt a pang of sorrow for her parents. How could they have been expected to know how to deal with the Elenil and their twisted bargains, their strange value system? Their statements were layered in half-truths, in lies, in misdirection. Even now she wasn't sure Hanali was telling her the truth. Vivi had seemed only kind in her brief interactions with him. But then again, Hanali often seemed harmless. He seemed to truly like her, like he really was trying to help her . . . sometimes, at least.

"Do you regret your time in the Sunlit Lands, then?" Hanali asked. Something in the way he said it . . . she sensed that a great deal was riding on this answer for him. She could see in his face that he deeply, honestly wanted her to have enjoyed being here. He wanted it to be a gift to her. He wanted her to be well, and she could see that he had never meant to harm her, as difficult as that might be to believe. He honestly thought he was doing the right thing, the best thing, the caring thing. So—did she regret the Sunlit Lands?

She smiled. "No."

She did not regret the Sunlit Lands. She loved them. She hated the way she had come here, but she had seen such wonderful things. She had flown on giant birds. She had eaten strange fruit in the marketplace with Shula. She had seen magic, had performed magic. She had walked with the gorgeous Elenil people, had put her hands on their graceful architecture, had heard the music of their fountains and listened to their stories. She had seen the beautiful Scim people, who hid their deepest selves from all but their closest friends. She had breathed the sweet air in Far Seeing and seen the Ginian Sea sparkling in the distance. She had met the Peasant King and spoken more than once with the Garden Lady. She had moved between worlds and had friends in them both. She had done all those things and many more, and she had done some good in the world . . . her own and the Sunlit Lands. In the end, she had been true to herself.

Madeline woke on the burned-out circle of ash that Shula had made for her. It had been a dream, yes, but maybe not only a dream. She didn't tell her friends about Hanali. She was finding it harder to speak, harder to stay focused. Jason and Baileya helped her to her feet, and they started through the forest again.

When they came at last to the end of the firethorns, Madeline made them keep walking until they had moved away from the noxious fumes of it. She could smell water now, and pine sap, and somewhere nearby a citrusy, floral scent from the woods. Baileya said it was night flowers opening now that the sun was going down. Baileya helped Madeline lie down beneath a broad-branched tree that was heavy with purple flowers. Baileya sat, making a pillow for Madeline with her lap. Jason lay down beside Madeline, putting his head in Baileya's lap too, and held Madeline's hand, and Shula sat on her other side, wiping the sweat and ash from her face.

No one spoke. They sat together in the quiet and listened to the gentle wind in the leaves above them. A bird called to another in the trees. Night insects started their evening greetings as the sun began to set. The cool breeze wicked away her sweat, but Madeline still felt hot. It was time. She wasn't ready, didn't know if she would ever be ready. Her friends sat around her like a shelter, like they could protect her from what was to come, but she knew better. What good friends they were!

It was Baileya who sensed it first. She rose and helped Madeline to her feet. Shula took the other side now, and Jason walked ahead of them. "We are not far now," Baileya said. "Courage."

29

THE CROSSING

If darkness falls while we labor,
let us light a lantern.
A small candle defeats even a great darkness.

FROM "THE SEED," AN ALUVOREAN POEM

✦

The water lay silent, unmoving, still. It did not gleam or sparkle—instead it seemed to swallow up light. A slight breeze moved the leaves in the trees, but on the water there was not so much as a ripple.

It was dusk when they arrived, moving on toward night, so Jason didn't think much of the dark water, not at first. The day had passed faster than he thought it should, as if every hour had been shortened by half. He mentioned it to Baileya, who nodded and said only that the magic of the Sunlit Lands which kept Far Seeing bright through day and night sometimes made the days strange in other parts of the world. So the dark water was the least of his worries when they arrived. But the longer they stood there, these four friends, the more the still darkness of the lake bothered him . . . like the feeling of someone standing in the shadows behind him, watching.

Jason wanted to lighten things with a joke, but he couldn't find one. He felt heavy and sluggish, like someone had sapped him of all his strength. "So this is it," he said. "The cursed river."

Shula knelt and touched the water. It moved almost like a normal pond, but not quite, as if the water resisted even giving way to a finger.

Jason took off his shirt, folded it neatly, and placed it on the ground.

"What are . . . you doing?" Madeline asked. She looked so pale and tired. He remembered, in a momentary flash, seeing her on the track team freshman year. He had tried out, back before he realized that he hated running, and he had seen her sprinting alongside their classmates, blonde hair streaming behind her like fire, a beaming smile on her face. She had been young and beautiful and full of life, and now she was so sick that even speaking four words hurt her.

"I'm going to swim across," he said.

"No," Madeline said, gently. So gently. Why was she speaking to him so gently? "It has to be . . . me."

"You won't make it," he shouted, and a pair of birds startled from the trees above them. "You can barely talk."

She laid the palm of her hand on his cheek. She was looking at him with a half smile, her eyes welling with tears. "You are . . . a good friend," she said.

"I'm not going to let you do it," he said. "I'm not."

She hugged him then, and he, not expecting it, almost fell backward, recovered, put his arms around her. She held him with a fierceness that surprised him, that told him maybe she had more strength than he thought. She put both hands on his face and would not let him look away. "I am so thankful for you," she said. "For your friendship. You have made so many things better in my life."

He tried to say something back to her but could only say, "Madeline . . ."

"I love you," she said, and he knew what she meant, knew that it had nothing to do with crushes or dating or getting married, it meant only what she had said. She loved him. And again, he couldn't find a way to say it back to her, could only think of her in that still, black water, and that he wouldn't—that he couldn't—allow it. "Take care of yourself," she said.

She squeezed his shoulders and turned to Baileya. She hugged the Kakri woman, and neither spoke, though the affection on both their faces was clear. In a low voice, Madeline said, "I'll need you . . . to hold him."

And before Jason knew what was happening Baileya had wrapped him from behind with her strong arms, and he couldn't get free. "No," he said. "Madeline, no!"

She was hugging Shula now, saying something he couldn't hear. They held each other for a moment, and Shula pushed Madeline's hair out of her face, and they hugged again.

"Baileya, let me go, you have to let me go!"

He struggled, and Baileya readjusted, held him so they were face-to-face. She didn't speak, but she didn't let him go, either. Just held him and let him watch Madeline.

Shula glanced at him, a deep sadness on her face, then got on her knees and helped Madeline untie her boots. She waded with Madeline into the water until they were up to their waists.

"No, no, Madeline, no. Let me do it!"

She looked at him again, standing with her back to the deeper water. She gave him that half smile, and a small, almost tentative wave. Then she lay down on her back and pushed off, floating into the darkness.

"Please, Mads, please don't do this." He struggled with Baileya, pushing against her arms, kicking with his legs. "Baileya, please. If you let me go now, I can still beat her to the other side. I can swim faster. Baileya, please."

Her arms didn't loosen. She didn't say anything. Shula stood in the water, peering into the darkness. He was crying, and he couldn't hear Madeline in the water. "I can't see her," he said. "Shula, can you see her?"

Shula did not turn, just shook her head.

"No!" he sobbed in Baileya's arms. "Madeline, it's not too late, come back, just follow the sound of my voice." But he knew she wouldn't, knew she was gone. A crushing sadness set in, and he gasped for breath.

"She is gone," Baileya said. "My dear Wu Song, she has left us."

"No," he said again, pulling at her arms. Then, in a sudden panic, he thought of Madeline alone in the dark water, on her back, looking at the rising stars of the Sunlit Lands, moving toward the far shore of the cursed river, listening to Jason sob and cry, and he hoped she hadn't made it to the far side yet, because he had failed to tell her everything he wanted. "I love you, too, Madeline Oliver!" he shouted, and the words echoed across the water, but there was no reply.

He lost all his strength, collapsed into Baileya's arms. She caught him, lowered him to the ground. She curled up beside him and stroked his hair. They stayed like this for a long time, until Baileya fell still and asked, "Do you hear?"

Shula turned to listen. She moved toward them through the water and the dark. There was the sound of water moving. A trickle at first, then a rivulet, then a stream. It flowed just beside them, picking up speed, growing in volume. "She did it," Shula said.

Only then did Baileya let him go, and he ran into the water, shouting Madeline's name.

PART 3

*The tides change with the moon, the sand rises
and falls with the seasons, the birds migrate,
the cliffs recede with the erosion of decades.
These things cannot be determined in a moment,
cannot be observed in an afternoon, cannot be
understood in a week's careful study.
This is to say nothing of the volcanic growth
of islands, the grinding shift of continental
plates, the meticulous motion of glaciers, or
the slow, careful metamorphoses of the heart.*

EXPOSITION ON A TRADITIONAL ZHANIN SAYING

30

THE FIRETHORNS

*The Sunlit Lands are not as they should be. The people fight
and argue. They have ceased to be the people of the Sunlit
Lands and have made for themselves other names.*

FROM "THE GOOD GARDENER," AN ALUVOREA STORY

✦

Elenil had surrounded the firethorns. Shula watched them from the
cover of the forest. They appeared to be on all sides, even where the
carnivorous forest began. Lamisap, the Aluvorean woman, shifted
next to her. "We must hurry," she said.

The woman had appeared soon after they had lost Madeline.
Jason was still in the water, shouting Madeline's name. Baileya stood off
to the side, watching over them both with quiet sorrow. There had been
a rustling in a tree back the way they had come, and when Shula stepped
over to investigate, Lamisap had stepped out of it. A hundred or so other
Aluvoreans had followed her, all of them with skin the color of the forest. Some had flowers twined through their hair. A cloud of faeries on

hummingbirds zipped around them. The Aluvoreans seemed drawn to the water. They stood on the edge of the lake or put their feet in the fresh river that had begun to run south. A great white bird had waded into the water, an eye turned toward Shula, and then flapped its long wings before circling once and flying away, over the trees.

"The annaginuk now wears the Heartwood Crown," Lamisap said in a reverent whisper. "Magic flows again! Now please come, for I need your help."

Jason didn't respond, didn't even look at the Aluvorean. Baileya turned to Shula and shook her head, then inclined it back toward Jason. She wouldn't be leaving him now, not when he was like this. Shula didn't want to go anywhere, didn't want to help anyone, either. Still, she found herself asking Lamisap, "Where were you when Madeline was leaving us? You're the one who asked her to come here, and you hid in the trees when she made her final decision?"

"We did not wish to interrupt your good-byes," the Aluvorean said. "It seemed disrespectful. But now that the annaginuk has been crowned, we need your help to make sure she receives the power due her sacrifice."

Shula was tired of these people saying things that didn't make any sense. "What is it? What do you need?"

"The old magic, the tainted magic, is draining away, but slowly. For Madeline's magic to take effect we must clear away the underbrush and the trees that should be dead but are not. We must release the firethorns. The heat of the fire will open the fireseeds, spreading the newly formed ways of magic into the Sunlit Lands. If the fires don't spread, the magic will change but slowly. Slowly enough, I fear, that the people of the Sunlit Lands will force it to keep its shape. The Elenil, of course, but also others who have grown used to the way things are."

"What keeps it from spreading? Why does the fire need our help?"

"The Elenil have placed a fire watch around the thorns, and their army spreads through the forest even now to keep the flames at bay and to kill any who try to help the first sparks of change."

"Show me," Shula said. At those words all the Aluvoreans faded into the woods again, except Lamisap, who led Shula on the long trek back to the firethorns. She hadn't said good-bye to Jason or Baileya. She couldn't bear the thought of speaking to them today. Their shared loss was too fresh, and she feared the raw emotion of it.

"What will become of the other Aluvoreans," Shula said, "when the flames spread? What about my Yenil and Madeline's mother?"

"They will be safe," Lamisap said. "This is when Queen's Breath is meant to be used." She showed one of the leaves to Shula, like a long oval oar. A fresh wave of grief hit Shula. Madeline wouldn't need those any longer. "If you wet this leaf and put it on your neck, you can breathe under water. Beneath Aluvorea there are caves that are safe. They can only be reached through the water. When the forest burns, we use Queen's Breath so we can swim deep enough to find the entrances. When the fire is done and the new growth begins, we return and find our new place in the world."

"Is someone with them? Taking them to the caves?"

Lamisap nodded. "Patra Koja will instruct them, I know. You and I will defeat the Elenil, and then we will go together."

"And the other Aluvoreans, will they help us?"

"The people of Aluvorea are not fighters. They will go to the caves."

But what about Jason and Baileya? Maybe they could swim to the Queen's Island, or just outrun the flames and head for the sea, or escape out of the forest. They needed to be warned. But first there was the problem of the Elenil.

There were far too many. They were glorious in their shiny armor, with their war beasts and bright swords and colorful cloth swatches. In another time and place, Shula would have been mesmerized by the pageantry of it all. Messenger birds of many sizes and colors flashed through the trees, taking orders to distant soldiers. Even in the smoke from the firethorns, the Elenil looked regal. The pops of flame made shining reflections on their armor.

An enormous elephant lumbered at the outskirts of the flames, squirting water on the ground. The Elenil dug trenches and moved buckets, and some were cutting back the brush, making sure a stray spark couldn't ignite the forest beyond the limits of the thorns.

"I can set the forest on fire myself," Shula said. She didn't see a way to get through the defenses of the Elenil.

"Yes," Lamisap said, "and that will help it to spread more quickly. But the firethorns must spread. If all of Aluvorea burns but the firethorns remain contained, then the magic will still be stunted. We have to release the thorns and then, yes, you can burn it all. But be cautious, for magic will cease completely for a time, and your bargain will not protect you from the flames then."

"The most vulnerable place may be where the firethorns and the stone flowers meet," Shula said. "The Elenil will not be able to hold the line if we can push them toward the stone flowers. When the line breaks, the firethorns can get through. But how long do they take to move? How big of an exit do the thorns need?"

As if in answer, a firethorn behind the Elenil lines grew so blazing hot Shula could feel the wash of heat from their hiding place. It glowed furnace white and made a loud popping noise. Sparks shot through the hollow stem, spurting twenty feet in the air, over the Elenil lines. Soldiers raced to the sparks and stomped them out.

Lamisap lifted her head with a look of alarm. "What's this?" She put her hand on Shula's arm. "Wait here. Do not move." She disappeared up a tree as quickly and silently as a squirrel.

Shula studied the Elenil near her. She quickly picked out several Elenil she knew. She'd met many of them during her time in the army at Far Seeing. In fact, she could almost certainly just walk up to them and have a conversation, which might be distraction enough for Lamisap to . . . well, to do something.

She debated how long to wait for Lamisap. It made no sense to speak to the Elenil if Lamisap wasn't there to do anything. That's when she saw Rondelo walking alongside the flames with his stag, Evernu. Here was an Elenil she knew well and considered a friend. No doubt he was the commander here, or at least near the top of the command chain. Shula clutched the branch of a tree, weighing the options. There was no reason for Rondelo to think of her as a traitor, was there? Was she included in the list of humans that the archon wanted captured or dead? She wasn't sure, but Rondelo almost certainly knew she had been there in the tower when Yenil cut off the archon's hand. She hadn't seen him since then. She had gone immediately back to Earth. Who knew what he would do if he saw her?

A hand on Shula's shoulder startled her. Lamisap motioned for Shula to follow, but quietly. They made their way through the trees, doing their best to stay out of sight of the Elenil. Most of them were focused on the fire. Hmmm. Shula wondered if starting a smaller fire would be enough to draw a few of them away. Lamisap led her down a narrow path that descended into a grown-over gully. "We have holes throughout the woods for when we need to hide," Lamisap said. "I have hidden them here."

"Hidden who?"

Lamisap pulled back a veil of vines and led her into a shallow cave carved in the rock—large enough to stand in, it was cool and dark. She couldn't see the back wall. She did, however, see the silver faces looming over her, and behind them the unmistakable shape of a Scim warrior, his stone ax held jauntily over his shoulder. She stepped backward, using her magic to light her hand on fire, casting a bright glow on the assembled soldiers. In the light she could see the black clothes on the masked men and see the Scim warrior more clearly: Break Bones.

Break Bones smiled, revealing his crooked yellow teeth. "Pray put out the light, Shula Bishara, lest thine old friends the Elenil come a-crashing into our tiny refuge."

She let the light fade. "What are you doing here? Where's Darius?"

The Scim stepped closer. "In Far Seeing, I hope, about to skewer the archon."

"Why isn't he *here*? Didn't he get the message we sent?" Her mind started to put new plans in place. With this many men, plus Break Bones, they had a real chance of doing this. She thought for a moment about Darius as the Black Skull, or even just with the Sword of Tears, and how much help it would be to have him here. "Well?"

"He received it, lady, but the battle at Far Seeing will take only a day or two. He will come to find his lady Madeline when the war is won."

Shula's stomach clenched, and her hands curled into fists. When the war was won. Of course. He could put Madeline on hold for a few days, why not? "She's dead," Shula said. "Just a few hours ago. If he had come when he got Madeline's message, he would have seen her."

Break Bones covered his face for a moment, then mumbled, "May the Peasant King welcome her into his courts across the sea." A fierce wildness came into his eyes. "Was it the Elenil who killed her?"

"In a way," Shula said. "She took the Heartwood Crown and reset the magic of the Sunlit Lands. All that remains now is to make sure the fire-thorns spread and burn Aluvorea to dust."

"Then we will fight the Elenil to make this happen. For the Scim and for Madeline." He looked at the oddly dressed soldiers and added, "For all the peoples of the Sunlit Lands."

It was strange to be on the same side as Break Bones. She had fought him many times on the battlefield, so to be standing beside him instead of in opposition to him felt backward. She had always respected his passion, his fury in battle. She realized it was partly because of how different he was from her father, who was mild and kind and generous to the point of personal harm. She wished he had been more like this unhinged warrior. But then, she supposed, he wouldn't have been her father. This reminded her, somehow, of Darius, and her anger rekindled. If Break Bones had been with him, how did he end up here? "Why are you here if Darius isn't?"

Break Bones hesitated. "Darius could not lay aside what needed to be done in Far Seeing. I told him I would meet him there, and he left before me, in the first wave of soldiers. As preparations were made, I realized I could not ignore Madeline's message. Though the message was to Darius, I made a pledge to serve Madeline every day of my life, for she returned the Sword of Years to the Scim people. I could not in good conscience ignore her words, which seemed to me a summons."

"Then you're a better friend than Darius," she said bitterly.

"We can discuss such things later," Lamisap said. "Now time slips away, and we are all hidden like wasps in a wall, waiting to sting. So let us fly!"

Shula considered the soldiers with Break Bones. "Who are these people? And can they fight?"

"They fight well enough, lady. They are soldiers sent by the necromancer king of Pastisia. They have crossbows and electric swords. I have a dagger to spare should you need one."

The necromancers! She stared at them a moment. The Pastisians were not well known—everyone Shula had met in the Sunlit Lands was afraid of them. But even if they were twice as fearsome as the rumors claimed, she wasn't sure there were enough of them here to do what needed to be done. "I'll use my own bare hands," Shula said. "Here is my plan: I'll set fires in the farther woods, drawing some of the Elenil away. When their ranks thin, you attack. We work to make a break in the line where the firethorns can begin to spread."

Break Bones asked Lamisap, "How fast will they spread, given the chance?"

"A fast walk, I'd say, without a wind to help it. With a good gust, at the speed of the wind itself."

Break Bones pounded his fist against the chest of one of the Pastisian soldiers. "We go to war, then!"

The soldier did not cheer or return Break Bones's excitement. Instead, he said, "There is an Earth politician who wrote that no matter how necessary, war is always an evil, never a good. We will not learn how to live together in peace by killing each other's children."

Break Bones turned away, disgusted. "You Pastisians and your books."

"Pastisians go to war for the sake of peace and in service to our king. We take no pleasure in it."

"All the more pleasure for me, then," Break Bones said.

Shula laughed. These were the warriors who terrified so many in the Sunlit Lands, yet they were reluctant in battle, or so it seemed. Reluctant, at least, to enter it.

Lamisap shifted from foot to foot, nervous. "Are we ready, then? The time, friends, the time."

"Give me three minutes," Shula said, and slipped from the hole. She climbed to the forest floor, watching carefully for Elenil. She didn't want to set the fires too close, or the soldiers would return to fight when the Pastisians came out, but too far and they might not see it in time to run to it.

She found a tree in sight of the firethorns and climbed into the upper branches. Then she lit it like a torch. She dropped to the ground, the Elenil already on their way. They moved faster than expected—definitely faster than her. She raced for another tree, lighting this one at the trunk. Then a third. Now the Elenil were peeling away from the firethorns, trying to intercept her before she lit another tree.

"Hold the line," Rondelo called. "You fools, hold the line! Stay near the firethorns!"

A crossbow bolt appeared in the chest of an Elenil soldier, knocking him backward into the flames. Sparks blew into the sky. Soldiers with buckets ran to put them out, while another pulled the Elenil from the flames. A shower of bolts rained down from the Pastisians.

Then Break Bones was upon the Elenil, a savage whirlwind of fury who swung his stone ax with unexpected speed and lashed out with feet and fists, his monstrous laugh striking fear even in Shula. She ran toward the battle.

Rondelo engaged with Break Bones, shouting at his soldiers to guard against the spread of flame. "Leave the trees," he shouted. "It is the flames from the firethorns we must protect against."

To see these two mighty beings in combat was like nothing Shula had witnessed in war before this. Break Bones, larger than a human, and Rondelo, slighter of frame but nearly as strong, attacking one another with brutal blows that would have felled a human instantly. In the firelight Rondelo's armor shone like a fallen star, and the black tattoos on Break Bones's grey skin seemed to shift and move like living things.

Evernu, the stag, bounded up behind Break Bones. Shula shouted a warning, and Break Bones, distracted from Rondelo, managed to turn in time to grab Evernu by the antlers and swing him toward the trees. The stag hit a trunk and fell, writhing, to the ground. Rondelo, in the same moment, sliced the Scim warrior's left shoulder. Break Bones stepped backward, using his ax to keep space between him and the Elenil. He examined his wound for the barest moment, and Rondelo burst forward, jabbing the hilt of his sword into the wound. Break Bones cried out and stepped back again, but Rondelo was moving forward, bringing his fist hard into the Scim's nose, driving him even further back.

Shula ignited herself and leapt between them.

Rondelo fell back in surprise. "Shula? You fight for the Scim?"

"I fight for the Sunlit Lands. Whoever is for the people of the Sunlit Lands, I fight alongside them. Rondelo, the Elenil are wrong on this one."

"Such is not my decision to make, Shula Bishara. I follow the orders of my archon. He knows far more than you or I about this situation, and I trust him to do right."

"We're going to burn this forest down," Shula said. "It will restart magic. It will put us all on equal footing for the first time in generations."

"What are generations to the Elenil? Less than nothing. And why should we desire equal footing? There is great danger in that sort of society."

So she wouldn't be able to convince him to let the firethorns free. A new idea came to her. The guards had thinned here near Rondelo. What if she turned up the heat to push people away? She shouted to them both, "Stand back!" and lit herself like a supernova, hotter than she had ever been before. Her hair rose in the updraft.

A warm wind stirred, and the firethorns advanced, like soldiers marching past her into the woods. "The wind!" she shouted. "Break Bones, the wind is here to help."

Rondelo yelled her name, but she could scarcely see him through the heat waves. "Do you know what this is?" he asked. She could barely see what he was holding—a small round shape in his palm. The firethorns were already spreading, a strange, magical expansion as they shot ash and flames near her feet, new sprouts growing in seconds. "A flood seed," Rondelo said. "Elenil magic that takes water from somewhere else . . . and brings it here."

He threw the thing to the ground, and a river sprang from it. It hit her like a solid thing, knocking her from her feet and carrying her away from Rondelo. She gasped for air. Her ribs hurt where the flood had caught her in the side, and then the wall of water pushed her through the trees, and the branches whipped at her head and back. She reached for a branch and just managed to pull herself out of the flow. "No!"

Break Bones was on his feet again, his massive grey hand covering his wounded shoulder. "The wind was not enough. The Elenil and their magic always win."

"That's right," Rondelo said. "Now throw down your weapons. It is time for you to come with me to see the archon."

Shula took quick stock of their situation. Several Pastisian soldiers lay crumpled on the ground, and a few others had been captured by the Elenil. At least one still fought an Elenil in the woods. Break Bones was wounded. The spread of the firethorns had been stopped by Rondelo's flood seed.

Break Bones threw down his ax.

"What are you doing?" Shula shouted. "Don't give in to him—we can still run!"

"We would run only to a place unchanged, despite all our sacrifices,"

Break Bones said. "I will live my life in an Elenil prison if I cannot return to my people with news of victory."

Then, to Shula's astonishment, a flying cat glided into view, hovering over the firethorns. At least, that's what her mind told her she was seeing. This was the Sunlit Lands, and anything was possible, but a flying cat? She studied it more carefully. She could not deny that it was a cat with wings. Maybe this wasn't a normal thing in the Sunlit Lands, either, because several of the Elenil stopped to stare as well, and Rondelo gave the cat the careful attention she had seen many times on the battlefield, assessing it to see if it was a threat. Break Bones seemed unconcerned.

"Excuse me," the cat said. "Did someone here say, 'The wind is not enough'? And why is no one bowing in my presence?"

Break Bones, Rondelo, and Shula exchanged perplexed looks. "I said these words," Break Bones said. "What of it?"

"What of it? Why, I am a Guardian of the Wind, and you, sir, have insulted the wind."

"Insulted the—? Begone, cat, we speak of weighty things here and have no time for your ridiculous interruptions."

"Cat?" Her eyes boggled. "DO CATS HAVE WINGS?" She began to beat her wings, hard, and a wind unlike any Shula had ever felt whipped around them, howling, drying her hair and clothes almost immediately. "I am a Guardian of the Wind. How dare you say the wind is not enough? Behold the power of the wind!"

The wind blew Shula backward, knocked Break Bones into a tree, and sent Rondelo tumbling away from them both. Then the firethorns began to move, writhing like snakes, curling in on each other, falling over, spitting sparks and seeds and smoke. They expanded into the forest, leaping over the water of the flood seed, igniting grass and brush and trees.

Lamisap appeared at Shula's side. She had multiple wounds on her arms—her blood was red. "We must run to safety or be burned. Run!" The Aluvorean didn't wait for her but leapt through the trees. Break Bones did not follow, turning instead to separate the captured Pastisians from their Elenil captors. The Elenil fell away easily enough, and he sent the Pastisians running from the flames.

Rondelo watched Shula from across a meadow engulfed in fire. Evernu stood beside him, then tugged at him to move away from the flames. He leapt onto the stag's back, and they disappeared into the forest.

Break Bones came to her, his left arm hanging useless. "Where is Wu Song?"

"North," she said. "Near the Queen's Island."

"Then that is where I must go. And thou, Shula Bishara? Whence away?"

She did not know. Her parents were gone. Her sister gone. Her brother, too. And Madeline. Now even the Sunlit Lands were burning, changing, becoming something else. Her eyes stung, whether from the smoke or the anger clawing its way out of her, she didn't know. It wasn't fair, none of it. She'd had to fight her old allies, even a friend like Rondelo. She had nothing left, nothing. The fury tore through her. "I'm going to make it burn," she said. The fire grew hotter and hotter, hot enough to melt metal. She could barely think, could barely see through the flames. Break Bones was gone, and she hadn't seen him go, had been so furious she hadn't heard whatever he might have said.

Then she was running, barely able to keep up with the magic flames of the firethorns. Everywhere she stepped blossomed into flame. She ran faster. The flames grew hotter and higher. She would burn it all, burn everything until there was nothing left.

31

INVASION

The magic of the Elenil has given me a deep knowledge of who you are.

FROM "JELDA'S REVENGE," A SCIM LEGEND

✦

The archon was not in his chambers. Darius pushed a plush couch against a wall so no one could come up behind him, and fell onto it. He was covered in sweat and gore, and his muscles burned with the exertion of fighting to reach the top of the tower. It had taken nearly two hours. The Pastisians were here now, the first waves having come via the gondolas, and more were arriving by the minute in airships, descending to the ground on long ropes. He watched them through a nearby window for a few minutes. He knew more Elenil would come upon him soon, and his legs were starting to stiffen. He needed to get up and move.

He had been wounded several times, but the adrenaline had kept him from slowing much. He had to keep going, had to find the archon. The sword, too, demanded that he continue. Rest was not an option when there was so much Elenil blood to be spilled nearby. He hadn't seen his mask and had no idea where they would keep it. It would be helpful if he could find it. It would prevent him from further harm. It should even heal the wounds he'd already received.

Not that it mattered much if he couldn't find the archon. Was it possible the ruler of the Elenil had left the city and gone with his army to Aluvorea? It seemed unlikely. He had never been much of a fighter. Darius had never seen him on the front lines. There could be a hidden room here, of course. Or a hundred hidden rooms. Far Seeing was a big city, too—he could be hidden away in any number of places.

A shadow moved over the tower. Darius slipped to the window and looked up in time to see the king's airship floating overhead. It was black and enormous—larger than any other ship in the fleet—with sturdy fins on the sides of the blimp and propellers on the fins. Ian had pointed it out to Darius in Pastisia, and even then he had been astonished by its size. Darius suspected they would use the archon's garden as a place to enter the tower. King Ian would be here soon. The garden was only a floor below, so Darius set off at a trot to meet him there.

A Scim servant barred the entrance. "You cannot enter here," he said. This sort of Scim had been "civilized" by the Elenil. Though they still wore their war skins—the intimidating public face of the Scim community— these had been softened and brought under control. They wore Elenil clothing and spoke with distinctly Elenil diction. Their tusks were nearly always shaved down or removed. Break Bones called them traitors, but Darius saw something else. He saw Scim who had been abused, broken, told they were worthless. He felt a mix of compassion and anger: compassion for them, anger at the Elenil, and anger, too, that they didn't break out and rebel, even though he knew that they had been worn down. But when he compared a creature like this to a glorious Scim like Break Bones, he scarcely could believe this was a Scim at all.

This servant did not make an intimidating doorman. He had none of the fire of the Scim left in him.

"Is the archon here?" Darius asked. "Hiding somewhere?"

The Scim's eyes darted left, then right. "N-n-no."

"My mask, it is here?"

"Your mask?"

"A black skull, with great curving horns."

The servant's eyes grew wide. The Black Skulls were the famous fighters of the Scim army. Even a civilized Scim would have heard their names often. Darius opted to take it one step further and showed him the blood-slicked sword in his hand. The Scim leaned forward. "The Sword of Years!"

"Yes, and it is here to bring justice at last, friend. So if you know where your master is, speak."

"I don't, sir, truly I don't."

"Then make way. I need to get to the garden. The invading king has arrived." He brushed past the Scim, who seemed too startled to do anything about it. He hesitated, then grasped the Scim's arm. "Find a weapon—even a kitchen knife will do—and join your people in this fight." But the Scim hurried away.

The airship was making lazy circles around the tower, moving closer with each pass. A black-clad airman was hanging from a bottom port. Darius waved to him, letting him know he could take a rope, and the airman threw one. The rope unspooled, landing in a rosebush. The garden still looked sick, half broken from the confrontation here two months ago, when Yenil had cut off the archon's hand. Darius tied the rope onto a dry fountain, then waved to the airman.

The airman didn't throw down a ladder, though—he jumped onto the rope and slid down, landing with a practiced flourish. He had no weapon, only big boots, a black uniform, and a bronze mask. "Darius," he said.

"Your Majesty?"

"Yes, it is I." Ian's voice boomed in the mask. He signaled to the airship, and more of his soldiers swarmed the rope, bringing a ladder and a series of ropes as they began to moor the ship. "Have you found the archon?"

"He's hiding," Darius said.

The king walked to the edge of the garden. The battle raged throughout the city. Smoke rose from several of the gates. Pastisians flew on gliders and dropped burning bottles from airships. A flurry of messenger birds filled the air. At the western gate, it appeared that the Elenil had built a significant force to fight back. Then the ground collapsed beneath them. "Ah," the king said. "The Scim's sentient tunnel friend, I think. The Elenil have never believed they were at real risk of an armed revolution, and now that folly has led to their overthrow."

"Regime change, surely," Hanali called. He descended a spiral staircase that had been lowered from the airship. He wore a more practical outfit than before, though this one still had a long cape which dragged on the ground behind him. "Not revolution, King Ian. Merely a change of leadership."

Mrs. Raymond was not far behind Hanali, with some of the king's soldiers. She said, "It was less than a season ago that the Scim breached the walls at the Festival of the Turning, and yet they have left the walls unguarded again. It is not like Thenody to be so careless."

"Where's Break Bones?" Darius asked.

"He went ahead to find Madeline," Hanali said. "He said he has certain obligations to her and to Mr. Wu. He said he would wait for you in Aluvorea or leave word of where to find him."

Darius's heart sank. Had he done the right thing in coming here instead of racing to Madeline's side? He thought so. They would find the archon soon, and then he could finish this business and move on to find Madeline. The sword sent warm feelings of affirmation to him. It would not be good to leave the archon unpunished.

The king spoke to his soldiers. "Every ornament, every brick, every stone of this tower is to be thrown down. It was built on ill-gotten gain, every piece of it squeezed from the lifeblood of the Scim or some other people of the Sunlit Lands. So tear it down, brothers and sisters, and let all people know that a time must come for all injustice to be undone."

Hanali's eyes widened. He leaned toward the king and said, quiet enough that the soldiers couldn't hear him, "Your Majesty? This is a grave injustice to the Elenil. Surely the tower should be preserved. Changed in its use, perhaps. But one unjust action is not negated by another."

The king regarded him coolly, then asked him to repeat his objection to the soldiers.

Hanali gladly took this invitation and said, "Pastisian friends! What good is it to throw this tower down? A wound to the Elenil will not heal the wounds of the Scim." Darius said nothing to this, but he couldn't help but think that this was precisely the way the Elenil magic worked. Hanali went on. "Let us take the tower and use it for some new, more noble cause."

When he was finished, the king said, "Hanali, son of Vivi. The archon had his hand cut off. Was this just?"

Hanali straightened his gloves. "I do not know. It was a child who did it. The archon had, of course, killed the child's parents."

"Oh? Why did the archon order such a thing?"

"Because the Scim attacked the city at the Festival of the Turning."

"Why, I wonder, did the Scim attack the city?"

"Yes, yes, I see where you are going," Hanali said. "I strike a blow, then another strikes a blow, and twenty years later we are still punching one another, and who is truly to blame?"

"Not at all," said the king. "I only say this. If two people came together with no history of violence or wrong-doing between them . . . let us say a Pastisian and a Kakri. If the Pastisian cut off the Kakri's left hand, would that be just?"

"For no reason? Surely not."

"Then would it be just for the Kakri to remove the Pastisian's hand in return?"

"I suppose."

"Wait," Darius said. "That's not fair, though. The Kakri didn't agree to lose his hand. It's not like they made a bargain. What if the Kakri had just wanted to keep his hand?"

"Even so," the king said. "So there should be a greater price for the injustice done to the Kakri. Perhaps we take two hands. But then the Pastisian thinks, 'Is this a fair price for what I have done?' He sees a debt between them."

"You are saying justice is complicated," Hanali said.

"I am saying that justice may be impossible," the king replied. "I am saying that unless the creator of the Sunlit Lands himself were to bring his wisdom into the situation, there may not be a true solution. One injustice imbalances the world." He looked out over the city. The smoke had begun to obscure the buildings below. "I am saying that mercy and forgiveness are deeper truths than justice, and yet we cannot set justice aside. We cannot allow the merciful and forgiving to be destroyed by the violent. It is an impossible question, best answered by those who have been wronged, not those in power. Yet this is the responsibility of kings." He took off his mask, looking into the eyes of his soldiers. "I say to tear down every orna-ment and brick and stone. I say this not to shame the Elenil. I say this not to punish them, or even to bring true justice, if such a thing were possible. If the Elenil choose to rebuild this place, so be it. But let them know that if they do it by thievery and deception and slave labor, we will return and tear it down again, and again, and again, until they build something that can last. We do this so that the Elenil may remember that justice does come, even if it does not come swiftly." He dismissed the soldiers, and they immediately headed into the tower to begin their work, armed with swords and sledgehammers.

Hanali's face had grown hard during this speech. "Your Majesty. You cripple my administration of the Elenil before it has even begun. How will I be known now? The Elenil who allowed the destruction of Far Seeing."

"No," the king said. "Rather you may be called the one who returned Far Seeing to glory. The Peasant King—or the Majestic One, as you call him—built the Sunlit Lands to be a refuge for those who were wronged. A place of peace, of mercy, of rest and safety. But the Elenil have corrupted this place and made it a mirror of all the injustices of the places we fled. Once every stone of this tower is torn down, your people will have to con-sider each stone as you lift it into place. You will meditate on the purpose of this building, of this city, and perhaps it will make you stronger, make you better, make you more aware of what you have been called to do."

"Mrs. Raymond, I do hope you can speak some sense to the king before he does this rash and terrible thing," Hanali said.

She shook her head. "He is king. He has spoken. It is already done."

Hanali sniffed. "So be it."

The king set his mask into place. "If I find the archon before you," the king said, "I will not kill him. Nor will I allow you to do so." He held out his hand to his wife. She took it, and they moved toward the interior of the castle. Though Mrs. Raymond wore light armor and a small sword on her belt, Darius wondered at how ill prepared she appeared. But then again, he had never seen her unprepared. No doubt she was more ready than he suspected. The king called back to Hanali, "I do not know what game you are playing, Hanali, son of Vivi. I shall do what I must to protect my people and to make the Sunlit Lands what it should be."

Hanali watched the king and Mrs. Raymond leave, his hands folded behind his back. When they had entered the tower, he turned to Darius. "I can, of course, sense the location of the Crescent Stone, which the archon keeps on his person at all times. Can your sword tell you where he is as well?"

Darius felt the sword's eagerness to spill more Elenil blood, but there were too many worthy targets in this tower. It did not prioritize. Or at least, not that Darius could tell. "No. But you know where he is?"

"Yes," Hanali said. "Are you ready?"

Darius was bone weary and ready for this all to be done. "Show me the way."

Hanali moved toward the tower, but as they walked, a white bird flapped in front of Hanali, landing at his feet. It was a tall bird, the sort you might see stalking in a marsh.

"Hail, archon-who-is-to-come," the bird said. "I am sent by an admirer who wishes you to remember him when you come into your power."

Hanali grimaced. "How gauche. Pray do not say his name. What news, bird?"

"The girl is dead," the bird said, "planted in the soil of Aluvorea."

"No," Hanali whispered. He bit the knuckle of one gloved finger. "Her life is past and just begun. She treads now in a clime of sun . . . in the land of the Majestic One."

"Who?" Darius said. "Who's dead?"

Hanali gave him a pitying look. "Don't be a fool, Darius."

"Madeline Oliver," the bird said simply, as if the words had no meaning in themselves, as if it didn't matter who it was or what had happened. Darius put his palm on the wall nearest him, holding himself up. No. He had just found out she was here. He wouldn't believe it, not until he spoke to someone who had seen her body. It could be a mistake, a misunderstanding.

"How did she return to the Sunlit Lands without my knowledge?" Hanali wondered aloud. "More importantly, what happened? How did she die? Who was with her?"

The bird turned its long head slightly to one side. "How did she die? A question that is not easily answered. Was it because of the curse you put upon her that stole her breath—"

"What?" Darius stared at the bird in disbelief.

Hanali scowled at the bird. "Oh, now I *do* want to know who sent you. He and I shall have words."

"—or the fact that you brought her here to the Sunlit Lands at all? Or the magical ecosystem which required her death if she was to reset magic?"

Hanali blanched. "She crossed the accursed river?"

"Yes."

"What of the firethorns?"

"When last I saw them, the firethorns were encircled by the Elenil and had not spread."

"That is some small comfort, then," Hanali said.

"What does the bird mean, that you're the one who stole Madeline's breath? Why would you do that?"

Hanali straightened, his face perfectly still. "It was my father, Vivi, who wove the curse, Darius Walker, though I admit he used my magic to do it. It was I who received permission to bring her here to the Sunlit Lands, to heal her, to undo her curse. How could I know she would reject that healing? My father gave her the sickness. He prevented the treatments from working. He made her name fall from the lung transplant lists. She was meant to come live here on her sixteenth birthday, to join our household. But her parents refused. Refused even though they agreed to the bargain all those years ago."

The sword was in Darius's hand. He didn't know how it came to be there, but his trembling fist was closed over the hilt, and the point of the blade hovered near Hanali's heart. "You killed her."

"My father did," Hanali said. "And you have killed my father. So the whole affair is done now, and all of my loved ones soaked in blood."

A look of true sorrow crossed Hanali's face, but that didn't stop the anger which flooded Darius. He felt hot, burning hot. His teeth ground into one another. He tried to keep the secret he had learned to himself, but the thought of harming Hanali with it was too tempting. Hanali was complicit in this. He may not have worked the curse, but he had been a part of it somehow. "Vivi wasn't even your father," Darius said. "He kidnapped you, you know. Just like he tried to kidnap Madeline. You weren't really his son."

"Nonsense," Hanali said. "I have lived with my parents my whole life."

"Do you even remember being a child?"

"No, but what Elenil does? We live centuries. It is only natural our memories of our childhood would be few."

"The Elenil can't have children," Darius said. "None of them."

"Except on the evening of the Turning," Hanali said.

Darius couldn't stop himself. He wanted Hanali to know. Wanted to hurt him with the knowledge he held. "Not even then. They can only have children by making more Elenil."

"Ha," Hanali said. "I think I would know if that were the case."

"No, you're not one of the magistrates, and you haven't had children of your own yet. The Elenil kidnap human teenagers from Earth—"

"It's not kidnapping, they are given a choice whether to come here or not."

"—and then they force them to drink addleberry wine. The addleberries make them forget. Their memories, their identity, and eventually, their shape. They're remolded. Taught how to change shape and become Elenil. They're left in seclusion for a short time, and then they are introduced to Elenil society. You're not—none of you are—any different than me or Madeline. You're humans. You've been twisted by magic, but you're humans."

"It's not true," Hanali said, but the tone of his voice made it clear he was uncertain. Darius imagined this new truth working backward through Hanali's life, making puzzling moments suddenly clear, transforming odd comments into perfectly understandable ones.

"It is true," Darius said, pulling the little book from his pocket. "The Pastisians gave me this. Quotes from your 'father,' Vivi, about you. How he chose you. How he brought you here. How he convinced you to leave behind everyone and everything you loved so you could be an Elenil. But you can't remember any of it, can you?"

Hanali straightened and looked to the tower. "None of this matters now. None of it. We must find the archon. We can deal with these lies after."

"It does matter, Hanali, because you've built your whole system on the idea that the Elenil should be in charge, that the Elenil were called to rule from Far Seeing. But the Elenil are just more humans. The Scim are as much Elenil as you are. The Elenil are a myth. You're human. The Scim are human. The Aluvoreans. You're all just humans twisted with magic."

"Wrong!" Hanali shouted, spittle spraying Darius. "The Elenil do exist. We made ourselves. However it happened, we became something more than human, something better. I am trying to change the world, and you are seeking to make it seem like those changes are insignificant."

"Change the world? You killed the woman I love for this?" He waved dismissively at the garden, the tower, the city. "You killed her, and I wasn't even there because I was with you." Darius grunted, disgusted with himself.

Hanali spoke, his voice cold. "You weren't there because you chose to seek after this revenge. You chose this over her. Now you are going to let your revenge slip away too. You cannot get Madeline back. But you can still kill the archon."

"I will kill the archon," Darius said. "Maybe I'll kill two." The sword sang for joy in his hand.

Hanali glared at him. "So be it. This way." He led Darius inside the tower, and they set off together to find revenge.

32
LOSS

Command me any task, be it possible or no, and I will perform it.

FROM "JELDA'S REVENGE," A SCIM LEGEND

✛

Jason had tried to swim to the island, but it defended itself with magic. The water spit him out. His feet sank into the ground if he moved toward the water again. He raged and shouted, but it wouldn't let him close. Baileya said it was to prevent anyone from interfering with the new birth of magic, but Jason didn't care.

When he eventually gave up, he knelt on the shore and wept. Baileya sat near him. Sometimes she put her hand on his back. Sometimes she wandered away for a time. She stood ankle deep in the water for a while, staring toward the island. By sunrise Jason was exhausted and had no more tears. Baileya appeared beside him with fruit she had gathered in the forest. They ate in silence—a red fruit with soft white flesh and bright green seeds—and he felt his strength returning.

"You should have let me go instead of her," Jason said.

Baileya closed her eyes, and he could tell that this hurt her. It was the first sentence he had said to her since Shula had left, hours ago. "She did not wish that," Baileya said at last.

"She shouldn't have died!"

Baileya's eyes flashed. "And you should have?"

"It would have been a relief," he snapped.

"You have taken a vow to be truthful," she said hotly. "Will you throw it away because of your grief?"

Jason blinked, stunned. She was right. He didn't want to die. It was only that he didn't want Madeline to be dead, and some part of him thought that his dying to prevent that would have been better. He took Baileya's hands. "I'm sorry, Baileya. You're right." He looked at his feet. "Thank you for staying with me. Thank you for breakfast."

She wrapped her arms around him, and they held each other. "You would given your own life for a friend. A friend who had little time left even had you saved her. It is a noble thing. You are an exceptional person. There are great things in store for you."

"You're literally the only person who thinks that," Jason said sullenly.

Baileya let him go and stalked to where she had left her weapon standing sentry in the sand. She pulled it out. "There are fires coming from the south. We should leave this place."

"Wait, are you angry at me? For that?"

"We do not need to speak of this now. Let us go. We can discuss this at another time."

"No, Baileya, I want to talk about it now."

"You are grieving."

"I've been grieving ever since you met me. First Jenny and now Madeline. Life is full of grief, unending, forever."

Baileya shook her head. "Life is full of *life*, Wu Song. Grief is reserved for when it is lost. Life is not defined by grief."

Jason wanted to believe that, but he didn't. "My experience tells me otherwise."

"Ah, Wu Song. We have lost Madeline, but did we not share fresh food a few minutes ago? Did we not hold each other and know affection? This is life, and something to be thankful for."

"It's so small compared to the loss," he said.

"Yes," she said. She took his hands again. "But sorrow is a gift. It is a sign that we have loved. If we did not love, we would not grieve."

He had nothing to say to that. He felt like all his reasons for being here were gone now. Why should he stay in the Sunlit Lands? What was he doing here? "Baileya," he said, "everyone I love dies, and it's my fault. My sister, and now Madeline."

Baileya's face grew hard. "How is Madeline's death your fault?"

"Remi told me about crossing the river. I could have come here myself and swum across, but I went to find Madeline and Shula instead. If I had come here directly, there would have been no one to stop me."

Baileya sighed. It was a long sigh, as if she were letting out all of her breath. A tear slipped down her face. "Wu Song. Sit with me." She sat on the sand. The fires were coming closer.

He lowered himself beside her. "What is it? What's wrong?"

"I have been considering your story."

"Our engagement story?"

Baileya winced. "Yes. I am thankful you shared it with me. I have thought on it these weeks. You have told me the story, that your sister, Jenny, was your closest family. That it was her and you against your parents. She became betrothed to a man—"

"Sort of. They were dating. I know you don't have that here."

"—a man your father disapproved of. So you did not tell your father when she had gone with him, even though she was late. When you found her, she lay dying, trapped in a vehicle."

Jason could see the car still, upside down at the bottom of a curvy road. Her boyfriend, Marcus, dead in the driver's seat, and Jenny trapped in the passenger seat, bleeding. "She blamed me," he said. "I lied to my parents about where she was. If I had told the truth, we would have found her, she would still be alive. That's why I only tell the truth now."

Baileya took a deep breath. "What did she say to you on that night?"

Jason's voice cracked, but he didn't cry. He had no tears left. "She said, 'I was waiting for you.' She knew I knew where she was. She knew I would find her. She was dying there, waiting for me. She blamed me, and she was right to do it, because it was my fault."

Baileya squeezed his hand. "I cannot accept this story."

"What?"

"I cannot accept it. Our betrothal is over. I will not accept this story. It is of great worth. It is a good story. But it is not true, and so I will not accept it."

Jason's heart beat so hard he felt light headed. "Are you breaking up with me?"

Baileya looked at him quizzically. "What does this mean?"

"Are you ending our engagement?"

"Yes, Wu Song. Our engagement has ended. It is done. We will not be married."

"What?" He looked at the small lake where Madeline had died. The sun shone on the ripples as it rose. The rivulet flowing south had become a full-on stream. Baileya was crying now. He wiped the tears from her face, and she didn't pull away. "What's wrong with my story?"

"A story is how we explain the world, Wu Song, and your explanation is wrong. You say your sister died because of you, because you were dishonest, and she blamed you. But this is not true. Your sister disobeyed your parents. She kept secrets. She trusted only you, true?"

"Yes, but—"

"She trusted only you. When her . . . her boyfriend?"

"Marcus."

"When Marcus destroyed their vehicle, they were trapped."

Jason didn't see where this was going. His hurt was giving way to confusion. "Yeah. I don't see—"

"Jenny kept secrets. Jenny snuck out. Marcus kept secrets. Marcus smashed their vehicle."

"I don't understand. This is all true—what are you saying?"

"But you say, 'Wu Song is to blame.'"

He felt like he had come up from deep-sea diving, getting a good breath of air, but the waves were threatening to draw him back in. What Baileya said made sense but was so contrary to how he saw it he could barely keep the pattern together in his mind. "You're saying that it wasn't my fault?"

"How could it be your fault, Wu Song?"

"But Jenny said, '*I've been waiting for you.*' She'd been hanging there upside down, knowing I could save her but I didn't."

"No, Wu Song, *she was saying she knew you would come.* She wasn't blaming you, she was praising you. She loved you, and she knew you would find her."

"She . . ." Jason couldn't get another word out. He shook his head. Baileya didn't get it. "No, Baileya, she was angry that I let her die."

Baileya jumped to her feet in frustration. "Was she dead when she said this to you?"

"No. Of course not."

"Then how could she blame you for her death? *You* blame yourself, but she did not. She *could* not. You don't see the depth of her love for you, because of your own lack of love for yourself. You say, 'Oh, she blamed me,' because you blame yourself, and you cannot hear her words of love which say you were a good brother and did all that could be done."

He thought he was out of tears, but they came again. "I loved her," he said.

Baileya crouched beside him, her eyes tinged with sadness. She took his face, made him look at her. "You have not only lost someone you loved . . . you lost someone who loved you. Why else would the wound run so deep? You do her a disservice, saying she blamed you. When you say these words, you deny the strength of her love."

Jason was sobbing now. Baileya's words felt like truth, but his mind rebelled against them, fought them, denied them. Baileya spoke again. "You say you are an ordinary man, and yet you convince my brother to let you live—an impossible feat—using only words. You say you are nothing, and yet you befriend a unicorn, you become betrothed to a Kakri warrior, you are at the center of the great changes coming in the Sunlit Lands. You have made fast friends with Break Bones, a Scim who has never loved a human before these days. You are loved by so many . . . David and Kekoa and Shula and, yes, Madeline, and do you not see that when you keep saying you are nothing, you are unimportant, that you make a mockery of their love?"

"You're ending our engagement," Jason said. "They love me, but you don't."

Tears sprang into Baileya's eyes. "How little you think of me! I have never loved so deeply as I love you. I have father, mother, brothers, sisters, cousins, and I have loved none of them—none of them—so deeply as I love you." She stood, went to her weapon, leaned on it for a moment as if she didn't have the strength to stand, then came back to him. She didn't crouch down this time. "I cannot have a husband who will not receive my love. You do not love yourself, and so you have no room in your heart for love such as mine. My love falls away. It is wasted on you."

"So we're done, then," Jason said. "You're going back to the Kakri lands."

Now she did crouch down. He couldn't look at her, but she didn't speak for a long time, until he did. Tears streaked her golden cheeks, and her face was twisted with sorrow. "Find a better story," she said. "Then come find me again." She kissed him, and he tasted the salt of her tears. He felt the sobs rise from within her, and her hand tenderly on his face. Then she stood and walked north.

"Baileya," he called.

She stopped. "Yes, Wu Song?"

"Before you leave . . . would you make sure Yenil and Shula and David are okay?"

A smile came to her lips. "Even now you are concerned for your friends, Wu Song. You are a good man."

"So you'll do it?"

"For you, my beloved, yes."

She walked away. He didn't call after her a second time.

Jason didn't know how much time passed. Hours. He still waited beside the lake. He couldn't see the sun, because the smoke had moved in, covering the sky. He had a hard time breathing. It reminded him of Madeline. He realized how bad it must have been for her. His chest hurt from coughing. He knew the Elenil could come across him here, or animals running from the fires. He didn't care. He didn't turn when he heard the crashing in the trees.

Break Bones came out of the woods, covered in soot and blood. His grey skin was black and red. He saw Jason but didn't say anything at first. He walked to the water's edge and sluiced off the worst of the ash. He splashed water on his face. "She was a good woman," Break Bones said. "Strong. Smart. Kind."

"She died to give the Sunlit Lands another chance."

"Yes."

"Baileya broke up with me," Jason said.

"This surprises you?"

Taken off guard, Jason actually laughed. "I guess not. I spent our entire engagement surprised she was with me."

"Was it because of your puny arms?"

Jason threw sand at Break Bones. "No!"

"Your big mouth, then. Or your disgusting breakfast food, the brown one. Pudding?"

"It was most definitely not the pudding, though I couldn't get her to try it."

"Then why, Wu Song?"

"Because she loves me too much, and I don't love myself enough."

Break Bones grunted. "She is a wise woman."

"She was too good for me."

"What would she say to that?"

"She would call me a fool. It's those sorts of comments that let her know it wasn't going to work."

"You need to learn a new story," Break Bones said.

"Yeah." He threw a rock in the water. "An old woman told me once that if I wanted to leave everything and come and learn, I could go to the desert. She said maybe I would find what I was looking for there."

"Then let us go there, friend. The fires are coming quickly and moving faster than you run. We will need to find a place to go."

"I'm not going anywhere while Madeline is still on that island," Jason said.

Break Bones raised his eyebrows. "Her body is still there?"

"I can't get there myself. The island is using magic to defend itself."

"I made you a promise once," Break Bones said. "Do you remember?"

"Yeah, you said you were going to murder me."

Break Bones laughed, remembering it fondly. "No, another promise. I promised I would deliver Madeline Oliver's lifeless body to you."

Jason regarded the Scim warrior. "It's not like you to break a promise."

"Indeed not. When I return with her, will you join us? We three? We will leave this forest behind."

A hundred replies danced through Jason's mind, but he just said, "Yes."

The Scim picked up his ax and walked to the water. It pushed him out. He tried again, and his feet sank. The third time he backed off a good distance, ran at the lake, and dove in, ax in hand. He didn't surface. Jason jumped to his feet and ran to the water's edge, where he could see Break Bones beneath the water, swimming. He didn't break the surface, he just swam with great frog kicks until Jason couldn't see him anymore.

The smoke was getting worse. Jason could hear the crackling of the fire moving through the forest now. There were big crashes as trees fell over, and a wall of increasing heat pushing at his back. Strange animals came running through the forest, panicked, headed north. Jason moved closer to the water. "Break Bones!" he shouted, but there was no reply. He thought he saw, once, Baileya watching from across the river, but he couldn't say for certain.

Jason stepped into the water, dipping in up to his chest, so he could pull the wet T-shirt over his mouth. His eyes burned. He couldn't stay here long. The fire made a sort of halo over the trees. There were popping sounds and bursts of glowing green sparks shooting up over them like fireworks. The magic, probably. He hoped Dee and Yenil and Shula were safe. And Baileya. Of course Baileya.

As the flames advanced, he moved farther into the water. It wasn't resisting him anymore. The moment he realized it, he swam as hard as he could for the island. Swimming in his clothes, with his sneakers on, was harder than he thought it would be. Plus the smoke and his general fatigue didn't help. He hadn't eaten since that fruit Baileya had given him, and he couldn't remember his last full meal. When he got to the shore, he pulled himself onto dry land. He couldn't see across the water in any direction, it was all smoke. "Madeline? Are you here?"

Break Bones came out of the haze, carrying something in his arms. Someone. Break Bones had been weeping, something Jason had never seen before. He knelt down in front of Jason. Madeline looked so small in his massive grey arms. Her head was turned to the side, her eyes closed, like she was sleeping, her blonde hair nearly dragging the ground. On her head was a delicate oaken crown, made of interwoven branches and just covering her brow. "Hold out your arms," Break Bones said.

Jason shook his head. He couldn't. He couldn't do that. But Break Bones said it again. Then a third time. He put his arms out, and Break Bones slid Madeline into them. He collapsed over her, putting his cheek against hers. Her cheek was cold . . . and stiff, like cooled wax. The weight of her in his arms reminded him of that day—it seemed so long ago now—when she had fallen in chemistry class. How he had picked her up to carry her to his car, to get her to the hospital. To save her. To be there for her. And where had he been this time when she needed him? Across the river, crying.

Break Bones stood and quietly walked away.

"Oh no," Jason said. "Oh no, no, no." He didn't know what he was saying, but he kept speaking to her, telling her what he liked about her, what he would miss, how she had changed him, repeating over and over his love for her.

A bearded man stood over him. He wore simple homespun clothes and a twist of holly on his head. He had the look of a woodsman, maybe, and his eyes were kind. "I am sorry, Wu Song, but I must take her now."

"Who are you?"

"Like you, I am one of Madeline's friends," the man said. "Now I must take her body. Do you see the glow?" There was a glow, a green light, coming from the center of Madeline's chest. "That is the Queen's Seed, and it is time to plant it."

"I can't let her go," Jason said.

"Walk with me awhile, then, and I will show you where to lay her."

The man helped Jason to his feet. Jason followed him, struggling to carry Madeline. Break Bones fell into step beside him, and he did not speak a word. Break Bones did not try to help Jason with the weight of his friend, and Jason was strangely thankful for this. They walked toward the center of the island, where there stood a very old, very tall tree, with golden fruit hanging from it and rotten fruit on the ground all around it. The core of its wide trunk was gone—it was a hollow space, dark and cool, with only maybe six inches of living tree under the bark. A throne was carved into the living part of the tree. It seemed to jut out from the main part of the trunk, beside the wide crack where the hollow center could be seen.

"This is the place," the man said. "We must tear down the old growth to make way for the new." His eyes went to Break Bones. "Will you push against the tree, friend?"

Break Bones did not answer, but he moved to the back of the tree and, grunting, pushed against it. It creaked. Break Bones strained against it, and it cracked in half, falling over and shattering into many pieces. Part of the lower trunk—including the throne—still stood.

"Here is where we must lay her. In the hollow space, Wu Song."

Jason stepped inside the hollow trunk and laid her gently on the ground. It was soft, like moss, and her body sank into it a little.

The man said, "It is time to say good-bye."

Jason kissed her on the cheek. "Good-bye, Madeline."

She sank into the ground, soft and slow, and she looked so quiet and still and at peace. The green glow from her chest increased as she sank, and soon her body was gone, but the green glow remained, spreading through the ground. A tender shoot sprang up from the center of the space, and in a matter of moments it thickened and grew taller and became the white trunk of a slender, beautiful sapling with golden leaves. Jason ran his hand over the smooth bark.

"She is called the annagini vasagi, the Queen's Tree," the man said.

They watched the tree as she grew. She continued to reach gracefully for the sky, and there was a sparkling shimmer to her bark. It wasn't quite white, Jason realized, but a golden color so light that it almost appeared white. When the tree reached about ten feet tall, she slowed and then stopped growing, at least visibly.

Break Bones came to Jason. "She was a good woman," he said. "I know she was a kind of family to you."

"Yes," Jason said. "I didn't even know her that long."

"I want to share something with you," Break Bones said, and as Jason watched, his war skin melted away. It was a bizarre sight, as if Break Bones had a thick layer of mud over his entire body and Jason was watching it be washed away. His tusks shrank and then disappeared. His massive forehead receded, his monstrous muscles sluiced away, to be replaced by smaller ones. He looked distinctly . . . human. Black tattoos covered his arms. His hair was black and plaited down his back, and his skin was a dusky brown, not the concrete grey Jason had grown accustomed to. "I have never shown my true face to anyone but the Scim. Not even to Darius, who is nearly Scim himself." He took Jason's forearm in his. "I am called Croion. From this day, we are brothers, Wu Song. When you call, I will answer. When you go to war, I will be by your side. I shall have secrets from you no longer. My true name, my true face, all these things are in your hands now."

"Croion. Thank you for sharing your true name. I will keep it safe," Jason said. "I am Wu Song. Everything you have said is true for me, too."

"You told me your name when we first met."

"I am a very trusting individual," Jason said, grinning.

Croion roared with laughter. "I will wait for you on the other side of the river. Think on where we will travel next, and I will chart a path for us." He bowed low to the bearded man and said only, "Your Majesty." Then he was gone.

Jason stood looking at the tree for a full ten minutes before the man spoke again. He said, "She loved you very much, you know."

Jason smiled. "I know. She told me." His eyes met the man's. He felt helpless, lost, without direction. Madeline was gone. Baileya, too. Even Dee was off with Yenil somewhere. Of course there were still people trying to kill him. One fewer these days now that he had talked to Bezaed, but still: the Elenil, the Scim, and the Zhanin. Still lots of angry magic people. He didn't even have to stay in the Sunlit Lands anymore. He could return home if he wanted. He wasn't sure what should be next. "Where will I go now?"

The man clapped him on the shoulder. "You have a good heart, Wu Song. Follow it."

33

ASHES

We must cast it in the flames
or be consumed ourselves.

FROM "THE SEED," AN ALUVOREAN POEM

✦

Flames. Fire. Death.

Shula ran through Aluvorea, bringing these three things with her. Flames crackled from her skin, lighting the underbrush on fire. Behind her, close behind, came the magically induced conflagration of the firethorns, exploding like fireworks . . . complete with the popping sound of the launch, the crack of the release, and the sizzling sound of magic falling to the ashen ground. And death? Death she always carried with her.

She did not know if she was crying, did not know if tears were trying to make tracks down her scarred face. If they were, they were licked away by the flames. She only knew that she must run, must spread this fire within her to every flammable thing she could find.

A small herd of white deer burst from the bushes in front of her, leaping and running and trying to stay ahead of the flames. She did not care, just kept running, the hot wind at her back, the sparks of the magic fire overtaking her, lighting the path ahead.

Soon the flames had passed far enough ahead of her that she could see only fire in every direction. The last time that had happened she'd been in her apartment. She saw the people jumping through the flames, catching on fire. Saw the man who had cut her face, the way he looked at her in the light of the flames.

Why don't you leave Syria? That's what people asked her. So many of her friends had gone. So many of the families they knew. But her father said he was a pastor, and he would stay. Her mother would say with some bitterness, "The question is why so many other Christians would leave."

Their church shrank away to nothing, but then the local imam said the mosque didn't have anything more to care for people, refugees or locals or anyone, and to "go see if the Christians will help you." They did. The church grew and swelled and grew again, and soon there wasn't room for more. Shula's youth group went from five to sixty, most of them Muslim. The volunteers and her father and others in the church kept reminding one another, "This is a blessing. When did we think we would have so many Muslims in our church?"

What else changed? Not much. It was harder to have enough toilet paper. People kept taking it, for one thing, but also there was just so much needed. They didn't have enough food, enough anything but air. The electricity came and went. The only thing that stayed was her family, and a few others.

The Russians were bombing them. The terrorists were on the streets. The government soldiers weren't any better. Shula's best friend moved when a tank set up in front of her house and started shelling another neighborhood. It's hard to believe that your family will be safe when a tank is sitting outside the entry to your stairwell.

The man with the knife—she couldn't even allow that story in her mind. Couldn't bear to see him coming at her out of the darkness, the knife in his hand. Didn't want to remember the smell of stale garlic on his breath, the feel of his gut as she punched him and ran, or the sound of his feet behind her. When he caught her . . . he thought the feel of his blade on her face would make her quiet, would make her stop fighting—and maybe on any other day the fear would have taken control, but on this night she had seen, she had heard the bombs, and they were in her neighborhood, and even though he threatened and cursed and then sliced her face, she fought him. Someone walked past them—walked past!—and did nothing, and she shouted and finally bit him, and when he dropped the knife, she picked it up and told him that if he came near, she would do more than slice a cut, there would be chunks.

She had hidden in an alleyway, panting. She could not stay for long, could not stop, had to get to her family, had to make sure they were alright. That's when Hanali had approached her. When she saw him coming out of the shadows in his pale-green jacket and cream shirt, she had prepared herself, holding the knife toward him. His gloves were scarlet, she remembered that.

"I am Hanali," he said. "An ambassador from the Sunlit Lands. I have an offer to make to you."

"Stay away," she said.

"I won't harm you," he said. "Nor ever touch you without permission."

"I have a knife," she said.

"I am well aware."

"What do you want?"

Then he explained in great detail—far too much detail—a war in his country ("not unlike your own"), where the best of all people, the Elenil, were harassed and harried by terrorists called the Scim. "Come with me," he said, "for one human year, and I will teach you to fight."

"I know how to fight."

"I will give you magic. Your heart's desire for a year. Then come back here and fight on whatever side you choose."

Her father was not a fighter. He had no weapons in the house, would not have them. Her brother, Boulos, had bought a long-handled knife, and their father, furious, had broken the blade off in the wall. Her father said to stay where they were, to try to help the less fortunate, and what happened when she followed a homeless family to offer them food? She was attacked by a soldier in an alley. She wanted to fight. Wanted to learn to fight better, wanted to be stronger. Wanted to follow this strange man, who seemed more dream than reality. She knew dreams were often true. She felt the stinging pain of the cut on her face, the blood mixed already with dust. She pressed it with the heel of her hand, still holding the knife's blade toward him with the other. "I can't leave my family," she said.

Hanali bowed his head. "You must leave them if you are to come to the Sunlit Lands. But only for a brief time." She could leave them, she knew, and come back. Could return knowing how to fight, how to protect them.

She found out later that the arsonist had set the fire in her apartment complex at the same time she was talking to Hanali. The bombs had missed their place—they'd hit two blocks over. But someone brought cans of petrol into Shula's building and lit them on fire. The conversation with Hanali had saved her life. If she had been home ten minutes earlier, she would have died too.

"My family," she had said. "I have to check on my family."

Hanali looked sad for some reason. "I will come back and ask you again. One more time, Shula Bishara. Be ready with your answer."

She ran then, ran like she had never run before, and she heard the explosion when she was less than a block away. The impact shook her, the sound reverberated in her ears. The apartment had caught on fire in a way she could not believe, that made no sense. It spread too fast, too far, climbing the building like it was alive, enraged.

She did not pause but burst in through the door. The smoke choked her immediately, the flames were unbearably hot. She raced up the stairs, her arm over her face, but she couldn't get to her door. It was too much, too hot, and she found herself outside again, enraged and helpless, her face bleeding and tears mingling with the blood.

And where was God in all this? The God her father had loved for so many years? Did he watch in disappointed silence? Did he refuse to intervene? Did he not have the power or not care enough? Or both? These are the questions that pounded through her brain. But maybe . . . could her family be at the church?

Of course, the church. So often her family was there. God had kept them safe, she knew it, and she ran, ran, ran again to the church to find it closed up, empty, dark. By the time she walked home again, it was lit up like a torch in the night. She knew then that they were inside still. Her sister and brother and mother and father, and she should have been with them. She wished she had been with them.

She saw the man who had attacked her standing in the crowd, watching the flames. She clenched the knife in her hand tighter. Someone asked her if she was okay, concerned about the blood on her face. Offered to help her find medical attention, but she could hardly hear them. She shoved the man, and he stumbled to the side. Not so tough when there was a crowd. She screamed at him, shouted, told the crowd what he had done. She could not stop the flames, could not find whoever had done this, but this man could be punished. He could be shamed, beaten, stoned.

And they did nothing. Some shouted at him, yes, or pushed him. One man spit on him. But then they turned back to the flames, watching their friends and neighbors rise to heaven as smoke. They prayed, yes, they cried, they called for help and cared for those few wounded who had escaped, found them a place to sit away from the flames. But all of this was nothing. Less than nothing. It changed nothing. The Russians would still bomb them tomorrow. ISIS would still roam the streets. Bullets and rocket launchers and bombs and all the other things people used to kill each other would still be killing tomorrow.

That's when Hanali appeared beside her again, only this time it was different. This time everything froze. Time stopped. There was a strange silence and something else: a coldness settled on her. She could no longer feel the flames.

Hanali started to speak to her, but she was already running for the stairs, through the frozen fire, and up to her apartment. She opened the front door and found her parents and sister where they had died: together in the kitchen. Why had they been there? Mama was cooking, probably, and maybe her father was doing the dishes. Maybe her mother had called Amira in, offering her a taste of dinner. She didn't know, but they were dead. She didn't have to kneel beside them to see. Her mother. Her father. Her sister. How could the fire have moved that quickly? How did it overtake them so easily? All that remained were burned husks, and the fire still raged throughout the building.

She felt a flutter of hope. She didn't see her brother's body here. She had to check the rest of the apartment, had to find Boulos. She jumped to her feet.

Hanali stood at the doorway of the kitchen, and he shook his head sadly. "Your brother is in the bedroom," he said. "He is gone. You will not want to see what remains."

No. That small bit of hope crashed to the ground. She collapsed beside her parents and sister again. Hanali was right. She didn't want to see her brother's body. Wasn't this enough? She closed her eyes and could still see the burned corpses of her parents and her sister, knew she would see them for the rest of her life. She had been right about that . . . all this time later and she still couldn't remove the memory. She had tried. Had drunk addleberry wine, which was supposed to erase memory, and whatever it took from her, it wasn't this.

"Come away from here," Hanali had said gently. He held out his gloved hand.

She hesitated, then leaned over her sister, taking the small metal cross from around her neck. Then she took Hanali's hand and followed him downstairs through the frozen flames. She didn't take anything from home but Amira's cross, none of the rest of it mattered. Hanali paused with her at the edge of the crowd.

"A year," he said. "In exchange I will teach you to fight."

"No," Shula said. "I don't know why you need me, but you do. You will pay me what I am worth."

Hanali smiled. "I knew I was right about you. So your heart's desire is more than fighting. You tell me the terms."

She saw the man who had cut her standing in the crowd. "Him. I want him dead."

Hanali scarcely glanced at him. "Done."

"Whoever set this fire. I want them dead. Burned to death."

"Done."

"And I want them to know why."

"Of course," Hanali said. "Is that all?"

"I want to be immune to fire. And I want to be able to bring fire. To fight people with it."

"That is a massive amount of magic to give in exchange for one year's service."

"I'll give you two years. Five. I don't care."

"Five years' service. So be it." He held out a thin silver bracelet. "Just slip this upon your wrist when you are ready to make the deal."

She slipped it on, and it constricted so tight it felt like it was burrowing into her skin. "When do we leave?"

Hanali raised his eyebrows. "People are not ready so quickly, usually. May I borrow your knife?"

She gave it to him. Hanali looked at it in the firelight. There was something strange about that fire. The color—it wasn't quite right. Hanali grimaced at the blood. He walked through the frozen crowd. When he came to the man who had attacked her, he slid the knife into him and left it there. "When I restart time, that should be it for him," Hanali said.

She wanted to say she had felt bad in that moment, but she had felt only satisfaction. Did he have a family? Probably. Who didn't? (Other than Shula—she had no family now.) She was glad his family would lose him, and she suspected they might be glad too. "When do we leave?" she repeated.

"Now, if you like," Hanali said, and they walked a while. Time rushed back in like water. He led her two blocks away, to the broken remnants of another apartment building. The white helmets were there now, digging out survivors. "You'll have to crawl through that," Hanali said, and she was going to ask why but decided it didn't matter. Something about how hard it was to get to the Sunlit Lands, she found out later, but in that moment the only thing that mattered was that she was leaving, she was done here, this was over.

Then the journey through the rubble that ended in a beautiful place unlike anywhere she had been before, the Sunlit Lands. She had learned to fight, with fist and fire, and had crushed the Scim at the side of others like herself. She grew a reputation as someone to be feared, the burning girl, the warrior, the flaming heart of the army. And over time she accepted it. All that had happened.

Or something like acceptance. Hanali told her he had burned the arsonist to death. She didn't know if this was true, but she liked to believe it was, and also felt guilty that she was pleased by it. And where was God in all this? She didn't know.

"Not in the flame," someone shouted, jolting her back to the present. She couldn't see who, and she wouldn't stop running. No doubt the flames had overtaken some Aluvorean or Elenil, but she didn't care. Something about the voice sounded familiar, though. She hesitated, then ran toward it.

Her father sat in a clearing on a burned-down stump. There were flames all around him and even going through him.

"Baba?"

He smiled at her. "Not in the flame," he repeated.

"What?"

"Do you remember that story? There was a prophet who wished to hear the voice of God. He hid in a cave. A great wind came that cracked rocks, but God was not in the wind. There was an earthquake that could knock down an apartment building, but God was not in the earthquake. A burning fire came, but God was not in the flames."

She knew the story, of course. She couldn't have grown up in her father's church and not known the story. "Is it really you?"

"But then he heard a quiet whisper, and he covered his head and went out of the cave and heard the voice of God."

"Is that you, Baba?"

He smiled again. "Not in the flame, Shula. You're looking for God in the flame, but that's not the right place. Not the earth-shattering destruction. Not the burning fires. Instead, listen for the quiet whisper. Do you hear the voice?"

"Is this . . . magic?"

Her father stood, brushing off his knees. He had always done that. As if dust had somehow accumulated in the time he was sitting down. He brushed off his knees and looked at her and said, "Magic will reset in a moment. When it does, you will have to make a choice."

She looked at where she was in the forest. She thought she was near where she had left Jason and Baileya. She tried to memorize it, to make sure she could find her way back here, try to see her father again. "Baba," she said.

But he was gone. Again. She stood alone in a circle of flame.

A howling wind came, and the fire burst into a thousand sparks, washing over her. The firethorns launched their seeded fireworks into the sky, and the pinecone-like pods throughout the forest opened up and fired magic into the air.

The earth shook, and Shula braced herself. Not well enough, it seemed, because she fell to the ground. Something moved on her arm. She jumped, startled. It was a silver bracelet. The bracelet Hanali had given her so long ago. It had disconnected from her. It was a bracelet again, no longer a tattoo.

She felt the flames now, felt them in a different way than she had a moment before. She was in danger of burning. The magic. It had reset. Of course. Which meant she had a choice. She could put this bracelet back on and submit herself again to the conditions of her bargain with Hanali. Or she could leave it off, lose her invulnerability to fire, lose her ability to summon the flame.

She thought of her father, of his insistence on peace, of how he would feel about her fighting. But what else did she have? She had discovered the Scim were not the terrorist monsters she had been led to believe, but she could still fight the Elenil. And when her time was done, she would need this power, would need the fire to return home to Aleppo, where she would bring justice to Syria. She would save the world.

That was when she heard the whisper. She could not see anyone, did not hear anyone walk up near her. Who said it? She didn't know. Maybe she said it herself. But she heard the whisper, and it only said one word.

"Yenil."

Yenil. The Scim girl Madeline had adopted when she was orphaned. The Scim girl Shula had come to love as her own. Now Madeline was gone, and who would care for the girl if Shula allowed herself to be wrapped up in the fight again? Who would take care of her, protect her, keep her safe? Could Shula do those things if she had a bracelet tying her to the Elenil, making her their slave? No.

A great crashing came from behind her. The main part of the fire was close. It would sweep over her in a few minutes, and she was suddenly vulnerable. The time had come. She had to leave the fire, leave her anger, and try to become someone who could build a better life and better world for her Yenil.

Shula gripped the bracelet in her hand. She looked for the place that seemed to have the fewest flames, and she ran. The fire crashed behind her, following her, chasing her, like a monstrous animal trying to devour her. Still she ran. She leapt over fallen branches, wove between flaming trunks. She was tempted to put on the bracelet more than once. She wouldn't survive without it, couldn't survive—she was crying, almost sobbing at the thought of laying her protection aside—but she could not be a good mother for Yenil if she was invulnerable. How could she let the child into her heart unless she was willing to be hurt? Unless she made herself vulnerable?

She burst out of the trees and saw the lake, the same water that had taken Madeline, and although her heart fell to think of her friend disappearing into that water, she felt an impossible lightness at the thought of escaping the flames. She ran as far as she could into the water before she dove, swimming away from shore. When the cool water was about to be higher than her head, she stopped, turned, and watched the forest burn. When she couldn't bear it any longer, she dunked her head and washed her face and hair, removing as much of the ash and blood and tears as she could.

Hours later—it must have been hours—when what remained of the forest lay black and smoking, she swam back to shore. The smoke rose from the ground, but already it was cooling. A gentle rain had begun, and to Shula's astonishment, green shoots were already pushing their way through the ash.

She turned back to the water, the bracelet still in her hand. She threw it as far as she could, watched it glimmer in the light before falling into the water. She left it there with everything else she had washed off herself. She would never need it again.

Then she walked to find Yenil, through a newly born landscape that was fresh and green and growing. She found the girl playing with Delightful Glitter Lady amongst a whole tribe of Aluvoreans, Mrs. Oliver gazing at her with a tired look on her face, and David keeping careful watch nearby. Yenil ran to Shula and leapt into her arms, wrapping herself around her like a sea star on a rock. "Shula, Shula, you're back!" she shouted, and Shula told her yes, yes, she was home.

34
THE ARCHON

"Farewell then, old friend," says she,
"for I have made a foolish mistake."
FROM "MALGWIN AND THE WHALE," A TRADITIONAL ZHANIN STORY

✦

anali led Darius through a warren of corridors. He shooed off any Scim servants who got in their way, and ordered Elenil to step aside. The servants gave Darius's bloody sword a sidelong look, but when Hanali spoke, people listened. Maybe not always, but today they certainly did. They passed through lavishly appointed rooms, rooms that appeared to be outside but were not, and at least one room entirely filled with water, floor to ceiling . . . even though the doors were off their hinges and the water should have flowed out. They passed a group of Pastisian soldiers bashing in a marble wall with what looked like power-assisted sledgehammers. Hanali almost paused for that, but then he hurried on.

He stopped outside a nondescript door in a long hallway full of nondescript doors. He put his palm against the door, his other hand preventing

Darius from entering. "The Crescent Stone is mine, once the deed is done. Agreed?"

Sick of agreements with Hanali, Darius pushed past him and threw open the door. On the other side was a small room with a fountain full of tropical fish. Darius spun around to find Hanali watching him with crossed arms and a disappointed look. "Agreed," Darius said.

Hanali smirked, then led him two doors down, across the hallway. He pulled the door open, and there he lay: the archon.

Archon Thenody did not look well. His face was drawn and haggard. He was propped up in a bed, weak enough that his breath was labored. His eyes moved to Hanali, then to Darius. "Come in, then," he said. "At least have the decency to sit and talk with me for a few moments before that blade strikes again."

"Do not bother to call for your guards," Hanali said. "I have already—"

"I have never thought you incompetent, Hanali. Come in. Sit." His eyes wandered to the sword in Darius's hand. "That blade. What pain it brings!" With his good hand he touched the stump of his forearm. "It is not only that it took my hand, but the wound will not heal. Medicine does not hurry it. Time does not help it." He saw the shackles on Darius's wrists. "My soldiers nearly had you, it seems."

"Very nearly," Darius said. The sword pulled so hard toward the archon that his hand had already begun to ache.

"Perhaps the shackles will remind you of me when I am dead," the archon said, and some life came into his face when he laughed. A shiver went through Darius. A cruel light entered the archon's eyes. "Is the girl dead?"

"Yes," Hanali said.

"Her name was Madeline," Darius said angrily.

The archon ignored him. "What of the boy?"

"Still alive, so far as I know."

"A pity. He has a special talent for being infuriating. Though he did me little real harm, I find myself picturing his death most often."

Darius stepped forward with the sword. But the sight of the archon like this—weak, sick, old—stopped him. He deserved death, no question. Darius looked forward to giving it to him. At the same time, grief welled up in him. He had given up a chance to see Madeline for this, and already he knew, he just knew, that he would trade this for another thirty seconds with her. Archon Thenody could have waited, might even have succumbed to death without Darius's help from the looks of it, and Darius had thrown away time with his beloved because his driving focus had been on bringing this one Elenil to justice. The sword urged him forward, but King Ian's words came back to him: *The sword whispers to you of justice and disguises the cost.*

"What of Nightfall?" Hanali asked.

Darius shook himself into the moment, looked at Hanali. "What?"

"I see the doubts in your mind, and I remind you, what of the Scim boy, Nightfall, murdered by the archon's soldiers? Should not Thenody pay for that?"

Thenody laughed. "I have killed my share of Scim youth, make no mistake. But that one isn't dead."

"What do you mean?"

"Did you see his corpse?" Thenody asked. "Did you feel his pulse slow and then stop? Put your face near his lips, feel for his breath? No?"

He hadn't. In fact, when they had gone back to look for Nightfall's body, it was gone. Darius had thought the Scim had come to bury him. "I saw him," Darius said.

"Grievous wounds can be healed," Thenody said. "And my dear Gilenyia was nearby. She fixed him and sent him to me. He's here somewhere, in Far Seeing, being educated. Civilized." He looked at Hanali. "It might be entertaining for you to send him back to see his family when he is civilized. If I were archon a year from now, I would do that."

"You're telling me Nightfall is alive. My whole reason in coming here," Darius said, though that wasn't strictly true. He had been fighting the Elenil for years, and he had every intention of lopping off the serpent's head this time. Nightfall's death was more catalyst than cause.

"I can call him if you like. I know what he will say, because we have taught him to say it. 'I misunderstood the Elenil. They only want what is good for the Scim, and have all along. We Scim squander our resources, and the Elenil want to teach us the right way. Here I get three meals a day. Here I have a bed, my own room, many changes of clothes. In the Wasted Lands I had none of those things.' And so on and so on."

Darius should have been happy about this news, but instead he was increasingly furious. If he had stayed with Jason to make sure he was safe in Aluvorea, he would have found Madeline. Maybe he could have altered whatever chain of events had ended in her death. If he had gone back when Break Bones did, maybe he would have seen her. But he had not done those things. His hatred, his passion for killing the archon, had kept him from someone he loved deeply. He had not been there for her, because he had filled his heart with the archon.

His heart was still full of the archon. He wanted nothing more than to use the sword—which was practically singing now as it stretched toward the Elenil—and end this whole thing. He was angry, furious, boiling with rage.

He was letting this Elenil control him. The anger was good, righteous. But it let Thenody and Hanali manipulate him, shape him, use him. If he wanted control of his own life, he had to get it back from them. Would killing Thenody make him less angry? Looking at the enfeebled wretch before him, he didn't think so. He didn't think it would change anything. Thenody was already collapsing, falling under his own weight, and Darius pounding on him along the way would change nothing. Then he thought of Vivi, who he had killed in the midst of battle. He hadn't known at the time that Vivi was the one who had made Madeline sick, he'd had no way of knowing that. So justice had already been served there, but it felt hollow. Hollow and useless. Madeline was still gone. His anger, his sorrow, was still here.

He could leave all this, go to Pastisia. Work for King Ian in a society set apart for something else. But if he killed the archon, he would always be that person . . . the human who came to the Sunlit Lands and killed the archon. But did that matter? He would be a hero to some, a villain to others, but at least it would be done. And someone else would take Thenody's place. Hanali. What then? Another assassination attempt? And on and on until someone took his place who was what? Better? Good enough? Enlightened?

The thought of Nightfall being re-educated to think that the Elenil were his benevolent patrons made Darius sick. He vowed to himself that whatever happened in this room, he would save that kid next and return him home.

"You want justice," the archon said, and he sounded amused.

"Yes," Darius said, grim, his fingers trembling from clutching the sword so hard.

"There is only one true justice, and that is death," the archon said. "A hundred years in prison would mean nothing to me. My hand being cut off by that child? Oh, yes, it made me furious, and I have every intention of killing everyone involved, should I live long enough. But did it bring justice? No. Even to kill me now, Darius, is that justice? I have killed far more than one Scim. Does my one death counterbalance all those whom I have killed? Does one Elenil life pay for a thousand Scim?" He paused and looked at Hanali. "We all pay the same price in the end . . . the just as well as the wicked. Death is our punishment. So bring your sword, boy, and get your measure of justice. What do I care now, when all that is left to me is pain?"

Darius clenched his teeth. "Maybe letting you live in pain is a better justice. I drag you from this tower, take you to Pastisia, let King Ian decide what to do with you. Or better yet, to the Scim elders. A hundred years in a cell might not be justice, but at least you'll be miserable. Maybe you'll even come to regret your crimes."

"Can the supreme ruler of a land commit crimes? I am the law, Darius, and I have been for these many years. I cannot do wrong."

"The prophecies are clear," Hanali said. "A human kills the archon, and he does it with that sword, the one in your hand."

"I don't care about your prophecies," Darius said.

"You should. You would not be here without them," Hanali said, his face darkening. Darius could see a vindictive cruelty looming in his eyes. "Oh, yes. Why do you think I would invite your girlfriend and Jason but not you? There was a pattern. A prophetic unfolding that would bring us to this room. A single misstep could take it all another way. So I didn't invite you, but I laid bread crumbs for you to follow. Another path. Another entrance. Do you not understand? I orchestrated Madeline's entrance to the Sunlit Lands. I brought you here, as well. Do you think you could come here without my permission? Foolish child. I decide who stays and who leaves the Sunlit Lands."

No. Darius didn't believe this. He hadn't followed bread crumbs, he had worked hard to get here. He had scraped and searched and fought his way into this world. It couldn't have been a trick. It couldn't be that Hanali had orchestrated this whole thing. Could it?

Hanali stepped toward Darius. "The prophecies say a human holding the Sword of Tears will strike the archon down and that I will be archon next, in his place. We are here, Darius, to fulfill that prophecy."

The archon laughed, rocking in his bed, holding the stump of his arm. "After all your scheming, the boy doesn't have the stomach to kill me. How long have you been building this plan, Hanali? Twenty years? Forty? Only to have it all fall apart when you were so close."

"I could kill you myself," Hanali said, his voice menacing.

"You are too true to the Elenil way of life," Thenody said, dismissing him. "You would plot and scheme and organize a coup, yes. Convince a human to take my life, I believe it. But you, as an Elenil, to take the sword in your own hand and strike me down? Not in a thousand millennia."

Hanali growled at Darius. "Kill him, Darius, or have done. What are you waiting for?"

Darius trembled. He had wanted this for so long, but the way Hanali pushed him, the way the archon encouraged it . . . It might be justice, maybe. It might ease his fury, he wasn't sure. But there was no doubt they would be controlling him. It fit Hanali's plan too well. "Why me?" Darius asked. "Tell me why it has to be me."

"You are the Black Skull," Hanali said. "When the other Elenil hear that I fought you, trying to keep the archon safe, my ascendance to archon is all but guaranteed."

"You're going to try to capture me. Or kill me. Show them that you were on the archon's side."

"He won't capture you," the archon said. "He cannot risk your story being told. Exile or death. If that is not his plan, I am disappointed indeed in my imminent replacement."

"I thought to send you home with Madeline and Jason," Hanali said. "If Madeline had done things the way she was supposed to all those weeks ago, I would have sent you all back, and she would have been able to breathe again. You would have lived happily ever after. But she came up with a new plan and made me fall back on this contingency. But I swear to you on my father's name, I will not harm you."

Darius knew he was lying, could feel it like an electric shock moving with startling speed through the soles of his feet and into his face. The jolt went into his hand, and with a cry, he dropped the sword. He stared at it where it had fallen, horrified. He knew he could not pick it up again, not in this room. What good could it do? Had killing Vivi changed anything? Had it accomplished justice for Madeline? Yes, maybe, in a way. But it had not made things better. It had not healed Madeline. It had not made Darius happy, or even satisfied. Now Hanali was using his anger, his grief, as a weapon to control him. But Darius would not allow himself to be controlled by Hanali, or the archon, or anyone.

Hanali stared at the sword, a look of genuine disappointment on his face. The archon was laughing, laughing, laughing. "Would that you had grown such a backbone before murdering my father," Hanali said.

The archon still laughed, and made as if to clap his hands, and laughed at that as well. "Oh Hanali, how delightful. It is as if you dropped a viper into my chambers, hoping to murder me, but the viper slithered free to kill members of your own household. You've fallen into your own trap."

"Yes," Hanali said, his voice cold. "It is a common problem with traps." He bent to scoop up the sword. Darius was shocked to see that the sword allowed it. "I fear the same has happened to you, Archon Thenody. I hope you know that for these many years I have served you faithfully. This plot is a new thing. Only a few decades old at best."

"Do not pretend to use the Scims' sword on me," the archon said, waving Hanali away. "Your own prophecies say it will be a human who kills me. Take a decade and find another one and come back again."

"My father," Hanali said. "You and he were friends for many centuries."

"Of course," Thenody said. "There was a time when there were no secrets between us, Vivi and me."

"Did you help him?"

"As often as I could."

Darius could see what was happening. Should he stop it? He stepped toward the door. Or he could run. He knew how this would end.

Hanali said, "Did you help him pick the child, I mean?"

"What child? My dear Hanali, you are rambling. Does that sword drive Elenil mad? What strange magics are on it!"

"The child. The human child. The one you kidnapped and brought here, to the Sunlit Lands. The boy. You know who I mean, surely. What was his name?"

Fear came into the archon's face now, and Darius realized that the archon had never really believed Darius would kill him. The archon was scooting back in his bed, trying to put distance between himself and Hanali. "You are an Elenil," Archon Thenody said, "and sworn to my service."

Hanali strode to Darius, yanked him back into the room, tore into his pocket, and pulled out the book. "My father's words, captured by the necromancers. His own words, Thenody. What do they say? Tell him, Darius. Speak the words."

Darius said quietly, "They say that there was a group of human children. Seven of them. Vivi chose one, his favorite, to be his son. He made him an Elenil and removed his memories, then raised him as his own."

"Human," Hanali said with disgust. "Human. Nothing more than this boy here, nothing more than this weak piece of filth. *Human.*"

Thenody started to shout something, to protest, but Hanali used him like a scabbard, and the magic of the Scim sword would not be broken by any Elenil counterspell. Thenody fell back on the bed, his mouth wide, his eyes blank and staring.

"Killed by a human," Hanali said. He shook his head in disgust. He yanked the sword out of Thenody and threw it at Darius. "I haven't much time, as there are a large number of necromancers to kill before they tear down my tower. The story is that you killed the archon. I tried to stop you but too late. I may have to kill a few of the servants who saw us together, as if anyone listens to them. But better safe than sorry. Is there anything you wish to say to me before this is all over?"

"Madeline," Darius said, but before he could say more, Hanali was in front of him, his hand clamped over Darius's mouth. He sneered.

"A rhetorical question, Darius. You murdered my father. I do not want to see you, I do not want to hear you. You have served your purpose. I give you your life as a gift, but if I see you again, you will go the way of the former archon."

He pushed Darius, knocking him into the wall. Darius struggled, trying to get his face free to speak. "What are you doing?"

"I told you, fool, that you walk in the Sunlit Lands with my permission. Consider that permission revoked." Hanali pushed against Darius's chest, and the wall behind him gave way like it was made of mud. Hanali shoved harder, and Darius couldn't breathe. The world around him went grey.

He tumbled to the ground, landing hard on his back. He took a breath, tried to gather himself, and stood, his legs still shaking. His first thought was Madeline. Oh, Madeline. He would go to her as soon as he could leave this place, whatever it was.

He didn't recognize it at first. He hadn't been here in . . . he wasn't sure how long. Eighteen months? Two years? It felt like years piled on years, serving with the Scim. The rumpled bed, the posters on the wall, a shelf of books. Madeline's books, the old ones, her childhood copies of the Meselia books. She had lent them to him. His backpack against the wall, near the desk.

Hanali had sent him home. He was back on Earth.

"No," Darius said. He threw open his bedroom door, slamming it against the wall. He ran out the front door and into the street. Cars passed him, honking. "No!"

He sank to his knees on the sidewalk. He had been kicked out. Exiled. Removed. The Scim, Jason and Baileya, Shula, Nightfall—they were all out of his reach now. Madeline, too. He had no way to return, no way back to the land where he had fought so long and given so much. He put his forehead against the concrete and wept.

35

A DOOR IN THE SIDE OF THE WORLD

*My companions the stars wheeling overhead, and
I listen to the gentle lap of water, the sigh of the wind.*
FROM "MALGWIN AND THE WHALE," A TRADITIONAL ZHANIN STORY

✦

Floating on her back, Madeline enjoyed the view of the stars. The stars were even brighter in Aluvorea than in Far Seeing. She could almost imagine she was looking down into a valley, and there were thousands of people below her, sitting around campfires, telling stories, enjoying one another. Or maybe she was the one below, and there were a thousand thousand people in a gigantic stadium looking down on her. Watching her swim, like it was an Olympic event. Like she was in a race. Cheering her on.

She couldn't hear Jason shouting any longer. It had broken her heart to hear him, but she couldn't let him go in her place, and she couldn't stay any longer. She knew Baileya and Shula understood, and she trusted that one day he would too. A cool green light was filling the water around her. She thought it came from beneath her at first, but then realized it was coming *from* her. From the center of her chest. She looked for the seed in her arm, but it was gone. Or rather, it had moved. Up her arm, into her chest. Strangely, her breathing was a little better. Not completely better but a little.

She reached the shore and stepped onto the island. A cloud of hummingbirds met her. She had never seen anything so beautiful. They moved like a school of fish. One of them shifted, and shining wings buzzed to make room in a rippling cascade of green and purple and red. "Hello . . . friends," she said. "Which . . . way?" The birds dipped in greeting, then zipped ahead a few feet. She took a step toward them, and a happy sort of buzzing came from them, and they zipped ahead again.

"So you made it after all," the Garden Lady said. "I wondered myself, I really did. I thought you might be happy to pass in that garden back home. No need to come back to the Sunlit Lands, you know. I thought, she may not want to cross the river."

Madeline smiled at her. The old woman wore that same big hat with the flowers around the brim, her grey hair sticking out like the straws of an ancient broom. "There is . . . happy . . . and there is . . . acceptance."

"Acceptance. Well, dear, that's a good word. You found it quicker than me, I'll say that much. Take my arm, Madeline, let me give you some of my strength. Hold on, girl, we're almost there."

They came to an old tree, its whole middle part rotted away. A throne was carved into one side, and the skeleton of someone long since dead sat on it. On the skeleton's brow was the crown she had seen in her dream with Patra Koja. A simple weaving of branches that looked like they had been alive once, growing taller, higher, curling in on themselves and forming something like gems. It was taller than she would expect a crown to be. "Must have been . . . tired," Madeline said. "To die . . . on the . . . chair."

The Garden Lady looked at the corpse fondly. "Allison was her name."

Allison. Wasn't that a name her mother had said? "She was . . . one of my . . . mother's friends?"

The Garden Lady smiled. "Oh yes. Thick as thieves, those two. Never one in trouble without the other, ha!" She looked at Madeline, as if remembering something from long ago. "These woods are named for her, you know. 'Aluvorea'—Allison Woods. Sweet girl, she was. Didn't deserve what happened to her, or how it came about that she wore the Heartwood Crown."

"Who does?" Madeline asked. "Deserve it . . . I mean." She pointed at Allison's remains. "I need . . . to sit."

"Of course, dear," the Garden Lady said. She took the crown first and pulled on the base, which came free from the upper part of the crown with the cracking of dead branches. What remained was a simple oaken circlet of woven branches. She placed that on one of the arms of the throne and then, somehow, lifted the skeleton away in one piece. She laid the bones reverently on the ground, and they collapsed into dust. The Garden Lady closed her eyes for a long moment. When she opened them again, she smiled at Madeline and brushed the dust from the seat of the throne. Madeline picked up the crown and sat in the chair, breathing heavily.

"So tell me . . . how it works."

The Garden Lady's eyes were twinkling. "You get to make everything new at last. You put on that crown, and the woods will stop being Allison's woods and become yours. Magic will drain away and restart, be redistributed, be made fresh and new. You can make three new magical plants, to get the magic moving in the new direction. Your direction. You can keep the old magic too, if you like—there are no rules."

Madeline smiled. "Then I . . . put on the . . . crown."

"Yes, dear, oh my, yes. You will be queen then. These woods will remake themselves to be like you. For a hundred years at least, whatever blessings and curses you lay down in this land will echo forward into the Sunlit Lands."

"Where will . . . I be? In a . . . tree?"

The Garden Lady's face fell. "You'll be dead, dear. Did no one explain this to you? I thought Arakam had—Arakam!" She was shouting now. "Arakam, where are you?"

"I'm here, lady, never shout. I am not far, what's this about?"

An enormous salamander came around the side of the tree. He was easily the size of an alligator but with soft, smooth skin and a wet look to him. He had wide yellow eyes the size of softballs that were surprisingly cute, like a cartoon drawing of a salamander.

"Did you tell Madeline what you were meant to?" the Garden Lady asked him.

"I had the words all lined up plain. All was prepared, but she never came."

"What?" The Garden Lady looked at Madeline.

"Jason," she said. "And something about . . . a cat."

"A cat?" The Garden Lady looked perplexed for a moment. "Who, Remi?" She laughed. "Our Jason tamed the Guardian of the Wind and sent her to do his bidding? Oh, he is full of surprises, that one."

"Would you like to hear my poem now? I worked upon it for many an hour."

"Oh, I hardly think that necessary, Arakam. Go on back to your waterfall. If all goes right, the forest will be burning soon, and you can take a long nap before she grows back."

"So begins another age, and poor Arakam cheated of his time onstage."

"Oh, you old ham. Go back to your cave."

The salamander closed its eyes once, slowly, then opened them again. To Madeline he said, "Lady, be generous to us." He moved away, lifting his feet carefully, and slipped into the lake.

"What does . . . he mean?"

The Garden Lady settled onto the ground, arranging her skirts. A hummingbird zipped around her face, and she swatted at it impatiently. "I know the time, I know. Get on with you! Go!" She smiled at Madeline. "Three new plants," she said. "Allison chose the stone flowers. She was angry at the people of the forest. She wanted to punish them. She felt helpless, and she wanted them to feel helpless too. She made the firethorns. Wanted to make sure the forest burned down faster than usual. She didn't want Aluvorea to last beyond its hundred years, though the Elenil made sure it did. And she made Queen's Breath, a plant to let the Aluvoreans breathe underwater. That one was almost a passing thought. Suggested by someone else, and she couldn't think of another curse against the people, so she took that. Thought it mostly useless, you know." The old woman looked sad, as if she were remembering something from long ago.

"Were you . . . there?"

The Garden Lady looked at her, surprised. "Of course, dear! Of course!"

"So I get . . . three plants?"

"Three to choose now. A farewell gift to the people, really. The rest of the forest will grow up alongside you, as the people say. It will be infused with you, with your character. I daresay, dear child, the forest will be a better place with you as the seed. We don't have much time, child, but think for a moment of what you want to leave, and we'll have done."

Madeline didn't understand all of that. "Okay," she said. "Ready."

"So quickly? What's your first plant, dear?"

"For myself," she said. "A plant . . . whose leaves unbind . . . undeserved . . . curses."

The Garden Lady beamed at her. "A beautiful gift, Madeline. Would that one had been here for you these many years." She held her hands over the ground, and a shoot of a plant came up. The leaves unfurled, and it looked like ivy almost, but with heart-shaped leaves. "Like this?"

"Yes," Madeline said, pleased. "The second. For Jason."

"Ah. And what shall it be like?"

"The fruit . . . tastes like . . . chocolate."

"He'll like that."

"Needs a . . . ridiculous . . . name."

"Like?"

"Pudding fruit."

The Garden Lady chortled. "Sounds suitably disgusting."

"Jason will . . . love it." She smiled. Tears were brimming in her eyes. "And . . . it grows . . . easily. Always stays . . . with you." She wiped a tear away. "When you . . . eat it . . . you can only . . . speak truth . . . the rest of the day."

"Ah," the Garden Lady said, and a small tree grew up between them, with beautiful, smooth fruit that caught the light. A bold red color, like a ripe strawberry dripping with juice. "Like this?"

Madeline nodded. "Last. For my . . . mother." She realized here and now that she was not angry at her mother. Her resentment had fallen away. She was thankful for her, and sad. Sad that her mother had lived so many years captive to her own past, working so hard to forget what had been done to her. And what she had done in response. She wished her mother happiness. She wished her joy. She had forgiven her at last, and she felt regret for the way she had spoken to her and treated her in their final days together.

"Yes?"

This last gift for her mother. She wanted it to be a healing one. "Fruit of . . . remembrance. When you drink . . . the juice . . . you remember."

"Remember what, child?"

"Whatever you have . . . forgotten," she said.

The Garden Lady nodded, and a bush grew, with wide yellow berries on it. "A remedy for addleberries," she said. "A wise gift to the Sunlit Lands."

Madeline's breathing was coming harder. It was almost time. Her body felt hot. So hot. Her mind was going slower, and it was getting harder to think. "Birds," she said. "Birds, come to me."

The Garden Lady's hummingbirds flocked around her, like a cloud of shining jewels. "Will you do . . . a favor for me?" she asked. The hummingbirds dipped and hummed around her, as if they were trying to come closer, trying to hear whatever word might fall from her mouth. "Find them. All the ones . . . I love. Tell them."

"Tell them what, child?"

"I want them to know . . . how much . . . I loved them. I didn't . . . I didn't say it . . . enough." The thought of not being able to say it again to them, to not tell them, to not be able to remind them . . . her eyes burned.

The Garden Lady put her hand over Madeline's. "You said it all the time, child."

"Not . . . enough."

Madeline's eyes flew open. The birds had started to disperse, but she called them back. "Darius," she said. "Darius especially." She searched among the birds, found the brightest green one. "You. You tell Darius. No matter how far away he is, no matter how hard you have to work to tell him. Make sure he knows." The bird dipped in the air, a small hummingbird bow, and then they were gone.

The Garden Lady watched them go. Madeline had slumped down in the throne, her strength all but gone. The old lady put her hands on Madeline's arms. "Sit up straight, dear. It's time for the coronation." She took the crown from Madeline and stood in front of her, holding it in both hands.

"Will it . . . hurt?"

"For a moment only, and after this, no more pain, dear."

She lowered the crown, and Madeline took one last, deep breath and let it out, let it all out, and was still, and then came the pain, followed by complete immersion in an ocean of peace.

The Peasant King took Madeline's hand and helped her stand. When she saw him now, for the first time in person, she could understand how the Scim would see him as a kind and accessible presence, and the Elenil as the powerful Majestic One. He was both these things and more. She looked back and saw her body, slumped against the tree, the crown on her head. Small tendrils of growth had already begun to sprout at the top of the crown. The seed glowed green in her chest. "Hello, Your Majesty," she said.

"Hello, Madeline." He nodded to the Garden Lady. "Allison."

"Your Majesty."

Madeline took a deep breath of the sweet air. She felt a lightness. A giddiness. Her fears and worries were falling away. She saw the hummingbirds scattering to the four corners of the world, carrying her message.

"Is there a white ship?" she asked, "Like in *The Return of the King*?"

"If you should like a white ship, I shall certainly bring one for you," he said, giving her a brilliant smile. "As it is, I have a door. A door in the side of the world."

"Where does it go?"

He squeezed her hand. "Where do you want to go, my friend?"

And she told him. And they went.

EPILOGUE

If one day you desire to leave all and learn from the desert,
come and seek what you may find among the sands.

MOTHER CROW

✦

The last few miles, Jason walked alone. Break Bones hadn't left his side in weeks, but this was something he needed to do alone. They said their farewells, and Break Bones headed back to the Wasted Lands, to see what had become of his people and to look for Darius. A hummingbird zipped around Jason's head, and laughing, he swatted at it. There had been a veritable plague of the things since they had left the forest, and they seemed to be attracted to Jason in particular. They were always nearby, and even when he made camp, one would perch in a branch and shout out its high-pitched chirp, often through the night. He hadn't seen any faeries, just the hummingbirds. He didn't know why, but the tiny birds made him think of Madeline.

Jason walked to the place that, as near as he could tell, was where the desert started. He stepped off the path and into the sand. He set aside his provisions. He put down his water flask. He took off his shirt and shoes. He was unbuttoning his jeans when he heard a familiar cackling laugh. He looked up and saw her, the Kakri elder who had told him once, at the Meeting of the Spheres, to come and learn from the desert. She wore the same outfit she had then, a sort of costume with a long cape made of crow feathers.

"Mother Crow!" he said.

"Why are you taking off your clothes?"

"You said I had to leave everything to come learn from the desert."

"Not your *clothes*."

"You said, and I quote, 'Leave all and learn from the desert.'"

Mother Crow laughed and laughed. "This is called a metaphor, Wu Song. Always wear clothes in the desert. Otherwise you'll be burned in the day and freeze in the night."

Jason frowned. This was not going the way he expected. He debated explaining to the old woman that this was not a metaphor. It was more like hyperbole or something. But this seemed like a bad way to start off when he was going to be following her into the desert. Instead he said, "So . . . I can put my shirt back on?"

"Please!"

He put on his shirt, then his shoes. "The water flask?"

"Unless you're a camel, you better bring it."

"I am not a camel," he said, slinging it back on. He picked up the bag of provisions.

"Not those," Mother Crow snapped. "You'll live upon food from the desert."

"Oh," Jason said, lowering it back to the ground, disappointed. "Okay, sorry."

Mother Crow laughed until tears squeezed out of her eyes. "I am joking, Wu Song—bring the food. Why feed the hyenas? Or worse yet, the wylnas."

He looked at the old lady to make sure she wasn't joking again and slowly put the food back over his shoulder. "I am going to bring this," he said. Some ash floated from the sky and landed on his shoulder. He brushed it off, and a shining spark fell onto the sand. Where it touched the ground, a small tendril of green grew. He bent to look at it. This had been happening for weeks now. Ash falling, and new plants growing where it landed. He put his finger under the tender young leaves.

Mother Crow had already started walking into the desert. She stopped and looked back at him. "Are you coming?"

The hummingbird chirped. Jason said, "Oh yeah. Also, I can't get rid of this hummingbird."

"And why would you want to? To befriend a bird is a great honor."

"Yeah," Jason said. "I guess it is."

"Come along then, both of you," Mother Crow said, and she trudged up a dune. Jason stopped at the crest of the sand to look back on everything and everyone he was leaving behind. Then he turned toward the desert and hurried down the side of the dune. Mother Crow walked with steady purpose, and Jason followed.

THE END

APPENDIX

ABOUT MARY PATRICIA WALL'S
TALES OF MESELIA

The Tales of Meselia is a series of six fantasy novels (with a seventh promised) by Mary Patricia Wall. It is considered a cult classic of children's literature, with many pointing to the missing seventh novel as the reason it has not risen in popularity to the level of other well-loved children's fantasies. Originally published in London between 1974 and 1979, the Tales of Meselia have been adapted several times, complete or in part, for radio, television, and the stage (Ms. Wall has refused to part with film rights).

The series follows a rotating cast of children who are called into the magical land of Meselia by Kartal, the Eagle King (he is, in fact, the "gryphon" of the first novel—he can appear as eagle, lion, human, or any combination thereof).

The published novels are:

The Gryphon under the Stairs (1974): Lily and her brother, Samuel, are approached by a gryphon and invited to come to Meselia, where adventure and danger await!

The Winter Rogue (1975): The beloved adventurer Karu appeals to the children of Earth to join him on a quest to foil the evil plot of the wizard king Kotuluk.

The Gold Firethorns (1976): Firethorns have begun to bloom across the land of Meselia, and in the ashes lies a fateful message: among the

Family there will be a traitor, a hero, a queen, and a corpse. (In this book, famously, Lily is exiled from Meselia, and Prince Ian disappears soon afterward.)

The Skull and the Rose (1977): Kartal, the Eagle King, turns to Prince Fantok, the young son of an evil necromancer, and sends him to discover why the source of magic is faltering. Fantok is joined by one of Kartal's servants, Rose Bragan of Earth. But will Fantok use what they discover to overthrow the Eagle King and take Meselia for his own?

The Kingdom by the Sea (published in the US as *Graceful Lily's Kingdom*) (1978): Graceful Lily finds her way back to the court of Kartal, the Eagle King, where she becomes a queen in the kingdom by the sea.

The Azure World (1979): The final defeat of Kotuluk is at hand as the Eagle King and Okuz the ox call together adventurers from across the ages for a final battle. The novel ends on a cliff-hanger (often altered in adaptations, with varying degrees of success).

The promised seventh and final novel, *Shelter at Eternity*, was due to be released in 1980. Wall had said this would be the last of the Meselia novels and promised it would include the return of several reader favorites such as Okuz the ox and the charming swashbuckler Karu and the conclusion of several dangling plot threads from other volumes, including the final battle with the evil Kotuluk and the final installment of the romance between Lily and the mysterious Prince Ian, who had disappeared in book 3 only to be revealed to have been married for political reasons in book 5. But Mary Patricia Wall disappeared, and her manuscript with her, shortly after the release of *The Azure World*.

The multiple unresolved plotlines of the Tales of Meselia impacted its popularity, but while it is not remembered as fondly as other children's fantasy series, it still has a small but devoted fan base.

LEXICON OF ALUVOREAN WORDS

ALAM: flower

ALLAE: the river of life; a waterfall; clear, running water

ANNAGINI VASAGI: the Queen's Tree; literally "the queen who brings life"

ANNAGINUK: queen

ANUKOP: a pond; also the name of the lake around Inyulap Anyar

ARAKAM: dragon of the underworld

AYARA: heartwood; heart; the center of a matter; "life's blood"

AYARA ARDHA: the Heartwood Throne, or the fruit of its tree

AYARA IKANNUTO: the Heartwood Crown

EMES ESUTOL: seed of hope

ENALANOK: hero

INYULAP ANYAR: the Queen's Island

ISAP: moss

KASKA SHRAM: the carnivorous forest

LIN: long grass that is good for weaving; productive

RASKAN: firethorns

UDUHUM KOB: literally "thirsty water"; the Ginian Sea

URUDAP: an Aluvorean beast of burden

VANA: a good and pleasant place

JELDA'S REVENGE

A Scim Legend

A great while ago, when evil wandered the land without opposition, a righteous woman named Jelda also wandered. She had a home once, but it had been burned to the ground, her husband murdered, her children slain. She wandered like a deer, her path repeating over the days, her feet making tracks through the woods.

So it was one day that she came across an Elenil man who had fallen into the river and become ensnared in the roots of a prison tree. In her youth, Jelda would have dived in to save him without a thought, but age and experience had given her wisdom.

The Elenil heard her move among the bushes on the far side of the river, and he called out, "Help me, dear friend, for I am trapped among the roots of this prison tree, and when the water rises, I will surely drown."

"How do I know you are a friend?" Jelda shouted. "This is a harsh world. If released, you may slay me or cause me harm."

Then the Elenil promised on his name that no harm would come to her, and Jelda trembled, for it was a name she knew well: it was this man who had murdered her husband and ordered his soldiers to set fire to her home, her two children still inside.

She stepped into the sunlight so he could see her clearly.

The Elenil's hands clutched the roots of his prison. "Fair lady," he said, "I see that life has used you ill, for you are more forest spirit than woman. Your hair is struck through with moss, your hands the color of dirt, your clothing in tatters. Still, set me free and ask what you will of me, and whatever service it may be, I will perform it. Bid me go to the roots of the world and bring back pure magic, or follow the humans to their other earth and bring back the cold, dead clay of that land, and I will do it."

Then it was that Jelda knew the Elenil did not remember her. She stood at the water's edge and said to him, "Elenil, if I free you, promise on your name that whatever three commands I give, you will follow."

He swore it on his name.

Jelda dove into the river and swam deep until she found the key knot for the prison tree. She turned it thrice, and the roots released the Elenil. Jelda grasped his shirt and pulled him to the bank and sat beside him on the emerald grass as he gasped and dried in the sun.

When the Elenil had regained his strength, he sat up and said, "Now, fair lady, what three commands have you for your servant? For you have saved me, and I must do as I have promised."

Now, in those days, a promise made on one's name was a promise bound with magic, and anything Jelda asked, the Elenil would have obeyed. Had she asked for great wealth, or to change shapes, or to be archon, he would have done those things for her, even if it had taken his whole life to do so.

But Jelda intended to get revenge on this Elenil, not to enrich herself, not to gain more magic, not to gain more authority in the world. Her first command, then, was simple. To the Elenil she said, "Know who I am."

In one moment, all his memories came rushing in. He remembered the Scim woman from the windswept plain, and how she had begged him over the corpse of her husband to spare her children. He could see in his mind her story, how she had fallen in love with a Scim man, and how they had lived happily together in their meager home, and the joy that had come with their children. He saw the sort of woman she must be to overcome her sorrow and still live, although she wandered the forest like an animal. He saw, too, that a woman such as this must have a bold plan of revenge against someone like himself.

With deep foreboding he said to her, "Jelda, I remember you well. The magic of the Elenil has given me a deep knowledge of who you are. Now speak! Tell me the second command I must obey."

The words leapt to Jelda's mouth, and she said, "Know what you have done."

In one instant, the Elenil knew all that he had done in those few moments on the windswept plain. Not only the death of this farmer and his children, but the consequences of it. The unworked soil, the food that was not produced and not sold to other families, the network of pain and longing that flowed to every person, every creature, every soul touched by the loss, the destruction of two young lives who might have brought greater joy to the world, cut off, destroyed, in a moment of power-drunk madness.

The Elenil could not bear the pain. He wept and cried out, tearing up the grass, tearing at his hair. The enormity of what he had done closed in upon him, as if the entire sky were a weight pressing upon his shoulders. He could not hide from it, could not pretend it did not exist, could not forget what he had done. He grasped Jelda's legs and begged for her forgiveness. He screamed to be set free, to be released from this pain. He snatched a dagger from his belt and prepared to slay himself, for he could no longer bear the full knowledge of his actions.

"Was I not promised three commands?" Jelda said, and the Elenil paused, the dagger in his hand.

Terrified and trembling, the Elenil dropped the dagger. "What is your third command, O Jelda? Command me any task, be it possible or no, and I will perform it. For my trespasses against you and against your family have been many."

Jelda did not acknowledge his speech but said only, "Live a long life."

Then, her revenge served, she left the Elenil upon the riverbank, weeping and cursing himself, and Jelda returned to civilization and did not think of him again in all her days.

Thus was her revenge complete.

Jelda was given three commands and used them wisely. So, too, this story shares three commands: one for the storyteller, one for the hearer, and one for the heart which understands.

HUMOR IN THE SOUTHERN COURT

From the book The Sunlit Lands and Their People,
found in King Ian's library

The people of the Southern Court are shape-shifters. There is some debate among sociologists as to whether they have a "default" shape, because they are highly secretive about their marriage, birth, and death rituals. In fact, for many years, some sociologists did not recognize humor in the Southern Court for what it was.

Humor in the Southern Court is generally recognized as funny because it is one of three things: 1) truth; 2) what is known as "truth in conflict"; or 3) so obviously false as to point toward the underlying assumption of what is true. I will share here an example of each form of humor.

One, truth. There is a famous story of a well-beloved comedian who arrived at a Southern Court marriage ceremony wearing the shape of one of the most hated enemies of the Court, Garnesh the Slayer. He arrived and immediately announced, "I will kill everyone at this wedding!" The comedian was met with riotous laughter because this was undoubtedly true (if someone had been so foolish as to invite Garnesh to the wedding). In some versions of the tale, he goes on to murder several members of the wedding party, with the guests and attendants laughing harder and harder as he slaughters the happy gathering.

Two, "truth in conflict." The idea here is that the comedian must juxtapose two ideas that are both true but appear to be in conflict with one another. In Southern Court humor, this is often accomplished by putting one's words and one's physical form in conflict with one another.

The most famous example is, no doubt, the comedian known as Lenia. She was well regarded as one of the most gifted shape-shifters of her generation, able to take on the shape of another person with such precision that a family member might choose her rather than their loved one if they stood side by side. She did this, she claimed, by not only taking on the physical attributes of her target shape but by actually emphasizing certain parts . . . making herself "more like them than they were themselves." A well-regarded act of Lenia's began with her taking the shape of a different Sunlit Lands race—for instance, an Elenil—and then standing in front of the audience and saying, "I am not an Elenil." The truth is that Lenia was not an Elenil, and yet all evidence of one's senses would say the opposite. This juxtaposition of a true statement while wearing what was, to all appearances, an Elenil body, is said to have created a wave of mirth that caused many in the audience to doubt she could top her opening sentence. Her second sentence is lost to history because of the crescendo of laughter. Her third sentence, however, was "This is not the Sunlit Lands"—a statement that was so boldly true and untrue that some in the audience that day do not remember the act continuing from that point forward. The truth here (the Sunlit Lands are much larger than just the Southern Court) and the competing truth (even a local territory like the Southern Court is, in some way, "the Sunlit Lands"), created a near riot of hilarity.

The third Southern Court principle of humor is to say something that is self-evidently untrue, with the express purpose of revealing the underlying truth. This is most often done through exaggeration to a ridiculous degree. For instance, the common human saying "I'm starving" when one is hungry is considered hysterically funny. Clearly the speaker is not suffering from starvation, but their statement points to the underlying truth that the speaker is hungry. Citizens of the Southern Court often break into uncontrollable laughter when speaking with humans.

The most famous teacher of Southern Court humor has a maxim that he says is the core of all Court humor (you will see it is partly based on the comedy routines of Lenia herself), and all of his students begin their course of study by memorizing these simple sentences:

This is not Aluvorea.
This is not the Sunlit Lands.
This is not the Southern Court.

The first sentence shows the value of truth as humor—the Southern Court is not Aluvorea. The second sentence is both true and untrue, as discussed earlier. The third sentence is a complicated exaggeration. The people of the "Southern Court" have their own name they use to refer to their territory. The term *Southern* is one the Elenil use, as the Court is to the south of Far Seeing. They are not, in fact, a "court" at all, since their government has no royalty as such, no sovereign, and in fact does not even have a judiciary. They employ a form of government very difficult to explain in a few sentences—it's a shifting form of representational democracy in which the person who makes a final decision rests on a complicated calculus of morphology, generation, gender, season, and chromatic awareness. Their "king" is a figurehead whose role is connecting to other political entities in the Sunlit Lands and, in fact, is not one person. Depending on the event, a different person will take the shape of the monarch and "play" the king. There was, in fact, considerable distress among the people of the Southern Court when deciding whether to use gendered language like *king* when the monarch might be, at any given moment, a female. So the term *Southern Court* is a political fiction embraced by the people for pragmatic reasons. There are undertones to the statement "This is not the Southern Court" that the Elenil (at least those who understand it) find troubling: it could also be a cry for complete disassociation from Elenil society. The Elenil concerns on this topic are, as you might imagine, hysterically funny to the people of the Southern Court.

For those outside Southern Court society, by far the most distressing outworking of not understanding Court humor is when they attempt to make jokes at public events. The people of the Southern Court love weddings, celebrations, and festivals of all kinds. It is common for a member of the Southern Court to arrive in the shape of, for instance, the mother of the bride, and to loudly declare, "I will break the legs of any who disturb this wedding!" While hilarious in a Southern Court context, this is considered uncouth by the other cultures of the Sunlit Lands.

THE GOOD GARDENER

An Aluvorean Story

It happened when the trees were still young—not saplings but not full growth, either. That was when the boy ran from the Sunlit Lands, for his family had been murdered. The boy was too young to know that the forest held no safety for him, and so he crashed through the trees and forded the river and found himself alone on an island.

Here he lived on berries and drank the fresh water of the stream. His bed was a carpet of moss, and at night he covered himself with a blanket of leaves. No one from his village came to find him, for in those days the forest still housed creatures that struck fear in the hearts of the villagers, for no hero had been found to empty the woods of monsters.

But the creatures did not harm the boy, perhaps because they saw in his heart a sort of kin, for what he had seen happen to his parents had sent his mind to different places than those walked by the people of the Sunlit Lands. So it was that the boy would hunt fish near the waterfall with Arakam, the dragon. Or climb the tallest trees and sit upon the edge of Fantol's dark nest. Even, it is said, he would swim down the river and join Malgwin and her dark brood in the Sea Beneath, though he returned home shivering and stiff from the cold. And most days he would walk through the forest with the man.

The man did not have any name that the boy knew, nor did the boy think to ask him for one. He was the man, and the boy was the boy. What else was there to know? He did not need to call for him, because the man came every day. He did not need to speak his name for attention, for who else would the boy be speaking to? When they were together, it was only the two of them.

The boy did not know, but it was the man who told Arakam and Fantol and, yes, even Malgwin that they were not to harm the boy. All the creatures of the wood knew to leave the boy in peace, for he had suffered enough already, and the man had not created the Sunlit Lands as a place of war and suffering but as a respite from them. True, the creatures of those woods had come to think of the boy as a peer and, it might be said, had even come to love him. But it was the man who had told them they must give the boy his freedom, and without the man the boy would have surely died in the woods.

One day as they walked through the trees, the man asked the boy a strange question. "Would you like there to be more people in the woods?"

"What do you mean?" the boy asked, his heart pounding in his chest. He could scarcely remember his own parents or the other people of his village. His life had been all wildflowers and berries and the creatures of the wood.

"The Sunlit Lands are not as they should be. The people fight and argue. They have ceased to be the people of the Sunlit Lands and have made for themselves other names: the Scim, the Elenil, the Southern Court, the Zhanin, and so on. They have forgotten that they are one people. There is anger. There is murder. There is even war."

The boy did not know this word, so he asked the man about it. "What is war?"

"War is when two groups of people kill each other until one group says 'enough.' Then that group—the one who says 'enough'—they are said to have lost the war."

The boy threw a stick into the woods. "But are they not the wise ones? Is not even one person killed enough? It is the smartest, then, who lose the war? The wisest?"

"A war does not end with only one death, though sometimes one death could start one."

The boy was amazed. "How many must die before a war is ended?"

The man looked sad and put his arm around the boy's shoulder. "How many do you think?"

The boy thought hard on this question. "Three?" he said, and when the man shook his head he said, "Five? *Seven?*"

"More," said the man. "Sometimes many more."

"Why would you bring such people here, then?"

"Not to wage war but to escape it."

"Because if they come here they will not be killed."

"Yes."

The boy did not have to think long on this. "Then they should come. I will teach them about the fruits that are good to eat, and I will show them where the wild berries grow. I will show them the cool places to lie on hot days, and the shady spots in the river that are best for catching fish."

"And you will not let them wage war?"

The boy was shocked. "No! Never."

"Good," said the man. "Then I will let the people come into the forest, and perhaps these woods will become what the Sunlit Lands were meant to be: a refuge for those who have been harmed by the injustices of the world."

The boy was troubled. "But if these people come, what will I call them?"

"They will each have a name," the man said gently. "Have no fear about that."

"Then what shall I call you? For now there are only we two in the forest, but in that day there will be many people, and I will need a name to call you by."

The man smiled. "I am called different things by different people," he said. "The people who call themselves the Elenil call me 'the Majestic One.'"

The boy laughed at that. "Do they never walk with you along the forest paths? You are majestic, I am sure, but it is too lofty a name for friends such as you and I."

The man was pleased with this answer. "There are those called the Scim who refer to me as the Peasant King."

"Are you a king, then?" the boy asked.

"Indeed I am, though not in the way the Scim think."

"And are you a peasant?"

"In a way. I walk among them without my wealth and power, to show them what they could be."

"So you are neither king nor peasant, but are both peasant and king."

"Indeed."

"So," the boy said, "the name is both true and untrue."

"For them it is true," the man said. "As they come to know me better, there will be other names. For truly, one name cannot hold the whole of a person."

They talked of other names the man had been called. Wind Walker and King of Stories and the True Man and the Magician and a hundred others besides, but none of them suited the boy. "These do not describe the man I know," he said.

"Then you choose a name," the man said.

The boy thought on this for some time and said at last, "I will call you the Good Gardener, for it is often I have come across you mending the branch of a tree or sheltering the tender shoot of a flower. I have seen you at the water's edge among the lilies, and you have never even broken a bruised reed."

The Good Gardener laughed at this name, so pleased was he. It had been many a year since such a simple and kindhearted name had been given him. "I shall call you a name too," the Good Gardener said. "I shall call you Patra Koja." (Patra Koja means, in the language of that day, "Bringer of Peace.")

Patra Koja, too, was pleased with his new name.

This is why the people of Aluvorea never fight in any war, for Patra Koja finds it evil and strange. Even today it is not uncommon to see him walking gentle paths with the Good Gardener, talking about their days and making plans for our future.

THE BEACH IN WINTER

A Traditional Zhanin Saying

(NOTE: A Zhanin will use the saying "It is only the beach in winter" to express when someone has discovered a partial truth and claims it as universal. Below you will find a typical exposition a Zhanin elder might make when reminding others of this truth.)

I return to the beach in winter.

The tide is high, and driftwood has been tossed casually onto the sloped cliffs. Algae foam slides up the sand, is caught by the wind, and is blown, rolling, to the east. A shoal of black basalt rises from the sand. The waves return to the ocean through rivulets cut in stone. Dark clouds sail through the sky like ships, their hulls punctuated with blue.

In summer there's deep sand, the black stone buried, the waves friendly and green, the sky wide and shining. The sand is dotted with a mosaic of bright towels. The seals pop up their glossy heads, watching the strange happenings on shore.

Sometimes we think we have found truth, but we have only found the beach in winter. We are tempted to say, "This beach has a vein of black stone that rises up from the sand," but in the spring it is less true, and in the summer not true at all. There are truths that cannot be discovered in one afternoon—there are truths that require a season's observance, a year's reflection to be understood.

The tides change with the moon, the sand rises and falls with the seasons, the birds migrate, the cliffs recede with the erosion of decades. These things cannot be determined in a moment, cannot be observed in an afternoon, cannot be understood in a week's careful study.

This is to say nothing of the volcanic growth of islands, the grinding shift of continental plates, the meticulous motion of glaciers, or the slow, careful metamorphoses of the heart.

MALGWIN AND THE WHALE

A Traditional Zhanin Story

(NOTE: Zhanin sayings can be challenging to the uninitiated. Some are obvious, such as the greeting "What tide?" or the farewell "Where goes the current?" Less obvious are sayings like "She has saved a whale but sunk the boat." This saying has several related meanings, depending on the context. It can mean that someone has "bitten off more than they can chew" or that someone is well meaning but ineffective. It can also be used in admiration for someone who will do what is right no matter the consequence. The origin of the saying comes from the story below.)

It is a moonless night, and I patrol the Big Deep, my companions the stars wheeling overhead, and I listen to the gentle lap of water, the sigh of the wind.

A seabird lands on the gunnel and says, "Sister, O sister, it is a dark night, but I see trouble near the horizon."

"What trouble?" I ask, for I see nothing.

"It is a quiet night," the bird says, "and yet I hear an animal in distress. Will you help, sister?"

And what am I to say? For a woman such as I—a woman who is not even entrusted with a living boat—always gives help when asked. So I tell the bird, yes, lead us to this trouble. In time we come upon a whale, whose head is rising out of the water and singing a mournful tune.

"What tide, sister?" I ask the whale, but she does not reply. I recognize her song then—it is a parting song. "Where goes the current?" I ask.

She turns her eye to me then and says, "How long, O Zhanin, have you and I been friends?"

"Since the world first turned," says I, for when have the whales and the Zhanin not been friends?

Great tears roll from her eyes, enough to turn the sea to salt. "Farewell then, old friend," says she, "for I have made a foolish mistake. One month past, old Malgwin caught me and said she would feed me to her brood. I begged her for a month's time to say farewell to old friends. She laughed

378

and said she would do me one better, and that if I could rise completely out of the sea for the space of ten breaths she would spare me on tomorrow's sunrise. She is a cruel beast to taunt me so. I have jumped and jumped all month and still cannot rise out of the water for more than the space of a breath or two. Soon she will find me here and take me to the Sea Beneath, where I will make a short meal for her foul children."

"Surely a big meal, not a short one," says I, but Sister Whale does not laugh at this. Sister Bird snaps her beak at me. But what a strange bargain Malgwin has made. She will not eat Sister Whale if she can get herself completely out of the water for the space of ten breaths. A whale can come mostly out of the water for maybe a breath or two when they breach, but they cannot fly like a bird. They cannot come upon the land like a turtle. It was a cruelty on Malgwin's part to offer a way out to Sister Whale, but one that was impossible.

Now Sister Whale has started her keening cry again.

"Now, now," I say. "All is not yet lost, for there are several hours until sunrise. You have a friend here, and the Zhanin have never lost so much as a toe to old Malgwin. I have a plan." I explain it all to the whale. The whale laughs to hear it, and I am glad for her lightened heart, and the bird says it will not work but still goes to get her cousins and siblings and parents and friends.

As for me, I dive down deep, down to the roots of the world, and I gather up long strands of kelp. Round and round I swim, then, and tie them to the whale.

Just then Malgwin comes upon me, out of the Sea Beneath, with her white skin and her jagged teeth. "What game are you playing?" she asks, but I know better than to slow my work.

"Only wrapping Sister Whale as a gift for your children," says I.

Malgwin smiles her sharp-toothed smile. "Then I will help you," she says, and she does.

Then the birds come, and I climb upon Sister Whale's back and tie the kelp onto their ankles. "What trick is this?" Malgwin asks.

I shush her. "The birds," I whisper. "They will be dragged down with Sister Whale, and what a treat for your children, to eat fresh birds."

Malgwin grins at this, and soon she, too, is tying the birds to the kelp.

When all is ready, I shout for Sister Whale to leap from the water, and I shout, "Fly, fly" to the birds, and Sister Whale breaches, and the birds lift her into the sky. Sister Whale is completely out of the water. Mostly.

Malgwin shouts, "What a filthy trick, you clever Zhanin girl! But look: the whale's tale is still in the water."

She is right! The birds are flapping and crying, and feathers fall around us in a great storm. Sister Whale is pulling on her tail, but it will not come out of the water. "Lift your tail," I shout, but Sister Whale can't lift it any higher.

Malgwin laughs and laughs. "It was a good trick," she says, "but in a few minutes Sister Whale will be our breakfast."

She is right, for the sun is just below the water.

I know what I must do. I paddle my boat beneath the whale's tail and wedge my boat beneath her. With a great deal of grunting and heaving and pulling, her tail is in my boat. She is out of the water!

For the space of one breath she hangs there, and the birds are suffering for it. Only nine breaths to go.

At five breaths a hole bursts in the boat from the weight. I shovel the water out quickly so Malgwin can't say Sister Whale is still in it. Only five breaths more, and Sister Whale will be saved.

At eight breaths the birds are beginning to fall into the sea. Sister Whale is listing to one side. Two more breaths out of the water and Sister Whale will live!

At nine breaths a bird falls, screeching, into my boat. That feather's weight is too much, and we begin to sink in earnest. Malgwin smacks her lip in anticipation. One breath more is all we need. But the boat is sinking, and Sister Whale's tail will be in the water!

At ten breaths I put my hands beneath Sister Whale's tail and push up. The boat is completely submerged, but my hands hold her out of the water. "Ten breaths!" I cry, and on eleven all the birds stop flying and Sister Whale lands on my boat, reducing it to so many splinters. A great wave crashes over me, and I rise, spluttering, to face Malgwin.

Malgwin sneers at me and says, "Clever Zhanin girl. But now you have no boat, and no boat means no fish, and no fish means no dinner. Tell that to your people when you swim home. The children of the Zhanin will fast today because of your foolishness." Then Malgwin swims away, back to the Sea Beneath, to silence the hungry mouths of her children.

As for me, ay me, I set about cutting the birds free from the whale before the long swim home.

THE OCEAN

A Zhanin Song

The storm is not love
The hurricane is not love
That is passion only
Passing from horizon to horizon in a day

The wind is not love
The breath of the world is not love
That is only shared life

The seabirds are not love
With all their comings and goings
They are only loud cries

The sun is not love
Though it brings many good things
Too distant, too fickle

Love is the ocean
It surrounds us
It sustains us
We dive deep
Or paddle in the shallows
Love is the ocean

THE PLANTING OF ALUVOREA

An Aluvorean Creation Tale

Here is the way it happened.

The Good Gardener made a place.

He shaped the crystal spheres of sky and sun and moon and stars.

He filled the inner sphere with ocean water, and he placed land in the center.

He made good, sweet water to flow upon the land.

He brought trees and plants and animals and people from the earth, and he said to them, "This place is safe. This place is home. This place is yours."

Then he took the people into the forest, where he had made an island, and he showed the people a seed. "This seed is full of magic," he said. "It will bring blessing to the people of the Sunlit Lands." He placed it in the ground, and its roots sank deep, and its silver trunk grew tall, and its branches reached high. "Every hundred years," he said, "we will plant another seed, and every hundred years there shall be three new blessings for the people of the Sunlit Lands." Then he warned the people, "Let no one hold on to their magic, or say, 'This is mine,' but rather use it for all people, and for the good of the Sunlit Lands."

Then the people were happy.

The roots of the tree went deep into the Sea Beneath, and it was there that the tree found the Good Gardener's magic. It brought the magic up through the roots, and into itself, and then out through its branches. The magic seeded and spread and planted and grew, and all the people of the Sunlit Lands were glad.

In those days the whole of the Sunlit Lands was covered in forest, and magic was everywhere. The woodsman and the king, the baker and the queen, the hostler and the duke, all had magic and were glad. Magic was the fruit of the trees, and all the people ate their fill.

THE SEED

An Aluvorean Poem

An enemy has planted fear
   in the orderly rows of our hearts.
An enemy has sown anger in our fields.

Fear is the seed of hate.
We must cast it in the flames
   or be consumed ourselves.

Anger is the seed of violence.
We must not be blinded
   by its knife-edged thorns.

Come, let us work together
   side by side. I'll tear out your fear,
   and you can weed away mine.

If darkness falls while we labor,
   let us light a lantern.
A small candle defeats even a great darkness.

We will work together
   through this finite dark,
   and see what crop of love
   will rise come morning.

ACKNOWLEDGMENTS

I'm deeply thankful to each person who helped make this book a reality. Here are a few of them:

Christopher Holman, Lauren Dodge, Kate Allen, and Michael Boncher helped come up with Jason's many names for a certain ill-tempered brucok.

Josh Chen gave permission to use both his name and his "what to do if you're pulled over" trick.

Elizabeth Kletzing, Lisanne Kaufmann, and Debbie King did the copyediting. I had them fact checking what possum teeth look like, asking questions about how magic works, and checking what I wrote in this book against what was written in *The Crescent Stone*. They had me feeling like George Lucas at a Star Wars convention in all the best ways . . . They care about the minutiae of this world and of this manuscript.

Once again, the incredible Matt Griffin (www.mattgriffin.online) did the art for the cover and the map, and Dean Renninger hit it out of the park with the art design.

Linda Howard opened the door to the Sunlit Lands and continues to champion the people and stories of this wonderful place. She's an exceptional person,

Jesse Doogan spends a lot more time in the Sunlit Lands than she needs to, I think because she loves cats, unicorns, books, and people (order may vary). Also, she takes the brunt of my constant texting, which I know everyone else appreciates.

Kristi Gravemann brings a lot of passion to getting the word out about these books! I am so grateful to have such a gifted person trumpeting the worth of these books to the masses.

Sarah Rubio is the main sociologist of the Sunlit Lands, and her constant curiosity about the characters and the world they inhabit makes the final product 93.7% better than those first drafts. Sarah, by reading these words, you agree to edit all Sunlit Lands books forever. Hooray!

There are a whole lot of other people at Tyndale who made this book possible. Books are a team sport, and I love this team. Thank you, Tyndale!

Wes Yoder, my agent, friend, and constant companion through all bookish adventures. Looking forward to many more years on the journey!

The whole Fascinating Podcast family makes my life better, and they are often my sounding board when I get stuck in life or in a book: Aaron Kretzmann, JR. and Amanda Forasteros, Clay Morgan and Jennifer Cho, Kathy and Peter Khang, and Elliot and Lauren Dodge.

My parents, Pete and Maggie, and my in-laws, Janet and Terry, support our family in so many different ways that I couldn't begin to list them all. We are deeply thankful.

Zoey! I love seeing this world through your eyes. Thank you for your questions, support, and ideas. Your insights are always great ones.

Allie! Thank you for your passionate love for the Sunlit Lands and the characters in it (except for that one guy). Thank you for always talking through the stories with me. You're a great help.

Myca! Thank you for inventing our amazing Guardian of the Wind, Remi. You are a creative and kindhearted person, and I am so thankful for you!

And of course, as always, my lovely wife, Krista, who makes sacrifices both obvious and unseen to make space for an entire fantasy world in our lives. Many thanks, and I love you.

Also: you, dear reader. We are making this world together. I am thankful for your part in it.

THE ADVENTURE CONTINUES IN

THE
STORY
KING

COMING SOON

FOR MORE INFORMATION, CHECK OUT
WWW.THESUNLITLANDS.COM

TURN THE PAGE
FOR A SNEAK PEEK AT
THE FIRST CHAPTER!

CP1498

1
THE ROBE OF ASCENSION

An unbalanced boat risks lives. Unbalanced magic takes them.

A ZHANIN SAYING

✛

The boats were nervous. The sail trees fluttered restlessly on the western side of the island, and last night the bay had glowed a brighter green than Kekoa Kahananui had ever seen. He took a deep lungful of the morning air. It was cool and crisp, but there was a whiff of smoke to it. Nothing was burning in the archipelago, so it had to be coming from the mainland.

Kekoa stood on the lanai of the royal palace, the highest point on the island. Below him the ground sloped away on all sides, covered in the bright, kelly green of sail trees all the way to the golden sand. He could see the boats paddling around in the bay and hear the lowing cries of their distress. A group of Zhanin was swimming out to calm them.

Kekoa gripped the balustrade. It was so quiet he thought he could hear the waves at World's End, something that was usually only audible when the crystal sphere of day moved below the Ginian Sea. He didn't know the waters here like he knew the sand and the sea of Hawai'i, but he knew enough that his fingers beat out an erratic tattoo on the balustrade, and his heartbeat quickened.

When he was a kid, he'd heard stories about the sea disappearing. Like, you'd be on the beach enjoying the waves, and then all at once the water went out and out and out like the lowest tide of all. If that ever happened, some of the haole might walk out looking for shells, sure, but all the locals would know to head for high ground. That water has to come back, yeah? And it's gonna be a big wave. Kekoa felt that now. Like the tide was suddenly far too low.

"What tide, majesty?"

A Zhanin man stood in Kekoa's room, wearing clothing made from surf-weave and sea-leather. If Kekoa had seen him back home, he would have thought he was a lifelong surfer, with his long hair tied back and the toned muscles of someone who regularly moved through water. He held a platter of fruits and dried fish. Breakfast. Kekoa hadn't even heard him enter, but that wasn't a huge surprise since the Zhanin didn't have doors.

"Oh hey, Fairweather. Howzit?"

The Zhanin names were all translated, maybe because of the magic of the Sunlit Lands that let people understand each other. They had names describing good things their parents wished for (Manyfish, Clearskies, Rain, Balance) or sometimes something about the family job in the clan (Leader, Chief, Fisher, Warrior—Kekoa had even met someone named Executioner, who he had promptly sent to another island).

"I am well, Chief."

"Don't call me that, brah. How many times I gotta say it? Call me Kekoa." He picked at the platter, pulling off some dried fish and wild hana—a tart citrus fruit with yellow skin and pink flesh—and throwing it in his mouth. "You eat already?"

"No, Kekoa."

Kekoa threw his arm around Fairweather. "Listen, brah, you're always acting like we're enemies, but we're not. We're friends. I want to be your friend."

Fairweather's face darkened, and the platter trembled. "Let me bring my sword in here, and I will show you what sort of friends we are."

Kekoa raised his eyebrows and took a step back. He checked the Ascension Robe, making sure it was on tight. He had been wearing it nonstop these last months, keeping it on over his clothes. A quick glance over the lanai didn't show him any major changes, but there had been some moments in recent weeks when the magic had stuttered. He went to the doorway and called for Ruth.

Fairweather moved to withdraw, but Kekoa put his hand on the Zhanin's shoulder. "Hold on a minute," he said. Fairweather scowled at him, so Kekoa added, "Please."

Ruth Mbewe, the young girl who had come to the islands with Kekoa, came in a moment later. She had worked her hair into two-strand twists, and she wore a blue-green shift made of surf-weave, with a cloth from the mainland folded and tied around her eyes. She was a strange girl, far too wise for her years, but in their time on the island Kekoa had come to think of her as his weird little sister. "Kekoa," she said. "Fairweather."

"Aloha, Ruth. Something strange is going on. I think Fairweather wants to kill me."

Ruth tilted her head to one side. "Of course he does, Kekoa. He's wanted to kill you since we first set foot on this island. Isn't that true, Fairweather?"

Fairweather set his jaw and didn't answer.

"Go on," Kekoa said. "Tell her."

The Zhanin man scowled. "I want to kill you both," he said. "You mis-use magic. You are unbalanced. The Zhanin keep the balance."

"Well," Ruth said. "I can't say I knew that he wanted to kill me, too. I'm not even using any magic. I've told you more than once that you should have taken off the robe by now."

Kekoa smoothed the robe. "Ruth. If I take it off, the Zhanin will kill us."

"Not necessarily," Ruth said.

"We will," Fairweather said under his breath.

"See?" Kekoa pointed at Fairweather accusingly, then was reminded of the fruit platter and took another mouthful. "The boats are nervous today too, and there's smoke on the wind. Something is wrong."

"What's wrong is that you didn't follow the Knight of the Mirror's instructions," Ruth said, repeating her daily reminder to him. They had been sent here by the knight, carrying the robe that Kekoa was wearing.

The Robe of Ascension. It was a long robe, just a shade darker than royal blue, with gold trim. Along the edges all the way to the collar a series of creatures danced: oxen, eagles, humans, and lions. It was a magical item, made by the Scim, and when someone wore it, they had to be obeyed, like a king or queen, like an emperor. When Kekoa had first put it on, it had felt strange—as if suddenly everyone around him were more agreeable, or as if they wanted the same thing as him, whatever that might be. The strangeness had worn off in a few days, and now Kekoa felt almost offended when Fairweather threatened to kill him. He knew the robe had kept him and Ruth safe, but it almost hurt his feelings that it was necessary. He had to keep it on so the more violent urges of the Zhanin were held in check. In the afternoon sun, though, Kekoa often wished he could pull it off. He got hot, even barefoot and wearing only a pair of shorts under it.

"Listen," Kekoa said, and for the fiftieth time he laid his case out. "We got here to the island, and we did what the knight said. We waited for the song of welcome. We reminded the holy ones of the knight's service to them long ago."

"And then?" Ruth asked, nudging him. "Then what did you do?"

"Then they tried to kill us!" He grabbed a handful of berries. "Back me up here, Fairweather."

"We tried to kill you," Fairweather said.

"He has to say that," Ruth said. "I think we may have misread the signs."

Kekoa laughed so hard and so suddenly that he coughed up his berries. He stumbled to a pitcher and drank water straight from the side of it. "They threw spears at us!"

Ruth frowned. She never had a great response to this particular fact, and the islanders had been less than forthcoming about what had happened, even under the influence of the robe's magic. The biggest issue with the robe was that the magic of the islands seemed to ebb and flow, like the tides, but not as constant. There were times when all the people obeyed Kekoa's standing orders (like "Do not kill me or Ruth") with unquestioning loyalty. But then there would be these moments like right now, when they talked back, made plans, whispered to each other. It made him nervous.

Kekoa and Ruth should have left, but every time they made it a certain distance from the island, the robe's magic stopped working on the Zhanin, and they started chasing them. It was only a matter of time until one of the Zhanin managed to skewer him or Ruth, or send one of their trained sea animals to kill them. The robe didn't work as well on animals. Kekoa had tried, at Ruth's insistence, taking the robe off a few times, but it always ended badly, with spears or swords or something sharp pointed at Kekoa's face. Or neck. Or heart.

"We should send another bird," Ruth said.

"We've sent a hundred birds!" Kekoa said. No one answered. The birds he sent to Jason rarely seemed to find him. They'd circle back within a week or so. No birds had found Madeline or Shula yet, and even David seemed to be missing. News from the mainland was dire, yes, but Kekoa didn't believe for a second that all his friends were dead or unable to respond. Ruth had sent birds to the Knight of the Mirror, but only one had returned, with the message that things were difficult in Far Seeing and that it might be safer to stay among the Zhanin. He had suggested that if they must leave, it would be wise to leave the Robe of Ascension with the Zhanin holy ones, but Kekoa had no idea how to do that and also escape with their lives.

Ruth put her palms together. "Kekoa. Let us speak in private."

Kekoa grabbed another handful of fruit and dismissed Fairweather, who exited the room half-bowed and walking backward. He stopped at the doorway and glared before turning on his heel and disappearing. Kekoa slumped onto a pile of pillows on the lanai and ate while he watched the water. Ruth stood beside him, her face turned toward the sun.

"We must leave here," she said. "Something is changing on the mainland. Something worse than last time."

The magic had cut out briefly soon after they had arrived on the islands. They'd had some trouble finding the archipelago when they first set out, partly because they were in an ordinary boat instead of a Zhanin boat, which was more turtle than watercraft, and partly because Kekoa had not realized that the archipelago *moved*. When the Zhanin wanted to change things up, they let the sail trees fill with wind and off they went. Kekoa had mostly kept them anchored since he had taken charge, because the few times he'd let them move the island, he had gotten the distinct impression the Zhanin were plotting something. He had discovered soon after their arrival that there was a troop of warriors out trying to kill some of his friends. The Zhanin had hidden it from him so he wouldn't be able to call them back, and now no one had any idea where the warriors were, and they couldn't be recalled at all.

"Something worse than the last time the magic went out?"

"How long was that?" Ruth asked. "Three hours?"

"Maybe." He sucked the juice out of a segment of orange and threw the skin over the side of the lanai. It had happened when he and Ruth had been trying to leave the islands. They had been among the Zhanin maybe three days, and birds had come saying that the attack of the Scim on the Elenil had passed. Kekoa and Ruth had packed up their non-Zhanin boat and slipped away at night to give themselves the longest head start possible. The timing of the whole thing had saved their lives. They were still in sight of the archipelago when the magic went out. The moment the Zhanin had realized the magic was gone, they had begun to hunt for Ruth and Kekoa on the island, and great horns began to sound as they communicated with one another across the water. Kekoa and Ruth had put a solid hour's rowing between them and the island before the Zhanin set out to look for them on the sea. They had been overtaken right as the magic set in again, which had been much too close for Kekoa's taste. They might have escaped altogether at that moment if not for the storm that had kicked up. The lack of magic had wreaked havoc with the weather of the Sunlit Lands, and Kekoa knew a storm of that size was going to prevent him and Ruth from reaching shore. They had returned to the islands, and here they were still.

"A messenger," Ruth said.

Kekoa didn't see it, but he had learned to listen to Ruth's insights. Perhaps she heard its wings. He scanned the horizon, and that's when he saw the black shape outlined against a wave. He had seen plenty of sharks back home. This thing was thinner and moved with a sinuous motion he found disturbing. It had slipped into the bay where the boats were kept and was moving toward the Zhanin who swam there. Kekoa shouted a warning, but they were too far. He saw the thing pull a Zhanin under the surface. He held his breath, waiting for the warrior to surface, but he knew by the way the water emptied of people that there was panic below.

"Come on," Kekoa said, and he grabbed his leiomanō, a traditional Hawaiian weapon he had found for himself in the Sunlit Lands. He didn't wait for Ruth—she always made her own way nearly as fast as he could, and this was no time to move slowly. As his bare feet slapped against the stone floor of the palace, he shouted for everyone to grab weapons and follow him.

He sprinted down the hillside, leaping over stones, weaving between the sail trees, the Zhanin trailing behind him like the tail of a comet. He burst from the jungle onto the sand by the beach, where people were screaming and shouting, "Malgwin! Malgwin! Malgwin has come!"

He knew what that meant in a second. Malgwin was a sort of half-fish, half-woman creature who haunted the waters of the Sunlit Lands. She was a symbol of chaos and trouble, and most of the stories Kekoa had heard about her included her eating people. Or whales. Or birds. Or really anything that came her way. There was a slick of blood in the water, and the Zhanin were screaming and pointing and shouting, and without a moment's thought Kekoa stripped off the robe and ran until he was thigh deep, and then he dove in, his leiomanō held out before him.

The Zhanin could say what they wanted about Kekoa, but he could swim like a dolphin. He didn't hesitate to use his weapon, either, and his shadow slid over the terrible mermaid creature, giving her a second's warning before he brought his toothed club smashing down toward her head. She moved as fast as an eel, and her fanged mouth, still red with blood, turned toward him. He didn't shrink back, but kicked toward her. She snarled and gave two quick flips of her tail, disappearing out of the bay and into the murky darkness of the wider ocean.

One of the Zhanin floated below, unconscious, blood streaming from a hole in his side. Kekoa recognized him—it was one of the boat keepers, a Zhanin named Brightstar. Kekoa slipped an arm under Brightstar's. The Zhanin was heavy—Kekoa would need two hands to get him to the surface. Here in the bay there wasn't too much risk in leaving something on the bottom, since the bay was built into the island and traveled with them. Kekoa let his leiomanō sink and put both arms around Brightstar, kicking them both to the surface. He didn't want to wait here too long in case Malgwin came back, so he moved quickly to one of the boats, which shied away at the smell of the blood, but calmed when Kekoa cooed to it. He hung for a moment on the boarding rope, giving himself three breaths to gather his strength, then hoisted himself and Brightstar onto the flat deck of the boat's shell.

Once Brightstar was on his back and breathing again, Kekoa let himself take a moment's rest. He tore off some of Brightstar's sea-leather and used it to stop the bleeding from his side. He'd need a medic, no doubt, but Kekoa thought he'd live. He blew out a big breath, and willed his heart to slow.

"Kekoa," a voice called to him across the water.

He stood. It was Fairweather. In one hand he held the Robe of Ascension, crumpled and possibly torn. In the other he held a knife. His knife arm was wrapped around Ruth, the knifepoint at her neck.

"Okay, then," Kekoa said. He looked at all the Zhanin who had raced down to the water with him. All the people he had commanded to come here, who he had commanded to grab weapons. Ruth struggled, and Fairweather tightened his grip.

Brightstar had a knife at his belt. Kekoa grabbed it. "Send the girl over to me," he said.

"Come and get her," Fairweather snarled.

Kekoa didn't answer. He just dove into the water. He wouldn't let them hurt Ruth. Not even if he had to fight the whole island. He didn't let anyone hurt his people. He burst from the water and sprinted toward Fairweather, the knife clenched in his hand. Kekoa had been fighting every night since he arrived in the Sunlit Lands. And yes, a lot of that had been using magic and skills borrowed from the Elenil, but he had been in plenty of fights growing up, and he had never once backed down when a friend was in trouble. Besides, though some of the Zhanin were warriors, scary ones, Fairweather was not one of them. Fairweather was a disgruntled butler.

Fairweather's arm tightened around Ruth's neck, but Kekoa didn't slow. He jumped as he came closer, driving both his feet into Fairweather's chest. As the Zhanin fell, his arms flew to the side, his knife spiraling into the sand. Kekoa snatched the robe from his other hand and flung it over his own shoulders. He pulled Ruth close to him and held his blade toward the assembled Zhanin until he felt the small jolt of the robe's magic taking hold. "Drop your weapons," he said, and they did, as if it were their own idea.

He rearranged the robe, checked on Ruth. She was unflappable, and this situation had done little to upset her. "We need to leave this place," she said. "Soon."

Fairweather got to his feet, rubbing his chest. He picked up his knife. Then the other Zhanin picked up their weapons, as if waking from a long dream. Kekoa and Ruth stepped backward, the waves slapping against their legs.

"The balance," Fairweather said, his eyes unfocused, as if he was feeling something far away and was studying it.

The other Zhanin started to murmur.

"Someone has reset the magic of the Sunlit Lands," Fairweather said. "A new queen wears the Heartwood Crown."

"I don't know what that means," Kekoa said. He took Ruth's hand in his own. He had a sinking feeling he knew exactly what it meant.

"It means that magic has ceased for a time," Fairweather said, smiling. "It means that the robe is nothing but an article of clothing now." He stepped forward. "It means the Zhanin are no longer under your control."

"Oh," Kekoa said, looking at the angry faces of all the Zhanin surrounding them. He pulled Ruth deeper into the water, hoping Malgwin had gone on her way. "We were just leaving, brah. Aloha. See ya later. Bye."

Fairweather stepped forward. He smiled, looking at his knife. "You know we never choose a new chief until the last one dies."

So it was going to be like that. Kekoa let go of Ruth's hand and pulled off the robe. He'd need to be able to move. He cracked his neck, pounded his chest, and exhaled a deep grunt. "Alright then. Let's do this."